The Language of Power

BY ROSEMARY KIRSTEIN:

The Steerswoman
The Outskirter's Secret
The Lost Steersman
The Language of Power

The Language of
Power

Rosemary Kirstein

ISBN-13: 978-0991354672 (Rosemary Kirstein)
ISBN-10: 0991354672

For
SHELLY SHAPIRO
who opened the road for the steerswoman

and
LISA BASSI
warrior, poet

ACKNOWLEDGMENTS

The author is grateful to many people, but most especially the following:

Laurie J. Marks, Delia Sherman, and Didi Stewart ("The Fabulous Genrettes), for knowing when to encourage and when to admonish; Shelly Shapiro, for indispensible editing; Brian Bambrough, for catching the dropped ball; Mary Ann Eldred, for approval on technical details; Ann Tonsor Zeddies, for reports from the trenches; Geary Gravel, for tolerance of enthusiasms; and my sister, Sabine, for everything.

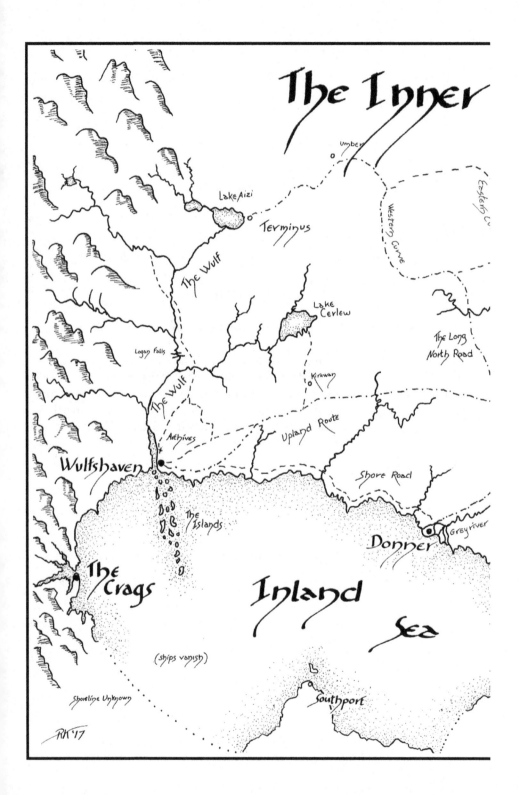

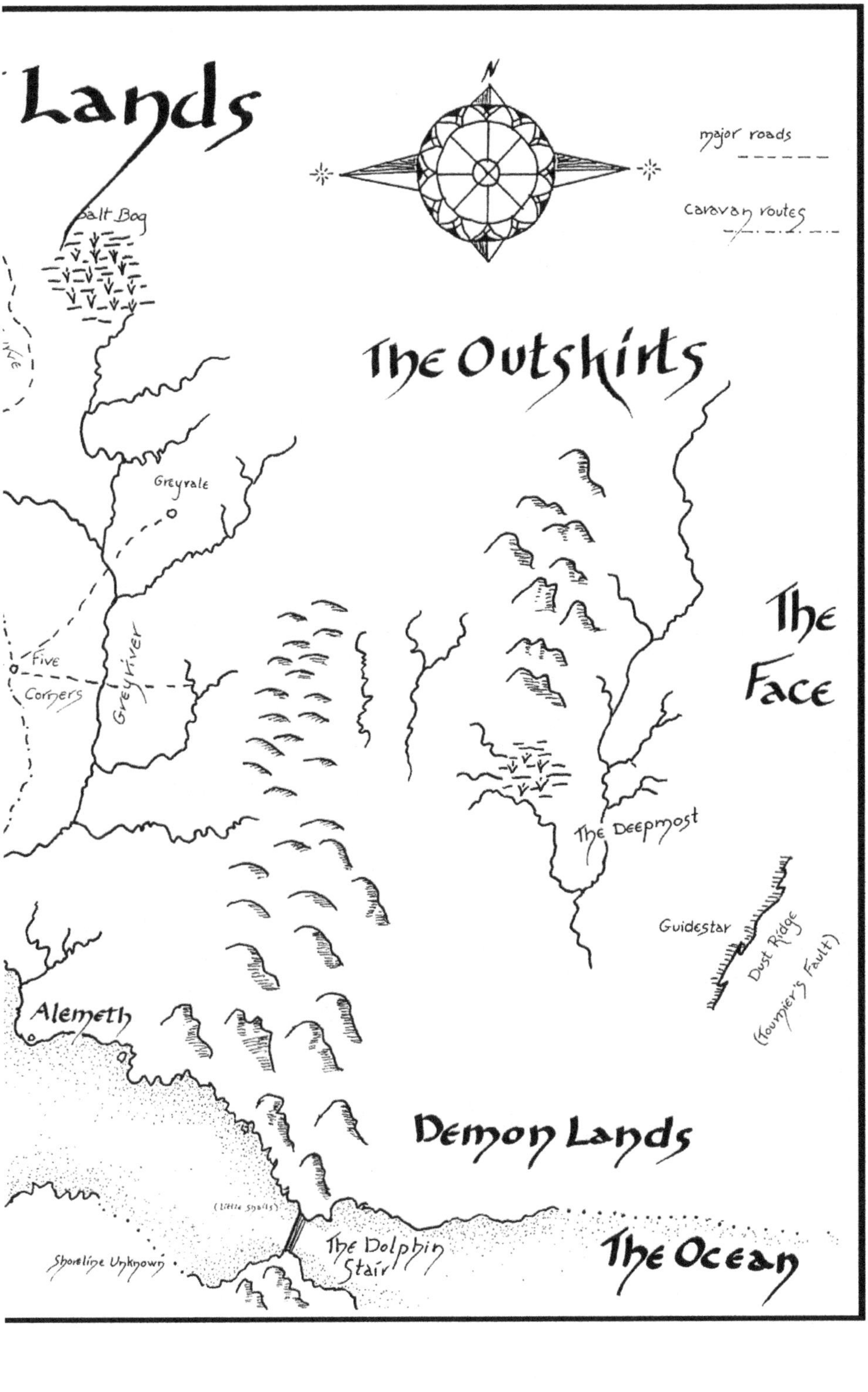

Lands

N

major roads
- - - - -

caravan routes
-/-. -/-

Salt Bog

The Outskirts

Greyvale

The Face

Five Corners

Greyriver

The Deepmost

Guidestar   Dust Ridge
(Founder's Fault)

Alemeth

Demon Lands

(Little Snails)

Shoreline Unknown

The Dolphin Stair

The Ocean

CHAPTER ONE

It was the first break in the weather.

The cargo ship had stood off from Donner for days; no barges had been able to cross the shallows to unload her, and the seas beyond had been high, and wild with wind. Early snow obscured the distance, and *Graceful Days* had been a glimpse, a guess, a dancing ghost behind curtains of spray and snow, until this morning.

Fortunate that she carried so few passengers. Only three, and two were ill: a large man and a small woman, now sitting huddled together in the center of the transfer barge, with an air of surrender and exhaustion that spoke of days of continual seasickness.

The starboard-side bargeman grimaced in sympathy, and attempted to pole more smoothly. The change only confused his partner, who tootled the whistle she held clenched in her teeth, admonishing him to work in proper rhythm.

The third passenger sat by the gunwale among a handful of the ship's crew members. The bargeman had thought her a sailor herself, at first; she was that easy on the water. But the captain of *Graceful Days*, sitting across from her, seemed to treat her as an equal, conversing in respectful tones, at one point angling himself to block the splashes raised by a set of small waves so that the map the woman held in her lap would not get wet.

The bargeman spared another glance from his work, to see what so interested her. He could not read; but the spread of streets, the jut of wharves, and the curve of a broad river identified Donner itself. The woman seemed to sense his gaze, and looked up.

She was not seasick, but she had been ill, in some other way, and not long ago. The clear gray eyes were too large in a face that showed its bones too well. Her short hair, brittle even in the damp air, was both dark and light: the color of wet sand, but tipped with remnants of sun-bleached yellow. She looked like a woman burned by years of light, paled by recent months of darkness.

1

He realized that he had been staring, and shied his glance away, putting his back into his work; but when he looked again, he found her studying him just as closely. "How old are you?" she asked abruptly.

The question took him aback; another toot from his partner reminded him where his attention should be. He poled once, twice, and could see neither why the passenger would ask such a question, nor why he should answer.

But there was no reason not to. "Thirty-one," he replied. A woman with a map—and, he now saw, a pack stowed behind her, with a map case whose end jutted from the top: a steerswoman? She did wear a thin gold chain, such as the Steerswomen wore, but showed no silver ring on her left hand, only a remarkable collection of small, old scars.

Still: "Thank you," she said, as if it were habit, as if she had the right to ask, ask any question at all. And with her question answered, she seemed to dismiss him, returning to her conversation with Gregori, the captain.

Gregori leaned over the city map, indicated. "There, about—Tilemaker's Street. Whole row of shops, and the jeweler's among them."

The crew member seated behind him spoke up. "Excuse me, sir, and lady," she put in, "but I've dealt with them; more dear than they need to be. There's another jeweler's, off near the tea shop. Found a pretty pin for my sweetheart, not so fancy, maybe, but half the price the other asked."

"Now, no one will charge Rowan—or they ought not, properly," the captain said.

"Properly," Rowan put in, "they have every right to charge me, if they insist. The rule only states that one must answer a steerswoman's questions; indulging a steerswoman's personal needs is entirely optional. If I find I must pay after all, the cheaper establishment will do." She rolled her map and leaned back to slide it in among the others in the map case.

The barge approached Tyler's Gully, a hidden trench in the bed of the shallows, and the barge tenders doubled their efforts to acquire the speed needed to coast past it. The change in motion distressed one of the other passengers, who suddenly clambered wildly over crates and bales of raw silk in order to be sick over the side. Wry comments from the sailors, and in one case, applause, but she took the jibes with remarkable good humor, and sensibly remained by the portside gunwale for the rest of the trip.

When the barge slid up to the wharf, Rowan leaned back to let the others disembark first, then accepted an assist from the captain. "Hup!" His hands on her waist, he lifted her bodily from the barge onto the wharf, a move that first startled, then amused her.

"It's been a while since last someone did that for me," Rowan said.

"Light as a feather. And are you all right with that pack? Seems a bit large."

"It's what I need. I'll get used to it again, soon enough." By way of demonstration she swung it up, neatly and smoothly, slipping her left arm, then her right, into the straps. A familiar movement, and a familiar, welcome weight.

Gregori stood back to admire her: pack, cloak, and grin. "Well. There you go, then." He clasped her hand. "And whichever one of us sees Zenna again first, will give the other's love to her."

"I believe that will be you."

"You're probably right. The sea's a wide road, and you're heading for narrow ones." He glanced about; no one else was nearby. He leaned closer, spoke more quietly. "And I hope your work here goes well."

He released her hand and turned away, calling instructions to the stevedores; and the steerswoman made her way down the long wharf.

Donner was built on flat land, and as soon as Rowan left the openness of the harborside, all sense of space vanished. The street before her seemed merely a corridor, the shops and homes to either side its rooms, an effect completed by the heavy white sky hanging close above like a low ceiling. Donner, despite being a city, felt today as if it existed within arm's reach only.

But when Rowan looked up, the low tower of the harbormaster's office was visible above, dimmed gray by the damp-laden air. Yet even that seemed two-dimensional, like a sketch of a tower, vague outline and shadow.

The office on the first floor was deserted. Rowan passed through to the back, and discovered a set of stairs leading above. She considered the steep ascent, winced, sighed. Leaving her pack below, she climbed.

At the top: a square room, occupying the entire top floor, with broad windows open all around. Rowan leaned back against the railing of the stairwell, nursing an ache in her left leg, and studied the view.

The southeast window looked out squarely on the harbor, where the barge was now plying its way back across the water, dimming as it neared *Graceful Days,* the ship itself a mere shadow. Northeast, low buildings spread to the river's edge, thinning to the north as they approached the mud flats, where a portion of Greyriver's broad expanse was visible, seeming to curl back around the city like a broad, protecting arm. Northwest, ornate residences crowded, then spaced themselves, and finally stood smugly solitary up against the edge of a grove of cultivated fruit trees that vanished into mist.

Southwest: the heart of the city, with a sweep of low and high rooftops, continuous, but for a sudden gap, large enough that a portion of the bare ground was visible. There, a crew of about a dozen people was at work, laying yellowish paving stones.

Inside the room, shelves ran along the walls beneath each window. Rowan limped over to check the contents, hoping that she would not find the package she herself had sent some months ago. Quite possibly it had never made its way past Donner at all, and the Prime still remained entirely unaware of Rowan's discoveries in the Demon Lands.

The package was not present, but Rowan was in no way reassured: seated in a wooden chair, its front legs tilted off the floor and his feet comfortably propped on an old crate, was the watcher on duty. He was fast asleep.

He had stirred not at all during Rowan's investigations, and she had not been quiet. Any passing thief or vagrant could easily have wandered in and made off with any of the various items. She resisted the impulse to kick the chair legs out from under the man.

She did, however, achieve a measure of satisfaction by standing behind him when she tapped his shoulder. He came awake with a start, dropped the chair forward with a *thump* and an outfling of arms and legs. "Oof!"

Rowan remained patiently in place while he looked about in confusion, left and right, and finally found her. He stood and shook down his skewed clothing, then stepped forward. "Well, what's your business?" he asked, now all brisk efficiency.

"I sent a package through here some months ago. I was wondering if it managed to get past Donner at all?"

The insult was lost on him. "From and to?" he asked, scanning the shelves as if whatever system organized them were invisible only to Rowan.

"From Rowan, Steerswoman, Alemeth. To Henra, Prime, the Steerswomen's Archives, north of Wulfshaven." And because his chair was now empty, and her left leg was protesting vigorously, she sat.

"A steerswoman, is it?" He studied her with new respect, which faltered when his glance reached her left hand. "You've got no ring..."

"No. I removed it in the course of a demonstration, and later found that it had been pilfered."

"Stealing from a steerswoman; some people have no shame! But that package, I do remember it now. We sent that out on the *Windworthy,* about five months ago. They were heading to The Crags"—he put up a hand to forestall Rowan's protest—"but they were planning to stop and stand off High Island on the way, and get met by a fishing boat, I forget why. We figured they could give it to the fishers and just have them pass it up-Islands to Wulfshaven."

Rowan's mouth twisted. "An attractive theory. I wonder if it actually worked?" There was intercourse among the Islands, often enough, but just as often the fisherfolk found excuse for disputes and occasional furtive vendettas. But with luck, her package might now be safe at the Archives.

"Here." Rowan removed a fat letter from inside her vest and, with a degree of reluctance, entrusted it to the watcher's care.

He made a show of squinting at the address, then placed it grandly on a shelf all by itself. "And there." He turned back. "Trouble with your leg?" he asked suddenly.

She had been unconsciously kneading her thigh, gently. She chose the short explanation. "An injury, last year."

"Ah, that's bad for a steerswoman, with all the walking you ladies do. Have a rest here, for a while, if you like. In fact"—he laid a finger aside his nose—"I think there's a bit of wine somewhere around, if you don't mind sharing the glass."

"Thank you; that's very kind."

"Not at all."

The watcher's "somewhere around" would more accurately be stated as "conveniently to hand"; it was tucked under the crate on which he had rested his feet. He pulled out a clear bottle and a single fine wineglass, and took the crate for his own seat.

The steerswoman studied him as he pulled the cork, which emerged with an encouraging *pop*, despite the bottle being only half full. "How old are you?" she asked.

He put up his brows and blinked. "A week away from forty-eight." He poured. "And that's an odd question."

"Not when it's followed by the next." She accepted the glass, sipped. "Oh, my." The wine was fine, clear, and effervescent. It tasted, lightly, of pears. Rowan could almost forgive the watcher for drinking on duty. She sipped again.

"The next being?" he asked.

She passed the glass back. "Do you remember a wizard named Kieran?"

He blinked in thought. "I can't say that I do. What's his holding?"

"Actually, Donner." His surprise was extreme; Rowan continued: "Forty-two years ago. He was the wizard Jannik's predecessor here."

"So that's why you wanted my age?" He pursed his lips. "Well, I was just a tyke then. Didn't notice much beyond my family, my dog, and my collection of wonderfully ugly bugs. You should have seen them, they were a spectacle!" He made to drink, but then stopped himself. "But no, no, wait a bit. I heard something, not then but years later, about the wizard who was here before Jannik. Some sort of trouble with the townsfolk..."

"You don't recall the particulars?"

"Sorry." He sipped the wine, turned the glass a gaze of respect and, it seemed, gratitude.

"Or perhaps you remember a steerswoman here, at about the same time?" Rowan asked.

"Ah!" Recognition, and he leaned forward. "A tall, narrow woman, dark, with curly black hair braided back from her face! She carried a bow, and caught me in an evil glare when I fingered it once. Can't remember her name—no, wait, hold up, here it comes, something with an L..." He closed his eyes for a few moments, smiled. "Latitia."

"That's her," Rowan said, although the description had not identified the woman. Latitia's logbooks had referred more to the world than to herself; Rowan was rather pleased to at last have a mental picture of her.

"So tell me, lady," the watchman began, using the formal mode, "what's your interest in two people from so long ago?" He passed the glass back.

The steerswoman considered before speaking. "There are gaps in the Steerswomen's records from that time," she said; and this was true. "Some of Latitia's lost logbooks were discovered recently in Alemeth, but her information was not complete. I'm here to remedy that." Also true. "Working in a city suits me, at the moment; I'm not quite ready to return to hard roads." All true, as far as it went—and caution warned her to take it no further.

"Hm. If you're looking to fill in news from forty-two years ago, you'd best be asking the old folks."

"I'll do that. But I'd be interested in speaking to anyone who remembers that time at all." She drank again, and the watcher refilled the glass. "Still," Rowan continued, "I ought to start with the likeliest source. Who is the oldest person in town, do you know?"

He considered as he poured. "I'm not sure... old Nid, maybe."

"Where might old Nid be found?"

"I don't know him well... I've seen him out at the docks up riverside, watching the eelers at their work. I think his granddaughter's one of them. Or, there's a mug-room where the steves dry out; I've noticed him there a time or two, and he did look like a fixture. Ah, wait, now that I think of it, hang about—" He closed his eyes again to search his memory; Rowan found herself wondering what sort of internal filing system he employed. "I believe..." He opened his eyes. "Yes, I once heard that he used to be mayor; maybe that could have been around that time."

This was very good news; a person in such a position would know a great deal about the town's doings while he was in office. "It sounds like Nid's my man."

"Sounds like."

Rowan received directions to the mug-room, and the conversation continued in a more desultory fashion. At last the steerswoman rose, finding her leg grateful for the rest; but she paused, and nodded toward the southeast window. "Isn't that where Saranna's Inn used to be?"

He turned to look. "Yes. They're putting down a plaza there now. And talking about a fountain, as well. You've been here before, have you? You must have heard about the fire."

"I know of it." The steerswoman did not volunteer more. "But I thought Saranna might have rebuilt..."

"No, we lost the inn and Saranna herself that day, more's the pity; we all miss her." He caught the change in her expression. "Did you know her?"

The steerswoman was rather long in replying; and then she sighed. "We met, briefly," was all she said.

"Well, it's a shame she's gone. Still, it could have been worse. The whole city could have gone up, if Jannik hadn't been here to stop those dragons. Took the trouble to move their nesting places, too, farther away from the city. We're lucky to have a wizard in Donner..."

He escorted her downstairs, carrying her pack to the street door, and held it as the steerswoman retrieved her cane, which was thong-tied at its side. She needed it only occasionally, but she used the cover of the movements to surreptitiously scan the street.

To the left, a pair of little girls in matching red-flounced dresses strolled arm in arm; a young woman in working attire hauled a cart of kindling down the cobbled street; a group of five sailors wandered aimlessly, gawking at the decorative moldings that each house displayed on every eave and window ledge.

And to the right—

"Hm." The watcher had noticed her glance, and followed its direction. "Don't recognize those two. Did they come in on the same ship you did?"

"Yes, they did," Rowan said; and by taking the watcher's hand to shake, she managed to turn him back toward her, shifting his attention away from the couple. "Thank you for the wine," she said, then donned her pack and departed, to the left.

First order of business: her letter, dealt with.

Her second order of business took Rowan on a very long but thankfully flat walk through the streets, northeast from the harbor. She arrived at

Donner's gracious Tea Shop, with its wide veranda overlooking the weedy estuary. The veranda was now deserted, but for a collection of disconsolate, hunch-shouldered gulls lining the railing. It began to rain.

Nearby: a small, shabby shop. Rowan entered, brushed wetness from her hair, slipped her pack from her shoulders.

The bell on the door called from a back room a small, squat woman with a bright eye and gnarled hands. After exchanging greetings, Rowan drew a silk handkerchief from her right vest pocket and opened it. "Can you size this to my finger?"

The jeweler studied the item Rowan passed, then turned up a sharp gaze. "Now, this is a steerswoman's ring."

"So it is. And I am a steerswoman."

"But this isn't yours."

"It is now. Its owner resigned, and I lost my own. I seem to have inherited it."

"Hm. Can you prove you're a steerswoman?"

"What sort of proof would suffice? I can show you my charts. You can read my logbook, if you like, or look at the soles of my boots."

The jeweler twisted her mouth in amusement. "I could do all that. Well, I don't suppose you've stolen all your gear; those boots fit you too well." She considered the ring again. "An hour. Will you wait, or come back?"

"I'll wait, if you don't mind. And may I pay you?"

The woman wrinkled her nose. "No, don't bother. Nice of you to ask, though."

Rowan tried on a few sizing rings, and the jeweler set to work. Finding no chair about, the steerswoman eased herself to sit on the floor by her pack, with her back against the wall, needing first to unstrap her sword. This she laid across her lap.

The jeweler glanced up. "Either you're stronger than you look or you inherited that sword, as well."

"As a matter of fact, I did." It was a bit chill on the floor; Rowan adjusted her cloak around her knees. "I hope to trade it for a lighter one." Her own sword was lost, and she missed it deeply; although plain to the eye, it had possessed subtle superiorities that she had learned to exploit well. She wondered if she would ever regain the level of skill it had allowed her.

The jeweler informed her of the location of the city's two swordsmiths, and of a pawnshop where weapons were sometimes found, and continued with her work, using incongruously heavy clippers to precisely cut a tiny section from the circle of the ring.

Outside, voices: happy exclamations, as if two long-lost friends were meeting by chance. Rowan thought the performance at least overdone, if not entirely unnecessary, and suppressed a surge of annoyance.

The jeweler noticed the turn of her head. "Someone you know?"

"They traveled on the same ship I did," Rowan said.

The jeweler crimped the ring around a sized rod, then used a pair of tongs to hold it in the heat of the tiny furnace at the back of the room. She was making a speedy job of it. Before the opportunity was lost, Rowan asked: "Have you lived here all your life?"

"I was born right upstairs."

She seemed the right age, barely. "Do you remember a wizard named Kieran?"

The woman suddenly straightened up from the furnace door and, to Rowan's amazement, tilted back her head, closed her eyes, and flung out both hands. "The Lion!" she announced. "The Eagle! The Winged Horse, and the Brothers, and the Sisters!"

"The constellations," Rowan said, bemused.

The jeweler dropped her arms, and returned to heating, her face now transformed with childlike happiness. "Oh, yes, I learned them all. What a wonder, to know the stars have names!"

"And… how does this relate to Kieran?"

"Oh, he loved the children, such a sweet old man. Once a month, just over at the tea shop"—she pointed with her free hand—"right at midnight, he'd have a little party, with cakes and sweet tea, and only children invited. And all the lanterns made red, so you could see the stars, he said. He taught us the star names, and told us their stories…"

Rowan was astonished. This was absolutely contrary to her understanding of the nature of wizards. "You weren't afraid of him?"

"Some were, you know how children can be. And some of the parents, they wouldn't their little ones come at all. But living right here, I never missed a single party. Me and about a dozen others, more or less, showed up every month, until the old wizard passed away."

Rowan considered this information silently. The jeweler continued her work.

"How did he die, do you know?" Rowan asked.

"Old age." A pause. "Well, I'm assuming. He looked to me to be about a hundred years old… Collecting information, are you?"

"It's what we do."

The conversation lapsed; Rowan leaned her head back against the wall. Her hair was still damp, but the room was warm, and she felt herself settle into comfort, listening to the quiet creaks and clinks as the jeweler worked, the hiss of rain, the distant cries of gulls…

She did not realize that she had dozed off until a hand on her shoulder woke her. She startled violently, and found the jeweler equally startled. "Jumpy, aren't you? But we're done."

Rowan rubbed her eyes, and clumsily regained her feet; her leg had stiffened while she slept. She winced. "Let's see." The jeweler laid it in Rowan's palm. The steerswoman picked it up, turned it over and over.

A smooth silver circle. Its only ornamentation: a twist in the band. But it was that twist, that precise half-turn, that made all the difference.

It identified the ring, immediately, as a steerswoman's, and altered the ring's geometry, subtly, from a simple circle into a lovely paradox.

What seemed to possess two edges had only one. And the two apparent surfaces—the inside of the ring and the outside—were in fact the same single surface, doubled back upon itself.

The jeweler had done well: there was no sign of the alteration. It was perfect. Rowan slipped it on the middle finger of her left hand.

To the Demon Folk, objects were words, and Rowan did not blame them for confiscating her own ring—she only wondered, often, what strange message she had passed on to them. Likely she would never know.

But she felt now, as sometimes she did, that she had perhaps caught a bit of their way of thinking. Because this ring did speak to her, and not of its own sad history. In pure silver it innocently declared its strange truth: smooth, hard, and bright.

Rowan's own history was written, permanently, on the hand that bore it: a complexity of tiny scars, the price of inattention. And on her leg: the deep burn of a stranger's ignorance. And invisibly, on her spirit: the wounds of anger, and betrayal, and desperation.

The cost of knowledge was struggle, and pain. But the reward, always, was clean, clear, bright…

"Need a hankie?"

"What?" Rowan looked up, found her vision blurred. She used her sleeve to dry her eyes. "I'm sorry. I've been a long time without my ring. I'm very glad to have this. Thank you."

The jeweler studied her, nodded. "You look tired. Where are you staying?"

"I haven't decided yet…"

"I've got a spare room upstairs."

"That's very kind. But I was hoping for something more central. I'll be doing a lot of walking."

"Hm." The jeweler took herself back to her workbench. "I can think of any number of people who'd be willing to put up a steerswoman. Or you could try the Dolphin, smack in the middle of town. Ruffo's a skinflint, but you might be able to shame him into it. Do you want this?" She turned back, a small chip of silver between thumb and forefinger.

"No…" Rowan glanced at her ring again. "You keep it. Perhaps you can find some use for it."

"Perhaps I will." The jeweler considered it speculatively, then laughed. "There, you see? You've paid me after all."

"Someone has," Rowan admitted.

The Dolphin was a sprawling establishment, possessing three wings of differing ages. Centrally, a large and comfortable sitting room faced the street through tall windows of real glass, behind which a number of well-dressed patrons were tended by graceful and solicitous servers, all safe from the drizzling rain.

Directly adjacent: a small entrance, announced by a life-sized model of a dolphin hung above the door. The detail on this was excellent, and Rowan surmised that the original artist had actually been privileged to observe the creatures personally. Unfortunately, later maintenance had been executed by a lesser hand, whose owner clearly shared Donner's local love of clumsy excess decoration. The fish was painted brightly, red on top, green below, with gold-gilt eyes and an entirely spurious line of wavelike markings down its length. Rowan felt she ought to apologize to it on the city's behalf.

Inside, Rowan found a simpler public room. The proprietor, one Ruffo, was occupied, and Rowan found a seat nearby and listened.

"Well, back again, getting to be a regular thing, isn't it. Just off *Graceful Days*, I suppose? And what's this? A lady?" Introductions were performed, at a rather high volume; around the room, heads turned to watch. By sheer will, Rowan forced herself not to do the same. "Your usual room is available, as it happens, but as you've got company this time, I suspect you'll want something a little finer—"

Eventually, the arrangements were completed; Rowan waved away the server who approached her, then rose and went to introduce herself to Ruffo.

He was a small, wiry man, dressed in fine green twill trousers with bright red piping, and a yellow silk shirt that did not complement his complexion. As mark of his trade, he also wore a white apron, but even this was of good, heavy linen, and sported a small embroidered red dolphin at the lower right corner. The apron was starched, and spotless.

When Rowan identified herself as a steerswoman, Ruffo grew wary. His suspicions were confirmed when she made her request: a small room, if one could be spared. She made no mention of payment.

Ruffo looked aside, scratched his ear, and embarked on a series of rambling comments regarding a sudden excess of business due to the ship's arrival, a caravan that would depart in two days, and more; he continued for some time. Rowan merely stood patiently, leaning on her cane.

The handful of patrons in the common room watched closely, said nothing, but visibly grew more and more outraged on the steerswoman's behalf. Finally, Ruffo succumbed to the silent social pressure. Likely the cane had helped.

A chambermaid wearing an extremely dubious expression escorted the steerswoman: up a broad, polished staircase; through a tangle of corridors; down a narrow, worn staircase exactly the same length as the first; down another corridor; and eventually to a door that opened on a room merely twice the size of its bed.

A rickety table stood under the window, holding pitcher and ewer and candlestick. A less rickety but even more ancient chair was tucked under the table. The maid departed for linens, and Rowan took off her pack, set it on the floor, and discovered that there remained in the room exactly enough space for one person to stand.

She thought a moment, exited the room, and continued down the corridor. Five feet, a turn to the right, and the steerswoman found herself at a door that opened directly to the outside.

A dirt yard, now hissing with rain and splashing mud; stables to the right; kitchen entrance to the left, and access to the street beyond. Excellent.

She shut the door and made her long and tedious way up and down stairs, back to the common room, where she requested a simple meal. When it arrived, its quality surprised her: eel in a tart lemon sauce; brown rice seasoned with scallions; a large mug of vegetable stew; and an entire bottle of the effervescent pear wine. Rowan nervously asked the price. The server, a slim, handsome lad of about fourteen, glanced about, gazed at the ceiling as if doing sums in his head, gave her a wink, and departed.

The cuisine on *Graceful Days* had been hearty, but artless. Rowan dined with deep pleasure, and, when her plates were cleared away, gathered up her bottle and glass, and took herself to a seat at a table closer to the fire.

The room slowly emptied of diners, until all that remained were a handful of locals by the hearth, and the occupants of the table directly behind Rowan. There, over one and then a second pitcher of ale, the conversation continued: loud, enthusiastic. One could not help but listen, and Rowan resigned herself to doing so. Eventually she heard:

"Now, didn't I tell you—finest ale to be had in Donner, and I know my ale. But, alas, even the best ale only comes to visit, never to stay. If you'll excuse me…" And Rowan heard the scrape of a chair, and the side door opening, then closing.

The room grew instantly quieter, and the patrons by the fireplace seemed to sigh in relief. Rowan waited a few moments; then she leaned back in her chair, and spoke quietly, without turning. "Bel, what exactly do you think you're doing?"

From behind her, the reply, as quiet, was amused. "I'm doing exactly what we planned. I'm watching your back."

"With Dan constantly at your side?"

"I've decided that he makes good cover."

The steerswoman brought her glass to her lips, sipped twice. No one was taking note of the conversation. She said: "He is large, loud, and attracts a great deal of attention."

"Perfect. The best place to hide something is in plain sight. And the best way to hide something in plain sight is to put it near something large, and loud, and distracting."

"I'm not attempting to hide!"

"I don't mean you, I mean me. I'm keeping a low profile."

"By maintaining a high one?"

"That's right. Wherever Dan and I go, everyone watches us. No one can accuse me of sneaking around."

"You're using him."

"So I am. And he's enjoying it. He thinks it's an adventure."

"I don't want him to enjoy it!" Rowan glanced about; no one had noticed her sudden vehemence. She moderated her voice, and studied her wineglass as if idly. "Bel, at some point, possibly soon, this may well become dangerous. Dan isn't a fighter or an adventurer; he's just a cooper from Alemeth. He doesn't have the resources to deal with real danger."

"Yes he does; he has me. If anyone makes a move on him, I'll kill them. Really, Rowan, it's all very simple."

"This was not in the plan." Rowan found she was grinding the heel of her hand into her forehead. She stopped herself. "Bel—"

"Rowan, I'm better at this than you are. You do your job; I'll do mine. I think it's lucky that Dan needed to come to Donner at the same time we did. I'm going to go on taking advantage of him for as long as I can. In a couple of days, he'll head upriver after his order of lumber, and you can stop worrying about him then."

At this point Dan himself entered the room, deep in conversation with someone he had met outside. Rowan and Bel quickly exchanged directions to each other's rooms, and the steerswoman addressed herself to the rest of her wine.

Much later, in her tiny room, as the steerswoman sat nodding over her notes and logbook, a soft sound startled her alert.

She sat, speculating. It repeated: a quiet knock on the door.

Rowan cautiously opened it. Bel slid inside and closed the door silently behind her.

She was smaller than Rowan, but muscular, and sturdy. Her hair was thick and brown, worn short over a wide forehead. Her nose was strong, her mouth small and mobile. But what one noticed first and last about Bel were her eyes: very dark, and large. On a person of her size they seemed completely to dominate her face, and whenever Rowan thought of Bel, the image she always had was of those great, dark eyes, looking up.

The dark eyes now regarded Rowan's chamber with astonishment. "Is this a room, or a closet?"

"I suspect it's served as both," Rowan said. "Have you learned something?"

"Yes, good news." Bel reached past Rowan, tested the mattress with one hand, and sat down. "I heard some locals talking. It seems that the wizard Jannik is out of town." She attempted a bounce. The bed did not bounce with her. "Ow."

Rowan leaned back against the door, thinking. Bel caught her expression. "Rowan, that is *good* news. We may get by without being noticed at all."

Rowan crossed her arms. "I suppose it must be coincidence—"

Bel threw up her hands. "Of course it's coincidence!"

"—but I do find it suspiciously convenient—"

"He's been gone for two days! If he were trying to lull you into a false sense of security, and lay a trap, he would have had to know already that you were coming here. Two days ago, you were on *Graceful Days*. Before that, you were in Alemeth, where no one has had contact with the rest of the world for months."

"No one that we know of—"

"You know everyone in Alemeth. There are no wizard's minions there!"

"And perhaps Jannik needs no minion to report my movements to him. He can watch me from the sky, through a Guidestar."

Silence. "But he can't tell it's you," Bel said at last. "Fletcher said, from so high up you can't tell one person from another."

14

"Yes. Still... magic." The steerswoman spoke it like a curse word.

Bel studied her long. "How's your leg?"

"Tired."

"So are you. That's why you're jumping at shadows." She rose. "Get some rest. I have to go; Dan and I are planning on making an amazing number of very peculiar noises in our room for the next hour or so. With luck, we'll be everyone's favorite topic of conversation tomorrow, and no one will bother to wonder about some steerswoman."

Rowan laughed, quietly. "Oh, very well." She checked the corridor outside, left and right, then stood aside to let Bel through.

Something occurred to her: she said, as Bel passed, "And will any of those peculiar noises be genuine?"

The short, strong woman paused in the light from the door, tilted her head, considered. "I haven't decided yet," she said; then she turned and slipped silently away into the dark.

CHAPTER TWO

Wizards and Steerswomen: there existed in the world no two categories of people more completely opposite.

The Steerswomen were collectors of information, students of the world, of nature, and people; the wizards, too, had their own store of knowledge.

Whatever a steerswoman knew was given freely, to whoever might ask. In return, one must answer a steerswoman's questions truthfully—or be placed under the Steerswomen's ban, with no question, even the most trivial, ever answered by them again.

But when asked about the workings of their power, the wizards declined to answer. They shared their knowledge with no one.

And so it had continued across long centuries. The Steerswomen had come to despise the wizards, and the wizards, for the most part, paid the Steerswomen the ultimate insult of ignoring them completely—until recently.

Recently, Rowan had uncovered certain facts, information both startling and disturbing:

She had learned that a Guidestar had fallen. Not one of the two visible in the nighttime sky, motionless points of light behind which the slow constellations shifted with the world's turning; but another, one previously unknown and unseen in the Inner Lands.

She had learned that the part of the world known as the Outskirts depended upon the intervention of magic, and had always done so. Every twenty years, a magical heat was sent down from the sky, sweeping an area east of the inhabited Outskirts, and destroying the dangerous creatures and poisonous plantlife common there. This spell was called by the wizards Routine Bioform Clearance—and its operation had ceased at the same time that the unknown Guidestar had fallen.

Without Routine Bioform Clearance, the redgrass that fed the Outskirters' goat herds would be unable to spread into newly empty lands; the Outskirters could not move to the east; and the Inner Lands would be unable to expand in the area left behind. The result would be famine among the warrior tribes, and overpopulation in the Inner Lands. A clash between two peoples seemed inevitable.

And finally, Rowan had learned that the single person behind these events was a previously unknown wizard, the master-wizard over all others, a man named Slado.

There Rowan's knowledge ended. She knew nothing else about Slado: neither his age, nor his appearance, nor where he dwelled, nor what he hoped to accomplish—nor why he had kept his actions secret even from the other wizards.

Those actions, inexplicably, seemed all designed to destroy. Slado had once even turned Routine Bioform Clearance against the Outskirter tribes directly, with results terrible to witness. And who knew what his next step might be?

He had to be stopped. To be stopped, he first had to be found—or at the very least, the nature and course of his plans must be discovered, so that they could be circumvented. With no other source of information available, Rowan had turned to the Steerswomen's Annex in Alemeth.

There, duplicate copies of steerswomen's logbooks were stored, covering centuries of travel and observation. There might, Rowan hoped, be some subtle clues buried unrecognized in the records. The hope was slim, but there seemed no other recourse.

It had been close on to midnight one spring night, with Rowan, still recuperating from the injuries she had received in the Demon Lands, half dizzy with exhaustion. She was collating and transcribing onto various charts some very odd information about unusual weather patterns when Steffie, a man who assisted the Annex's new custodian, appeared at the worktable.

He was nearly as weary as she—and dusty. He and Zenna, the custodian, had been at work in the attic, sorting through trunks apparently untouched for decades. With an expression of suppressed outrage, Steffie wordlessly set a single logbook on the table in front of Rowan, then stalked back upstairs. Rowan glanced up from her work at the book, then stopped short.

The book's cover was worn and scratched, the leather stained dark in places from handling; the thong that tied it closed had been broken and re-knotted twice. The book had been used hard, and had traveled long.

It was an original logbook, one written by the hand of a steerswoman during the course of her journeys—and the Annex was no place for it.

Such books were precious, and were preserved in the Steerswomen's Archives, north of Wulfshaven. The residents there would make two copies, to send to each of the far-flung annexes: safekeeping against the possibility of some disaster striking the Archives.

But this was not the first original logbook that had been found in Alemeth; there had been several. The previous custodian had neglected her duties—to a criminal degree, in Rowan's opinion. But the old woman had died, leaving others to sort out the chaos she had left behind.

Rowan made a small, weak noise of anger. Suddenly, inexpressibly weary, she considered retiring for the night; found her cane inconveniently far away; decided to wait for Steffie to return and retrieve it for her; organized her papers; cleaned and set aside her pens; took up the logbook and opened it. She read the first lines:

I've just been told that the wizard Kieran passed away two weeks ago. My entire trip to Donner is a waste of time.

Moments later, the entire house had been roused.

The comment was at the beginning of the logbook, and there was no later mention of Kieran at all; the reason for this steerswoman abandoning her assigned route, for her interest in a wizard, must have been recorded near the end of the previous volume. But three days of near-continual searching failed to produce, either in original or copy, the logbook that preceded Latitia's mention of Kieran.

Rowan was left with only two pieces of information, both equally compelling:

First, that something about Kieran had drawn the steerswoman Latitia to Donner.

And second, the date—two weeks after the fall of the unknown Guidestar.

Whether or not Dan and Bel's performance of the previous night did in fact monopolize the morning's gossip, Rowan never discovered; she rose too late.

It was halfway to lunch, which disappointed but did not surprise her. When she had lain down the previous night, her leg raised such vigorous complaint that Rowan had found it necessary to take a small draught of poppy extract. She disliked the drug intensely, but knew she must rest, and reasoned that if there were any night where it might be safe to sleep drugged it would be this night, and possibly no other.

After attending to her morning routine, she climbed and then descended to the common room. It was deserted. Noises led her into the kitchen, and a request for some breakfast resulted in every member of the kitchen staff being introduced one by one as their duties brought them near her—and Rowan found herself adopted.

Kippers produced themselves as if by magic, seeming to regard in startlement the fans of sliced eggs arranged about their heads. Lemonade of exactly the best degree of tartness was presented in a fine crystal glass. The first bread prepared for the noon meal was ready, flavored with fennel and poppy seed, and Rowan enjoyed it hours before the paying customers.

She sat by the edge of a preparing table, using fine linen and fine silver, observing the action of the kitchen crew as she ate. It seemed almost a dance, an orchestrated swirl of activity. Pockets of motion spun inward and outward, from one end of the kitchen to the other, under a cacophony of conversation, not one word of which pertained to the duties at hand. No one, it seemed, required verbal direction.

Rowan found the entire performance deeply satisfying, and spent her breakfast lost in happy analysis of patterns of flow. Eventually, she noticed a single small discontinuity, and watched as it moved, generating minuscule disruptions in its wake. Amused, Rowan projected paths, crosscurrents, amplifications—and so was not surprised when, in three different parts of the kitchen, a pan of salt-covered turbot clattered and crunched to the floor; a basin of silver crashed, sending butter knives sliding to every corner; and an entire basket of rolls leapt into the air, causing four persons to collide in a flurry of snatching hands.

All motion ceased. A moment of silence, then laughter, and cries of "Beck!" "Beck!" Rowan wondered if this were a local curse word, until the source of the original discontinuity—her young server of the previous evening—rose up from the crowd of knife retrievers. Beck blinked about in seeming innocence, then conceded his guilt with an elaborate bow, executed with many flourishes.

The kitchen began to recover, and Rowan addressed the undercook, who was sharing her preparing table with the steerswoman. "Do you remember a wizard named Kieran?"

The undercook, a woman of late middle age, was using heavy shears to trim tails and fins from a stack of five turbot. The question made her pause, causing a five-year-old boy, standing on a stool beside her, to offer a white handkerchief for her to scratch the tip of her nose against. This was his only duty, which he took very seriously.

The cook declined the handkerchief with a jerk of her head, chewed her lip in thought, and began on the turbot again. "Killed a little girl," she said.

The handkerchief boy gaped, dumbfounded. Rowan was herself a moment recovering. "One of the children at his star parties?"

"No... No. No, no." She shook her head. "No. Before he started those up." She finished trimming the last turbot. "Years before that, twenty, twenty-five or more..." As if on cue, an assistant arrived with a stack of five square pans. The undercook transferred one fish into the top pan; it fit, edge to edge, as perfectly as if it had been measured.

"Do you know how it happened?" Rowan asked.

The stack of empty pans began to transform into a stack of fish-filled pans. "Got in his way," the undercook said.

"Surely there was more to it than that?"

"I don't know." The last turbot made its journey. "Stay away from the wizard, my dad told me." She tilted her head, beaming cheerfully at the completed stack, her expression rendering her next sentence freakishly incongruous: "Because he kills little girls who get in his way."

The pan carrier departed; Beck arrived, placed a heavy bucket on the table, and left. "Is your dad still alive?" Rowan asked the cook.

"No. Years gone, him and my ma both." The cook peered in the bucket, glanced up as if consulting an internal list, nodded, then extracted double fistfuls of clams from the water.

The dance of the kitchen crew had recovered, and was quickening: lunch was nearing. Rowan disliked the idea of possibly interfering with the lovely flow, but managed one further question. "Would you happen to know where an elderly man named Nid lives?"

"Rose Street. Off Ambleway. Third on the left. Tub of geraniums just outside. Take the staircase down." The cook took up a clam knife and began plying it with a will.

"Thank you." And the steerswoman scanned the patterns of motion for an appropriate opening, sidled neatly through the moving staff members, and exited by the back door.

Into the yard, around the corner, through another door, and she was at her room in moments. There, she strapped on her sword, collected her logbook, pencils, pen, and ink, loaded them into a shoulder-slung satchel. She made a point of climbing and descending the two staircases, so as to depart the inn publicly through the front door.

When she reached the street, Rowan looked back and sighted Bel, nursing a cup of tea behind the windows of the ornate sitting room. Bel looked extremely comfortable, sitting with both legs folded beneath her, in ostentatious disregard for elegant sensibility. Rowan wondered what the dubious servers who watched askance would think if they knew that they were waiting on a member of a barbaric Outskirter tribe.

Rowan walked away, knowing that Bel would not be far behind. It was good to have someone to watch one's back.

Rose Street was easily found, and the basement dwelling of the venerable Nid. Nid, however, was not present.

The watcher at the harbormaster's office had suggested riverside with the eelers, or the stevedores' mug-room. Because it was nearer, Rowan chose the latter.

Inside, a small iron stove threw out more heat than the day needed, but the dampness retreated from the blast, so that it served its purpose. Off to one side, three beefy men sat in chairs pushed against the wall, their hands wrapped around mugs of soup. They leaned toward each other, their heads close together, and spoke in low tones, occasionally casting sidelong glances at an equally beefy woman who sat alone at the sole, tiny table. She was working a bit of bone with a delicate rasping-file, whistling soundlessly, nonchalant, her own cup beside her.

No proprietor was present. Rowan decided that the woman was the most approachable of the customers.

"Nid?" The stevedore showed surprise at Rowan's question. "Not here, not today. Was he supposed to be?" She considered this seriously, as if it were a difficult question. "Did Susan send you?"

"No, I'm a steerswoman. I have some questions about the history of Donner, and I understand that Nid might be a good person to ask."

The conversation on the other side of the room ceased. Rowan found all present looking at her in puzzlement. "Is there something I don't know about this that I ought?" she said.

"Going to ask *Nid?*" one of the men asked, while another acquired a look of immense astonishment.

Rowan became suspicious. "Is old Nid still in possession of his faculties?" The question caused merely perplexity in the listeners. Rowan clarified: "Gone soft in the head?"

Comprehension. "You can't get the time of day out of him," one of the men confirmed.

"Always mistakes me for some old sweetheart or another," the female stevedore put in. "Most of them dead thirty, forty years now."

"Ask him a question, he'll answer what he thought you've said instead of what you said."

Rowan sighed. "Do any of you happen to know of any people near Nid's age who have lived in Donner all their lives, and can think clearly?" Some discussion, and a joint reply in the negative. "And have any of you lived here since you were children?"

Again in the negative, with several attempts to amplify and discuss at length. Rowan managed to extract herself from the premises before having to sit through anyone's entire life story.

When she reached the street, she spotted Bel seated on a doorstep halfway down the street. The Outskirter was conversing cheerfully with two little girls, who examined with shy fascination the sword Bel had unsheathed to display to them.

Rowan turned away and passed down the street. With Nid apparently useless as an informant, Rowan found herself briefly at a loss. Strolling with no particular goal in mind, she stepped into a provisioner's and acquired a small loaf of black bread and some cheese for her lunch, taking the opportunity to question the proprietors. Both were in their forties, the man a recent immigrant, the woman a longtime resident who nonetheless could recall no mention of a wizard named Kieran.

Outside, the sun was finally dispersing the high mist. The sky lightened to a pale blue, and Rowan wandered toward the docks, planning to eat her lunch by the water; but on impulse she turned aside at Tilemaker's Street.

The workers whom Rowan had seen from the tower the previous day were present again. They were now taking their own lunches, dining out of buckets and satchels they had brought with them, ostentatiously ignoring a lone, disgruntled entrepreneur who had established himself and his steaming cook-cart at the completed end of the plaza.

Rowan considered the layout of the streets, the surrounding buildings, matching them against memory.

There had, in fact, been a cobbled square here five years ago, but much smaller, and with many businesses crowded around it. Rowan and Bel had sat at the old watering trough, conversing, watching the stars; later, they had pushed through a bucket line leading from the well, as they fled from the burning inn.

Now Saranna's Inn and at least seven of the surrounding buildings were entirely gone. The ground there was two-thirds bare earth and one-third brick cobbles, of the pleasant yellow-brown of the native clay. The well was unharmed, although its stone edges were blackened, but the watering trough was new.

Rowan abruptly recalled a young woman, whose name she had never learned; who, wakened from sleep, wearing only a night shift, armed only with a splintered board, had stood side by side with the steerswoman, the two of them trying to fend off a swarm of Jannik's dragon hatchlings while Bel and another stranger created an escape route.

Fire, all around, and collapsing walls, and falling debris. And then the woman, caught in the breath of a dragon, was wearing new clothes, bright clothes, clothes of flame—

And how many others had died that night?

Rowan hoped desperately that Saranna—strong, dignified, kindly Saranna—had, at the least, met a quicker end.

All this, Jannik's doing, at Slado's command. All this, merely to rid the world of one inconvenient steerswoman. It seemed to Rowan that wizards had no greater regard for the lives of the folk than they did for the lives of insects.

She must be cautious. Even with Jannik out of town, he might have minions among the townsfolk.

And it was for exactly this reason that Bel must continue to follow Rowan. If the steerswoman's actions attracted surreptitious scrutiny, Bel would notice, and they could leave Donner.

Assuming, that is, that the matter of Kieran and Latitia was of any significance at all. In fact, Rowan did not yet know.

She settled herself on the edge of the new watering trough and unwrapped her lunch. She made to take a bite of the bread; but then she paused, set it down again, and thoughtfully pulled out her logbook and a pencil.

She reversed the logbook and opened it from the back: a method steerswomen sometimes used to keep scratch notes separate from more finished records. On an empty page, she drew a horizontal line, and labeled the right end *Present*. She divided the line into increments: -10, -20, -30... back to -100.

At the point representing -42, Rowan wrote: *Kieran dies*. On the basis of the undercook's information, Rowan counted back twenty-five years from that point and added: *Girl murdered*. Between the two, hovering above the line, with no date indication: *Star parties*.

Hugo, an elderly steersman living at the Archives, had been the Steerswomen's expert on the nature and history of the wizards. From old conversations with him, Rowan knew to add *Kieran arrives in Donner* at approximately -95.

Rowan wished she could consult Hugo now; unfortunately, he had passed away a year and a half earlier. The steerswoman Sarah had taken over his work. What had once been an obscure area of study was now a subject of continual and urgent importance.

Weeks or months from now, when Rowan's new letter completed its journey from the harbormaster's office to the Archives, Sarah would begin an analysis similar to Rowan's. She would have Hugo's own notes, and the wealth of the Archives itself to aid her.

Or, quite possibly, Sarah's task would begin and end by simply removing from a shelf one of Latitia's many original logbooks, and there find recorded, toward the end, plainly stated, the reason a steerswoman became interested in a wizard.

A shout. Rowan looked up.

The brickworkers were waving her over, enthusiastically. She had been recognized as a steerswoman. They wished her to join them.

Rowan waved back, took bread and cheese in one hand, clumsily, and stood. But before she slipped her logbook and pencil back in her satchel she took a moment to quickly notate, in the same year as Kieran's death: *Guidestar falls*.

The workers had a bucket of beer, and invited Rowan to partake. She accepted, and politely offered in return a portion of her hard cheese—and suddenly found herself in the midst of a very lively trading session, apparently a daily ritual. When the flurry was over, her lunch now consisted of: half a cold pastry filled with smoked fish; a sweet red plum; slices of her own black bread, spread thick with goose grease; and a handful of fresh string beans, to be crunched raw, like candy. The group settled down to eat, Rowan companionably accepted among them.

Two of the workers were middle-aged, and Rowan wasted no time. "Do you remember the wizard Kieran?"

The woman of the pair immediately indicated eagerness to speak, but she had just taken a very large bite of pastry, and had to deal with it before she could talk clearly. Her workmate had the leisure to consider before replying. "I remember the parties," he said. "Kieran used to hold parties, just for the children, out by the Tea Shop, where it's all so open. He told us the names of the constellations, and stories of how they were named. And how to tell time by the Guidestars."

"Who's Kieran?" one of the others asked.

The woman had cleared her mouth to speak. "Wizard. Used to live here. It was before your time."

"Before yours, as well," the man put in.

"Not at all! I was just a tiny thing, but I can remember him." She wiped her mouth on her sleeve. "He was tall and thin, and his beard was like a great white cloud." Her eyes shone with remembered delight. "He had the bluest eyes I've ever seen, a really deep, dark blue. He could make fire come from his fingertips. And smoke came out of his mouth!"

"That was a pipe he was smoking."

"Well, it was magic to me." She took another, more manageable bite of pastry. "I don't remember much else. Just that it was fun, and mysterious, and a little scary, to be with a wizard. And he served cake, I liked the cake."

"I remember the star-names..." The man acquired a look of concentration. "The Hero, that was named for the strongest man who ever lived. And the Hunter, he was the best hunter. The Hound was his dog. The Lion... I don't remember what the Lion was, other than a lion..."

"The stars are distant suns," the woman added, addressing the comment to the group as a whole, with an air of self-satisfied superiority. "Did you know that?" In fact, Rowan did, as did all the workers, who indicated so by means of deprecating noises and gestures. The statement was common knowledge throughout the Inner Lands. Although it could not be proven, steerswomen treated it as fact; it was hardly possible to imagine what else stars might be.

"Were there no adults at the parties?"

Both Rowan's informants paused to think, and shook their heads. "None that I ever saw," the woman said.

"It was only for children, is what I heard," the man put in. "He liked children."

Another member of the group, a bony woman with her hair in many braids, made a long and unpleasant noise with her mouth. A few of the other workers laughed.

The noise carried no meaning for Rowan, but the man defended the wizard. "No, not at all, nothing of the kind," he insisted.

The older woman confirmed: "He acted just like a grandfather to us. He was spooky, but he was nice. I think he gave those parties, and talked to us, just because he enjoyed it. He was just a nice old man who liked children, and happened to be a wizard."

Rowan said: "But I heard that he killed a girl."

The woman gaped. "Never! Someone told you wrong, lady!"

"Perhaps that's the case," Rowan conceded—then caught the expression on the man's face.

The man's co-workers caught it, too, and they turned to him with interest. He noticed their attention, and dipped another cup of beer for himself. He took the time to drink deep, then nodded to the crowd at large. "It's true. Long before the star parties. In fact"—he drank again—"it was my own dad's sister." Excited murmurs from the workers.

"Kieran killed your aunt?" Rowan asked the man.

"That's right."

"And you were allowed, later, to go to his parties?"

"Well, I wasn't allowed, not at all. In fact, I was exactly forbidden to go. I slipped out on my own. My dad never caught me. But he told me, plenty of times, how it happened with his sister."

People edged closer, settled in, eager for the story that would surely follow. Rowan said, before the tale could begin: "My information places the event about twenty-five years before Kieran died."

"That's about right."

"Come on, tell it!" someone called.

"Well." He passed his cup for refilling. "My dad always told it to say, *Don't be too curious, because you might not like what you find.* Seems his sister was a wild and lively girl, and liked to poke about. Always into some sort of trouble or other.

"One day, Ammi—that was her name—she tells all her little friends that she wants to see some magic, and she's going to go look in the windows of the wizard's house, and come back and tell them about it. Brave and wild, she was, and that was the bravest and wildest thing she could think of doing, what with everyone so scared of the wizard—"

"Wait," Rowan put in, "everyone was afraid of him?"

"That's how my dad said it."

"But surely she knew he was fond of children."

This took some thought. "I don't know. Maybe he wasn't, back then. But when Dad told the story, it was always *Everyone was afraid of the wizard.* And when those star parties started up, he told me, *You keep away, that wizard is a dangerous man.* Because of what happened."

The listeners disliked Rowan's interruptions, and the steerswoman allowed the tale to proceed.

"So, one day when Kieran was off tending to his dragons at the mud flats, Ammi slips away from her playmates after lunch.

"And dinnertime comes, and she's not home.

"And bedtime comes, and that's when the family went asking at her friends' houses—and they hear what she had planned to do. My dad's older brother—he was a grown man, nearly—he was all wild to go and fetch her back, but the family stopped him—"

"Because everyone was afraid of Kieran," Rowan said, annoying the listeners again.

"That's right."

She leaned forward. "*Why?*"

The man shrugged. "Sensible to keep clear of wizards, isn't it?"

And it was, as Rowan knew well. But wizards who lived in a town within their holding generally had some interaction with the townspeople. This could hardly be sustained if the people were in continual fear. Perhaps events even earlier had given them reason—some contemporary of Nid's might have the answer.

She found the workers gazing at her with disgruntlement. "I'm sorry, do go on."

The tale-teller continued. "Next day, someone comes to the house around noon, saying Kieran's back from the mud flats. And the whole family goes over, not to the wizard's house, but near. That little plaza around East Well. You can see the house from there. And they all wait, watching the house.

"It goes past lunch, and it goes into the afternoon, and more and more people show up as the word gets around. And just before dinner, the wizard comes out of his house." Little stirrings among the crowd as the man paused to drink more beer. "And he's dragging Ammi's body behind him." Appreciative shivers from the listeners. "By her hair." Soft cries of delighted horror.

"And he drags Ammi along, right down the street, right up to East Well, with all the people gone quiet and watching. And when he got there he let go of her... My father was right there, and he saw it. He said he remembered how it sounded when his sister's head hit the ground, and he cried because he thought it must hurt... but she was already dead.

"And Kieran looked around at all the people... My father said he never saw anyone look like that, like there was nothing at all behind his eyes... Just looked at the people, all around the square... and then walked away."

The crowd sighed appreciatively, and relaxed, satisfied by the eerie tale—but there was more. "And here's the thing," the storyteller said, leaning forward. "When they were laying Ammi out to bury, they could tell she wasn't just fresh dead. She was a day dead, at least. That Kieran, he had killed her from miles away, with magic."

The people returned to their lunches, commenting to each other on the excellence of the tale. The bony, braid-wearing woman spoke up. "Maybe it was the house itself killed her. A magic house."

"Could be." The storyteller bit into a plum, leaning forward to let the juice drip on the ground.

"Were there any visible injuries on the girl's body?" Rowan asked.

The man nodded as he swallowed. "Holes." He indicated on his own torso, using his fist to show size. "Each about so big."

Rowan could not help commenting: "You don't seem very distressed by the death of your aunt."

He shrugged. "It's stupid, isn't it, messing with a wizard's house? Everyone knows that. Anyway, I never knew her."

"And after hearing this harrowing tale from your father, you slipped away yourself, to attend the murderer's parties?"

The man could not miss her accusatory tone. "That happened ages ago," he said, annoyed. "And the girl brought it on herself, didn't she? But being asked by a wizard to go look at the stars, and hear stories—well, that's something wonderful, isn't it?"

"He invited you personally?"

The man nodded, caught the eye of the woman who had also attended the parties; she nodded as well.

"Both of you specifically? Did he invite only particular children?"

"No," the woman said. "I was with a crowd of my friends, under the veranda at the tea shop, playing in the mud. He looked down over the edge, and he asked us all to come. I remember it well, I was so surprised and excited."

"Same for me. I was playing soldier with some cousins, by East Well. He passed by and asked us all, too."

The workers continued their lunch, contemplatively; Rowan did the same.

Across the plaza, the cook-cart had acquired a customer: Bel, who passed a coin over and received a cone of brown paper, steam rising from its top. She peered into it with interest as she ambled over to the watering trough.

Rowan said to the workers, "Do any of you know how Kieran died?"

"Old age is what I heard," the storyteller said. "No surprise, I suppose. He looked about a thousand years old to me."

Some in the crowd chuckled, but Rowan knew that wizards aged differently from the common folk, and could not help wondering at Kieran's true age. "How many star parties were there? They ended when he died; but when did they begin?"

Neither of her informants could identify a specific date. "I was so little," the woman said. "Days just ran into each other."

The man was no more helpful. "Once a month, they were, but how many months altogether? I don't know."

The proprietor of the cook-cart had another visitor, one far less welcome: a tall man, wide-shouldered but otherwise thin, his clothing many layers of rags, his white hair a wild tangle. One hand held a bamboo rod, too long and slim for a supporting cane, and there seemed to be a bandage wrapped around his head. The proprietor was attempting to shoo him off. A beggar, apparently.

Rowan needed clearer information. She turned back to the storyteller. "Is your father still living?"

"No."

"Your mother?"

"She married again. They moved upriver, he has a farm somewhere."

Unfortunate. But other adult family members would certainly hold a grudge against Kieran, and perhaps would have watched him carefully for the rest of his life. "You mentioned an uncle, your father's older brother. Is he still alive?"

Nods all around: success. "And where might I find him?"

"Rose Street. Just off Ambleway. You can't miss it, there's a big pot of geraniums right in front of the door."

Rowan sighed. "Nid?"

"Nid," the bony woman said, before the man could speak, and the workers cheerfully took it up: "Nid." "Nid." "Nid."

"Nid," the man himself confirmed.

The steerswoman sighed again. "Your father had no other siblings?"

"No."

She asked the older woman. "Is either of your parents living?"

"Both, I suppose, but where? I couldn't say, other than west. They bought out a caravan captain ages ago, they travel all over."

Across the plaza: protests growing more vehement from the area of the cook-cart. The workers craned their necks. A handful of passersby paused to watch. One of these continued on, crossing toward the workers.

The storyteller noticed. "That's it, then, let's go," he announced, rising to his feet with an authoritative air.

The response from the group was largely hoots and jeers. No one budged from their seats, save one muscular woman who pointedly made herself even more comfortable, lounging full length on the ground.

"Come on, if Jenny's coming back, then old Sam's not far behind." The workers grudgingly and grumblingly conceded the truth of this, and slowly began to collect themselves.

"How old is old Sam?" Rowan asked.

"Younger than me," the bony woman informed her, as she upended her lunch bucket to shake out the crumbs; she was about Rowan's age. "He's just in charge, that's all. It's a joke. Why did you ask about that dead wizard?"

"I'm interested in the events during a particular time in Donner's history," Rowan told her. "Do you know of anyone still living who was an adult, or close to it, during that time? Someone perhaps fifty-five years old, or older?"

The worker gave the matter some thought. "There's my gran... no, she moved the family here from upriver, that must have been after that wizard died. But seems like I see a lot of oldsters about... just ask around, I suppose." She strode off, back to the uncobbled edge of the plaza; but halfway there an idea struck her, and she called back: "Ask my gran! Oldsters like each other's company, she knows everyone her age. She'll know who to talk to."

This was an excellent idea. Rowan quickly got directions, and headed off toward the street. But before she reached it, her steps slowed; she paused and turned.

A small crowd had collected around the cook-cart, watching as the beggar, half stumbling, backed away from the cook's continuing curses.

Rowan strode over, brushed through the crowd, interrupted the cook's performance. "One portion, please."

"Of course!" A glance at her ring and chain identified her as a steerswoman, and he cheerfully waved away the coin Rowan held out.

She took the steaming paper cone in one hand, and forced payment on the man. "It's not for me," she explained, and turned to the beggar.

The reason for the cart cook's displeasure was already obvious: the beggar stood in the midst of an acrid stench so strong Rowan felt it ought to be visible, like some sort of foul cocoon. The combination of this with the scent of fish and fried potatoes was far from appetizing. The beggar's various layers of clothing seemed extremely well used, possibly by several different persons previous to him, and apparently never cleaned between owners. The light cloth bandage around his head covered his eyes.

Mastering her fastidiousness, Rowan took his rag-wrapped left hand, placed the cool end of the cone in it, said: "Be careful, it's hot," and walked away.

Halfway across the plaza, she could not help but glance back again.

Some of the watchers were now laughing, one of them shoving another's shoulder in mirth. Others were gaping after the steerswoman, including the cart cook and the beggar.

As she continued on, it occurred to Rowan to wonder why a blind man, surprised, would bother to turn in her direction as she left.

She chuckled to herself, and considered that she might have just rendered assistance to a confidence artist.

Possibly.

She managed not to stop short at the thought.

Surely, it was too soon... Still, as she drew near to Bel, and gave the sort of nod one gives to strangers, she said, quietly: "I may have attracted interest already."

Bel smiled into her paper cone as if charmed by the local cuisine, extracted a fried potato with her fingers. Just as the steerswoman passed by she said: "I've noticed."

CHAPTER THREE

*R*owan found the grannie seated out in front of a tailor's shop run by the mother of the bricklayer. From her, the steerswoman acquired eight references, and a promise that the question would be passed around to older friends and acquaintances. Rowan thanked her, then set off to investigate the names she had been given.

The owner of the first name was out working in the orchards, Rowan was told by his granddaughter; a long walk there and back. Rowan decided to try again in the evening, or visit the orchard the next day, if other leads kept her occupied that night.

The second person proved to have left town to visit family upriver, and would not return for months.

The third, a frail, ancient woman nearly totally deaf, regaled the steerswoman for more than an hour, endlessly plying her with thin, sour tea, addressing her by three different names, none of them correct, and never once touching the subjects of Kieran or Latitia, despite Rowan's repeating the questions at full volume. Attempts to question her in writing proved useless: she was illiterate.

The fourth person, unfortunately, had passed away that very morning, and the steerswoman had to ease herself awkwardly out of a room full of his mourners.

During her wanderings, Rowan sighted Bel only twice, although, interestingly, on the second occasion the Outskirter actually seemed to be following from in front: pausing at, and then casually passing by, the home of the deaf woman, before Rowan had identified it herself. She must have overheard the conversation with the bricklayer's grannie while remaining unseen by Rowan.

The steerswoman also noticed the beggar: once tapping down the street where the orchard worker lived, and later immediately underfoot, when Rowan literally tripped over him as she exited the mourning-house. He was curled up by the foot of the front steps, seemingly asleep. He did not stir.

Back at the Dolphin, Rowan was late for dinner, with the dishes

31

already being cleared from the tables in the common room. The diners remained, enjoying ale and wine, apparently in anticipation of an evening's entertainment. A small band of musicians, tinkers by the style of their apparel, were organizing themselves in one corner of the room: a fiddle, a lap-harp, and a bouzouki.

Rowan attempted and failed to flag down one of the servers. She had just resigned herself to a trip to the kitchen, when she turned back to discover a meal already before her: turbot, cold but sweet, its juices sealed by roasting in a crust of salt; buttered beans sprinkled with marjoram; a light, airy bread, delicate as sea foam, that collapsed under her fingers and melted on her tongue. Presently, the handkerchief boy delivered a pitcher of ale, walking carefully across the room, with great concentration, using both hands. Rowan thanked him politely, which caused him to gape, erupt in giggles, and then flee to the kitchen. A moment later Beck arrived with the mug the boy had forgotten, and another wink.

Bel and Dan came down from their dinner in the formal dining room, and settled themselves at a table in the company of a narrow, dark-haired woman who, by the loud conversation Rowan overheard, had a business interest in a lumber mill upriver. Music began, and when Rowan's plates were cleared away, she joined a group of locals at a long table. None was old enough to have been an adult when Kieran had passed away, and the steerswoman passed the evening in more casual conversation.

The music was as excellent as the food, but the tinkers, typically, ignored all applause and sneered at requests. However, they accepted tips.

Eventually, Bel separated herself from her dinner companions and went to stand alone to one side of the room, as if to gain a better view of the musicians. She had chosen a likely spot, and Rowan felt that anyone might sensibly do the same; so she did so herself.

Bel indicated the musicians with her mug of ale, as though about to remark on their skill, but said: "Don't stay by me too long. If you are being watched, the watcher is here now."

"Really?" A twinge of tension in Rowan's stomach; she covered any outward sign by sipping at her ale. "I'm surprised Ruffo let him inside, considering the smell."

Bel did not turn to Rowan, but her brows knit. "Him? No, *her.*"

Rowan blinked, permitted a verse to pass before saying: "Who?"

"The stout woman sitting in the corner, at our five," Bel said, using Outskirter orientation.

Rowan did not look, but from memory reconstructed the room behind her, and its occupants. At the back, to Rowan's right: a strong-bodied, gray-haired woman, drinking alone. "Interesting. Not the beggar?"

It was Bel's turn to be surprised. She hid it well, changing a suppressed impulse to turn to Rowan into a sideways motion, repeated, as if rocking a bit to the music. Another stanza passed. "If they're working together, that would explain why neither one of them was always there."

Rowan drained her ale. "I'm going to my room." And she nodded politely to Bel, waved at her drinking companions as she passed, handed her empty mug to a passing server, and left through the front door.

Around the side of the building, past the kitchen door—but Rowan was stopped short by a very distinctive smell.

No one was in the yard. The steerswoman cautiously followed her nose, and discovered the beggar in the stables, asleep in the straw in the far corner of an empty stall. Rowan backed out silently and continued to her room.

Bel was already there, standing by the table. "Can you tell if anyone's been looking through your things?"

"Yes." A glance told the tale. "The maid has cleaned, and made the bed. My pack's been moved, but it wasn't opened. The papers on the table haven't been disturbed."

Bel looked dissatisfied, pulled out the chair, sat.

Rowan took the bed. "Was either the beggar or the stout woman always with me?"

Bel wove slightly, side to side: a movement typical in her of calculation. "The woman wasn't. I saw the beggar twice, but I wasn't really watching out for him."

"You didn't notice that he's not blind?"

A disgruntled sound. "No. And he couldn't find you if he were. It's got to be him, or both of them."

"Not necessarily." Rowan rubbed her leg, purely out of habit; thankfully, it had given her no trouble today. "He might be a confidence trickster, who's simply identified me as an easy mark he plans to hit again."

"I wonder where he is now?"

"Asleep in the stables."

"I don't like that."

"Stables are common dossing places for vagrants."

Silence.

"How many times did you notice the woman?"

"She was at the plaza, in that group of people watching when you gave the beggar lunch. She was outside the first house you went into, but she left before you came out."

"Which way did she go?"

"Northwest. Don't ask me the street name."

"She might have thought I was going to the orchards."

"She was gone for a while. But she was looking in a shop window when you came out of the last house." A pause. "Where you tripped over the beggar."

Both women considered.

"If they're Jannik's minions, they're very alert to have noticed me this soon."

"And serious about their duties. He's not here to tell them what to do."

"He may have given them spells to speak to him at a distance."

Bel frowned. "Like links?"

"Or something similar." Fletcher, the wizard's minion Rowan and Bel had met in the Outskirts, had carried a link: a small magical device with which he could paint colored lights in the air, schematic representations of the land below, as seen through the eye of a Guidestar. The link had allowed the Guidestars to track Fletcher's movements, and was also used to report back to his master or masters—but Fletcher had been executed by the Outskirters before Rowan could learn more.

And this was unfortunate. It seemed to Rowan that the common folk would one day need an ally with magic at his or her command, and with Fletcher gone, there remained only two slim chances for help: Corvus, the wizard in Wulfshaven, who, thanks to Rowan, knew something of what was occurring; and Willam, a boy of the common folk, whom Rowan and Bel had befriended on the road, and who was now serving as Corvus's apprentice.

But Corvus had declined to commit himself, and his own goals and motives remained unknown. He might yet choose to side with the master-wizard.

And young Willam—who knew what he might become under Corvus's influence?

Fletcher would have helped. Rowan was certain of it.

But as ever, when thoughts of Fletcher arrived unexpectedly, the steerswoman needed a moment to settle her emotions. She forced herself to consider her lost lover merely in the light of the information provided by him and by the fact of his existence.

She was, slowly, becoming rather good at this.

Rowan recovered her train of thought. "If every minor wizard's servant carried something as powerful as a link, the fact could not have been kept secret for this long. I suspect these watchers are using something simpler."

"Or nothing at all."

"Which means that they had advance warning of my arrival—"

"—or already knew that anyone asking about Kieran and Latitia must be on to something very important."

And that was exactly what they had been watching for, the reason for all caution and urgency.

Without knowing why Latitia had visited Donner so close in time to the fall of the unknown Guidestar, Rowan could not know whether the matter had any significance at all. But evidence of scrutiny was proof of importance.

Rowan had planned to conduct her investigation as quickly as possible, for as long as she was able. And should the wizard Jannik become interested in the investigation, the plan called for Rowan and Bel, quite sensibly, to flee.

But without Jannik himself present—

Rowan said, reluctantly, "This is just too unclear..."

More silence.

Rowan said, "Is it possible that neither of those people is watching me at all?"

"Yes. The beggar might keep himself underfoot for the reasons you've said. The woman might be a coincidence."

"It takes three to know," Rowan muttered: a Steerswomen's adage.

Bel had heard it often. "Well," she said, and rose to leave, "if you trip over the beggar two more times, let me know."

The next morning, Rowan found the elderly orchard worker among a troop of others, all ages, who were engaged in the odorous task of spreading manure throughout the pear orchard. The man, stooped and gnarled but remarkably strong, was definitely not inclined to converse. Nevertheless, custom required that he reply to any question asked by a steerswoman, and he did so, as tersely as possible. Rowan trailed along behind him for an hour, trying to inspire him to expand on the subject of Kieran. Despite the effort, she acquired only information that she had already received from other sources.

Eventually, her frustration became complete. She laid down her cane, which had proved unnecessary that day, folded her cloak on the ground, and joined in with the workers.

This astonished everyone. After some shuffling, the steerswoman ended up working alongside two children, a boy of nine and a girl of about twelve, who were occasionally instructed, in shouts from the old man, how to correctly discharge their duties. Rowan took his instructions to heart, and led by example. The children worked much harder, and more efficiently.

35

This freed their attention somewhat, and they found time to question Rowan endlessly: about distant lands, strange people, the sea, and monsters.

At lunchtime, all the workers congregated on the ground beside a donkey cart holding a large water barrel. Rowan continued her conversation with the children, describing to them the magnificent, mysterious Dolphin Stair, and how the great fishes leapt down the steps, from level to watery level, eventually reaching the unexplored Outer Ocean.

Her audience now included all the orchard workers, all of them enthralled, as they munched on bread and cheese and fruit from sacks they had stored on the water cart. When the story ended, they continued dining, silent and thoughtful. Rowan dipped into her own shoulder bag, pulling out a small wicker box, which had been handed to her by the server who cleared her breakfast dishes. She opened it.

A crispy pastry filled with sweet turnip cubes and tarragon beef; a dark yellow triangle that proved to be a bread impregnated throughout with sharp cheddar cheese; a pear; and, individually wrapped in twists of blue tissue, three pink frosting candies.

These last she distributed: one to the girl, one to the boy, one to the elderly worker. The children gobbled theirs, emitting happy squeals; the old man held his under his nose, eyes closed, breathing in the sugary scent, in apparent rapture. Finally he popped it past his toothless gums and held it in his mouth, sitting completely still, his ancient face transformed with pleasure. The other workers watched, amazed and clearly jealous. The old man took his time chewing, and when at last he swallowed, said: "The Dolphin."

Rowan laughed. "I'm staying there. The kitchen staff seem to have taken me under their wing."

"Hm." He studied her, squinting, his eyes mere black chips barely visible within nests of wrinkles. "And how is young Beck doing?"

"Working hard and cheerfully. Are you related?"

"My great-grandnephew." He continued to study her, then seemed to reach a decision. Reaching into his shirt, he pulled out a flat silver flask, used his shirttail to wipe it down, opened it, and handed it across to the steerswoman.

She took a sip: malt whiskey. She closed her eyes, held the liquor in her mouth, thinking, then swallowed. "High Island," she said, and passed the flask back.

He laughed. "My own dad laid down two dozen bottles, and never touched a drop 'til the day he turned seventy. Took a sip a day after that, and only lasted one bottle. I thought it was the anticipation kept him going, so I didn't start on it until I hit eighty. By then, I thought it was worth the risk."

"Thank you for sharing it. You inherited it entirely yourself? You must have had at least one sibling to share claim."

He wrinkled his nose. "Marisa. She didn't like the taste."

"Is she still living?"

"Forty years dead." He eyed her. "And you asking about that wizard, you're forty years too late, yourself."

"Forty-two, in fact. Still, some new information seems to be coming to light." She took another bite of beef pastry. "Those star parties he held for the children, for instance. That was not very typical of wizards, and it's not mentioned in our records. I suppose that the steerswoman who was here at that time didn't stay long enough to learn of them."

Then: "Ah!" the old man said, with great feeling; and to everyone's amazement, and with sudden energy, he pantomimed an immense arrow shaft piercing his breast. He fell back, to lie on the ground with eyes closed and arms spread, a beatific smile on his face. Laughter all around, but for Rowan, who watched the performance, perplexed.

"Lowry's dead!" the boy cried, overcome with giggles; "He's in love," the girl corrected, in mock-seriousness. Playing along, she knelt by the old man's head, leaned her ear near his mouth. Theatrically, old Lowry breathed, as if it were his last breath: "Latitia..."

"Actually," Rowan said, bemused, "yes."

Lowry broke his pose, reached up to tousle the girl's hair, then used her shoulder to pull himself up again.

Rowan said: "May I assume that you were lovers?"

"Oh, no!" Astonishment. "Ah, if only that were true, but no, no. She wouldn't look at me twice, me such a scrawny little man and her so..." He sighed ostentatiously. "... magnificent."

"Really?" Rowan was delighted. "What was she like?"

"Tall, tall, and slim as a willow wand. Skin so dark that blue light seemed to shine off it. She moved lovely, regal, long graceful steps with her head held high, like a princess from some strange land. And eyes like cool stars in the night sky..."

"Oh, my," Rowan said. "And did you ever speak to this veritable paragon of beauty?"

He threw his head back and laughed. "Constantly! What a pest I was! Ah, but she was a steerswoman, and all I had to do was ask, and she had to answer. Oh, I asked and asked..."

"Did she ever mention what brought her to Donner?"

"Well, steerswomen travel. I don't think I ever asked her that one. Mostly, lady, I just asked to hear the sound of her voice. Never paid much attention to what she was saying…" His voice trailed off; the self-mocking air faded; he acquired a contemplative look.

Interested, Rowan waited, and when Lowry looked at her again, it was with a tinge of speculation. "Might have been that wizard."

Rowan could not help leaning forward eagerly. "Do you know that for a fact, or are you reasoning it?"

"A little of both, maybe. She was mad at him, I knew that."

"Really?" This was unexpected. "Why?"

"For dying. That's how she said it. She was angry, underneath, the whole time she was here, and I couldn't help noticing it. So I asked her straight out: *Tell me, lady, what's made you so angry?* And she said: *Kieran*. And I asked: *What did he do?* And she told me, *He died too soon.*" He thought long, and hard, and Rowan waited; but at the end of his thoughts, he only shook his head. "If the conversation went on from there, lady, I don't know what was said. It's a long time ago, and really, I was just listening to her voice."

Rowan said: "Something about Kieran brought her to Donner."

His gaze became sharper. "And it's brought you, too, hasn't it?"

She sighed. "Yes. But I have no idea what, or why."

Returning from the orchard, Rowan caught sight of a pair of figures standing on a bridge that crossed one of the many streams flowing down from the hills. Even from so great a distance, Rowan easily recognized Bel and Dan. The two seemed to be conversing idly, but Bel had arranged it so that she was facing the orchard.

From Rowan's vantage on the low hill, she could see quite a distance across the flat land: down toward the stream, across northeast to where Greyriver curved around the city. In the fields and in the visible streets, there was no sign of either the beggar or the stout gray woman.

The steerswoman continued down into the city.

The owner of the next name on Rowan's list was not at home, the house shuttered and apparently abandoned. Instead of proceeding directly to the next address, Rowan rambled, in a widening circle, turning left and right in the close streets, occasionally pausing just past corners to glance back. Neither of her suspected followers was present, but eventually Bel and Dan appeared in the street ahead. They stepped into a pawnshop, which reminded Rowan that she ought to see about replacing her sword. She decided not to enter the shop while Bel was there; tomorrow would do.

But she could not resist, as she passed the open shop front, glancing inside. Dan was in some discussion with the shopkeeper; Bel leaned back against the counter, as if idly gazing out into the street. Rowan caught her eye, as was apparently Bel's plan, and the Outskirter leaned slightly forward, so that her face could not be seen by the shopkeeper. So swiftly that it would have been easy to miss, Bel's face showed a knit-browed half squint of uncertain suspicion, and her right hand flashed three fingers. Then she turned away and joined Dan's conversation.

Rowan passed on by.

Three. Maybe.

A third watcher?

It was a busy street, with shops and shabby residences crowded against each other. Many people were about. Rowan mentally subtracted the obvious residents: half a dozen children; the tinsmith lounging outside his own shop front; the woman who came out to berate him, apparently his wife; three men and a woman absorbed in decorating a horse cart with festoons of flowers and ribbons, for what reason Rowan did not know; and a young woman of obvious mental deficiency, sitting half-sprawled on a doorstep beside a disgruntled young man of about eighteen, who was feeding her soup.

Rowan cataloged the remaining persons; she would know if she saw one of them again.

At the next house Rowan found herself trapped for the better part of two hours. The old couple who lived there answered her questions cheerfully, but provided no new information; and then they began questioning her in turn.

As a steerswoman, Rowan was required to answer. Apparently the couple's many children and grandchildren had dispersed themselves across the entire Inner Lands, and after determining that Rowan had not actually met any of them, the pair interrogated the steerswoman as to details of the areas in which they had settled.

Eventually, she managed to extricate herself. At least the tea had been good this time.

The last address provided by the bricklayer's grannie brought the steerswoman to the harborside, and Rowan arrived at a prosperous-looking three-storey building, clumsily and ostentatiously decorated in the native Donner style. She climbed the front stairs and entered, leaning aside to allow three ledger-carrying clerks to brush past, nattering numbers at each other.

Inside: a murmur of quiet voices, an air of constrained bustle. The first floor was a single large room, with counters and open storage areas to the right, cabinets and worktables to the left. Rowan sidled past persons obviously intent on their duties, trying to sight someone who seemed to have a spare moment.

The person she found proved to be a secretary. When Rowan asked after Marel, he led her behind a rank of tall filing racks that obscured the rear of the room, their pigeonholes bristling bits of colored paper.

Beyond: more light, from broad, unshuttered windows at the back of the building. A huge open yard was visible outside, with a warehouse behind. Horse carts were being loaded with newly-made crates, the wood yellow-fresh.

Marel occupied a corner of the main room, with open windows to both sides behind him. He had three tables for his work, set up on three sides of him with ledgers, loose sheets of figures, and on one table a bamboo box with many compartments, all empty.

The old man divided his attention among three different tasks, turning from table to table and back again, and work seemed to progress at equal speed on each. Rowan and the secretary stood quietly, waiting for him to take notice of them.

"I hope I'm not interrupting something important," Rowan said after introductions were made and the secretary had retired. "I could as easily come back later, or tomorrow, if that's better."

"Not at all." Marel was bone-thin, but moved with crisp efficiency. His scalp was bare and pale, and, it seemed, a bit dusty. Nose and eyebrows jutted; green eyes in which the squint of hard thinking had become a permanent feature now showed pleasure and interest. "I do it all by rote. Five minutes after you've gone, I'll have caught up again, without a moment's strain. I hardly have to pay attention to myself at all."

Rowan liked him immediately. "Your business seems to be doing well," she commented; the secretary returned with a tall stool, and Rowan perched herself on it, leaning her cane against the central worktable. "I've just come from Alemeth; I can't help wondering if the silk that rode with me is coming through your offices?"

"Silk." He blinked twice, then became animated. "No, more's the pity! Dunmartin's got it, I've heard, and it'll caravan up the Long North Road."

She nodded. "I'd like to ask you about some events that occurred in Donner some years ago."

He spread his hands. "If it's after eighty years ago and before today, I'll know about it! Although, I admit, I'm a bit hazy on the first three years…"

"The wizard Kieran."

His brows rose. He leaned back in his chair, steepling his fingers. "Strange for a man to change like that," he said.

Rowan leaned forward, hands on her knees. *"Did* he change?" she asked intently.

"Oh, yes. Yes, indeed. Never saw the like. When I was a lad, one steered clear of Kieran. A strange, grim man, as I recall. But just before he died…"

"Star parties for the little children."

"Yes."

"Didn't people think it odd? After what happened to Nid's sister?"

The old man's brows rose higher; he whistled silently. "Now, that is going very far back indeed. I was just a lad myself. Just turned thirteen, and Nid a year or two older."

"I'm surprised anyone permitted their children to associate with Kieran at all."

"That's the thing, do you see? We were all so very young when Ammi died, and later, when Kieran started being friendly… well, most of us hadn't seen the business personally, just heard about it. I hardly knew the girl myself. But Nid was my friend, so perhaps it stayed with me more."

"Did you keep your own children away from Kieran's parties?"

He scratched his ear. "No, they were grown by the time those started. My youngest was eighteen, nineteen. They weren't invited to the sky parties."

"Did Kieran actively keep them away?"

"I don't think so… Here, boy!" He called across the room, and gestured someone over.

The "boy" addressed was a tall and angular man in his fifties. Marel continued when he arrived: "Now, those old star parties that Kieran the wizard hosted; your lot never went to them yourselves, did you?"

"No. We weren't invited." He turned an uninterested pale green gaze on the steerswoman, then back on his father. "Stupid, really, to bother a wizard uninvited."

"It was only the little children he asked, then?"

The son considered. "He would make a great show of performing formal and gracious invitations. But as I recall, any little child could show up, anytime, whether she'd been asked or not."

Rowan nodded. "We've met," she said suddenly.

"Excuse me?"

"Reeder, isn't it?"

His gaze remained impassive. "Yes."

"I was on *Morgan's Chance* with you, six years ago, traveling from here to Wulfshaven." His expression became even more blank, and intentionally so. Rowan instantly regretted reminding Reeder of the circumstances of their meeting, but found she could not gracefully exit the conversation without some further, more formal comment. "I was sorry when I learned what had happened to that boy who traveled with you. He wasn't your son, I hope."

He paused before replying. "No. The son of a friend." And he departed without another word.

Rowan watched him cross the room to return to his own work, and turned back to find Marel studying her sadly. "A lively lad, and quite a handful," he said; and she was a moment realizing that he was not referring to Reeder. "We thought to bring him into the business; no one else in the family seems interested in the daily running. His dad and my son were very close."

She nodded, but chose not to mention how near she had been to the events that caused the boy's death. She was quiet for a long moment; Marel sat watching her, patiently. In the pause, a stocky, disheveled woman hurried up to Marel, an open ledger with two bookmarks clutched across her breast, a sheet of paper filled with close writing in one hand, and a bolt of cloth jammed awkwardly under one arm; Marel gestured the clerk away without shifting his gaze.

When the steerswoman completed her own train of thought, she returned her attention to Marel, but he spoke before she did. "And now that's twice we've talked about children being killed by magic, I can't help noticing. Is that coincidence?"

"Nothing else," she informed him. "In fact, such things are common enough to make me wonder why Kieran suddenly became the exception. I can't help but wonder at his sudden interest in children."

Marel mused, pursing his lips. "Age, perhaps. When you can see the end of your own days coming, you become more interested in the young. There's an impulse, I think, when you know that you won't see the future yourself, to start recruiting ambassadors..." Rowan made a sound of amusement; Marel put up a hand. "But no," he went on, "it wasn't only children, really. He became... nicer, in general. Took more of an interest in people..."

"Suddenly, or slowly?"

He puzzled, blinked, shook his head. "Not easy to answer. I noticed it suddenly, myself; but maybe some others noticed little things, slow trends, earlier. As for me, he came right here one day, asked to talk to me, confidentially. He told me that I should get ready to absorb some losses, because a shipment of embroidery and glassware from The Crags had just gone down in a storm."

"And it had, I assume."

"Oh, yes indeed. With the warning, I was able to do some creative borrowing, invested here and there… by the time the news reached Donner in the normal way, I'd even managed to turn it to my advantage." The thoughtful squint appeared. "And I couldn't help wondering: What's in it for him?"

She twitched a smile. "Spoken like a merchant. Perhaps, nothing more than the pleasure of doing a good turn?"

He smiled himself, broadly and with deep insincerity. "And you believe that?"

"I do not," she assured him.

"Nor I." He became intent. "Lady, in my experience, there are very few people in the world who do things out of pure goodwill. Maybe he was one. Probably not."

What does one gain from acts of general goodwill? What does one gain from kindness to children?

Nothing tangible. Friendship? Amusement, perhaps? Admiration? Loyalty? "Perhaps he felt regret at murdering Nid's sister, and was trying to… atone, somehow?"

"Twenty-five years later?"

"That does seem rather long."

"A man of slow conscience, perhaps. Still, I first noticed the change when he did something nice for me personally."

"And did he continue to do you favors?"

"Oh, no. Not directly, that is. When the East Well went dry, he set it going again, but that was good for everyone. And he suggested we dig another, right outside Saranna's old inn. Pulling up old cobbles, quite a job; but we did it." He squinted again. "And he had us, that is, he *made* us change over all the outhouses around Tilemaker's Street. From pit-style to pot-style." He was suddenly amused. "Old Greydon—he's dead twenty years now—he decided that he wasn't going to do it."

Disobeying a wizard—but Rowan was reassured by the humor in Marel's green eyes. She gave an anticipatory wry smile. "And what happened?"

The green twinkled. "Greydon gets a knock on his door one day, and he opens it up—and it's the wizard himself. And Kieran just pushes by him, walks straight into the house, straight through it, straight out the back—by now the whole family's following behind—and straight to the outhouse.

"He gets in; he shuts the door.

"A few minutes go by. Then the wizard comes out, and looking neither left nor right, walks straight through the family to the back door and out the front again. But he says to Greydon as he passes by: 'Don't go in there.' "

Marel chuckled. "And they all just stood there in the back yard, staring at the outhouse… and then—"

He clapped his hands suddenly, causing Rowan to startle. "The whole thing went straight up in the air! Over the rooftops, and flying in a hundred pieces!" He laughed openly now, and Rowan could not help but do the same. "What a mess! Everyone in the neighborhood was a week cleaning it all off the roofs! We had a few words to say to Greydon, I'll tell you! Oh, and we never let him forget it, either; for years after, we all would show up on his doorstep on the anniversary of the date, and force a celebration on him, willy-nilly. 'Flying Turd Day,' we called it." He gave himself over to laughter, eventually pulling a neat white handkerchief from a drawer to wipe his eyes. "Ah, me."

The steerswoman found the tale more than simply amusing. It was not safe to have pit-style outhouses anywhere near wells or other underground water sources; contamination could pass through the ground into the water, especially in a damp environment. The well water would be foul at the least, and a source of disease at the worst.

Kieran had done the city a kindness. And interestingly, he had done it in a way that provided amusement to the residents, a tale to tell to others— long past the wizard's own demise. It seemed almost an intentional augmentation of the wizard's personal legend. "Do you think," Rowan asked, "that people in Donner tend to remember Kieran kindly rather than otherwise?"

"I don't know… some do, certainly. I expect, if he'd lived longer, we all might have come to." And it seemed that this thought had not occurred to him before, and he gave it some consideration.

Rowan said cautiously: "How did he die?"

"How? Old age, or so we were told. He seemed elderly."

"Can you remember whether Jannik appeared in town before, after, or at the same time as Kieran's death?" If Kieran's death had not been natural, Jannik, as the next master of this holding, seemed a likely suspect.

"Jannik? Oh, after. Hard to pin down, but I'd say, at least a month, maybe two."

Rowan was taken aback. "So long a gap? How did you deal with the dragons, with no wizard to keep them in check?"

"Oh, there was no problem with the dragons, none at all."

"I find that rather interesting…"

"Still," Marel said, "I expect they were never completely uncontrolled, really. I have to assume the apprentice took care of that."

"Apprentice?" Rowan asked. Wizard's apprentices were, if possible, even more mysterious than their masters. They appeared, apparently from nowhere, served and studied for a length of time, and then vanished. Some resurfaced as wizards elsewhere, years or decades later; most were never heard from again. But she had not heard of Kieran possessing an apprentice...

Her puzzling stopped short; she felt cold. "Apprentice?" she said again.

"Oh, yes," Marel continued. "In fact, we'd assumed that he would stay on; but when Jannik showed up, there was no argument at all—"

"—What was his name?"

Marel waved his son over again. "Reeder, I can't recall; what was the name of Kieran's apprentice? You spoke to him a few times, didn't you?"

Reeder flicked his pale, bland gaze from his father's face to the steerswoman's, and Rowan thought: *No. It cannot possibly be this easy.*

But it was.

"Yes," Reeder said. "You mean Slado."

CHAPTER FOUR

*M*arel maintained an apartment on the third floor of the building and among the chambers, a private study: small, slant-ceilinged, comfortably appointed. The single unshuttered dormer window faced west, where now the yellow-brown roof tiles of the city of Donner were tinged red where they faced the sunset, smoky blue in the shadows. The window threw a glowing orange rectangle up onto the opposite wall, like a tilted doorway composed of insubstantial light.

Marel sat behind an old mahogany desk. Reeder slouched in a red leather armchair to the left of the window. The steerswoman paced.

He had been here, in Donner: the man she sought, the one behind all the new troubles of the world. Secretive, immensely powerful, casually murderous, evil. Here, at exactly the moment when it all had begun, with the falling of the unknown Guidestar.

The steerswoman had hoped for more small clues and hints as to his plans, his goals, his nature; she had found instead the man himself.

But only in the past. "I need to know everything you can remember about Slado."

Reeder steepled his fingers, regarded them with lifted brows. "That's rather an open-ended request," he said, seeming to address his hands. "One hardly knows where to begin—or how to end, for that matter."

The steerswoman stopped, turned to him. Where could one begin?

And because it was suddenly important to her, she asked, "What color are his eyes?"

"Gray." Reeder tilted his head a fraction, as if studying her for comparison. "More gray than yours. Less blue."

"Hair?"

"Reddish brown. Auburn, really. He wore it to his shoulders."

"How old?"

Reeder gazed at the ceiling, in an affected show of thought. "My age, perhaps, or a bit younger," he said, indifferently. "Eighteen, nineteen... He looked younger still, from wearing no beard."

So young. And merely an apprentice.

To bring a Guidestar down from the sky must require very powerful

46

magic indeed. Could an apprentice do such a thing?

"How long had Slado been in Kieran's service before the old wizard died?" How much time had he had to learn his craft?

There was a pause. It was Marel who answered. "I don't know. It seemed not long. Reeder?"

A longer pause. "Hardly any time. It was less than a year, I'm certain. More than six months, perhaps. But, really, so long ago—I'm afraid it's difficult to be clear."

"And Slado did not stay on, once Jannik arrived?"

"I don't know that they ever met at all. I never saw them together. Jannik arrived, and Slado was never seen again. One has to assume he left some time before…"

Rowan discovered herself facing the wall, and realized that she had begun pacing again. A habit of hers when agitated. She composed herself and turned back.

If Reeder had himself met Slado, then others had, as well, perhaps some who would remember more clearly. "Did Slado make any friends among the common folk?" she asked. Someone to whom he might have said goodbye, and to whom he might have mentioned something of his future plans. Eighteen years old? "Perhaps he had a sweetheart?"

The pause was considerably longer. Both men were regarding Rowan dubiously. "I'm sorry." With her pacing, and her unexplained intensity, she must seem very peculiar to these men. "But this is important. Was there anyone Slado might have been close to?"

Reeder replied, "It's hard to remember, lady. I do know that there were girls who looked on him with some interest, but I don't know if he ever returned it. As for friends… No one close that I saw. I spoke to him fairly regularly, but not at any length."

Rowan was instantly, sharply attentive. "On what subjects did you speak?"

Reeder made a dismissive gesture with one hand. "The sorts of things fellows that age say, when they have nothing in particular to say. Insulting observations of the passersby, for the most part." Something occurred to him. "He didn't like Kieran," he said, seeming surprised at the memory.

"Did he say why?"

"Well… I believe that he thought he was soft."

Rowan found Reeder's expression interesting. "And you agreed."

He shifted uncomfortably, seeming puzzled; then glanced at her sharply, as if remembering her presence. His pale green gaze again became masked, indifferent, impenetrable. "I suppose it seemed rather silly to me at the time. Cozying up to people, when you have so much power—why bother? He was a wizard. He needed no one's approval. He could do as he pleased."

"And Slado didn't bother to 'cozy up'?"

"No. And it was clear he found Kieran's behavior annoying. But Slado was only an apprentice. He didn't cross his master."

Marel took up the other side of tradition's privilege. "Tell me, lady," he said, in the formal way, "why so great an interest in a wizard's apprentice from so very long ago?"

The steerswoman turned to him. "Because," she said, "Slado is now the most powerful, dangerous, and evil man in the world. Because the harm he is causing with his magic is far worse than anything we ever thought possible." She paused. "And because something must be done about him."

The implications of this last statement took time to sink in; then both men grew disturbed, Marel slowly sitting upright behind his desk, Reeder, blank-faced, pressing himself back in his armchair.

Marel said, "That's... not the sort of thing one generally hears from a steerswoman."

"Yes."

"And exactly what do you intend—"

"*No!*" Reeder had risen. Rowan, startled, stepped back a pace. Reeder said to his father, vehemently: "No! We do *not* want to know about this!" He turned to Rowan, fists clenched at his sides, and spoke through his teeth. "Steerswoman—get out of here!"

"Reeder!" Marel's tone was sharp.

"We want nothing from the wizards, and nothing to do with them. If you're planning to actually cross one—then get far away from us, and keep us out of it!"

Marel thumped the top of his desk. "*My* home," he declared, his bright green eyes now sharp on his son. "*My* office. And if I may remind you, Reeder, *my* business. If you do not like the company I keep, if you cannot speak politely to a guest in my home, then it's you who should—*politely*—excuse yourself."

"Father—"

"Merchant's honor, Reeder. Value rendered for value received. I cannot count the number of times this business has benefited from information that ultimately came, directly or indirectly, by short route or long, from the Steerswomen." Marel folded his hands, composed himself; but he still held Reeder's gaze, and the son seemed locked in its grip. "Now, this woman is asking questions," Marel said tightly, "and for the sake of everything we've gained from the Steerswomen's knowledge, we must reply to the best of our ability—or declare ourselves hypocrites and swindlers!"

Reeder hissed once through clenched teeth. He said, "There has been trouble enough from wizards lately—"

"Lately?" Rowan was taken aback. "What trouble has there been lately?"

Marel released Reeder from his glare; the son stepped back loose-kneed, as if the release had been physical.

The old merchant replied, "No trouble in Donner itself, lady—although if events continue, perhaps we can expect some difficulties." Reeder made an abortive gesture, perhaps of protest, then spun away and threw himself back into his seat. Marel went on: "I find that several of my smaller competitors upriver have been run out of business. Jannik has been commandeering materials, whether or not the suppliers and merchants can afford to lose them. Certain staple foods, grain for the most part; cloth and thread; ores—not the sort you'd expect, not the precious metals. Tin, copper, some iron. The raw stuff, not worked."

Rowan considered. "How odd," she said.

"Those who protest are dealt with rather more harshly than has been Jannik's habit. And interestingly, a similar thing seems to be happening in Olin's holding—where there is less local organization to draw on. He has been commandeering people as well as materials."

Rowan grew more disturbed. "Is Olin gathering an army?"

"If so, an odd sort of army. Two towns by the Salt Bog have been completely emptied, with their citizens, children included, sent somewhere north, for no reason anyone knows."

The steerswoman cast about in her mind, seeking patterns, explanations, and discovering none. She emerged from her ruminations to find both men watching her: Marel speculatively, Reeder with suppressed anger.

Marel, Rowan believed, would gladly help her, if he could. But it seemed to her that Reeder knew far more than he was saying, and he, in fact, could help her—if he wished.

But his dislike of her went beyond this room, and this moment. It was personal.

Steerswomen and sailors were said to be immune to certain types of spells. On *Morgan's Chance*, the boy who had traveled with Reeder had watched from hiding while a navigator demonstrated to Rowan that this was true. The navigator, and then Rowan, had touched a magic trunk carried in the hold, one being shipped to a wizard. No harm had come to them.

But later, all alone, the boy had attempted the same act. The guard-spell had killed him.

Rowan crossed the room to Reeder's chair and stood before him, looking down. She wished that she could sit as well, wished she did not have to loom over him so. "I'm sorry about what happened to your young friend. It broke my heart when I heard of it. But Reeder—*I* didn't do it. He died by the hand of a wizard."

He looked up at her. His gaze narrowed fractionally. "Which one?"

"I don't know," she said. The chest could easily have been Slado's, but: "I'm sorry, but I don't know and can't guess." She drew and released a breath. "It's not common knowledge, but the wizards do have one authority over them all, one person whom even they must obey. They fight amongst themselves—who knows why? They work their magics at whim, and they do not care how it touches us, whether for good or evil. We have no choice. We have no say. Each wizard seems a law unto himself, beyond control or command."

And because she suddenly could no longer continue looking down at Reeder, Rowan dropped to one knee, resting her folded hands on the other. She looked up, into pale green eyes the color of sunlit seawater. "But I know, and now you know, that the wizards have over them a single master. His name is Slado. Will you help me?" *Whom do you hate more: the wizards, or me?*

His gaze had become unreadable, impenetrable. He studied her from the distance that lay behind his eyes. It took some time.

At last he said, "Are you capable of acting with... discretion?"

"If necessary."

"As condition for my assistance."

"Reeder." Marel's tone was warning; Reeder ignored him.

"You'll have to be more specific," Rowan said.

And as she watched, the man's facade reassembled itself: the shuttered gaze, the supercilious tilt of the head, a shift in his body as he regained balance, and dignity. Rowan found it rather an interesting performance.

"I am referring," he said, "to casual, innocent conversation. Without pointed questions, dire revelations, or talk of interfering in wizards' business."

"Actually," Rowan said, "I've become rather good at extracting information from casual conversation."

Reeder glanced down, adjusted one trouser leg at the knee, flicked an invisible bit of dust from it, and rose from his chair. The steerswoman stood up.

To Rowan's amazement, Reeder offered his arm. "I hope you have no plans for dinner," he said.

The couple greeted Reeder first with stunned, silent astonishment—and then, to Rowan's amazement, cries of delight. They pulled Reeder through the door by both arms eagerly; there was laughter, and embraces, which Reeder accepted with a slight smile and a cool dignity. Bemused, Rowan entered the house in their wake, wondering if she would escape notice entirely; but when Reeder inserted a pause in which to introduce her, the couple welcomed her easily.

He was dark; she was light, and freckled. His hair was long, and iron-gray, worn in thick, wild locks about his face and down his back; hers was short, of corn-yellow fading into white. He was Naio; she was Ona.

Their home was their workshop. A long main room, and high, with ranks of shelves occupying the front and back walls, climbing up into the shadows, displaying plates, urns, vases, mugs, tea sets. On the far right wall a kiln stood, still radiating warmth. Two potter's wheels were set at a comfortable distance from it, one to each side. On the opposite wall: a hearth, where a small fire hissed and sparked cheerful flame. A low table before a faded divan held the settings for the couple's simple dinner.

Naio and Ona bustled about, finding more plates, more utensils, another chair, and wineglasses when Reeder, with what Rowan considered an unnecessarily supercilious air, proffered the two bottles he had acquired en route.

All four settled down to dinner by the hearth. There was stew and bread, plain but hearty. But Reeder, in heavily formal phrases, praised the meal far in excess of its actual quality, causing Rowan to grit her teeth in annoyance.

Naio seemed not to notice Reeder's tone at all. He listed for Reeder the stew's various ingredients: all rare, all esoteric—and, if Rowan's taste was any guide, all definitely absent.

Puzzled, the steerswoman very nearly corrected him, but caught a side-glance from Ona. A suppressed twinkle in the pale blue eyes—and Rowan suddenly realized that she was in the midst of a performance.

Inspired by Naio's list, Reeder's praise became wildly extravagant. Naio then entered into a detailed explanation of the cooking process, one apparently delicate, demanding, and, as nearly as Rowan could tell, completely impossible to accomplish. Reeder interjected comments on other dishes equally arcane—and even less likely—whose preparation he, urbane and wide-ranging traveler that he was, had the good fortune to observe during the course of his many adventures in distant lands—

When the two men had reached the point where Naio was attributing the recipe's origin to an ancient tradition handed down from the court of the mythical King Malcolm, Ona could contain herself no longer. She suddenly leapt up and began batting Reeder about the head with her flapping napkin, laughing.

He threw up his arms, fending her off. "Ho! Cease! Hold off! Really, Naio, you must control your woman!"

"Of course, immediately; but first, I'll have to ask her permission to do so. That's always best, I've learned…"

The men were old friends of long standing, and their act had long practice. They positively baited each other to more and more outrageous comment, Reeder with his heavy-handed air of superiority, Naio with a sort of cheerful artlessness.

It dawned on Rowan that Reeder's usual exasperating manner was not what it seemed. It had a natural context, a place where it was at home. It needed a second voice; it needed Naio. Without him, Reeder was like the first half of a joke that, lacking its second half, had become puzzling, meaningless, and on endless repetition, annoying.

And Naio's cheeriness could find no better foil than Reeder's stolid formality. The two men were more than complementary; they were, in some way, a unit, each incomplete without the other. The steerswoman found herself wondering why they were not always together, and what had happened to separate them, and why for so long?

They nattered; they rambled; local politics, gossip, the odd weather. Opinions were aired, scandals discussed, all in the same practiced rhythm of escalating absurdity. Rowan was amazed to find herself enjoying Reeder's company. She laughed often, and at one point long and helplessly. This Reeder watched with lifted eyebrow, as if affronted; Naio, with a sort of beaming pride.

Eventually, the men turned to reminiscing. Their acquaintance with each other was far longer than with Ona, and they were soon discussing people Ona barely knew at all. Rowan began to listen closely, hoping for mention of Kieran and Slado, but Reeder could not have more effectively avoided the topics if he were doing so intentionally. She began to realize that he was. She had been told to follow his lead; she waited for that lead to appear.

The women were now entirely outside the conversation, and Ona shot Rowan a wry glance. Reeder noticed, as if he had been waiting for this moment. "Naio, these poor women can't possibly be interested in our childhood history. Rowan, why don't you ask Ona to show you some of her work? Really, she's quite the more talented of these two."

"Due to my training," Naio interjected proudly. "I taught her everything she knows."

Reeder shook his head sadly. "No, Naio; I'm sorry to say that you merely taught her everything *you* know…"

Ona protested politely, but the steerswoman insisted, equally politely. With a fond smile as her husband and his old friend returned to their conversation, Ona led Rowan away from the hearthside.

"I suppose," Ona said shyly, "you've seen some very good pots and ceramics, traveling about the world as you do, much better than these…" She hesitated, reached up, and brought down from one shelf a delicate vase, which she set on a small display table.

Rowan said, spontaneously and sincerely: "This is beautiful."

The vase was pale white, translucent. A painted branch of pear blossoms swept across its side, curling up the neck. Petals trailed across the open spaces as if caught by a soft wind. Rowan found herself holding the vase, turning it around and around in her hands.

She set it down reluctantly, then scanned the shelves above for more treasures—and abruptly burst out laughing. "What is that? Am I seeing it right?"

Ona gave a cry of delight and scrambled to bring over a step stool. She climbed, reached high, passed the items down to Rowan, and the steerswoman laughed at each as she took it.

A fat tea pot, in the shape and color of a calico cat, one raised paw serving as spout. Six mice were the tea cups, with curled tails for handles, cheese slices as saucers. Each mouse showed a different expression of terror at the presence of the cat, but for one fat mouse, asleep on its back, a smile of satisfaction on its face and its painted whiskers full of cheese crumbs.

Ona laughed, too. "Oh, you like it, I'm glad! I've been working on another similar idea… She glanced about, sighted what she sought, and went to fetch it: a fat folder, bursting with papers. Ona opened it, flipped through the pages. "Here." She passed the sheet to the steerswoman.

Rowan looked at it. "Hm," she said, dubiously.

Ona took no offense. "Yes… It doesn't quite work with a dog and cats. I'd have to make the cats kittens, to be good tea cups…"

"One can't help but feel sorry for them." But the drawing was marvelously well executed. The imagined tea set seemed as real as the existing one.

Rowan understood why she had been brought here. But—*casual conversation*, Reeder had insisted. Rowan would need to maneuver events.

She reached out one hand. "May I?"

With shy pride, Ona passed the folder over. Rowan scanned through the drawings, then looked up to study Ona's delicate skin, her faded hair; the woman was at least in her mid-fifties. "Have you been drawing all your life?"

"Oh, since I was a child. Unfortunately, nice pictures don't pay the bills."

"I'd really like to see some of them," Rowan said, with sincerity. Ona hesitated. "Steerswomen have to draw quite often." And this was true. "I think I might... learn something."

Ona allowed herself to be convinced, and she led Rowan through a door beside the hearth, into a small room with its own little fireplace, cold. The room was used for storage, but a small, dusty cot with a bare mattress stood against one wall. Rowan sat on this, as Ona scanned the various boxes and crates that filled most of the chamber.

Ona sighed, selected one at random, opened it. "They're not organized at all, I'm afraid. Most of these are old studies for pots." She sifted through the contents quickly, abandoned it for another. "I suppose I'm the sort of person who just can't stand to throw anything away."

"You never know what might come in useful," Rowan commented.

Ona received no satisfaction from the box, moved it to the floor to gain access to the trunk beneath it. "Oh, this is old..." She pulled out a leather folder, opened it. "Here!" Ona was first delighted, then hesitant, as she passed a folder over to the steerswoman. "I was rather young then..." Prepared to be patient, Rowan opened it and examined the contents.

Several awkward drawings of flowers, the same arrangement, seen from different angles: then suddenly and startlingly, a single bloom executed perfectly, to the spark of sunlight in a drop of dew on its petals, with all its companions in the vase, and the vase itself, mere outline and shadow. "This is lovely!" Rowan declared, immediately.

Ona demurred. "It's unfinished."

"No... No, it's perfect." It was as if the artist had captured, not the outer world, but the seeing mind, as it focused closely on one chosen detail.

Rowan felt an undeniable tug of longing. In her own work, when she was required to draw objects or scenes, she did so with precision and accuracy. But she felt that this single flower, alone and glowing with reality, more truly captured Rowan's own sight, her own heart, as she apprehended with crystal precision some small portion of the wider world.

She looked up at Ona in amazement. "How old were you when you drew this?"

Ona sat down beside her. "Nine, I think."

The other drawings in the folder were more typical of a talented child: static depictions of various adults, perhaps family members, simple landscapes, and many, many drawings of cats. Ona retrieved a second folder, opened it. "I was older here." She passed it to Rowan.

The difference showed immediately. The artist's hand was sure, and Ona now used selection of focus as a tool, at will, to very good effect. "I wish I could do this…" Passing through the drawings, Rowan found a face that interested her, paused.

A thin man with white hair, a long beard… She recalled the bricklayer's description. "Is this the wizard Kieran?"

"Yes, it is." Ona was delighted. "Now, how did you guess that?"

"Actually, I'm here in Donner to fill in some history… And Kieran is an interesting case… Are you aware that he altered his behavior? That people used to be afraid of him?"

"Marel and Nid used to talk about Ammi."

"Nid's sister."

"Yes… but that was so long ago. People do change."

Rowan held the sketch carefully, lightly resting it on the fingers of both hands. "He hardly seems malevolent." With eyes closed, chin on his chest, the old man might have been anyone's elderly grandfather, dozing in the sunshine.

But most drawings, and especially drawings made by persons of real talent, more closely reflected the artist's own evaluation of the subject than objective fact. "Did you like Kieran?" Rowan asked.

Ona shrugged, sifted through the other pages. "Well enough, I suppose. He had an interesting face." She paused at another drawing, a half smile on her face.

Kieran again, and a child, about three years old, tugging at the hem of his cloak, a mischievous spark in her eyes. Ona had captured the child's bravado, the wizard's feigned unawareness, the varying degrees of interest and uninterest on the part of persons nearby, themselves mere vague silhouettes.

Rowan laughed out loud. "That's Reeder!" An adolescent, but instantly recognizable among the shadowy watchers by the back-tilt of his head, an arm at particular aspect to the body, an air of disdainful superiority. Rowan found Naio beside his friend, leaning against a wall, arms crossed, ostentatiously casual. By shaded outline only, Ona had rendered both easily identifiable.

Rowan indicated the child. "Who is the little girl?" she asked.

"That's Saranna." Ona saw the change on Rowan's face. "Did you know her?"

"Not well." But Saranna seemed determined to haunt the steerswoman. *I'll find your murderer*, Rowan promised the girl in the drawing.

Rowan's compliments inspired Ona to pull out a second chest, while the steerswoman continued to leaf through the thick folder.

Tucked among the separate sketches was a slim folio of soft leather, tied with silk ribbons. Rowan opened it.

A face she recognized: Reeder's traveling companion on Morgan's *Chance,* the boy who had died by wizard's magic.

Rowan looked up: Ona was sifting through the trunk, her back to the steerswoman. Turning the pages quietly, Rowan glanced at the other drawings in the folio. The same boy, at a younger age; again, and younger yet...

The last showed a chubby-cheeked infant, wrapped in a blanket, cradled in Naio's arms. Father and son were fast asleep in the same high-backed armchair that Rowan had used during dinner. Their faces were soft with sleep, half shadowed, half revealed by gentle firelight. Of all the drawings, only this one bore a title, in a neat, slanted hand: *First Night.*

Rowan closed and tied the folio, gently laid it beside her on the small, cold, dusty cot, and returned to sifting through the other drawings.

As she neared the last, Ona suddenly emitted a girlish squeak, and a longer, more mature laugh. Rowan looked up to find her yanking from the trunk one ribbon-tied stack. Ona caught Rowan's glance, inexplicably turned red, laughed again, and held the folder protectively behind her back, attempting to look innocent. But she could not hold the pose, and covered her eyes with one hand, laughing harder.

Rowan was bemused. "A collection of nude studies, I presume?"

"Oh, no—" Ona assured her; then, "no... oh!" She suddenly recalled something, and grew even redder. "Well, but just my imagination, really—honestly, I can't believe I kept this..."

Rowan half smiled. "An old sweetheart, then," she said; and she felt the smile vanish.

She heard Ona's reply only distantly. "Oh, no, just an infatuation... but I was thirteen, you know how girls are. And of course I drew all the time back then, and dreamed a lot..."

Rowan found that her hands had dropped, holding the folder limply, elbows on knees.

She was surprised at her own tiredness; she was tired to her soul; she had been treading a very thin line between honesty and deceit; it was no place for a steerswoman; the strain of it suddenly exhausted her.

Rowan said: "Is it Slado?" There was an odd quaver in her voice. She looked up at Ona.

The potter was surprised. "Do you know him?"

"No. But I'm interested in him, and his history. I'd like to know what he looks like."

Rowan stated these words simply; and then merely waited. She no longer knew what expression was on her own face—hope, or hatred; anger, weariness, or hunger—but whatever it was that the older woman saw, it made Ona pause, made her think, made her puzzle.

Then it made her, very visibly, decide not to ask.

Instead, Ona untied the ribbon and seemingly at random pulled out one sheet. She handed it to Rowan.

The steerswoman gazed, silent, for a long time. "How idealized is this portrait?"

Ona stepped nearer and tilted her head. "A lot, I suppose..."

A young man, not tall, but well formed, gazing into the distance with a noble expression. Wind sent his long hair flowing back from his face. A cloak was thrown over one shoulder. His left hand rested lightly on the ornate hilt of a sword hung at his waist.

Ona searched through the other drawings, selected another. "This one is more real."

The same young man seated at a small table, nursing a cup of tea. He was gazing off to his right, at something that was not depicted. His hair was now shown with the more typical crisp auburn texture, and his face was less perfectly symmetrical. His expression was one of cautious evaluation; Rowan wondered what he was watching.

She studied him, feeling no sense of identification at all: the man she had been searching for, for these last years—but nothing startling, no sign of power.

Such a very young man. "Did you ever speak to him?"

"Only once. Right then, in fact. He saw me, and saw I was drawing him. I started to put my things away, but he said he didn't mind, I should go on... But I was so flustered—" Ona slipped a third drawing over the others.

On a page nearly blank, faint, preliminary lines: the set of shoulders, the shape of the head, positioning marks for the features. The inner edge of the hair was present, with one stray lock falling past the broad cheek. The left eye had been started, the lower lid from inner to outer corner—

—and from there, a dark, slashed black line to the edge of the page and off it, as if at a sudden jerk of the artist's hand.

Ona said, "I just couldn't bear him looking straight at me... I swept up my things and ran out. He laughed."

Ona sat down beside the steerswoman and considered the aborted portrait. "Do you know," she said, "I'd forgotten about this one. So long ago... You think of the feelings of your youth with a sort of fondness, I think. Across these years I've remembered only that I had a sweet infatuation with the mysterious wizard's apprentice. But seeing this again, it's like I'm right back there…" She paused. "I stopped drawing him, after this." Ona took the sketch from Rowan's hand, held it at arm's length, regarding it as one regarded the face of a person standing nearby. She shook her head. "The way he looked at me… I don't know… I'd never seen anything like that. Not like you look at a person. He looked at me like I was… some sort of *thing*. Some interesting thing." She handed it back to Rowan.

"I suspect," Rowan said, "that the wizards hardly regard the common folk as persons at all."

"But Kieran wasn't *like* that." Ona spoke with feeling. "I'd heard the story of Ammi, and all, but really, I thought that Nid must have told it worse than it was, because Kieran *loved* children. And… And he was kind, too, often, to anyone."

Kindness, again. Always, it seemed, in his last years, kindness from Kieran.

Rowan sighed. "I don't suppose you're willing to part with these?" She held up the two drawings.

Ona winced. "You take them. Now that I've seen them again, I won't miss them. I think I'd rather remember that dreamy girl, so sweet on the magical boy."

CHAPTER FIVE

"And that, I suppose, is what you consider 'discretion,' " Reeder said bitterly.

The steerswoman did not reply. They passed one street lantern, another, candles glowing softly behind oil-paper panels. Beyond and around, silhouettes of dark buildings stood, with the occasional gentle light leaking from slitted shutters.

Some explanation to Naio and Ona had been necessary. Rowan had chosen, again, the simplest: a steerswoman's log-book from forty-two years ago, information from that time incomplete, and Rowan's job being to fill the gaps. Perfectly true, and Naio had accepted it easily, even with some interest in how one went about solving such a problem. Ona had seen Rowan's reactions in the back room, and clearly knew that there was more to the matter; but she had not pressed for details.

"If this man is as dangerous as you say—"

"You'd rather I had continued callously to manipulate your friends, to treat them like tools?"

"Yes!" He spoke quietly, but vehemently. "They've had misery enough from wizards. If you've placed them in any danger, I'll—" He balked at exactly what he might do. Really, he could do nothing, short of violence. And the steerswoman was armed; he was not. Rowan did not bother to reply.

They walked in silence for some time. More street lamps, where moths tapped softly against the oil-paper. Rowan recalled the magic street lamps at Wulfshaven harborside, a gift to that city from the wizard Corvus. She wondered briefly how he and his own young apprentice were doing.

Reeder stopped abruptly, and turned to her. "What do you plan for this former apprentice, this most evil man in the world?" His tone was harsh with sarcasm. "You want to find him, that much is obvious. What will you do when you do?"

"Are you certain that you want to know? You didn't earlier."

"I don't care anymore."

"Very well then." She planted herself solidly, looked up at his shadowed face. "I do intend to find him, if I can. When I find him, I plan to speak to him. When I speak to him, I shall require him to justify every evil act he has undertaken; and if he cannot, if I find his reasons insufficient to the destruction he has caused, I will see him dead." She stood, merely waiting for him to speak.

His pale green eyes were now dark in the darkness. "And what evil is it that he is doing?"

"Murdering people. In very large numbers. Some quickly, by magic directly. Others, slowly, by starvation and forced conflict. Us, eventually."

" 'Us'?"

"The folk of the Inner Lands. So far, only the warrior tribes of the Outskirts have suffered."

"Barbarians," he said, disparaging, uncaring. "They're all far away."

"As you say. But Slado's magic will one day render the Outskirts uninhabitable. And at that point, far away will become right here. The Outskirters will move inward. They will be hungry. They are warriors. They'll take what they need. Do you think that can happen peaceably?"

"And exactly when will these great hordes of barbarians descend upon us?"

"I don't know. But think of what Jannik's been doing lately, and Olin. Watch them. I believe they are preparing for war.

"Slado is the master of all wizards," she went on. "I don't know to what extent he directs their everyday actions, but I know that when he speaks, they must obey. That being the case, I regard him as personally responsible for their indifference to suffering, and their casual cruelty.

"The Outskirters have children, too, Reeder. I've seen their children, dead. I watched one girl die, weeping from pain, because Slado had sent magic down from the sky, and she had gotten in the way."

"And you." Ironic, condescending. "One steerswoman, one wandering question-asker. The judge, jury, and executioner of the master of all wizards?"

She flared anger inside, at his tone; but she answered him simply and directly. "If need be." Above Reeder's head, moths gently battered at the light, tapping; from behind Rowan, far up the street, in the deep dark, another tapping, faint.

The pool of lamplight did not extend far. "And I'll continue to ask my questions—as any steerswoman would," Rowan said, more quietly. "People answer steerswomen's questions—that's known, that's accepted. Any blame that falls will fall on me, the asker. And now, we ought to part, and we ought to do so in a manner that looks both casual and friendly." She put out her hand, spoke louder. "Thank you for dinner, and the wine, and the company." Reeder ignored her hand. The tapping had ceased. Rowan noted the last location: thirty feet away, behind her.

In full sunlight, the beggar must see through the thin cloth over his eyes, to some degree; in lamplight, far less, unless he had removed it. Rowan doubted he would risk compromising his disguise. He would be unable to discern her and Reeder's expressions.

Rowan assumed control, took Reeder's slack hand in her own, shook it, clapped him on the shoulder, and walked away, in no hurry. Eventually, she heard Reeder's steps crunch as he departed. Somewhat later, at the limit of her hearing, the tapping resumed.

Rowan made absolutely certain that the beggar was following her and not Reeder before altering her course to lead more directly to the Dolphin.

The common room was crowded, despite the late hour. The caravan would be leaving in the morning, and its captain was occupied with last-minute details. He sat at a long table with his drivers and guards around him and a collection of excited travelers hovering about, asking questions, checking their arrangements. Dan sat at the end of the table, and seemed to be standing drinks for the entire lot.

The group occupied fully half the room; the other half was empty, but for a lone drunkard snoring by the fire. Beck, looking very sleepy, was on his knees beside the man's chair, mopping a spilled mug of ale.

Rowan chose a small table on the empty side of the room, against the back wall, far from the firelight. One candle in a red glass bowl cast a dim puddle of light, faintly pulsing, like a heartbeat, on the tabletop. Rowan sat.

From her left: noise, laughter, some argument; the creak of benches shifting; the *thunk* of mugs on tabletops; the *clink* of coins. To her right: a cool, thick quiet, populated only by echoes. Rowan remained, motionless, suddenly weary to the core, gazing at nothing at all.

And it seemed to her now that the world had slowed, somehow: voices were distant, and the walls of the room dim, half-seen, mere outline and shadow…

Something waved for her attention: she brought her gaze back with difficulty, and found Beck signaling with a cupped hand to his lips, and a questioning expression.

He seemed unreal; she found she could not reply. Beck hesitated, studying her face, then he carried his rag and the empty mug into the kitchen. Rowan returned to staring at emptiness.

Eventually she pulled her logbook from her satchel, opened it, and removed Ona's drawings.

On the page before her, the vague shape, the empty face, the slashed line of the artist's panicked flight.

Despite its emptiness, Rowan thought: Slado, exactly as I know him. All guess, blankness, and fear. She sat gazing for a long time.

Somewhat later, a presence at her side. Rowan was several moments recognizing Beck.

He placed something on the table before her, not wine, not ale—

A delicate tea cup and saucer, decorated with tiny purple irises; an odd, fat, round, yellow tea pot; and a scent, warm and welcoming, bright with mint, rich with honey.

Rowan breathed in deeply, and felt a sudden sweet rush of gratitude. She grinned up at Beck, and said, almost inaudibly: "Perfect."

He tilted his head, eyes half closed, basking in her approval, then gracefully eased himself away again.

Rowan poured, tasted, sighed.

A latecomer entered the tavern, made for the fireplace, discovered the sleeping drunkard, and instead chose a long table to the fire's right, in the empty side of the room. He studied the crowd around the caravan captain, glanced in Rowan's direction, glanced away again.

She recognized his face from her catalog of people outside the pawnshop. The possible third watcher.

Bel entered by the street door and scanned the room, ostentatiously searching for someone, and equally ostentatiously discovering him: Dan. They greeted each other with glee, and Bel settled cozily into his lap, allowing one quick glance to tell Rowan that she had sighted her in the dim corner.

Two serving girls and Beck brought three more pitchers of ale to the caravan crowd. Young Beck noticed the lone man at the long table by the fire, and nudged one of the girls, who hurried to take the man's order.

Rowan turned back to the sketches, covered the shadow of her enemy with the second drawing.

There the apprentice sat, much as Rowan sat, both hands around a tea cup, exactly as if he occupied another table in this very room.

It occurred to Rowan that this might actually have been the case—and that she and he were separated not by space, but by time.

She wondered if this was what magic felt like. The young man with his tea cup could not see her, but she saw him, and more: she, like some tinker fortune-teller, knew his future.

So young.

He was watching something off to his right. Feeling herself to be facing him, Rowan involuntarily looked to her own left—

—and observed the entrance of the stocky, gray-haired woman, overdressed in a heavy green cloak that might or might not conceal any number of weapons. The woman swept the room with a quick gaze, completely failed to notice Rowan, and approached, stepping sideways, her attention on the caravan crowd, only turning back when she was a mere five feet from the table.

She startled immensely at finding Rowan occupying her own usual seat. The steerswoman sat regarding her expressionlessly.

The woman was a moment finding words. "Hai, what a shock! Sorry I am, lady, not seeing you there, sitting so quiet like that." She laughed, one hand on her chest as if quieting a fluttering heart; it was a very good performance. "I'll just be leaving, no need to disturb you. You want your peace, I can see it." And she glanced about the room, her gaze pausing almost imperceptibly on the lone man at the long table, then settling on the fireplace. She sidled away around the smaller tables and sat in a chair next to the snoring drunkard.

A very distinctive accent: The Crags, held by Abremio. Among those wizards known to the common folk, Abremio was considered the most powerful.

Across the room, Bel laughed, overloud. Rowan looked, and Bel's eyes caught hers briefly, as behind Dan's back, shielded from onlookers, the Outskirter flashed three fingers.

But the steerswoman already knew: the solitary man, the stocky woman, and the beggar, now certainly waiting outside. All three watchers, all close by.

Time to go. For safety's sake, she must abandon this mission.

But she was so close.

The steerswoman turned back to the drawings, pulled the first sheet from behind the other. And it seemed different to her now, no longer fraught with dark meaning. Merely lines on a page, drawn by a girl, decades ago. Merely a quick attempt at capture, failed.

The steerswoman needed more information.

And there was more than one way to get it.

Rowan replaced the pages into her logbook, returned the logbook to its satchel, slung it over her shoulder. She checked to see that the lone man and the gray-haired woman were not currently looking at her, then turned to watch Bel.

When the Outskirter glanced in her direction, she noticed Rowan's attention.

When Bel looked back a moment later, Rowan was still regarding her, steadily.

When Bel managed to look again, she gazed longer. As she watched, Rowan glanced: at the woman by the fireplace, the man alone at his table, and at the door. Then Rowan waited.

Bel knew the steerswoman very well indeed. The Outskirter's eyes acquired a brief, hard glitter, her mouth a quick, small smile. Her chin lifted once, almost imperceptibly, in Rowan's direction; then she turned her attentions back to Dan.

Slowly, Rowan drained her tea cup, rose, swung on her cloak, picked up her cane, crossed the room, and left through the front door.

She paused under the carved dolphin. Against a wall, under the ledge of the tall windows of the formal parlor, the beggar lay curled up, apparently fast asleep. Only his smell distinguished him from a pile of rags.

Ruffo kept lamps lit through the night, all around his inn. Beyond, only growing dimness, then near-dark.

Rowan arranged in her mind a diagram of the surrounding streets and selected a straight route toward a wide intersection, which she and Bel had both passed many times in the last two days and knew to be surrounded only by business and warehouses. At this late hour, all would be shut.

The steerswoman breathed the night air, looked up to the Western Guidestar, just above the rooftops, and walked out into the night.

CHAPTER SIX

*A*t the intersection Rowan turned right, then flattened herself against a stone warehouse wall and waited, listening.

Distant laughter from the direction of the Dolphin. Somewhere far to Rowan's right, the clop of horse hooves. A small clack from high up—a cat on loose roof tiles, perhaps.

Nothing else.

The steerswoman unclasped her cloak, shrugged it to the ground, drew her sword. With her other hand she tested the heft and balance of her cane.

Above, between the rooftops, stars: the Hunter, the Hound, and the Western Guidestar. Rowan wondered who among the wizards might now be watching through that high eye.

She waited.

Minutes later, she was still waiting.

More minutes later, footsteps. But Rowan recognized them, and when Bel emerged from the street, the steerswoman waved her over. The Outskirter tucked herself beside Rowan, leaned close. "No one."

Rowan whispered back: "What?"

"No one's interested at all. The man and the woman are still ignoring each other. The beggar looks asleep."

Rowan digested this information, confused. "Can we have been completely wrong?"

Bel was definite. "No. The man and the woman are working together. I saw them speaking to each other when they thought no one was looking. The beggar... he just seems to be underfoot too often. And whenever I see him, either the man or the woman seems to be nearby."

The steerswoman and the Outskirter both waited, listening. Under the roof eave above, a flutter and scrabble as some bird adjusted its perch. The horse hooves were somewhat nearer, and the creak of a cart wheel could be heard.

Nothing else.

Bel made a quiet noise of amusement; with her face so close, Rowan could feel the huff of her breath. "Maybe they think you've just gone to the outhouse, and they're all waiting for you to come back."

"Why would I take my cloak to visit the outhouse, on a fine night like

65

this?"

They listened some more: still nothing. "Then," Bel said, "they're lazy. They're comfortable, they're enjoying their ale, and they don't want to stir. They think they'll catch up with you in the morning."

"That beggar can't possibly be comfortable."

"Then they know it's a trap."

Rowan shut her eyes and listened even more intently. She stepped slightly away from the wall, clearing a path for the sound from up the street.

Steps, distant, approaching.

Rowan moved quickly back, tapped Bel on the arm, and indicated the opposite corner. The Outskirter slipped past Rowan, peered around the edge of the building, then jogged across the intersection and took her post.

The steps paused at the point where the light from the Dolphin's lamps grew dim; then began again, now accompanied by a faint scratch-and-tap.

The Outskirter and the steerswoman waited.

The steps continued, slowly—and then there were more, two more sets, and they were running.

Rowan heard a startled cry; something clattered to the ground. Feet scuffled on cobbles. A series of thumps; a choked sound of anger; the flutter of cloth.

Rowan stood listening, utterly confused, so completely so that she said out loud, "What?" as if Bel were beside her and able to reply. But Bel was invisible, at her post in the dark at the opposite corner.

The sounds continued; sounds of a struggle, which now seemed to include blows. Rowan peered around the corner but saw only a vague knot of twisting shadows halfway up the street.

Then someone grunted, hard, and the sounds became quieter. "There, like that," a woman's voice said; "No, wait—" a man replied, and the struggle suddenly renewed, wilder, more desperate.

Rowan found that she had stepped completely away from the corner and now stood in the center of the street, watching. Only two followers, after all? she speculated; and... one simple confidence artist—

Who happened to get in the way.

And from up the street: the unmistakable hiss of a sword being drawn.

Aghast, Rowan said, "No—" Then she ran, toward the fight, calling to Bel, "Come on!"

Then Bel was beside her, and then she was not: the Outskirter swiftly outpaced Rowan. A moment later there came a clash of swords, and a silver flicker in the starlight. Beyond, the other two figures were a tangle of shadows.

The ringing became rhythmic; Bel had one attacker occupied. Rowan reached them, passed them by, reached the others, rounded on them, struck overhand, not with her sword but with her cane.

Two male voices cried out in pain; one figure fell sprawling, then scrambling away. The other man acquired a small silver flash: a knife.

Rowan swung her sword at a point just behind it, connected. A hiss of pain; but the flash arced up and over, came at her from the other hand. She back-stepped, swung at the flash; it dipped, came again from below. She slashed, down, and across. A weird, quiet wail, and the clatter of metal falling on stone. Rowan stepped back.

Wet noises; the smell of blood, and offal. The figure collapsed. And because, by the signs, the wound could not be survived, Rowan quickly finished the man.

Ringing sounds behind her; she turned. Bel was still engaged, her opponent's back to Rowan. Rowan moved to assist.

But the beggar had regained his feet; he was in Rowan's way; he made some movement with his arms, she could not see what. Then he took three steps forward, slapped Bel's opponent on the back, and, stepping away quickly, cried out: *"Bel, get back!"*

A soft *thump*, a hiss, a sudden wild flare of brilliant white light. The woman's shadow was huge, flailing against the stone walls. The white light on her back was small, sharp, almost too intense to look at. Rowan squinted in pain, half-shielded her eyes with her arm, backed away.

The woman dropped her sword, convulsed, fell, taking the light to the ground with her. She thrashed, once, and was still.

The hiss continued. Other than this, only silence.

The beggar was beside Rowan, breathing hard. He turned to her, looked at her once, his eyes uncovered now, and wide. He seemed as horrified as Rowan felt. Then he turned back and watched as the white light slowly dimmed to blue.

Beyond the fallen woman Bel stood frozen, her face pale, her dark eyes huge, her sword, loose in her hand, reflecting blue light. Then blue jumped as her grip tightened; she closed her mouth, made a strangled sound of fury. She leapt over and past the corpse and came on the attack, her sword ready for a backhand slash—

Rowan interposed herself. "Bel, no!"

Another sound from Bel, a choked sound of pure hatred. And because it was the only way to stop her sword, Rowan raised her own, met Bel's stroke, and hoped that sheer surprise would halt the Outskirter's attack.

It did: Bel took a step back, her guard completely dropped. She let out one shriek: "Rowan!" Then, quieter, between clenched teeth: "He's a wizard!" She made to attack again.

From behind Rowan: "No, Bel, please—"

Rowan flung out both arms, protectively. "Bel—wait!" The blue light hissed on, down to dimness, down to darkness.

But Rowan had seen, clearly, in the white light of magic: the eyes, the unmistakable wide, copper gaze—

"Bel," Rowan said. The Outskirter was breathing heavily in the dark, deep gasps. "Bel… it's Willam."

CHAPTER SEVEN

In the wake of the white light, Rowan's vision was a complexity of overlapping afterimages. She could see nothing, nothing. She dropped her cane, reached her left hand behind her, found the rags of Willam's sleeve. His arm turned under her hand; his fingers gripped hers.

From somewhere before her, Bel's voice came. "… Willam?"

Willam drew a breath, released it. "You know," he said in a shaky voice, "whenever we're all together, it seems like one of you has to stop the other from killing me. I really wish we could get that sorted out." His voice was different from their last meeting: a man's voice now, deep.

A weak sound of amazement from Bel. "Willam?" She started coming forward. "Curse it, I can't see a thing!"

"It'll pass," Willam said. "If your sword is up, please lower it. I'd hate to lose any more fingers, groping for you."

Then Bel laughed out loud. "Will!" They found each other in the dark; but Bel gagged and stepped back again. "What a stink! When did you last bathe?"

"I think it was Wulfshaven. It's part of my disguise. I can't believe you're both here—what are you doing in Donner?" He seemed more than surprised: he was urgent, distressed.

"The same thing we're always doing," Bel told him. "Rowan is finding things out, and I'm making sure she doesn't get killed for it. But what are *you* doing here? And why are you in disguise? And who were those two trying to catch you?"

Rowan put a hand on Bel's arm. "Quiet a moment." They silenced, startled. Rowan listened.

A man's voice in the distance, another's replying. A pause, then both voices in conversation, approaching.

Rowan leaned in to whisper. "Anyone awake can't have missed that light. We shouldn't be found in the company of corpses. And the corpses shouldn't be found at all."

"They're too heavy to carry far fast," Bel pointed out.

Rowan looked about, blinking past the dwindling ghosts of Willam's magic fire. "There." She crossed the street, tested a double gate; it was bolted. "There are stables here."

They used the dead man's knife to jimmy the bolt, and dragged the corpses inside, Willam sacrificing a layer of his rags to sop up the worst of the blood on the cobbles, and to wrap around the man's slashed abdomen. Inside, they waited with their backs to the closed gate, breathing shallowly, in the deep warm horse-scented darkness.

The voices paused outside near the scene of the struggle. Shifting light shone from the cracks in the gate: a lamp. One man exclaimed: he had discovered the woman's sword. Quiet discussion as the two men examined it, apparently pleased with their good fortune. Eventually, they departed.

They had called no alarm. Rowan released a pent breath.

"We could use a lamp ourselves," Bel said.

"Wait a moment. There must be one about."

Rowan moved cautiously, navigating by feel, sound, and scent. Horses greeted her with snorts and curious whickers. She passed them by, and eventually found the tack room. As she had hoped, a tin lamp was hung just inside the door, but Rowan could find no tinderbox or flint. She almost left the lamp behind, but thought twice.

Back at the gate, she located her friends, placed the lamp in Willam's hands. "Can you light this?"

"Yes." He set it on the ground, scrabbled in the dirt a moment, then rose and seemed to be fumbling about his clothing. Whatever it was that he sought, he found; then he stooped down to the lamp again and, unmistakable by the sound, spat.

Between his fingers, a little twist of straw flared with a tiny white light, then immediately settled into natural yellow flame. This Willam used to light the lamp.

Watching, Rowan said: "So... it seems you spit fire, now."

Willam adjusted the flame low, then looked up at her. Underlit, his face was all weird angles and slanting shadow, unrecognizable; not the face of the boy she had known, but that of a man, a stranger. She could not see his eyes. "No," he said, sounding embarrassed. "I spit spit, the same as you." He rose, lifting the lamp, and the light rose with him. "But there are some things that, if you wet them, they burn."

Rowan looked up at him; he was quite a tall man. "How very odd."

"That explains why you don't bathe." Bel seemed delighted by Willam's new talents.

They undertook the grisly and laborious task of carrying the corpses to the river. The steerswoman carried the lantern, shuttered to emit one small splash of light ahead of her feet. Bel and Willam carried the woman from The Crags, supporting her limp form between them as if she were drunk.

"We were hoping to question these people," Rowan said, "to find out why they were following me. But it wasn't me they were after at all, was it?"

"No." Willam's voice came from behind her, from the dark. "It looks like they wanted me."

No one else was about in the street; they were far from any taverns or other places of late entertainment. It was safe to speak. Rowan said: "Why?"

A pause, long enough for Rowan to wonder whether Will intended to refuse a steerswoman's question. "I think the other wizards have heard that I've left Corvus."

Rowan stopped short and turned back, lifted the lamp higher.

He made a very eerie sight: a tall figure in filthy, blood-streaked rags, and with white hair a wild tangle, supporting what was very obviously not a drunken friend, but a fresh-dead corpse. He looked, in fact, like a ghoul out of some macabre story told to frighten children on just such dark nights as this.

Only his eyes, the beautiful copper-brown gaze, were familiar, unchanged across the years, but startling in their new setting, as if this strange creature had cruelly snatched them from the face of the boy Rowan had known.

"Why—" Rowan began; but Bel cut her off.

"Later," the Outskirter said, and she shifted awkwardly, pulling the corpse's limp arm tighter around her shoulder. "A steerswoman's questions can go on forever, and this woman isn't getting any lighter. And we have another to do after this."

Rowan regathered herself. "Yes, of course." She turned and led them on.

Their grim work completed, they returned to the Dolphin, entering by the back door; and immediately upon reaching Rowan's room, found the atmosphere unbearable, due to Willam's stink. He excused himself, and when he returned had shed several layers of rags, and many degrees of stench.

"What were you carrying?" Rowan asked him. She was vigorously swinging the window shutter, urging the remaining traces of the odor to depart.

This was not entirely successful: the smell still lingered on Will's clothing. "Some fish heads and part of a dead raccoon," he said. "I've cached it all behind the outhouses."

"An excellent choice." Rowan abandoned her attempts and sat on the bed, shifting herself back to lean against the wall.

"How's your leg?" Bel asked.

"Not pleased with the night's work," Rowan said, rubbing her thigh distractedly.

"What happened to you?" Will asked. "I've seen you using that cane sometimes. Were you hurt?"

A bloody, ragged ghoul, asking after her health; but the copper gaze was openly distressed. "Yes," Rowan said, "but it's really not so very bad any longer; it happened more than a year ago."

"It's a long story," Bel said. "And so is yours, I suspect." She tilted her head. "Look at you, all grown up—and stinking to the skies!" She ostentatiously held her nose and backed off the single step that the room's size allowed, waving her other hand before her face. "I'd give you a hug, but I'm afraid it would rub off on me."

"Actually," Will said, "I wish that you would." He leaned back against the table, regarded the Outskirter with an odd, helpless relief. "I'm so glad to see you alive. After all that trouble in the Outskirts—I just didn't know what became of you."

Bel opened her mouth as if to make some light remark, perhaps an Outskirter's *Ha!* She closed it again. She said, simply, "I survived."

"We both survived," Rowan said. The memory was not a pleasant one. "And so have you, just. Those two who attacked you—are you sure they were wizard's minions?"

"I can't think of anyone else who would be after me."

Bel climbed on the bed beside Rowan, and folded her legs. She studied Willam, dark eyes curious. "And how did you know you'd find us in Donner?"

"I didn't! I didn't know you were here at all, until Rowan bought me lunch!" He laughed. "That was a shock, I'll tell you!"

"And you stayed close by after that," Rowan said.

"I was trying to decide whether I should let you know who I was…"

"Why would you not?"

Bel answered for him. "Because he's in trouble, and he didn't want it spilling over onto his friends. It's a kind thought, Will, but if you've run off from Corvus, you're going to need help. I think we just proved that. You didn't even know those two were following you, did you?"

"No," he admitted reluctantly.

"What made you leave Corvus?" Bel asked.

Willam was a few moments replying; and during those moments, his expression grew dark. He said at last: "Routine Bioform Clearance." He noticed the chair tucked under the table, pulled it out, turned it, and sat.

"Hardly routine, as Slado uses it," Rowan said; and Willam nodded silently.

When Slado had turned the spell called Routine Bioform Clearance against the Outskirters themselves, only Fletcher's warning had saved Rowan and Bel, and the tribe with which they had been traveling. They and the entire tribe had fled, and for months after, Rowan kept dreaming of that flight, of three days of nearly ceaseless movement, by daylight and darkness, across the dangerous Outskirts.

And after: the dark, half-buried tent; the tribe members crowded against each other; the screaming wind, and screaming wind again, as tornadoes, one after another, tore across the landscape.

Willam, and Corvus, knew of these events because Rowan had informed Corvus herself—

"Willam," Rowan said, "in my letter to Corvus last year, I did say that Bel and I both escaped from the magic heat. That we both survived." What then was the cause of his concern for Bel in particular?

"Yes," Will said. "But you also said that you'd left Bel behind in the Outskirts."

"But—" Rowan began; then, of itself, the answer came to her. "Oh, no…"

Quiet in the room. Eventually, the Outskirter said, almost inaudibly, "He did it again?"

"Yes. Last summer." Willam leaned toward her, the memory of pain on his face. "And Bel, I didn't know where you *were*—"

"He did it again?"

Willam startled; and the very small room became a great deal smaller.

"Where?" Bel demanded, her dark eyes darker now, and hard.

"North. Much farther north than the first time—"

"And people? Were there tribes there?"

Willam hesitated; he was not glad to tell it. "Yes. Three tribes. They all died."

Bel became utterly still.

Willam waited, but when Bel did not speak, he went on. "Corvus knew it was going to happen… he said he'd seen the Clearance listed on the upcoming schedule—I told him that we had to *do* something, we had to stop it! But he wouldn't. And I… I couldn't." Willam looked down at his two hands, clenched them. "I watched. From the Eastern Guidestar. I didn't want to, but I couldn't help it. Everything calm, everything normal, and all the people down there, shining like stars… they do that, when you look at them right, they shine just like stars… And then the land, lit up like it was burning. And afterwards, everything growing dark… and all the little stars gone…" He opened his hands, dropped them to his lap, looked up at Bel helplessly. "And I didn't know where you were."

The Outskirter stared, past Willam, past the walls of the room; stared as if blind. Rowan nearly laid a hand on Bel's arm, to try to comfort her, but stopped herself.

Not wise. Not when Bel was like this.

When Bel spoke again, her words were slow, her voice carefully controlled. "Willam," she said, "do you know where Slado is?"

"No." Earnestly. "I'm sorry, but I don't."

"Does Corvus?"

"Yes… but he wouldn't tell me."

"And Corvus… he *could* have stopped the magic heat. If he'd tried."

"Not without Slado noticing—"

"He's a coward."

Willam did not respond immediately; and this won him a glare from the Outskirter. "The wizards…" Will said uncomfortably, "… they don't think like we do. Things don't mean the same to them as they do to us. I think there are some things they don't understand at all." He turned to Rowan. "Corvus *is* trying to find out more, to figure out what Slado is trying to accomplish, with all this, this trouble. But he's moving so slowly! He's being so cautious, he's not willing to risk anything. But we can't just wait and see, not while people are dying!"

"And that's why you left him, and came here," Rowan said.

Willam's urgency subsided. He looked distressed, then ashamed, and Rowan surmised that the decision had not been an easy one. "There's a chance," he said, "that I can find out more, right here in Donner."

Bel's eyes narrowed. "What chance? Why Donner?"

Rowan took her shoulder sack from the table. "Here," she said, and pulled out her logbook, opened it, drew out one loose sheet, and passed it to Bel.

The Outskirter took it suspiciously, regarded it briefly, then looked up at Rowan. "Kieran's apprentice," Rowan said, "at eighteen years of age, as drawn by a local girl."

Puzzlement; then comprehension. Bel looked again. And all that had been absent on Rowan's first viewing—the meaning of this stranger's face; the sense of identification; the knowledge of what he had done; the *hatred*— all of it was there, in Bel's eyes.

The Outskirter gazed on the face of her enemy for a long time.

Then she passed the paper back to Rowan, unfolded her legs, and rose. "When I see him again," Bel said, "I'll know him." And she left the room.

Silence in her wake.

Eventually, Willam said: "I suppose it's not a good idea to go after her."

"No." Rowan sighed, deep. "You've just told her that hundreds of her people have died, with nothing done to help them, while she was living comfortably in Alemeth. She needs to be alone." She handed the drawing to Willam, said simply: "Slado."

Will turned in his chair to tilt the drawing to the candle-light. He studied it grimly. "He doesn't look like much. You could pass him on the street and never notice."

"I don't know how age has changed him. But I do believe that I will be able to recognize him."

Willam shrugged. "He might wear a beard now. And... forty years later? He should look just a little older than you are." He turned back. "This is why you thought people were following you. If you're investigating Slado, you're probably jumping at every shadow." He passed the page back to her.

"But you knew," Rowan said, "you knew that Slado had been here."

Will nodded. "Corvus mentioned it, years ago. I didn't think much of it at the time. But I've learned a lot since then." He leaned forward, nearer to Rowan, but past the candle; light was now behind him, his features in shadow. "Lady, there are only three places in the world where there's the right combination of magic to bring down a Guidestar. Donner is one of them."

"Where are the other two?" the steerswoman asked immediately.

"One is on the other side of the world. No one lives there. The third one... I don't know where it is, I just know that it exists." The candle flame flickered, then steadied. "And I'm fairly certain that's where Slado lives now."

Stirrings overhead: footsteps down the hall, approaching Rowan's door, then passing. A sound outside caused Will to half rise, half turn, to look out the window. "There are some people about..."

Rowan gestured him back, knelt to reach across and close the shutter; she did not want him seen in her room. "There's a caravan leaving at dawn. A lot of the travelers have been staying here, and they'll be rising early. It's just as well you aren't sleeping in the stables again; you'd certainly be discovered."

He made a sound of amusement. "It wouldn't be the first time. I've been chased out of a lot of places." He paused. "I wonder if I can get rid of the disguise entirely?"

Rowan said, "Is that wise?"

"Well..." He thought. "If there were only those two people after me…"

"There were only the two," Rowan said with certainty. "With you following me so closely, Bel would have noticed anyone else following you."

"Then it might be a while before their master notices that they're gone."

"If Corvus sent them, I suppose that's true. But could they be Jannik's people? He would notice their absence immediately, I should think."

"Actually," he said, with a touch of amusement, "Jannik happens to be out of town at the moment. And he won't be back for, oh, three, maybe four days."

"Really?" Rowan sat on her heels, folded her hands, tilted her head. "Is this an example of magical scrying?"

Now Will could not suppress a grin. "No," he said. "It's an example of magical sabotage. I set a group of spells around the dragon fields. They don't all activate at once, so Jannik will be a while chasing them down. Until he finds them all, he can't control his dragons."

Rowan's own amusement vanished. "Will—is the city in danger?"

He was surprised. "No." He sat straight, spoke earnestly. "No, the dragons only attack when Jannik tells them to. Without instructions, they do nothing, or they—they just move around, in patterns, over and over."

"How odd." But, as she had thought, Jannik was no protector of the city after all. "Won't Jannik wonder who set those spells around his dragons? If he's heard that you escaped from Corvus, won't he suspect you?"

"He'll suspect Olin." The wizard whose holding lay north of Jannik's. "I made them to look like Olin's work. I know his style, and it's just the sort of trick he likes to play."

A thought came to Rowan, one that flared warning. "Are you carrying a link?"

"No," Willam assured her, seriously. "Anyone could track me, if I had a link. Well, any wizard could."

According to Fletcher the links allowed one to request information from the Guidestars, and to view schematic charts, among other magical uses. "If those people were Jannik's, could they have used a link to pass a message to him?"

"Not while the jammers are up." He saw her confusion. "The spells that I set. They don't just stop commands to the dragons, they stop every kind of magical message. While Jannik is in the dragon fields, he's out of communication entirely."

Magic.

Rowan struggled with the idea of an escaped apprentice being able to thwart the power of a full wizard. "You're certain?"

He nodded. "Absolutely."

"Well," she said, "perhaps the beggar can be safely retired after all."

Will said, with feeling: "That would be nice."

Rowan surprised Dan by knocking on his door and requesting some spare clothing. Bel was not there; nor did Rowan expect her to be. Rowan explained Bel's absence, briefly, reassured Dan as best she could, and, because she would not see him again before the caravan departed at dawn, bid him good-bye.

Back in her room, Rowan found Willam engaged in the task of shedding layers of rags, which seemed rather a long process; he was still completely clothed. Somewhere within the rags on the floor, a fragment of dead raccoon must have adhered. Exposed to the air, the smell was so appalling that two night maids paused outside Rowan's door to hold a muttered conversation. Will and Rowan stood silent while this went on, and when the maids left, Will slipped out again to dispose of the offending material.

"I'm afraid the stink has sunk into my skin," he said, as Rowan, amused at his modesty, stood at the door with her back turned as he changed.

"You can't magically get rid of it?"

"No. Well, yes, I could. I mean, one could. But soap and water is actually easier. I'm done."

She turned back. "Cleaner, but no less disreputable, I'm afraid." Dan's clothing, while suited to Will's height, flapped about his body loosely; and he was barefoot.

"I see that it's been a while since you did any blacksmithing," Rowan said. At fourteen, Will had been stocky, and had shown all the signs of growing toward burliness. The structure of his bones still suggested that mass and strength ought to be his natural configuration; but Willam the man was clearly not a person who engaged in regular heavy labor.

Still, his shoulders were wide, and the folds of Dan's shirt fell across lean muscles on the chest and arms. The sleeves were too short; Willam's wrists showed, and seemed very strong. The steerswoman tilted her head. "But," she continued, "apparently you've decided to remain an archer."

He grinned. "You can't hide anything from a steerswoman. Corvus —" he began; then he looked down at his outfit, assessing his own appearance, and pushed the sleeves up past his elbows. His right forearm showed an old burn along its length, and his right hand lacked the last two fingers. "Corvus used to tell me that practicing archery was a waste of time. Now I'm glad I kept it up." He moved back to the chair, and pulled it out to sit again. "A bow is useful, when you're traveling alone."

His movements, too, were those of a person at home in his body, expecting and trusting its strength, a quality usually found in those who were physically powerful. Will had learned this in his youth, and the signs still remained. But in the slim twenty-year-old man, the effect was now incongruous, seemingly inexplicable, and striking: an easy physical confidence, and a grace that spoke of strength.

"I've recently learned the value of a good bow, myself," Rowan said, leaning back against the door. She considered his appearance, indicated the white hair. "You should get rid of that, as well."

Will tugged at one tangled lock, and his grin became a grimace of distaste. "I think there are parts of it that will never unravel. And I'd hate to face a barber like this; I just don't know what he'd find in there. I don't suppose a steerswoman carries scissors?"

Her jaw dropped. "That's... not a wig?"

"No..."

And despite the fact that it was merely folk rumor, that the Steerswomen could never verify the phenomenon, Rowan could not help but blurt out: "What frightened you?"

"Nothing." He laughed. "Or, nothing that did this. I changed it myself. I could have done any color, but white is the easiest to do, and the easiest to keep up."

Comprehension. "But you couldn't change the color of your eyes." The beggar's blindfold had hidden the unfortunately memorable copper-brown, a color not unnatural, but very rare. Rowan had seen it in no one else.

"I could have. But it's harder. And you need perfectly clean water, every few days. That's hard to find on the road."

Reasoning that it might be useful if no clue remained to connect the former beggar with the present Willam, Rowan decided to use her field knife on the worst parts of the tangled hair herself. She had Will turn the chair and stood behind him, lifting the candle high to survey the task at hand. It was daunting indeed. "I believe," she said over his head, "that some portions of that raccoon have migrated."

"It's possible."

Rowan set down the candle and picked up her comb, but found herself stymied: there seemed to be no place to begin. She lay the comb down again. "The last time we were together," she said, "it was every wizard in the world, looking for me. Now it seems our positions are reversed, aren't they?"

Will was silent for a long moment. "Maybe not."

"If not yet, then soon." Mastering her distaste, she thrust her fingers directly in amid the greasy, gritty tangles, attempting to sort them. "Surely by now they all know you've escaped."

"Maybe… But it's not the sort of thing Corvus would advertise. It makes him look a little foolish."

More or less at random, Rowan selected a knot on the right side and began cutting it away, her blade crunching audibly against embedded bits of grit. "That's good to hear. You may have some time before the rest of them join the search." She placed the severed lock on the table, selected another.

Small movements of his head under her hands betrayed his uneasiness. "Actually… they might not care. The rest of the wizards don't take me very seriously."

With the first cut made, the rest began to move more quickly. Rowan concentrated on matching length. "Why would they not?"

"I'm not Krue."

"I don't know that word…"

"It's the name the wizards use for themselves. Not just the wizards that you see, that the common folk know about, but all of the wizard-people."

Rowan had known that the wizards considered themselves a separate people; it was interesting to learn their name. "How do you spell that?" She moved the candle to the other side of the table, hoping to better light her work. It was too low, and cast confusing shadows. She began again, using touch more than sight.

"I don't know," Will said. "I've never seen it written down."

The texture of Will's hair seemed to have altered along with the color. Between her fingers, it felt both stiffer and finer than its previous appearance had suggested, and slightly brittle. "But the other wizards didn't believe you were capable of learning magic?" Rowan asked. "Because you're not Krue?"

He paused, long enough for her to add two more tangled locks to the pile on the table. Eventually, she prompted him. "Will?"

"The other wizards don't believe that Corvus would even *try* to teach me magic," he said. "Because I'm not Krue."

And now Rowan herself paused, comb in one hand, knife in the other. "But they knew you existed?"

"…Yes…"

"How did Corvus explain your presence?"

And Willam said immediately, as if it were a practiced phrase: "Corvus told me that they all assume he just kept me around as a catamite."

Rowan laughed. "A convenient explanation." But she could see why they might assume so. After all, Willam had been only fourteen years old when he entered Corvus's service, and quite an attractive boy. "And," Rowan began, meaning to say: *And did Corvus never correct that impression?*

She noticed that Willam had become very still beneath her hands.

She wondered—but no. She forced the question aside. Willam was a grown man, and it was not her business. A steerswoman's privilege ought not to be used to pry into private matters. And whatever the facts may have been, Willam was now beyond the wizard's reach.

For the moment. "Well," Rowan said, beginning again to work at the tangled hair, "Corvus knows you're here—assuming that those minions had a link and used it." Will said nothing. "How soon do you think it will be before he sends more people after you?"

Will was rather long replying. "I don't think he sent anyone after me at all."

Rowan stopped short. "If not Corvus, then who?"

"Probably Abremio. He and Corvus are always spying on each other."

"But Corvus himself... He would just... let you go?" She found this very hard to believe.

"Yes."

"But, surely—" Surely an escaped apprentice, especially one who was a member of the common folk, would be far too great a threat to the wizards' power—

Rowan abandoned her work, came around, sat on the edge of the bed. She studied Willam's face carefully. "But Corvus *was* teaching you magic?"

"Yes," Will said, immediately, definitely.

"Not merely—" She did not say: *Not merely a few simple tricks to keep his pet amused?*

"Rowan," he said seriously, "I know a *lot* now. Not everything. You can't learn it all in six years. But no wizard knows *everything* about magic. Some of it is still beyond me—but there are certain parts of it that already I know *better* than most wizards. And a lot better than most of the Krue."

"How is that possible?" She discovered the comb still in her hand, and handed it to him.

He looked at it blankly a moment, then began using it. "The Krue take magic for granted," he said. "Some spells are always there, always operating, and people just call on them without thinking about it. But usually they don't know a thing about how the spells really work, on the inside..." He paused to clear the comb's teeth of debris, then plied it again. "And because it's all so familiar, when they do start to learn, they have to... to unlearn things first, and throw off old attitudes. A lot of them can't manage to do that at all."

She considered this. "But you started fresh?"

"More or less. I had what I'd figured out on my own. And that's really what convinced Corvus to take me on. Ow." This as the comb met a knot behind one ear. He used his fingers to work it apart. "It takes a certain kind of mind to make magic work from scratch," he went on, "and you can't always find it, even among the Krue."

Rowan found that odd; but whatever talent might be required, Will certainly did have it. She had seen it demonstrated. Six years ago young Willam, entirely untrained, had shattered and partly destroyed the great fortress of the sibling wizards Shammer and Dhree.

She noticed that Will was growing uneasy under her scrutiny. It came to her that it must be obvious that she was now considering him in the light of the potential power he represented, and not as simply a friend.

"Have I mentioned," she said, "how happy I am to see you again?"

He grinned, set down the comb, and pushed his ragged hair back with his fingers. "Not yet."

"Well, I am. And I'm also glad to have another intelligent mind working on this problem." He acknowledged the compliment with a tilt of his head, a small shrug. "But you: you came here all alone," Rowan said, "with whatever magic you do know… what exactly are you planning to do?"

He became serious. "Find out why the Guidestar was brought down out of the sky," he said. "Whatever else Slado may be up to now, that's where it all started."

She leaned back against the wall and crossed her legs on the bed. "Assuming that it was brought down intentionally." Proper Steerswomen's precision impelled her to state all the possibilities. "It may be that the Guidestar's fall could not be prevented."

"No. The Guidestar," Willam said, definitely, "was brought down on purpose."

"How do you know that?"

She waited as Willam took the time to think very carefully before speaking; and as Rowan watched him, it slowly dawned on her that he was organizing and preparing to communicate ideas that he believed were beyond her comprehension.

It was something the steerswoman had done herself, many times, when answering questions posed by simpler members of the common folk. She found it very strange to suddenly be on this side of such a conversation, and stranger still that it was Willam on the other.

"Well," he began, "first off, the place where the Guidestars are—that part of the sky—if you can put something up there, it tends to just stay. Once it's there, you don't need magic to keep it up."

"Motion," Rowan said. "Mass. The Guidestars are constantly falling, but in such a wide arc that they miss the world completely, and moving at exactly the speed that keeps them in lockstep with the world's turning. With nothing impeding their fall, they should continue indefinitely."

He smiled as if relieved. "That's right. So, they'll stay, unless something else up there hits them—or if they're told to move out of the stable place."

Rowan found her thoughts stumbling, then halting, at the idea of *something else up there*. Then she recovered. Something, she decided, like a shooting star.

"But," he went on, "if one of those things did hit a Guidestar, it would be accidental."

The Guidestars watched, and made records of what they saw, Rowan knew. "There would be records from the other Guidestars. A wizard would be able to review the records."

"Yes, that's the thing." He relaxed further. "The relay would be interrupted, there'd be queries and warnings all over, and requests for commands—someone would have to answer. All that ought to be in the records. And the falling Guidestar itself—unless it was completely disabled, it would be asking for help. And there'd be a record of that, too. But there just isn't."

Rowan was completely lost, left only with the image of the huge, jeweled Guidestar crying out silently and piteously for help as it fell across the sky, burning. She wondered if it felt pain.

She struggled back. "But... a Guidestar can be told to move out of its position." Told, in effect, to die.

He nodded. "And if someone did that, they'd be sure to cover their tracks."

"They'd erase the record." She knew from conversation with Fletcher that this was the correct phrase.

"Or prevent it being recorded in the first place, if they were clever enough, and had the right clearance."

"Clearance?" She puzzled. "Routine Bioform Clearance?"

"No, not that. It's something different..." Will showed a trace of disappointment. He said with such careful patience that she felt abashed: "There are some spells that are so powerful that only a few people are allowed to use them. And other spells that recognize who you are, and know whether or not you're allowed to use the most powerful ones. And secret words you have to speak, even before trying."

And it seemed to her that this must be a very simple idea; but she felt that she could not hold on to it. Some part of her was rejecting this.

Recognition: that was it. The idea of a spell that saw—but *what* was doing the seeing?—and recognized a face—but with what eyes, or by what means? Something that listened, for secret words, like a soldier on guard, challenging intruders. *Who goes there?*

And it was the thought of soldiers that settled her: a hierarchy, a graduated scale of authority. A sergeant could order a soldier to scrub the pots, but only a general could send the army into war.

"'Clearance' means authority," she said to Willam.

He seemed a bit bemused. "Yes…"

"You might have said so immediately." He was using the terms to which he was accustomed. "Forty-two years ago, Slado was an apprentice. Would he have had that much authority?"

"No. But Kieran had top clearance, the highest there is. Slado might have stolen the words from him, and somehow fooled the recognition process."

She stumbled again at that last phrase; she could not help it. Will had spoken almost as if the very process of recognizing someone was something that could operate by itself, could exist and act independently, entirely unsupported.

A soldier, she told herself. Think of a soldier, and an intruder with a clever disguise and all the right passwords.

"Then the Guidestar was brought down intentionally. But we still don't know why. What can you do here that you cannot do elsewhere?"

"Find the records."

He was contradicting himself. She was lost again. She found it exhausting. She shut her eyes. "But," she said, and rubbed her forehead, "the records were erased."

"The records that the *Guidestars* made were erased." She looked at him, now speculatively. "Some records," he said, "are records that are shared, that all the wizards can look at, if they want to… as if they were written down, say, in a book, and put on a shelf for anyone to pick up and read. The Guidestars make that kind of record, and those were erased. But there are other records that a person can keep to himself, as if… as if that book were hidden away, in a drawer."

And because he was stating it as a metaphor, Rowan realized, for the first time, that the records of which they had been speaking were *not* words on a page, not written down at all; that there existed some other way to record events; that she had been understanding even less of this conversation than she had assumed; and that even the familiar words that Willam used so casually represented concepts outside her own understanding.

Willam had not only grown up, he had grown beyond her. She wondered how great a distance now lay between them; and how hard she would have to work to cross it; and whether it were even possible to do so.

And then, quite abruptly, she realized exactly what this entire discussion had been leading toward.

She said, with no regard for the inaccuracy of metaphor: "Records in a book, the book in a drawer, the drawer in—"

"Yes." And he leaned back, soft candlelight falling full on the serious face, the copper gaze; and Rowan saw in the man the same grim certainty, the same unwavering determination that she had seen so often in the boy.

Willam said: "I have to break into Jannik's house."

CHAPTER EIGHT

*R*owan found Bel in the formal dining room upstairs from the glass-windowed parlor, seated alone at a small table by an open window. There were no other diners, but a few servers moved about quietly, clearing tables of the remnants of many early breakfasts. Rowan pulled out the chair opposite Bel, and sat.

The Outskirter glanced up from her meal. "Have you decided to let everyone know that you know me?"

"Since no one was following me after all, yes. Jannik himself won't return for several days, I've learned."

"That's good. You weren't very happy, sneaking around your steerswoman's morals."

"I never am. That smells good." The dish before Bel held a trio of artfully circular fried eggs, each with a sprig of dried rosemary and a dollop of blood-red sauce on its center; a single huge, fat sausage, still hissing steam, and seeming about to burst its skin from sheer enthusiasm; and a crisp triangle of cheese bread. Another small and elegant plate held an apple, rendered into slices that were half-tilted into a red-and-white spiral pattern around the upright and perfectly cylindrical core. The core's stem held a single leaf, dry but gay.

"Dan's gone," Bel said around a mouthful of egg. "He's paid for my room through the week. You can move in, if you like. The bed is huge."

Rowan helped herself to a slice of apple. "Well. Even with no one actually hunting us, it still might be convenient to have a room so close to the back door. I think I'll keep it." Her wave caught the attention of one of the servers, who nodded and slipped down the service stairs leading to the kitchen.

Bel continued to eat. She was pale, her eyes were too bright, her movements a shade too controlled. A long night, with no sleep, Rowan surmised.

Bel's responsibilities must have lain very heavily upon her at the moment: responsibility, but no immediate recourse to action. And the one thing Bel could not abide, Rowan knew, was inaction.

In the two years that Rowan and Bel had spent apart, Bel had established herself as the leader of the Outskirters—possibly the first single leader of them all ever to exist. And while Bel now traveled in the Inner Lands as apparently merely Rowan's aide and companion, in a way the reverse was true. However strong and deep their friendship, Bel was here now, with Rowan, because it was the steerswoman who stood the best chance of learning how to save Bel's people.

Bel's people, and Rowan's own as well. But to the Outskirters, the danger was far more immediate.

But now, in this quiet dining room, bright with morning light and filled with every accoutrement of civilization, there were only the two individuals, regardless of their larger roles. Rowan wished, simply, that she could say or do something to help her friend.

No help was possible. The event had occurred: huge, bizarre, distant, magical. People had suffered and died. Nothing could change it.

Rowan said only: "I'm sorry."

Bel glanced up once, nodded, looked away, out the window.

It was a warm day, unseasonably so. And a few days ago, a blizzard had kept *Graceful Days* from unloading...

Rendezvous weather, as the Outskirters called it: one of the signs of recent use of Routine Bioform Clearance. Really, Rowan ought to have suspected. "Do you know where Kammeryn's tribe was, last summer?" Rowan did care about the Outskirters as a whole, but among the warrior tribes, only Kammeryn's people possessed, for her, faces.

"South," Bel said, regarding the empty air outside the window. "And I'm glad Willam's left Corvus." She turned back. "The wizards are too evil. I'd hate it if Will became like them."

Rowan sighed. "Yes." She folded her hands before her on the table, sat gazing at them a moment. "But." She looked up at the Outskirter. "Bel, no matter how clever we are, no matter how much we can discover, I believe that the common folk will, at the end of this, need magic. Even if we defeat Slado, or kill him, Routine Bioform Clearance will have to be reestablished according to its proper use, and maintained, and intelligently so. And who knows what other damage exists, somewhere out in the world"—here she gestured toward the window—"and still unknown to us." Outside, a dog barked; a girl's voice replied, in an aggrieved tone, exactly as if the animal had admonished her. A flock of pigeons, startled from the ground below, appeared briefly, vanished upward, and the window was empty again.

"It's not enough for us to stop Slado," Rowan continued. "We need to correct what he's done. It will take magic to do that. And I don't know how to get it, other than from the wizards themselves. I wish we had a hundred apprentices, all of the common folk, learning what the wizards know." A serving girl arrived at the table, smoothly slid dishes in front of Rowan, departed.

"And what the wizards know best," Bel said, "is evil. Maybe that's what your apprentices would learn from them, in the end."

"All we would need is for just one of them to stay true." Rowan looked down at her meal. "Oh, my."

Bel regarded the food, amused. "Do you have enemies in the kitchen?"

"No… Exactly the opposite, or so I thought," Rowan said. Before her: a bowl of gruel. She picked up her spoon and hesitantly tested it.

In fact, it was excellent, as gruel went: salted and buttered, with a hint of some other flavoring that Rowan could not identify. Upon investigation, the tea pot proved to hold chamomile. The mug standing beside the tea cup seemed to contain milk.

Rowan tasted. It was watered, tepid, and carried a trace of vanilla…

She suddenly felt herself back in Alemeth, propped up on pillows, weakly sipping, from a mug held by a solicitous Zenna, exactly this same flavor—

Rowan suppressed sudden laughter, which nevertheless escaped as a peculiar snort. The noise caused Bel to look at her askance. "I believe," the steerswoman said, attempting to control herself, "that the staff think I'm ill."

"Why?"

Rowan put down the mug, rubbed the side of her face with embarrassment. "Will spent the night in my room…"

It took Bel a moment to understand; then she laughed, as well. "The smell!"

"I'm afraid so."

Will said, as he pulled a chair from an adjacent table, "We heard a couple of night maids muttering about it outside the door." He sat. "And the people at the bath-house had a few things to say to me, too."

Bel gaped at him. Eventually, Will said: "… It's the hair, isn't it?"

"That wasn't a wig?" the Outskirter asked.

"No." He ran his fingers through it, close to his scalp. The barber had corrected Rowan's clumsy work, and Will's hair was at least all of one length, but of necessity it was extremely short. Now clean and stark, pure white, its new texture sent it bristling in every direction. With his copper eyes and dark brows, the total effect was very unusual indeed.

"What did you see that frightened you?" Bel asked him. Will repeated the explanation, as Rowan signaled again to the servers.

"Well," Bel said, "now that you don't stink, I can greet you properly." She rose. "Come on, stand up."

Will laughed, and did so; Bel flung herself at him, caught him in a bear-hug, and literally lifted him, briefly, off his feet. "Oof." Then Bel switched to back-pounding, which elicited similar sounds. "Cease, woman!" he cried at last. "I'll be bruised for days!"

Bel stepped a pace back, grinned up at him. "You're so tall!"

"No, I'm not. I'm just taller than you are."

"My turn." Rowan rose and gave him a quick hug. He smelled of rosemary-scented soap. Rowan's head reached only to the center of his chest; at their last parting, they had stood nearly eye to eye.

She released him and studied him a moment. He was no longer dressed in Dan's spare clothing. He had acquired, from somewhere, a dark green cotton shirt, secondhand but freshly laundered; gray felt trousers; and a pair of very old gum-soled sailor's boots.

"Where is your bow?" Bel asked, as Rowan and Will reclaimed their seats. "Or don't you use it anymore?"

"I do," Will said. "I hid it at the west edge of town, along with the rest of my gear." The serving girl arrived and delivered Willam's breakfast, watching him sidelong and wide-eyed; then she spared a speculative glance first for Rowan, then Bel, and then departed.

Rowan watched her go; immediately upon her rejoining the other servers, the three female members of the group separated from the males and gathered into a clot to conduct an urgent whispered conversation.

Rowan recognized the signs—as did Bel, apparently. The Outskirter reached across to poke Will in the ribs. "I think the ladies are finding you interesting."

Will's mouth twitched. "It's my hair. They're wondering what frightened me, too." He picked up knife and fork.

"Not at all," Bel said, sitting back to regard him with an almost proprietary pride. "You're a handsome man. You should make the most of it."

"It's not always the advantage you might think..." Will began on his eggs. "And now," he announced with a determined expression, which seemed incongruously directed at his breakfast, "since we've managed to say hello properly, we're going to say good-bye." He looked up at Bel's astonished face. "You can finish your breakfast first."

Rowan said: "Will and I seem to have a slight disagreement on this—"

"What we have," Willam said, "is a *complete* disagreement. But it's no good. You're both going to leave town, as soon as possible."

Bel recovered, and her eyes narrowed. "I hope you have a very good reason for giving me orders. Because I don't take them well."

Willam did not flinch in the slightest; and this, Rowan thought, was a new thing in him. "I know. I understand. But you do have to go. I'm about to do something fantastically dangerous, and if it goes wrong, neither of you must be anywhere near me. You can't be connected with this."

Rowan glanced about: there were no other diners present, and the servers were well out of earshot. She said: "Will is going to break into Jannik's house."

Bel showed surprise, then intense interest. "The house that killed that little girl, when Kieran owned it."

"Yes." Willam had heard the story from Rowan. "If she tried to go inside, she was dead as soon as she entered."

"But you think you can get in, yourself?"

"I know I can. And once I'm in, I can get out. It's what I'll do in between that's the problem."

"And what is that?"

Willam glanced once at Rowan, then returned his attention to his meal. The steerswoman recounted for Bel the relevant portions of her conversation with Will the previous night. She was halfway through the explanation when it occurred to her that she herself had, naturally and without thought, just taken an order from Willam—albeit an unspoken one.

Bel listened; and when Rowan was finished, she turned to Will again. "And while you're in the house, among these secret records—can you find out where Slado is?"

And Rowan was frankly astonished that this very simple question had not occurred to her.

It caught Will by surprise, as well, and he immediately lost the stubborn expression that he had maintained during Rowan's recitation.

He sat for a moment, jaw dropped. He closed his mouth, blinked, then discovered his fork, with a sausage slice, still in mid-air. This he carefully set down on his plate; and he gave himself to thought.

His face passed through a series of evolutions: speculation; caution; a sudden displeasure at one particularly disturbing idea; a growing interest as he pursued another; disbelief; tentative reevaluation. At one point he made to speak, then stopped himself, and seemed to pass through the entire analysis a second time.

Eventually he came back to his surroundings, looked at Bel, Rowan, then Bel again, and said, slowly: "I think I can locate the place where he lives, generally... In fact"—here he showed a disbelieving astonishment again—"that should be ridiculously easy... But I'm fairly sure that a lot of people live there, or nearby, so it's probably a very big place. I can't tell you where he is inside it, or even whether or not he's there at the moment."

Rowan could hardly believe this turn of luck. "That much by itself would be immensely helpful," she said, with feeling.

Bel emitted a satisfied "Ha!" and sat back. "Now tell me how to kill a wizard."

Will became serious again. "By surprise," he said. "It's the only way."

"Good," Bel said. "That's my plan, exactly."

Rowan did not comment; simply killing Slado might not be the proper solution. It remained to be seen.

Bel went on, "Now tell me what might go wrong when you're in Jannik's house."

"There will be guard-spells."

"And those gum-soled boots won't help?"

Will was surprised. "You know about that?"

"Rowan told me. Sailors and steerswomen. But it's just the boots."

"Well, there's more than one kind of guard-spell. If I'm not careful, and clever, anything might happen."

Bel said: "You could die."

Will winced, nodded. "And then Jannik comes home to find Corvus's runaway apprentice, dead in his house. But even if I do get out, if I haven't done everything perfectly, Jannik would know that someone had been there. And *that's* the thing." He became urgent. "Rowan, you haven't kept quiet about being here. By now, half the city probably knows about you. If Jannik finds that someone was in his house, among his records, at the same time that a steerswoman was asking questions about Kieran, and about Slado—Specifically, the steerswoman named Rowan, the one who caused so much trouble six years ago, the one—" Bel raised one hand slightly, to warn him to moderate his voice. He continued, very quietly. "—the one who Jannik was ordered to kill, six years ago. The one he *failed* to kill."

Silence. Then Rowan said, cautiously: "But when I spoke to Corvus, after all that, he said that no one was interested in me any longer."

"That's right. Because they thought you were some wizard's secret minion, and they were more interested in who that might be. But if you're in Donner, at exactly the time someone manages to break into Jannik's house, then you're a minion who has too much power. They'll start looking for your master again—but they won't wait to find him. They'll deal with you right away. Probably Jannik himself will want to do it. He'll drop everything else."

Unfortunately, Rowan could find no flaw in Will's reasoning.

Bel said: "So, Rowan has to leave town. And she has to do it before you make your attempt. And she has to do it in plain view of as many people as possible."

Will said, "That's right."

The Outskirter nodded. "I agree." She resumed eating.

Rowan sat slack in amazement. "Bel!"

"No," the Outskirter said through a mouthful of sausage, "he's right."

Willam showed immense relief. "Good. It's really the best thing—"

"We are not leaving the city!"

"Who said 'we'?" Bel asked Rowan. "You're the problem here. You go, I stay."

Rowan's astonishment was complete. "What?"

Willam looked from one to the other. "No, Bel, you ought to go, too. There's no reason for you to be involved."

"Yes, there is." The Outskirter continued on her breakfast, nonchalant. "You're about to do something fantastically dangerous. That means that you need someone to watch your back. I've been watching Rowan's back for the last two days. It's one of the things I'm good at."

He shook his head. "But Bel, this is magic—"

"I have no intention of leaving here!"

"Your own magic didn't stop you from being jumped in the dark," Bel said to Willam. "Where would you be now if you'd been alone, as you'd thought?" She indicated him with her knife to make the point. "Dead. Or being dragged back to Corvus, for who knows what sort of punishment?"

"But once I'm inside, there's nothing you can do."

"What about outside the house? What if someone sees you going in?"

"Bel—" Rowan said.

"Or coming out? How can you tell if some couple hasn't ducked into the shadows to play tickle? And won't they be surprised to see you?"

"Bel. Willam."

"Or some lost drunkard hasn't stopped in the middle of the street to get his bearings? Who knows who he'd tell?"

Will became thoughtful. "That's true."

"If you give me a signal, like a whistle, when you're ready to come out, I'll whistle back when the way is clear—"

"*Pardon* me—"

"You're starting to make sense..." Will admitted.

"Good. Then it's settled. The steerswoman goes. In fact, *Graceful Days* is still in port. If everyone sees Rowan climb on board and sail away—"

"*Excuse* me!" They stopped, turned to Rowan. "I am definitely not leaving."

The others traded a glance. "I was hoping she'd be sensible," Will said.

"I think you're asking that of the wrong person."

They studied her. "I guess dragging her away by force would be visible enough—"

"That's true."

"People might comment, though."

"And may I point out that I am actually still present in the room!"

"Do you happen to have some sort of sleeping spell?"

"Not on me. But the apothecary probably has some poppy extract. That should do just as well."

"There's some in her pack."

"Really? I say, that's handy."

"We'll just slip it in her tea."

At this last exchange, Rowan's outrage vanished. She knew for certain that Bel would never attempt such a thing; the Outskirter's sense of honor would forbid it.

The steerswoman composed herself, spoke seriously. "Willam," she said, "how sure are you that you can actually enter the house?"

He answered with reluctance, but obvious honesty: "I'm absolutely sure of that much."

"Bel, if Willam is going to be rifling through a wizard's records, learning something of Slado's past actions, and possibly his future plans, not to mention the chance of finding out where Slado lives when he's at home—I intend to be present."

"Wonderful. And if he makes a false move, you both die."

"Will? Is that true? If a guard-spell inside the house catches you, would it kill us both?"

He was forced to admit: "I don't know."

"Then it seems to me that we'll increase the chance of one of us escaping with the information. And Bel, with you outside, even if the worst happens and we both die, you at least will be able to tell the Steerswomen what we've learned so far."

Bel considered. "It does improve the odds..."

Willam disliked this line of reasoning very much. He made to speak twice, angrily, stopped himself, and when he turned to Rowan, she expected a glare; but instead there was, again, that open concern, that pleading distress, that she remembered so well. "Rowan, listen to yourself—'If we both die.' Tell me, lady, is this information worth dying for?"

She held his gaze. "Death is a risk," she told him, "not a certainty."

"People have already died," Bel said. They turned to her. "My people. And soon enough, yours. We have to stop Slado. You know that. Otherwise, you wouldn't be here."

Two men entered the dining room, carrying a large wicker basket of fresh linen tablecloths between them. The serving girls observed their arrival with annoyance, broke up their conversation, and set to replacing used tablecloths with fresh.

"I don't like this," Will said, his gaze on the empty window. He seemed to be addressing only himself, with quiet vehemence. "This was supposed to involve only me. No one else should be hurt, no one else should be put in any danger."

Bel said: "You can't make that choice for us."

"We *are* involved, all three of us," Rowan said. "That being the case, perhaps we should get the whole thing over with as soon as possible."

Will brought his gaze back from the distance with difficulty. "No," he said. "Two days from now."

"Why then?" Bel asked; then suddenly leaned aside to look past Rowan's shoulder in surprise.

A tug on the steerswoman's sleeve. Rowan turned, looking up, then down.

It was the handkerchief boy from the kitchen. He stood before her, silent, wide-eyed, hands behind his back.

"Yes?" No words, and no change in expression or posture. "May I help you?"

Moving only his eyes, the boy studied first Bel, then Willam, then brought his gaze back to Rowan. Then he hesitantly pulled out one hand and held it at arm's length, leaning forward precariously so as to approach no nearer.

The hand held a rolled paper tied with a ribbon. Rowan took it. "Thank you."

The boy dropped his hand, gaped as if stunned, then abruptly flashed a huge grin, remarkably similar to Beck's. Then he was gone, off through the tables and out of the room, trailing a stream of giggles like bubbles in his wake.

"Expecting a message?" Bel asked.

"Not especially." Rowan untied and unrolled the paper. A glance told her: "This is Ona's." She flattened it against the tablecloth.

A drawing, very old, by the condition of the paper. It showed a garden in full bloom, with banks of rhododendrons and ranks of daffodils, a cherry tree, a stone bench, the back of a house. In shaded outline: two figures, one standing, one stooped. Rowan turned it over.

Freshly written in artist's pencil: *Lorren and Eamer, Old Water Street, three doors past the pawnshop, blue house front.* Not in Ona's handwriting, Rowan saw; she assumed Naio's.

93

Rowan reversed the page again. "And that would be Lorren and Eamer themselves." She slid it across the table for Bel and Willam to see.

"That's the back of Jannik's house," Willam said. "But the garden is different."

"From forty years ago?" Bel speculated. "Ha. Kieran's gardeners."

"So it would seem. I really must speak with them." Rowan began to rise, realized she had not touched her breakfast, sat again, regarded her gruel with distaste.

"How's your leg?" Bel asked.

"Uncomfortable. That was rough work, last night." Rowan downed her mug of milk.

Bel said to Willam: "That's her code word for agonizing pain. You should have seen her while she was recuperating. She'd drag herself down the staircase by sitting on each step and sliding down, one by one, stagger over to the worktable, collapse in her chair, sit with her head on her arms for ten minutes, and when you asked her how she felt, she'd say she was 'uncomfortable.' "

"In this case"—Rowan reached over to snatch the remains of Bel's sausage—"it's merely accurate. My leg hurts, but if I don't work it, it will just stiffen up. Oh, my." This in response to the flavor of the sausage. "And it's a flat walk to Old Water Street," she continued around a mouthful. "I'll be fine. Bel—" Rowan had been about to ask if Bel was ready to go, but the only watchers so far had been for Willam, and not the steerswoman. There had been no other sign of interest in Rowan's investigations from any threatening party. Jannik himself was still out of town, still entirely unaware of the steerswoman's presence. There might well be no need for caution at all, and certainly none for urgency.

"I think you both should get some rest," Rowan said. "Bel, I suspect you didn't sleep last night, and I believe Willam hasn't, either."

"I dozed for about half an hour, until I thought the bath-house would be open."

"You probably need sleep more than either of us," Bel pointed out to Rowan.

"You may be right," although she did not feel drowsy at all, "but..."

Bel grinned. "But you're dying to hear what Kieran's gardeners have to say."

"I am," Rowan admitted. "And they're elderly. Perhaps they'll be napping in the afternoon. I'll do so, myself." She scanned the table for tempting remnants, and discovered that Will had entirely neglected his cheese bread. She confiscated it, and the last of his apple slices.

The servers recognized the signs of imminent departure, and two approached, with trays and apologetic expressions. Bel rose, gestured expansively. "All this on my tally, please. Come on, Will. You really have to see the room they've given me."

The three left the dining room together. In the hall, by the staircase, they paused: Rowan would be going down, Bel and Willam up.

No one else was present. Rowan said to Willam, "Why two days from now?"

Will rubbed his eyes; apparently the anticipation of sleep was causing its lack to catch up with him. "Regular maintenance and updates," he said. "Certain systems will be down." He forced himself to more alertness. "Some of the biggest spells need to be adjusted," he explained. "While that's happening, no one can use them." He was unable to suppress a yawn. "I can handle the house, but if any wizards try to see what I'm doing, it'll be harder for them... with the updates running..."

Bel took his arm. "Explain later. Sleep now." She led him away, up the staircase.

CHAPTER NINE

*T*he young woman who met Rowan at the door of the blue house on Old Water Street was amazed by the steerswoman's request, but admitted Rowan and led her up a long, polished oak staircase. During the ascent, Rowan studied with interest the collection of odd objects displayed in niches along the wall: a blown-glass vase holding glass daffodils; a marionette of a tinker dancer, very realistic with its golden curls and flounced skirts, seated companionably beside an equally realistic evil imp; an empty bottle of lemon liqueur, chosen perhaps for its artful and ornate label; and an old book—no longer in its niche but being read by a young man seated on the stair beneath it. His only reaction to Rowan's presence was to shift his knees aside as she and her guide passed by.

In the musty dimness at the top of the stairs, the woman crossed the landing and opened a door. Clean, bright light spilled out, and she stood aside as Rowan entered space that seemed all light, color, and fresh air.

A white room, with two beds, neatly made, on opposite walls. Broad double windows with glass panes stood open to the yard below, brown with autumn, but for splashes of asters and chrysanthemums, purple and pink, yellow and orange. A table directly under the window held more asters, freshly cut, in a blue vase.

On either side of the table in huge cushioned armchairs sat two ancient persons, quite the oldest Rowan had ever seen in her life. The one on the left seemed asleep, chin on chest; the other gazed out the window with an air of deep contentment.

Rowan glanced back, hoping the young woman would perform introductions; but she had departed. Rowan approached the pair tentatively, regretting the need to disturb them. "Excuse me?" It was the sleeper who reacted first, opening faded brown eyes to regard her curiously; the other turned from the window, blinking perplexity. "My name is Rowan. I'm a steerswoman—"

"Ah!" one of them said.

"Oh!" said the other.

"Don't see many of those."

"Traveling far and wide, all over the world."

Rowan was relieved by their alertness. They were obviously at least not completely senile. "I wonder if you would mind answering a few questions?"

"Oh," the one on the right said, in a dubious tone.

"Well," the other said, "busy day, don't know if we could fit you in…"

"There's the roses to cover."

"Pruning that apple tree."

"Those daffodils. Got to plant 'em."

"Three dozen of them, altogether." Rowan became disturbed; for persons of such age, these plans were completely impossible.

"And," the one on the right reminded the other, "the Grand Ball at the Dolphin tonight."

"Oh, yes!" Brown eyes under raised brows caught and held Rowan's gaze. "We intend," their owner informed her, "to drink an entire keg of ale between us, kiss all the prettiest dancers, and kick up our heels until dawn."

And Rowan laughed, half with humor, half with relief; they were obviously jesting. Her laughter pleased them, and they traded broad smiles.

With a lift of the chin, the one on the right indicated a straight-backed chair standing by the door. Rowan fetched it, placed it near, and sat.

She regarded them. "I'm sorry, I don't know which of you is which."

Laughter, in ancient, cracked voices. "I'm Lorren," the one on the left said. The head that had been tilted down in sleep remained tilted; Rowan assumed it a permanent condition.

"Eamer," said the other, with a lift of one hand, bird-boned and blotched with brown.

Age had rendered them virtually indistinguishable from each other. Both were tiny, frail, and almost entirely bald, with a few sparse white hairs remaining on the top of yellowish pates, somewhat more behind the ears and across the backs of their heads. They seemed not to possess a single tooth between them.

They were dressed identically, in fine blue quilted silk house jackets, buttoned to the chin. Wool blankets covered their legs, home-knit, but of excellent work. The colors of these were brown, gold, green, and yellow, with small points of pink, echoing the flowers in the vase, and the autumn world outside the window.

Rowan realized that she absolutely could not determine their genders, and could find no polite way to ask. Even their voices gave no clue: Lorren's was more creak than voice; Eamer's name had been spoken by its owner in a fuzzy baritone, such as even a woman might acquire at such an advanced age. Rowan decided that the matter was irrelevant to her purposes.

Because she thought it would please them, the steerswoman pulled Ona's drawing from her shoulder sack and passed it over.

Eamer took it, held it close to examine it, displayed pink gums in a grin, then leaned across to show it to Lorren.

"Ah," Lorren said immediately, "Ona. That's Ona's work."

"Yes, what a lovely girl."

"All grown up now, of course. She married that fellow, what was his name, the dark one with all the hair—"

"Joly."

"No, the other one. Naio."

"Of Reeder-and-Naio, that's right! Ho, that was a surprise."

"Bigger surprise when the baby came. So late in life for Ona." This with sympathy.

"Even later for Naio, not that that matters. But that baby was already on the way, wasn't it? That's the thing."

Rowan said, "That's Kieran's garden, isn't it?"

Eamer nodded thoughtfully.

"Yes… ," Lorren said, laying the drawing down on the knitted brown-and-gold. "We were with him, what was it, twenty years?"

"No. Seventeen, altogether."

"That's right. Fifteen before, and two after."

Rowan was about to inquire concerning "before" and "after", then realized. "After he changed," she said.

Both old persons nodded.

"Can you tell me about that? You seem to think there was a very clear division."

"Oh, absolutely."

"We were working—"

"It was morning—"

"Early. We always started early. We were planting marigolds that day."

"We didn't think he was up yet."

"Well," Eamer said to Lorren, "he'd been up all night, hadn't he?"

Lorren nodded to the degree that the bent neck allowed. "By the look of him. Long, hard night."

"Came out the back door, and just stood there."

"Looking like he'd had a hod of bricks dropped on him."

"Then he sat down on the back steps."

"And me and Eamer, shooting glances at each other, and trying not to stare."

"Didn't want him to notice we'd noticed."

"And when I looked at him again," Lorren said, and raised one hand, as if indicating the scene, "he was looking straight at me. Nearly gave me a fright, because I thought he'd seen us watching. But no. He looked at me like he'd just noticed I was there, and didn't know who I was."

"And he looked at me the same. I just went back to work. But then"—here Eamer squinted in thought—"when I glanced up again, he was looking at me like he *did* know who I was. And he got up and walked over."

"And we just didn't know what was coming. So we stood up.

"And I took your hand. I remember that..."

"And when he reached us, he didn't say a thing, for a bit."

"And then he *did* say a thing, and he said it like he'd never thought of it before."

"He said: 'How do you support yourselves?' "

"Wait," Rowan said, and looked from one to the other. "He paid you no wages?"

Both heads shook. "Fifteen years," Eamer said. "Not a penny."

"He'd seen us, you see, putting in that little garden over by East Well. Told us he liked our work, and from now on we'd do his garden."

"And that was that."

"The family supported us, all those years."

Eamer sighed. "Hard times, all around."

And the steerswoman realized what was coming next. "He started paying you for your work."

Eamer leaned forward, despite the fact that it clearly took great effort. "He walked back into his house, came straight out again, took my right hand, and poured a fistful of silver and copper into it."

"It was a lot of money!"

"It wasn't fifteen years' worth of wages—"

"No. But a lot of money, still, all at once."

"I don't think he'd counted it out at all. I think he just snatched up whatever was on hand..."

Rowan found this extremely interesting. "And did he begin paying you regularly after that?"

Lorren's faded brown eyes grew wide, and the tilted head came nearly erect. "A silver coin, each and every week after!"

Rowan was amazed. "That's an excellent wage indeed."

"Yes, it was!" Eamer said, with feeling. "With an extra silver, each Winter Solstice!"

"Two Solstices, that was, and then he died."

"What a shame, the little children were so sad..."

Rowan sat forward, elbows on knees, folded her hands. "Do you know how he died?"

Outside, clouds slipped past the sun, and the window edge permitted a narrow block of light to fall on Eamer, painting the right side of the blue silk jacket with a light sheen of gold. Lorren lifted one arm, laid an ancient hand on the fine white cloth that covered the table, spread fingers more bone than flesh. The cloth seemed to glow with sunlight, seemed to reflect light and heat back upward, through the translucent skin. "Old age," Lorren said. "So we were told."

Eamer's head shook, slowly. "I don't believe it."

"No..."

"Why not?"

Eamer said, "He wasn't old. Not really. We thought so at the time, of course. He looked a hundred years old to me, then. But now..."

"We know what old is, now," Lorren said, still quietly regarding the cloth, the light, the glowing hand. "He wasn't old. Not like this."

"He was tall," Eamer said, eyes gazing into the far distance beyond Rowan. "He was thin, but he stood straight. He had all his teeth, and he had all his hair."

"Well, not everyone loses their hair..."

"Yes, they do." Eamer said, returning to the present, and directed a twisted smile at Lorren. "Everyone. If they last long enough." And Lorren chuckled.

"Perhaps magic kept him strong," Rowan suggested.

"Now, see," Eamer said to Rowan, emphasizing the point with one raised finger; the entire arm trembled. "That's the thing. If the two of us can last this long, all on our own, it wouldn't be age that takes someone with magic in his hands. No..."

"How old *are* you?" Rowan asked, suddenly needing to know. She felt herself in the presence of some wonderful natural phenomenon, like a tall, spreading waterfall, a trackless expanse of deep forest, a wild cliff of many peaks, cutting the sky, eternal.

Both Lorren and Eamer had to think long on this question. "I've seen a century, at least..." Lorren ventured.

"And I'm five years older."

Rowan nodded, deeply pleased. She decided that she loved them. And it seemed to her that they certainly were a couple, but she remained unable to guess who possessed which gender—or, for that matter, whether their genders were opposite. She tried to recall what local custom prevailed in Donner concerning such matters, and discovered that she had not the slightest idea. And local customs did vary wildly across the known world. Rowan decided not to disturb these lovely people with a possibly upsetting question.

She returned, instead, to the matter at hand. "If Kieran did not die by natural means—" An immediate reaction on both faces stopped her.

Lorren said: "Slado."

"Now, we don't know that..." But Eamer clearly suspected, as well.

"Bet he did it." Lorren's brown eyes receded and vanished behind a squint of distaste. "I bet he thought he'd get Kieran's holding."

"No, he was too young. He couldn't have learned all that much, yet."

"And that's why he didn't know any better."

"What was he like?" Rowan asked.

Identical expressions of deep displeasure. "Like Kieran," Eamer said. "The Kieran-before. Exactly like."

"No, not exactly. The old Kieran never went about town the way Slado did. Though the new Kieran did, a bit."

"Well, that Slado, he was hardly more than a boy. A lad that age would, wouldn't he? Out to the taverns, off riding..."

"He had a horse."

"Who tended the horse?" Rowan asked, hoping for another informant.

"He stabled it at the Dolphin, same as Jannik does."

Rowan decided to ask among the stable hands; perhaps their predecessors' names were still remembered. "Did Slado have any friends among the folk?"

This took some thought. "None that I ever saw," Lorren said. "Saw him chatting, sometimes. People his age, for the most part."

"Did he ever speak to you?"

"Hm." Eamer squinted. "Can't recall..."

"Yes, he did. You remember. He complimented the roses, that time."

"Ah, that's right; but the roses were terrible that year! He didn't know what he was talking about."

"He was just saying it to say it. I think Kieran told him to be nice."

A grunt. "Like that would work. Slado paid out that compliment like it pained him to do it."

"But wasn't it Slado who told you that Kieran was gone?"

They shook their heads, the movements almost synchronized. "No," Lorren said. "That was Jannik."

"And Kieran had already been gone some time, I think."

"Six weeks, at least," Eamer said. "Less than seven."

"Now, how do you remember that?" Lorren inquired, pretending disbelief.

A smile. "Six paydays with no wages. I was counting."

"But he might have been off with his dragons for part of that..."

"Can you give me the range of dates for those six weeks?" Rowan asked.

Surprise, and long thought, with much blinking on Eamer's part, and *hm's* from Lorren.

"It was summer…"

"Pruning the cherry tree…"

"But I think we had to do that twice, that year…"

"What about the day Kieran first paid you?"

They looked at her, and in perfect unison recited year, season, month, day, and day of the week. They laughed, and Eamer added: "Around five o'clock in the morning."

"We're not likely to forget that!"

"Nor to forget the wizard himself. It's interesting… fifteen years of rudeness, arrogance, and even sometimes cruelty, and only two of kindness. But it's the kind wizard we remember best, in the end. That's a lesson for us all, I think."

Lorren nodded. "Yes. Hearts can change. Even the heart of a wizard."

Rowan found it interesting, as well. Given more time, possibly everyone would have come to feel as fondly as the old gardeners did toward the wizard of Donner. "And when he died," Rowan prompted, "it was Jannik himself who gave you the news."

Lorren sighed. "Yes. We came to work one morning, and found some things had already been done…"

"The flats of tulip bulbs we'd left there the previous morning. Some of them were gone…"

"Planted. So we started on the rest…"

"And after a bit, I noticed there was someone behind me. I thought it might be Slado, because his shadow was too small for Kieran…"

"But it was a stranger."

"A little round man, with a pointy beard—" Eamer's hand pantomimed the shape, knuckles to chin, fingers moving stiffly. "—dressed in green. And he told us that our services were no longer required."

"Because he liked to keep the garden himself."

"And he does, too. Not as well as we did, of course…"

"But you've got to respect a man who likes to keep a garden."

"You do. All the magic he wants, but he just gets right down on his knees and puts his own fingers into the dirt. Got to respect that."

"And he specifically said that Kieran had died of natural causes?"

"That's right. 'The old wizard has finally passed on.' "

Apparently Jannik himself did consider Kieran to be old enough to simply pass away—or at least, in front of the gardeners, made a show of seeming to think so. "How did Slado react to Jannik's presence?"

"We never saw that."

"Hadn't seen the young fellow at all, for a couple of days…"

"And we never saw him again."

"But you did have opportunity to watch Slado and Kieran interact, earlier?" Indications in the affirmative. "How did they seem toward each other?"

Further conversation, and the picture began to emerge.

On Slado's arrival, Kieran had made a point of introducing Lorren and Eamer (" 'The finest gardeners in the Inner Lands!'—and he should know, being a wizard, so it must be true…"), to which simple social nicety Slado reacted with perplexity, and glances askance at the old wizard.

During the first few months, when the two were seen together in the garden or about the city, it seemed that the master regarded the apprentice with a kindly interest. There was no comradeship displayed, but neither was there evidence of the sort of close discipline that sometimes was enacted by masters of more common professions—although what conditions prevailed when both were out of sight, during Slado's actual instruction and training, no one ever saw. Still, Kieran seemed not to dislike his apprentice.

Somewhat later, the gardeners on occasion noticed Kieran observing Slado, from a distance, with an expression of vague disappointment.

On Slado's part, there was first careful respect, then a respect rather more hesitantly granted; then one both carefully formal and emotionally neutral—when the master was looking. Behind Kieran's back, or in his absence, when the wizard was mentioned in conversation: a clear and unmasked disdain.

One summer afternoon when Kieran was taking his tea in the garden, as was his habit on fine days, Eamer, working alone, observed the wizard deep in thought. Whatever subject Kieran was considering, it was one that disturbed and saddened him; and his tea grew cold in the pot, and the sweet-cakes that he so enjoyed were entirely ignored.

Young Slado wandered out of the house, book in hand, to sit on the stone bench under the cherry tree. As he passed into Kieran's view, the wizard glanced at him, once, then looked away; but during that glance and after, as Eamer noticed, Kieran's expression did not alter in the slightest. The gardener could not help but think that the subject of Kieran's contemplation had been Slado himself.

Then followed a period when Slado was never seen in public without Kieran being present. The master kept the apprentice close by his side during every sort of casual interaction or activity that Kieran routinely engaged in—which Slado seemed to endure, but never enjoy.

At one point the two were observed—not by the gardeners, but by an acquaintance who reported it to them—outside Saranna's Inn, where a celebration was in progress. They were at some distance from the crowd, and Kieran, who was facing the observer, was speaking to Slado at length: very sternly, but calmly, and with no apparent rancor.

"It was after that that Slado told us the roses were lovely," Eamer said.

Lorren nodded. "Kieran was telling Slado that it doesn't hurt to be nice."

"A possibility," Rowan admitted.

Some time after that Slado's free time became his own again. And Kieran continued as before, benevolent, cheerful, seeming happy with the world in general, conducting his star parties for the children.

"I assume those only started after Kieran's personality altered?" Rowan asked.

"That's right. After that, but before Slado turned up."

Then came the period with only the apprentice on hand, seeming to go about his days as usual; then Slado was absent; and then Jannik appeared.

"But, you know," Lorren said to Eamer, "there was one day, before then, when Kieran came out in the morning again."

"He always came out in the morning, to bid us good day."

"Yes, but this was early, like that first time, when he gave us the money. I remember, because I was worried he was going to change back."

"Did he look like he'd been up all night?" Rowan asked.

Lorren thought, but came to no clear conclusion. "If he had, it wasn't a hard night, not like that first time. He looked happy enough... no, more like pleased. Like he was pleased about something, some particular thing."

"I don't remember that..."

"It was early. All the stars were still out, but he had that magic lamp lit in the garden, the red one, so I saw him well enough. He lifted his hand hello, but I thought he wanted to be alone, so I waved back, but didn't say anything. I think... I think it was close to the end, then. Close to when he passed on..."

"Was that the last time you saw him?"

Lorren indicated in the negative. "There was a puppet show in town, and I saw him handing out some coppers to a group of children, so they could go. That was the last time, for me."

"What about you, Eamer?"

"The last time? Can't pin it down. Might have been right in the garden, him taking his tea one of those afternoons. Or maybe at Saranna's Inn. He'd go there, now and then, just for the beer and the hearthlight."

The three sat quietly, contemplating the gentle final years of the wizard of Donner. And perhaps, Rowan thought, perhaps it was merely this that had piqued Latitia's curiosity: a good man, where there had been a bad one. The heart of a wizard, changing.

Changing suddenly. Changing overnight.

"Do you have any idea," Rowan said, and she sounded to herself almost pleading, "can you even guess, why Kieran did change, what happened the night before that one particular morning?"

Both the ancient gardeners shook their heads. But: "Thoughts, I suppose," Eamer said. "A lot of hard thinking goes on in the dead of night. All your sins catch up with you, and he had more sins, and worse, than the common folk get."

"Ammi's murder," Rowan supplied, musingly.

"And others," Lorren said. "And that war."

"The one when Kieran first came here," Eamer said. "A lot of trouble over that; we had the wizard Olin's troops, right in sight of the city. Just a child, I was, but I remember it well. Standing right at the end of Old Water Street, gaping across the river, smoke on the other side, and fire, and soldiers in blue, trying to cross in boats... I lost two uncles and an aunt in that war."

Rowan could hardly believe that she was actually speaking to persons with firsthand experience of so ancient an event. "Wars are usual, when a new wizard is first established... but there was none when Jannik came."

"No..."

"None."

"How odd... Fortunate, but odd." She wondered if this were significant, but could come to no conclusion. "I'm also interested in the doings of a steerswoman, whom perhaps you might have met. A dark woman; her name was Latitia."

"No... You're the only steerswoman I've ever met at all. Lorren?"

"No... But I heard about another." Lorren squinted in thought. "Hm... was that the one who died?"

"What?" Rowan sat up. "Are you sure?" But no: Latitia's Donner logbook at the Annex continued for at least six months after her leaving the city...

"Yes, now that I think of it, I did hear... Oh"—a sigh of exasperation—"it's the recent years that run together..."

"Recent?"

"Yes... Ah, that's right: the fire. Dragons got into town, and Saranna's Inn was burned to the ground. My niece told me about it. There was a steerswoman among the guests. They never found her..."

"Actually," Rowan said, oddly embarrassed, "I believe that was me."

They regarded her with new interest. Then Eamer turned to Lorren. "See? We've been sitting here all this time, talking to a ghost."

"Ah! That means we've finally crossed over!"

"And we did it together. How clever of us!"

Rowan laughed. "I'm pleased to inform you that we are all three still in the land of the living."

Rowan was sorry to take her leave of them. She made them a gift of Ona's drawing, which gesture delighted them far out of proportion to the act. Rowan wondered how often they had visitors, and considered that perhaps the greater gifts to them had been merely her presence, and the conversation.

As she paused by the door, and because she suddenly simply had to know, and because she had finally discovered a question that might serve to satisfy her curiosity while remaining open to alternate interpretation, Rowan asked: "Are you married?"

"Ah!" Lorren said. "Oh, my... must be more than seventy years now..."

"Every day a treasure," Eamer said, reaching across the white tablecloth to take Lorren's hand.

"Every day."

"I saw her," Eamer said, turning to Rowan, "one spring morning, kneeling in the turnip patch. Felt like I'd been hit on the head with a shovel, and the only thought I had was: That's got to be the most beautiful woman in the world."

"And I saw *her*," Lorren said, "standing in the road, and all I could think was: That is the ugliest woman I've ever seen in my life"—she laughed and turned back to Eamer, her faded eyes shining—"but I *do* like the way she's looking at me!"

Outside on Old Water Street, the steerswoman paused.

The blue house before her was tall, clean, dripping with bright white trim as ornate as a party cake. Comfortable, and prosperous, courtesy of the kind Kieran's generous wages.

Old Water Street was in the north quarter, tucked up against the curving arm of Greyriver. The street ran to the riverside, where decaying docks, some reduced to pilings and rubble, pointed out to the opposite bank.

Rowan gazed down the street at the water. There, nearly a century before, the little girl who had been Eamer had stood watching the fire and destruction of Kieran's personal war.

The steerswoman turned away, and slowly made her way up Old Water Street, lost in thought.

At the intersection she paused, crossed two streets over, and continued east, away from the river. Eventually, she reached a small open square, where a pair of boys were working a crank to draw a bucket of water from a wood-roofed stone well. The boys regarded her suspiciously, then filled their two smaller buckets from the larger one and carried them off, grunting and staggering at the effort.

Rowan approached the well, considered it, sat on its edge.

East Well.

She imagined the kindly, white-haired man from Ona's drawing; imagined him real, and standing before her. A gentle face, a smile and coppers for the children, so that they might attend a puppet show.

Rowan imagined him walking down this street, walking up to this well, where waited, all around, a silent crowd of people. Walking, empty-eyed, and dragging by its hair the corpse of little Ammi.

Although perhaps Kieran had not yet been white-haired. Rowan wondered, vaguely.

Before her, one empty gap between two fenced house yards: a pocket garden, now gone to weeds and bramble. There, Kieran had first spoken to Lorren and Eamer, had simply informed them that they now worked for him.

The steerswoman looked left.

The street curved up and slightly right, with houses more widely spaced. Two intersections ahead, half obscured by the last home on the right: Jannik's house.

She rose, walked up the street with as much nonchalance as she could manage.

The house was brick, three storeys, and its decoration far more modest than was the Donner norm. The windows were small on the ground floor, and shuttered, larger on the upper storeys, with glass panes glaring white where sunlight reflected, pitch-black where it did not. There was no porch, but a small shingled portico shaded the front door. The roofline and peak of the house were edged with pigeon-chasers, rendered in decorative spikes. Half hidden by the roof peak, part of a curved object was visible, gray, like stone or old ceramic.

The house stood alone on its corner lot, with no others adjacent. In the next yard over, a wreck of grayed timber and the tumbled remnants of brick walls suggested previous neighbors, long departed.

Keeping to the far side of the street, Rowan strolled casually on. Jannik's backyard was walled, but not to any great height. The bricks stood only as high as Rowan's waist, and the garden was easily visible.

It was huge, occupying the equivalent of four of the neighboring lots. Sections of lawn fell and rose gently, their borders outlined with white stones. Fieldstone paths wound among flower beds, between ornamental bushes and under a lattice arbor, where climbing roses, past blooming, cheerfully displayed bright rose hips. At the far end of the garden, a fair-sized shed stood, with a red wheelbarrow nearby, half-tilted on its side.

Most attention had been paid to the areas nearby the house. Only chrysanthemums still bloomed, but these were bright and abundant. Still, their arrangement and brilliance felt regimented to Rowan, and over-controlled, oddly sterile. Not at all the exuberant opulence shown in Ona's drawing. Lorren's and Eamer's talents were missed.

As Rowan continued down the street bordering the garden wall, more details were revealed. An ornamental iron lamp with glass panels stood on a pedestal directly in the center of one flower bed. One would need to step on the flowers to light it—but Lorren mentioned a magic lamp, red. To be lit, perhaps, by a word or a mystic gesture.

In a section of lawn unnaturally bright green in the autumn landscape, a cherry tree stood. Beneath this, a curved stone bench.

There, Rowan thought: there he had sat, Slado himself, reading his book, studying his craft. Plotting, perhaps, the murder of the one good wizard in the world.

Rowan found that she had stopped, and was gazing steadily. She hoped, belatedly, that she did not appear suspicious; but Jannik was not at home.

The steerswoman glanced back at the house, captured the view in memory, and studied it after she turned away, walking on.

Only two entrances to the house. Probably the back door, in the garden, would be best. Less chance of being noticed.

Larger windows upstairs: rooms most often used, perhaps. More important rooms, away from street-level prying eyes.

The shape of the house, arrangement of windows, the roofline: these gave her a general idea of internal layout.

And that ornament on the roof, stone or ceramic: Rowan's glance had caught its shape clearly. A birdbath, perhaps, but neglected and out of use, tilted badly out of skew. Or a sundial: the small central spike would cast an adequate shadow.

But there were no doors or landings on the roof. And it was not visible from any window.

Regardless: if a birdbath, the birds were out of luck; if a sun-dial, it was useless, as it was oriented incorrectly. It was tilted to the east-southeast.

Facing, she suddenly realized, exactly toward the Eastern Guidestar.

Wizards spoke to the Guidestars, commanded them. The Guidestars obeyed, possibly even replied...

A voice, then, to speak to the sky; and the bowl, like hands cupped around an ear, to listen to the distant answer of magic.

CHAPTER TEN

*A*t the Dolphin, Ruffo had moved half a dozen small tables out onto the cobbled square before the glass-windowed sitting room. All tables were in use, by locals and a handful of sailors whom Rowan recognized from *Graceful Days*, all enjoying lunch or tea out in the pleasantly warm autumn day. Some customers were observing with blatant interest a lone patron of the gracious parlor, who sat twirling a glass of wine in his hand, pretending not to notice the scrutiny.

One of the outside tables was occupied by Bel.

Rowan sought for and failed to find another chair: all had been confiscated for adjacent tables. The Outskirter considerately relinquished her own seat, and perched herself on the low brick window ledge nearby. "Were the gardeners useful?"

"Extremely," Rowan said, and prepared to relate her experiences, but asked first, "Is Will still asleep?"

"No. He's gone off to retrieve his gear." Bel shifted. "I think it's a good thing he met up with us. I'm not sure he's safe traveling alone."

Rowan became disturbed. "Was there more trouble?" Someone appeared at her elbow: the handkerchief boy, with a fistful of cutlery, which he shyly placed in front of Rowan, in no particular configuration. At the common room door, Beck stood watching in parody of stern supervision.

Bel waited until the boy had departed. "No. But he's hard to wake up. I tripped over him twice, on my way to and from the outhouse, and he never stirred."

Rowan had been arranging the cutlery; now she hesitated. "You tripped over him?"

Bel nodded. "He slept on the floor. He absolutely refused to share the bed. I think he's secretly a prude."

Will had also slept on the floor in Rowan's room, but that bed was hardly large enough for one person. "Perhaps he simply prefers privacy."

"Maybe. But if he slept that hard on the road, then he was lucky. Any thief or bandit could have made off with his possessions, or even cut his throat, and he'd never have noticed at all."

"Then he probably slept lightly, for all that time." The boy arrived

110

again, with a single plate that he placed before Rowan with an air of ceremony. The act so delighted him that he stood for a moment, regarding the result with a sort of gleeful self-satisfaction, and then departed. "And," Rowan continued, "now that Willam is finally someplace safe, his body is probably catching up on what it's missed."

Bel made a noncommittal sound. "And he has nightmares."

Rowan stopped short. "Really?"

The Outskirter nodded again, thoughtful. "Not the sort where you wake up screaming. But he did make enough noise to wake me."

The steerswoman leaned back in her chair. "Well," she said, "I do hope that you tried to wake him."

"Yes, but not very hard. When I shook him the first time, he didn't wake, but he did settle down, so I let him go on sleeping. The next time it happened I noticed that all I had to do was rest my hand on his shoulder. He went quiet right away."

Rowan found that this small detail saddened her deeply. Bel went on: "I asked him later, but he wouldn't talk about it. He changed the subject." She glanced about cautiously: no one was attending the conversation, but Bel leaned closer to Rowan, to speak more quietly. "He's worried about that woman he killed."

Rowan was immediately concerned. "Is he expecting some repercussions?" she asked. "Does he think that—" She was stopped by a look from Bel.

"No," Bel said. "He's sorry that he did it, and it's weighing on his mind. He wonders if she had family." Rowan was suddenly ashamed; she had dismissed both the woman and the man, she now realized, as merely a problem solved. Even wizard's minions did not deserve such indifference. "And he wishes there had been some other way to handle it," the Outskirter continued. "He agrees that it's probably safer that she's dead. But it still bothers him."

Rowan recovered. "I believe that speaks well for him."

Bel nodded, waited while the boy brought a tall glass of lemonade, which splashed over his hands with every step. Rowan took it from him, and placed it on the table herself. "Interestingly," Bel went on when the boy had left, "he's not as bothered by the man you killed. You were defending someone, the man turned his attack on you, you stopped him. You were justified."

"But, Bel—very similar circumstances also held in the woman's case."

The Outskirter nodded broadly. "But in that case, it was Willam who did it."

Rowan considered. "Then he's holding himself to different

standards."

"That's right. And he should." Bel spoke definitely.

"I believe you're right." Someone with power beyond the scope of common folk ought not use it by whim, ought not impose it on weaker persons. "He's a good—" Rowan nearly said *He's a good boy,* but realized that throughout the entire conversation she had in her mind substituted the younger Willam, the stocky, awkward, earnest, copper-eyed boy. She corrected the image. "He's a good man. He's managed to hold on to that."

"Yes." And Bel added quietly, "But I'm glad he got away from Corvus."

The steerswoman sighed. "So am I."

Rowan's meal arrived: a bowl of soup delivered, wisely, by Beck himself. Rowan thanked him distractedly, and the young man departed.

Rowan was about to begin on the soup when she noticed Bel's attention caught by something; the steerswoman followed Bel's gaze.

A young, dark woman, slightly disheveled and wearing a harried expression, was making her way through the tables, oblivious to the complaints of persons she jostled. Once at the door of the Dolphin's common room, she peered inside, and apparently found no satisfaction. Looking about in annoyance, she sighted a serving girl attending a group of sailors, went to her, asked a question. The server immediately indicated Rowan, and the woman hurried over, with a distinct air of exasperation.

Rowan and Bel observed her approach with perplexity. Arrived, the woman spoke politely enough. "Excuse me, the steerswoman Rowan, is it?" She seemed someone who had quite a lot to do, and was not pleased to be doing this.

"Yes…"

"Here." She passed over an envelope. "From Marel. Will there be a reply?"

"I really must read this before deciding," Rowan pointed out. She untied the ribbon and unfolded the paper. Bel spied a vacated chair nearby and fetched it, pulling it close beside Rowan to read over the steerswoman's shoulder. The messenger, less than pleased, scanned the area, found not a single free seat, and resigned herself to perching on the window ledge.

There was no greeting or preamble; Marel got down to the matter immediately.

After our conversation, I recalled that one of my previous employees had the regular assignment of delivering to Kieran any items of his shipped through our establishment. It seemed to me that the fellow might have had opportunity to observe the wizard's or Slado's daily doings, so I invited him to tea.

In fact, he had seen very little, other than two occurrences that struck him as odd.

When delivering packages, the procedure was to place the item in front of the door, and wait. (One never knocked.) By some means, the wizard, if he was present, always knew when someone was at his door, and would arrive in short order.

On this occasion, the wizard did not arrive, which was of itself not unusual, as he was occasionally out of town, dealing with the dragons. The door was opened by the apprentice Slado, who accepted the package without a word, and took it into the house.

One would not necessarily regard this as remarkable; it seems quite reasonable to me. But apparently—and here Rowan had to turn to the second page; Bel snatched up the first, which she had not finished reading—*on the next delivery, three weeks later, the same thing occurred. And Kieran had not been seen at all between those two events.*

After the conversation, I sent one of my clerks to look through our old files, which are stored in another building, and it seems that those two deliveries were the last ever to Kieran. Marel provided the exact dates. *About three weeks later, Jannik arrived— which I remember distinctly, as I was in the Dolphin chatting to a rival of mine whose business I was attempting to acquire at a frankly cut-throat rate (I was successful), when the news made its way through the room.* Marel had added the date of the acquisition.

"Excuse me?"

Rowan found herself regarding a thin, graceful woman of late middle age, wearing fine attire and an expression of suppressed outrage. "I heard you were asking about Slado?"

The steerswoman was bemused. "Yes..."

A diner nearby vacated a chair; the woman appropriated it instantly, pulled it over to Rowan's table, and sat. She said, with no preliminaries: "I slapped him."

"*What?*"

"And you survived?" Bel asked.

"As you can see. But it was a near thing."

Rowan's astonishment was immense. "You *slapped* him? Was he taking liberties with your person?"

"He was doing exactly that, and I endure such effronteries from no one, not even at the age of seventeen!"

"Were you leading him on?" Bel wondered.

The woman turned the Outskirter an evil glare. "I was conversing with him in a somewhat flirtatious manner," she said stiffly, "but with no particular intensity. No person of normal social perceptivity would have mistaken my behavior as bawdy."

"Maybe Slado lacked normal social perceptivity," Bel remarked to Rowan.

"Or considered it irrelevant," Rowan said. "But," she continued to the woman, "I'm frankly amazed that you didn't, say, immediately catch fire. Or vanish in a flash of light."

"Or get turned into a weasel," Bel said.

"Well, he would have done that to me, or some such, I'm sure; but Kieran arrived instantly, pulled Slado aside, and gave him a serious talking-to."

"I see," Rowan said and, with no effort on her part, her information began to interlock. It was rather an interesting internal process, which she observed with pleasure. "This would have been at the celebration at Saranna's Inn?"

The woman seemed surprised that Rowan knew this. "In fact, yes. The occasion was the mayor's inauguration."

"Was that Nid?"

"Nid? No, the council had just voted him out. The wizard would never have been invited to any function Nid held. This was Elena's."

"Is Elena still living?" A possible new source of information.

"Who knows? They left, she and her husband, when the council put up Joly in her place, twelve years ago."

"And that would be the dark fellow with all the hair," Rowan said, recalling Eamer's and Lorren's comments.

The woman eyed her. "Yes… he keeps a lot of it. Elena was so distressed, she left the city altogether. They bought a caravan, of all things."

Rowan could not help enjoying herself. "And their daughter is a bricklayer?"

A disparaging sound. "A general laborer. When she's not gaming in the back rooms. It's her debts that keep her from rising in life."

Bel was observing the conversation with something like pride; apparently she found Rowan's performance impressive. The steerswoman went on. "Then, that night, Kieran's attention lapsed briefly, and Slado immediately caused a problem."

"Well, the old wizard kept him close, generally, that's for certain."

"For a period of time. Later, Slado moved freely again."

"I wouldn't know. I generally steered clear of both of them. I didn't trust that wizard."

Rowan hesitated. "You mean Slado."

"No, I mean Kieran. It made no sense; first he's cruel and dangerous, and then suddenly he's getting invited to social events, protecting innocent maidens, and playing with little children. People don't change overnight like that."

Rowan said, musingly, "Apparently, Kieran did…"

Bel noticed her tone, became curious. "*Literally* overnight?"

"So it would seem... I believe I possess the exact date." Across the street, Rowan saw Willam arrive, carrying an unstrung bow in one hand and a knotted burlap sack in the other. A bedroll was slung across his back, to which a quiver of arrows was tied. He studied the group at Rowan's table, hesitated, then placed the bow on the ground, and the sack—using no great care with it, Rowan noted. Then he sat down beside them in the dirt, his back against one of Ruffo's lampposts.

Rowan returned to the woman. "I don't suppose you managed to overhear the substance of Kieran's remarks to Slado?"

"No, I went off in a huff, found a nicer dancing partner, and married him that year."

"Thank you, you've been very helpful..." Rowan realized that the messenger was still waiting, slouched back against the windowpanes, arms crossed, eyes narrowed to a squint. Rowan said to her: "No reply, other than 'Thank you.' " The messenger threw up her hands, emitted an inarticulate noise of frustration, and departed. The middle-aged woman remained in place and waved at Beck, apparently planning to dine. With no other tables available, Rowan could hardly chase her off. Instead, she set to her own neglected lunch.

Chicken soup, now nearly cold. Bel considered it with amusement. "Are you going to tell the staff that you haven't been sick after all?"

"I suppose I should. But frankly, I'm finding all this concern rather flattering."

"Ha. Deception by omission."

"I'm not required to volunteer information."

"You steerswomen draw a fine line sometimes." Bel glanced past the tables. "Finish your lunch. I think I'll chat with our friend over there."

She rose and departed; her chair was instantly claimed, and occupied. "Ah, there you are!" It was Naio. "I was looking for you in your room. Sherrie told me you were under the weather."

The steerswoman was bemused. "Sherrie?"

"My niece. She's a chambermaid. Here." He placed on the table a slim cardboard folder.

Rowan took two more spoonfuls of soup before setting down the silverware and taking the folder. "More of Ona's work?"

"Yes. We had quite an interesting discussion, after you and Reeder left." He seemed pleased, and deeply amused. "You know, it's amazing what you can not know about your own wife. But Ona and I never really knew each other at all until, oh, our forties. I wonder, sometimes, what she was like as a girl. A whole history that I never knew about."

Their tablemate made a disgruntled sound. "I was under the

impression that you were one of those fellows who didn't notice the girls at all. Had I thought otherwise, I'd have given you a run for your money."

He beamed at her. "I'm sure you would have, Irina. You were the prettiest thing in town, and knew it well."

"You should properly be saying that about your own wife."

"My own wife has other fine qualities, which I've come to find I cannot live without."

"Ah!" This from Irina, as Rowan opened the folder. "There's the nasty little man!"

"He was short?" Rowan asked.

"Yes."

"No," Naio said. "Irina, you forget how tall you were."

Irina gave him an arch look. "It merely added to my grace."

"So it did," Naio assured her.

Rowan considered the drawing. Slado was not its subject, or rather, had not been planned to have been. It was a scene on a wharf, with lobster pots piled artfully askew. Ona had apparently been fascinated by the complexity of the inner workings of the traps, and the knotted strands were shown with that luminous clarity that Rowan had come to love in Ona's work.

A handful of bystanders were sketched in the background, and it was clear that Ona had shifted her focus. Among other persons composed merely of outline and shadow: young Slado, depicted with obsessive detail, his face in light, his left shoulder shadowed by the overhang of an adjacent building.

Rowan called to mind the various wharves in the harbor, identified which one was shown, and found that she knew exactly where the apprentice had been standing, and by the shadow, the time of day.

"Hmph," Irina said. "Felicia."

"Felicia?"

"That girl he's talking to." Irina indicated the shadow-shape of a buxom figure with wild curls. "A much better subject for his attentions than myself, I assure you. A wanton little thing she was." Rowan found Slado's expression interesting: evaluative, as in the tea-cup portrait, but with a shade of intensity perhaps understandable under the circumstances. A young man, after all, with natural inclinations and urges.

"I don't think I knew her," Naio said.

"You hardly would. A much lower class of person. I was certain she'd end up in the bawdy-houses; she had no other talents to speak of."

"But she didn't?" Rowan asked. "End up in a bawdy-house?"

Irina sniffed. "Well perhaps she did after all, but not one in this city.

Wild girl that she was, she wandered off one day, probably following a sailor or caravan worker or some such riffraff. No one ever—" And she stopped.

Silence at the table.

Eventually, Rowan said: "In other words, she vanished." On the page, the young apprentice regarded the shadow-girl, and his intensity seemed to have acquired a darker cast. "I believe," the steerswoman said, "that you had a much closer call than you'd thought, Irina."

Irina sat very still. "My word," she said quietly.

"And so did Ona," Naio said. His eyes were wide in his dark face.

Irina turned to him, astonished. "Your wife had an interest in this creature?"

"A girlish infatuation. She was hardly more than a child."

Rowan said, "Perhaps it was her youth that saved her."

Later, Rowan crossed the street to where Bel and Willam waited.

Will looked up from his seat on the ground. "Were the gardeners helpful?"

"Yes, very." Rowan leaned back against the lamppost. "And Naio seems to have become interested in the subject, as well. He's promised to ask around, and about Latitia, as well. I'm starting to feel like information is seeking me out, instead of the reverse." She considered the burlap sack beside Willam. "And either you're not carrying any of your destructive charms, or you've learned to make them less unstable. You practically dropped that sack on the ground."

He grinned. "They're a lot safer now. And some of them have delays, so that I can set them and get out of range before they go off. I don't need to use flaming arrows."

"Far more convenient," Rowan commented. She noticed that Bel sat unnaturally still and quiet.

The Outskirter glanced up at her once, a dark glance, then looked away. "Will told me an interesting story about his time with Corvus."

Rowan hesitated. "Oh?" She was not certain she wished to hear it.

Bel nodded, gazing off across the square. Then she said: "That minion of Shammer and Dhree's who we questioned, the one with the speech-garbling spell—Will watched Corvus put that spell on someone."

"A house servant," Will said. He looked distressed. "They all have it —"

"Please," Bel said vehemently, "don't tell it again, I don't think my stomach could take it." Rowan found it difficult to imagine a process that would be considered too gruesome to discuss by a woman who had herself been able and willing to apply torture to a man.

"If you want the details, I can tell you later," Will offered.

"And bring a diagram of the inside of a human head," Bel added, through clenched teeth. "And expect to have nightmares for a week."

Rowan changed the subject. "Well, we've made a lot of progress." And she handed Ona's drawing of the lobster traps and Slado to Bel, gave Willam the note from Marel.

Will read with growing interest—and very rapidly indeed, Rowan noted, seeming to take in both pages in only five separate glances. "It does look like Kieran was probably dead before that first package… unless he was off doing maintenance on the dragons," he said.

"Yes," Rowan said. "And there's more." She outlined the content of her conversation with Lorren and Eamer.

Bel forgot her nausea entirely, and became fascinated. "He *did* change overnight," she said when Rowan finished.

"So he did."

"Something happened. Right then, that very night."

"Yes—but I can't guess what."

"If I can get into the records, I'll look for that date," Willam said. "But there might not be anything. If it was something personal that happened, and not magical, it will only show up if Kieran kept a diary."

Rowan considered this. "But all magical events are recorded?"

Willam thought. "Do you want a long answer, or a short one?"

"A short one, please."

"It depends."

Bel said: "If the records the Guidestars make can be erased, couldn't the ones in the house be erased, too?" Will opened his mouth to reply, but Bel quickly added: "And give me the short answer."

He made a sound of amusement, then said: "There are two ways to erase records, a hard way and an easy way. If you do it the easy way, pieces can still be left behind."

Willam did not expect to find complete records, as he had explained to Rowan the previous night. They would be fragmentary, scattered, tucked away in spaces between current records, spaces assumed to be empty.

Spaces in what, and where, Rowan did not know. Will had attempted to explain; Rowan had understood not a single word.

"At least we do know that it was Slado, and not Kieran, who brought down the Guidestar," Rowan said.

Will was dubious. "Well, that would make the most sense. But we can't be absolutely sure—"

"It happened between those two packages," Bel said. "Kieran was dead. Slado did it."

Will looked at Bel, then up at Rowan. "I've got the Guidestar's fall narrowed down to somewhere inside a two-year range—"

And Bel said, rather smugly: "Rowan's narrowed it down to two weeks."

He was astonished. "How did you manage that?"

"By the application of good Steerswomen's techniques," Rowan said.

"Good, *boring* Steerswomen's techniques," Bel amplified. "And *I'll* tell him about it. *You*"—here she climbed to her feet, slapped dust from her trouser seat, and took Rowan's arm—"are going to get some sleep. If we're going to be sneaking around in the dead of night, doing something fantastically dangerous, we all need to be rested enough to be alert. It will be the dead of night, won't it?" This to Willam.

He nodded. "An hour before midnight. And I have three hours to get everything done."

"Then we have two days to get used to being awake all night," Bel informed Rowan. "And you're exhausted. Shut up; you are."

Rowan laughed. "Far be it from a steerswoman to deny the truth."

Bel began to usher Rowan back across the street; Willam gathered his gear and followed. "We'll wake you at dinner-time," Bel said. "Will and I can find something to occupy ourselves until then—and I'll fill him in on what we've done since we saw him last. Then after dinner, we'll all carouse until dawn, sleep until noon, and do it all over again. Then we'll be set."

"Oh, if you insist."

"I do."

"Use Bel's room," Willam suggested. "You won't fall out of bed if you toss in your sleep."

"At the top of the stairs," Bel said, releasing Rowan's arm, and indicating a window above. "The door on the left."

"Actually—" Actually, all Rowan's gear was in her own room, including logbook, pen, and ink. She planned to take some time to record the information she had just acquired. "Actually, I think I'd prefer my own room."

"How's your leg?" Bel asked suspiciously; she obviously assumed that it was the climb that daunted Rowan.

"Fine," Rowan said, with emphasis, and perfect truth. She recovered her arm, made a show of resetting her shirtsleeve. "And I will see you both later. Try not to get into any trouble."

CHAPTER ELEVEN

*R*eason, precision, patience: good steerswomanly techniques that had served Rowan well during her research at the Annex in Alemeth.

For a wizard, look for magic; for magic, look for something otherwise impossible; for a *secret* wizard, one unknown to the common folk, look for impossible events that no known wizard could claim.

The copies of the steerswomen's logbooks in the Annex held centuries of observations. Any steerswoman observing an inexplicable event would be certain to record it. By the condition and location of the Guidestar fragments that Rowan had found, she was able to place the event somewhere within a four-year span.

Steerswomen traveled wide, and were few. Not all logbooks successfully made their way back to the Archives, and not all of the copies made subsequently found their way safely to the Annexes. Nevertheless, Rowan managed to locate fifty-two books covering the relevant period.

She read them. She began generating notes, charts, and in one case, a graph. After a while, and quite incidental to her planned search, she began to notice something odd.

It was the weather.

Steerswomen routinely, in every day's first entry, made note of the weather. The collation of this information by the residents of the Archives, steerswomen past the age of traveling, had resulted across the centuries in quite a lot of useful knowledge about climate, and the movement of weather patterns.

Late one summer, every traveling steerswoman described identical weather.

The women had been widely scattered: Terminus in the north; Southport in the south; a mountain peak west of The Crags; the edge of the Outskirts east of Five Corners; the empty lands northeast of the loop of the Long North Road. Two others, at sea; the rest, at various locations within the great circle of the Inner Lands.

All reported the same phenomenon: heavy, dark clouds that moved in from the north, remained for many days, occasionally emitting thunder and brief deluges of rain—and then dissipated.

There could not be individual pockets of foul weather miraculously choosing to hover over each and every steerswoman. It took no great leap of logic to assume that everywhere, across the entire Inner Lands, the sky had been completely obscured.

For fourteen days. And this was impossible.

Rowan had already known that the Guidestar did not simply drop to the ground. Its fall had been long, and bright. It had crossed the sky, burning. And yet, in all the Inner Lands, there was not even a rumor of any person seeing it fall.

This was why. Weather had shielded the Guidestar from human eyes. Only during this specific two-week period could the Guidestar have fallen with no Inner Lander witnessing it.

Magic, hiding magic.

In the darkness, Rowan startled, struggled, struck out.

The shadowy figure stumbled back. A *thump* against the table, a clatter, a splash of water spilled. "Rowan, it's me!"

"Willam?" The white hair was barely visible, seeming to float in the darkness. Rowan calmed down. "I'm sorry—" she said as he simultaneously said: "Sorry—"

She climbed to her knees, took the wash towel hanging on her bedstead, located by memory the vase of fresh-cut flowers that the day maid had placed on her table, began sopping. "Are you all right?" She didn't think she had struck very hard.

"Yes. Are you? You didn't answer my knock. And—"

"Yes... A dream, that's all." She considered lighting the candle, decided that it was not worth the effort.

"It sounded bad," Will said. A pause. "Nightmares don't give you much rest... if you want to sleep some more, I'll tell Bel."

"No." Rowan handed him the towel, sat back on her heels, rubbed her forehead, watching the ghost-hair dip as he went on his knees to find the rest of the spill. "Actually, it wasn't so very bad." It had been one of those peculiar dreams wherein nothing particularly dreadful occurred, but that nonetheless filled one with an inexplicable terror. "I dreamed you were a Demon." She cast about on the foot of the bed for her clothing.

"One of those, those strange people?" Apparently, Bel had gone a long way toward filling Will in on Rowan's experiences. He rose, set the towel on the table. "The ones who burned you?" He sounded distressed.

Rowan knew how one sometimes felt a vague responsibility for the actions one's imagined self took in others' dreams. "You weren't trying to hurt me," she reassured him. She found her shirt. "You were trying to talk to me." She pulled the shirt over her head. "But, being a male, you didn't have the necessary equipment."

He had politely turned his back, despite the fact that the room was almost completely dark. He made a noise of amusement. "I guess I wouldn't, would I ?" He must have been told of the nature of the female Demons' organ of communication.

"It did present a quandary," Rowan said, sliding from the sheets to put on her trousers. In the dream, Rowan herself had been speaking, at length, in human language; but as she spoke, each word transformed itself into a solid shape, like a Demon utterance. The shapes appeared, and then hung in the air about her head, unsupported. And the Demon-Willam was attempting to communicate as Demon males did, by collecting and rearranging word-objects uttered by females, in this case snatching Rowan's words from the air instead of off the ground.

The dream-Rowan had been watching this behavior with interest, and commenting—rather pontifically, Rowan now thought—on the cleverness of the process by which the speechless males circumvented their inability. Each sentence the dream-Rowan uttered allowed the Demon access to more words.

But the Rowan who observed the dream, who seemed entirely separate and with separate knowledge and emotions, was terrified, filled with a desperate urgency. She knew, with perfect certainty, that the dream-Rowan must speak *differently,* must use more words, other words, that the words being said were not the ones the Demon-Willam needed. But despite all effort and strain on Rowan's part, despite her rising panic, the tedious steerswoman continued to pontificate, using very similar words, over and over; and the little male continued, patiently, to collect, to test new arrangements, discard, collect, and test again.

"What's the time?" Rowan asked, rising, groping under the bed for her boots. "And is dinner imminent?" She found that she was famished.

"Eighteen thirty," Will said, "and yes, and it smells wonderful." He stopped short, made a small noise of surprise. "I mean, half past six."

"I knew what you meant," Rowan said, and found and donned the boots. They left the room, proceeded down the corridor. "Is Bel in the dining room upstairs, or the common room?"

"The common room. Upstairs is filled, I think some event is afoot. The innkeeper said that we could dine in Bel's room, for a surcharge, but Bel said no. I think she's starting to worry about money."

"It can't last forever." Bel had spent the last season working with the silkworms in Alemeth, largely because there had been very little else to occupy her. With no need to pay for lodging at the Annex, she had acquired a tidy sum.

"Well, I have some. Since I got here, I've mostly begged for food."

"Very effectively, I'm sure. You were truly pitiful."

An event was afoot after all: two roast boars with all the trimmings, with entertainment to follow. In the common room, every table was occupied, despite the caravan's departure that morning. Bel had managed to claim a small table herself and defend it against all comers. The Outskirter waved Rowan and Willam over.

When they arrived and took their seats, Bel leaned down and with a cautious glance around the room passed something surreptitiously to Willam under the table. "Here, take them," she said to him quietly. "They make me nervous."

"They're perfectly safe. Unless you drop them off a cliff, or throw them into the fireplace." He shifted, arranging the object between his feet.

"And you should find someplace to put them. Carrying a burlap sack with you everywhere you go looks too suspicious. You might be taken for a thief of some kind."

"I don't like to leave them alone, with people about."

Willam's destructive charms. "No one has bothered my pack in my room," Rowan began. Then: "No…" The fact that the maids had so far been honest did not guarantee the same in the future.

Will leaned back as a burly serving man arrived with fistfuls of knives and forks, which he distributed gracelessly; apparently the most experienced servers were working in the formal dining room.

Will gestured Rowan and Bel closer, to speak above the clash of cutlery and rise of conversation all about. "When I was in the stables the other night, I noticed a place up in the rafters that should make a good hiding place for them, if I can climb up there without being noticed."

"Later tonight, then," Rowan said. "There should be no one about at all by midnight."

A sudden crash and clatter as silverware escaped from the server's overloaded grip, inspiring a cheer from a table of sailors across the room.

Something nagged at the back of Rowan's mind; she identified it, and stopped short, puzzling.

Will was watching the serving man scrambling about on hands and knees, searching for lost silverware; some customers were cheerfully directing him toward far-flung items. Only Bel had noticed Rowan's reaction. "What is it?" she asked, causing Will to turn back in curiosity.

"Eighteen thirty," the steerswoman said, thoughtfully.

The others traded a glance. Bel said, "No, midnight is twenty-four hundred. You know that."

"Wait, let me think." Rowan closed her eyes. The serving man was voicing petulant complaint; apparently some of the directions provided were intentionally spurious.

"Are you all right?" Will asked Rowan. "Rowan?"

"I'm trying to remember something…" So long ago…

Six years back, and Rowan a captive of the wizards Shammer and Dhree. Rowan had told them of the fallen Guidestar; she had described the pattern of fragments; maps had been brought out. Maps of incredible detail, and seemingly impossible beauty of execution… Rowan tried to ignore the din around her, concentrated harder.

Numbers, everywhere on the wizards' maps: measurements, Rowan had thought at first, elevations. But she had seen, then, that the numbers attached to landmarks that she knew well did not in any way match elevations on her own charts.

She tried to remember some specific number from the wizards' maps, any number at all. But it was no use: it was too long ago, and the numbers had been meaningless to her, and she had not retained them.

She opened her eyes to find Bel and Willam watching her dubiously. "Will," Rowan said, then checked to ensure that no one else was attending the conversation. "The Krue… do they measure length in centimeters and meters, distance in meters and kilometers?"

The question surprised him. "Yes."

Bel turned to him. "So do we."

"And the Outskirters count twenty-four separate hours in a day, instead of twice twelve."

"So do we," Will said. "Except, midnight is zero hundred."

"How very interesting." Two such different peoples, standing, it seemed, at utter opposite points in both society and location. "The Outskirters must have learned it from the wizards."

Bel caught and held Rowan's gaze, an extremely stubborn expression on her face. "No," she said, and stressed the next words. "The Outskirters were the first people." This was a very old disagreement between them. "If, as you say, our line names resemble your Inner Lands women's names, then you got your names from us. And if the wizards use our time and distances, then they got *those* from us."

Rowan decided not to repeat the argument. "Regardless. There was, at some point, a connection between your people and mine. And now it seems that there was also a connection between the Outskirters and the Krue. Will—" She turned to him. "Do you know anything about that?"

He shook his head. "No, I never heard anything. It never came up.

But I think you must be right. Spells need very precise timing and measurement. Our way is a lot easier to calculate than inches and feet. Outskirters and wizards must have at least met, long ago, if they're using our measurements."

A hush fell over the room, and all eyes turned to the kitchen door, from behind which came a sudden bustle, voices, clatters, and *thunks*.

Bel alone seemed uninterested. She turned to Willam. *"Their* measurements," she said.

He looked at her. "What?" The bustle in the kitchen quieted.

The room was nearly silent. Bel leaned closer. "You said 'our measurements'," she said quietly. "You mean 'their.' You're not one of them, anymore. And you were never really Krue at all."

He blinked. "You're right." He gave a small laugh of embarrassment. "I guess I've gotten used to thinking like them."

"Just try not to think too much like them."

"Until two nights from tonight, at"—Rowan internally adjusted her thinking to Outskirter modes—"twenty-three hundred."

Across the room, someone gave a plaintive cry. The reason was immediately evident: from beyond the kitchen door, perfectly audible in the near-silence, the sound of stairs creaking as some extremely heavy object was carried upward, accompanied by no less than four sets of ponderous footsteps.

All listened as the sounds diminished. Then, from somewhere in the distance and upward, a cheer, followed by a rising rhythmic noise, thumpings, and voices, resolving into: "The boar! The boar! The boar!"

Groans of frustration in the common room, and sighs of resignation. Conversation resumed.

"It seems we're a bit early after all," Rowan remarked. "Apparently upstairs gets first choice."

Bel eyed the common room, tilted her head. "I like it better down here."

Young Beck had been given charge of the proceedings in the common room. He took his assignment very seriously, and attempted graciously to direct the other servers by subtle nods and gestures only. Unfortunately, the new servers were not accustomed to picking up the cues. There was stumbling, and awkwardness, requiring Beck to move quickly here and there, correcting and adjusting as needed. But his calm and persistence were impressive, and Rowan decided that the young man definitely had a bright future in the business.

Eventually, the food arrived, and the crowd let out a cheer. For a space, there was only appreciative silence, as the portions were dispensed, and then dispatched by the happy diners.

Roast boar, not the best cuts, but plentiful. Also: buttered beans; cubes of potatoes and turnips cooked together with bacon; a side dish of pickled fruit; and for afters, white-frosted pumpkin cake. The steerswoman's slice, delivered by Beck personally, arrived decorated with a tiny drizzle of rare chocolate. Dinner was long, and delightful, and conducted in a reverent near-silence.

When the dishes were cleared, everyone stayed for drink, and for entertainment, which the crowd provided for itself. There was music, but not here: it drifted faintly down from the formal dining room. Occasionally, the melody was recognizable. Whenever this happened the common room crowd dropped all other pursuits and sang along, for as long as the tune was audible. New lyrics were sometimes improvised.

New arrivals swelled the crowd, and Rowan, Bel, and Willam were required to share their table. Their tablemates were the female bricklayer Rowan had met on the first day; a narrow blond man in his thirties, who by his own cheerful admission possessed neither occupation nor permanent abode; and a squat, muscular young woman with huge callused hands, who served as apprentice to one of the city's swordsmiths. With the dinner dishes cleared, there remained just enough room on the little table for six mugs of ale, and the occasional pair of elbows.

With the strangers present, Rowan, Bel, and Willam could no longer discuss their mission. Rowan fell into conversation with the swordsmith's apprentice concerning the steerswoman's need for a new weapon. Willam listened to the bricklayer's bitter tale of bad luck in recent wagers, and expressed his opinion that the rat races were fixed. Bel professed an interest in the underside of city life, and the vagrant became her eager informant.

Some time later, Rowan noticed Naio descending the main staircase then pausing to scan the crowd. Suspecting that she was herself the subject of his search, Rowan stood and waved him over.

"Quite a gathering tonight," he commented, nodding to the others at the table. Rowan could not help noticing that he held a rolled and ribbon-tied paper.

"Were you dining upstairs?" Rowan asked.

"Yes. Ona is still there, I'll go back in a moment." Finding no empty chair, Naio lowered himself to sit on his heels beside Rowan. "We've been going through her old drawings together—and that was an interesting experience, I'll tell you!" He paused to suppress a grin; it took all his self-control to do so.

Rowan guessed what inspired the amusement. "Including," she asked, "the nude studies?"

"All of them completely from her imagination, of course." He raised his eyebrows. "She was, let's say, an extremely innocent girl."

"Oh?" Rowan played along. "And was her subject"—she sought a delicate way to phrase it—"imaginatively endowed?" She sipped her beer.

"Well, that's the thing. Being so innocent and sheltered, Ona was completely ignorant… She ended up depicting the subject in question with, ah, no endowments whatsoever."

Caught off-guard, the steerswoman choked and snorted beer up her nose, then succumbed to a coughing fit that required the assistance of Bel, pounding on Rowan's back, to quell.

Naio waited for the fit to subside. "On the one hand," he said, "poor fellow. On the other, serves him right, I say."

Rowan gestured weakly toward the paper in his hand. "Please, tell me that isn't—"

"Oh! No! No, lady, I wouldn't do that. This—well, I thought you might find it interesting."

Rowan took the paper, untied and unrolled it. She was briefly stymied, then fascinated. "Is this Latitia?"

"Part of her, at least."

In ink: a standing figure seen from behind, only vaguely and rapidly outlined. Young Ona had lavished all her attention on the subject's thick black hair. Pulled back from Latitia's face, it was held close to her head by a complicated interweaving of braid, then allowed its freedom past the nape of her neck. It must have been very wiry; it stood out like a small thundercloud behind the steerswoman's shoulders. Of Latitia herself, there was only the suggestion of leanness and grace, and a few draping folds of a steerswoman's cloak.

Rowan was delighted. "I'm beginning to feel that I know her."

"And I've managed to find out where she stayed when she was here."

She turned to him, astonished. "Naio, I hardly know how to thank you. I think you're doing as much work on this question as I am."

Her gratitude pleased him. "Well, it's entertaining. I do love gossip. And gossip from forty years back—that's a challenge! A steerswoman, a wizard, an evil apprentice—it's too much to pass up." He rose, and winced as he stretched cramped legs. "Now, the fellow you want actually used to be mayor here—" He stopped when Rowan's face fell.

"Not old Nid?" she asked.

"As a matter of fact, yes—"

"But, I understand that he's senile."

"So he is. But he also rambles. If you invest a little time, and use a lot of patience, you might be able to get some details from him."

It sounded worth the attempt. "Thank you," Rowan said. "I believe I'll look Nid up after all." And there would be plenty of time to devote to the project, tomorrow.

Naio took his leave, and Rowan returned to casual conversation with her tablemates.

The steerswoman's glass was never empty, thanks to Beck's attentions. The others were required to pay, but Willam drank slowly and little, and Bel, seeing the vagrant come up short, poured half her own beer into the man's empty mug, inspiring him to gallantly kiss her hand. Out of sheer good spirits, the entire table adopted him, and followed Bel's example. The man did not lack for drink for the rest of the night.

Time passed; the evening grew quieter, but no less convivial. Obeying one of the universal laws of such gatherings, the crowd began, subtly and spontaneously, to grow more unified.

At the sailors' table, a wiry young woman, oak brown and blond from the sun, rose and sang "Jamboree," with her crewmates clapping along and the locals enjoying puzzling over the lyrics—except for Rowan's table, where, to her own discomfiture, the steerswoman was asked by the swordsmith's apprentice to translate "Jinny keep your ring-tail warm."

Bel rolled her eyes at the explanation; then, as soon as the song ended, and with no warning whatsoever, she rose and stood on her chair.

She sang. The room grew immediately attentive, then noisy with appreciative laughter.

It was an Outskirter song, one familiar to Rowan. Called "The Queen of Three-side," it concerned a she-goat who became so outraged at the inept care rendered by the tribe's herd-master that she began to berate the man in words. At each new error, she corrected him, at length, in rhyme. The tune was rollicking, the insults hilarious—and the detailed information on the proper raising and care of goats perfectly accurate in every detail.

Looking up at her friend, listening to Bel's rich, dark voice made light now by the skittering melody, it came to Rowan, as if she had forgotten: this, too, was a steerswoman's life.

For the most part, a steerswoman's days were equal portions of hard work and hard traveling, with much solitude. But there were interludes such as this one, with warmth, good food, good drink, and the goodwill of strangers.

Rowan's life recently had lacked these interludes. But Jannik was occupied with his dragons; no one had been following Rowan after all; Will's dangerous mission was two nights away. The steerswoman was astonished to find herself with nothing to do but enjoy herself. She gave herself to it.

When Bel climbed down from her chair, to the applause of the crowd, Rowan amazed her friends by climbing up on it herself. She stood a moment, gazing at the faces around as the crowd quieted; then she sang.

The tune was "Greenwood Sideyo," an eerie little song, one of the few well suited to Rowan's plain voice. The audience was in the mood for it; they shivered in all the right places, and experimented with strange harmonies.

When it was over and Rowan climbed down, the applause was as enthusiastic as Bel's had been. Bel clapped her back; Willam laughed; then he thought, shrugged, and rose to his feet.

He did not sing. Instead, he recited a folktale native to Wulfshaven, concerning two rival Island fishermen, who repeatedly, in alternation, captured and recaptured the same magic fish. Each fisher used the wish granted him to cast some misfortune upon his opposite number, and with each passing day the curses grew more and more unpleasant and bizarre. Eventually, one fisher decided that he would end the cycle by killing and eating the fish; but first, as his final wish, he wished upon his enemy "Perfect misery for the rest of his life."

The instant he swallowed the last bite, he discovered that he had been transformed into a woman; that he was now the wife of his enemy; and that they possessed nine venomous children—with one more on the way.

The tale was familiar to the sailors, but not to the locals, and was a great success. Someone sent the performers a pitcher of beer. They shared it with the whole table.

A tug at Rowan's sleeve; she looked down.

The handkerchief boy, a shy smile on his face, stood by the steerswoman's elbow, holding out a folded piece of paper.

Rowan took it from his hand. "Thank you very much," she said, seriously.

The boy grinned hugely, and stood wriggling, nearly doubled over in transports of joy. Then he made his departure, stamping his feet with each step, apparently merely for the pleasure of the noise.

"A message?" Bel asked.

"Possibly," the steerswoman said. She unfolded the paper, and everyone present leaned close to see.

After a long moment, the bricklayer said: "That's a tree. Got that in one."

"Well, yes, several trees. And a number of..."

"Dogs?" Bel guessed.

"They look... dead," Willam said.

"I'm not sure they're dogs," Rowan said. Apparently the handkerchief boy had noticed that Rowan enjoyed receiving drawings. This was his own contribution.

They puzzled over the crude depiction. The swordsmith's apprentice pointed. "What's them black specks in the air?"

"Flies," Willam decided. "For all the dead dogs."

"Unpleasant," Rowan said, with a wince. "But this one animal seems happy enough." Indeed it did; not only was it the only creature standing, it also sported a toothy human-like grin situated at the very tip of its snout.

"It's the victor," Bel declared. "It's vanquished all the others."

"Perhaps the others are only sleeping." They were scattered about, stiff-legged; still, the artist was just a child.

"That would be nicer," Willam said.

"I think it's a horse," Bel said. "Either that, or it's standing on four wooden blocks."

"And the other horses lying down." Rowan had it, and laughed. "It's a night scene! The black specks are stars!"

"Stars should be white," the vagrant said.

"But the paper is white," Bel said. "White on white wouldn't show, so he made the stars black."

"All the horsies fast asleep," Willam said, "except for one happy fellow, just enjoying the starry night."

"Well. I'm very much relieved; the alternative was just too grim." The steerswoman carefully refolded the drawing and placed it in her vest pocket.

"Everyone's trying to help," Bel observed.

Eventually, the evening faded, and the crowd dwindled. The bricklayer departed, then the apprentice. Even the vagrant finally left, with a parting kiss of Bel's hand; and at last only the evening's most stubborn revelers remained.

"Ruffo may throw us all out soon," Rowan commented.

"In a city this size, you'd think there would be something to keep us occupied until dawn," Bel said.

"There are some gaming rooms," Will said. "Four of them, but one is illegal, and nasty; you wouldn't want to know what goes on in there. Two of the others are considered honest." He raised his brows. "There are also two bawdy-houses, if you're interested. I'll pass, if you don't mind. And there's one unregistered pub, with only hard liquor. Most of the people who go there are hiding from spiteful spouses."

He seemed to know the city well. "How long have you been here?"

"I was here for two weeks at first, checking out Jannik's routine, and what the city was like. It's amazing what you see, when no one thinks that you can see at all. And for some reason they always act as if you're deaf, too." He sipped from his mug. "And then, I went to the dragon fields and set my spells. They didn't start up at once, I used a delay, so I got back here in time to watch Jannik leave."

Rowan called over one of the servers to ask the time, and was informed that it had gone past midnight. The friends decided to go to the stables and cache Will's charms.

But when they arrived, there was a light inside, and a voice.

Rowan listened. "It seems to be only one person." The words, and the tone, were of the sort used when addressing animals.

"Can you distract him?" Bel asked.

"I think so," Rowan said, then smiled. "In fact, I have the perfect excuse."

Willam and Bel slipped around to the back of the building; Rowan entered by the open double doors.

She followed the light and the voice down the rows of stalls, eventually reaching an open stall on the left, two-thirds of the way down.

Inside, a man was at work on a horse, crooning to it in a happy voice. Rowan said, "Hello?"

"Ho, ha!" He startled, peered at her. "What's on, then? It's late!"

"I'm sorry to bother you..." Rowan stepped farther into the light. "I wonder if I might ask you a few questions."

"Questions in the middle of the night?"

"Well, we both seem to be up and about; I thought there'd be few distractions." She became distracted herself, by the horse. "Oh, that's a lovely animal!"

"Yes, she is, isn't she?" the groom said with deep pride. It was a mare, white-haired but dark-skinned, so that her face seemed tipped in black at the nose, around the eyes, inside the swiveling, curious ears. Her white mane was shot through with black strands, with her tail more black than white. Rowan reached out to stroke the mare's nose; the horse permitted this, nuzzling her fingers, then her palm, then abruptly biting, hard. "Ow!"

"Hey, you!" This to the horse. "Now, now, be nice. Sorry," he said to Rowan. "She's back home, expects her treat." He dug in a pocket, inspiring immediate intense interest from the mare, and handed Rowan a lump of sugar. "Here."

More cautious now, Rowan placed it carefully in the center of her palm. With gentle delicacy, the mare's soft lips sought and found the gift. Greatly pleased, the animal then leaned her entire head against Rowan chest, and shoved playfully. The steerswoman laughed, shoved back, stroked the mare's neck, rubbed her ears.

"See?" The groom came forward to run his cloth down the mare's chest. "She likes you. She's a darling, isn't she? Give us a kiss." Rowan was relieved to find that this, too, was addressed to the horse, who turned her head and nibbled sloppily on the man's nose and chin. The groom wiped his face on his sleeve, and returned to brushing the mare's flanks. "Questions, you said?"

"Yes," Rowan replied. "I'm a steerswoman—" Up and past the man's shoulder, Rowan noted a shadow shifting, just above the farthest stall. "And I'm interested in some events taking place forty-two years ago—"

"Oh, I wasn't born yet, then." The shadow resolved into Willam, apparently being boosted up from below by the unseen Bel. Will grasped a crossbeam, pulled himself onto it, lying prone to reach one hand back down.

"I assumed as much." Rowan moved to the opposite side of the mare, to keep the man's attention in her direction. "But it occurred to me that you might know of some elderly stable hand, perhaps not working any longer, who might have been on hand during that time."

"Hm." The man paused in his work, resting his arms across the mare's back. Behind him, Will was now standing on the beam, his sack in hand, scanning the rafters above. "Hum," the groom said. "Andry, maybe. Old as the hills, he is, and he worked here when I first came."

Rowan recognized the name. "Does he live on Iron-and-Tin Street?" Up above, Will caught her glance, flashed a grin—then stopped short.

"Matter of fact, I think he does." The groom stooped to wipe at the mare's rear hocks.

Rowan looked away quickly, then could not resist looking back; the groom could not see her face. Willam was now lying on the beam again, gesturing urgently to Bel down below.

"You should ask old Andry," the groom said.

"Um..." Rowan recovered. "Actually, I suppose you haven't heard yet, but he passed away"—it took her a moment to calculate, with her sleep pattern skewed—"yesterday morning." Will passed the sack back down, shot one wild, wide-eyed glance at Rowan; then, moving urgently, he shifted his body, hung from his hands, dropped out of sight.

"Well, no surprise there. On the one hand, I'm sorry he's gone. On the other hand, he was a sour old thing, and wasn't above using a stick, on horses and stable hands both. Still, it's a shame. No one should die; then he'd have the time he needed, to mend his ways."

"I suppose you're right," Rowan said distractedly, casting about for a polite way to depart immediately.

"Hey-oh!" Bel's voice called from the stable doors. "Good, someone's still up." She arrived, slightly out of breath, looked at Rowan in apparent surprise. "And you're here, too, that's good." She addressed the groom cheerily. "Now, I just had a notion, in the middle of the night, while drinking my last beer, which is often the case, isn't it? It came to me that my friend the steerswoman, here, has been working far too hard, and could use some recreation, so I thought: Why don't we hire a pair of horses and spend a day in the countryside?"

"Hire a pair?" The man shrugged. "Plenty for hire, here. Are you a good rider?" Rowan was completely at sea, and could only watch the exchange, trying not to let her confusion show.

"I'm terrible!" Bel declared, as if proud of the fact. "I hope you can find me some animal old enough to be gentle, but not so old that it will die under me. But Rowan, here"—she clapped the steerswoman's shoulder— "she's good with horses. Let's get the best you have for her. In fact"—and here she eyed the mare—"I like this one. How much, to hire him and another for the day?"

"Her," Rowan corrected, which was the only contribution she could muster.

"Her. She's beautiful. I like the idea of the steerswoman up on a beautiful white horse."

"That's not a white horse," the groom informed Bel. "That's a gray horse. And she only boards here, she's not for hire."

"Really? Well, perhaps I can talk to her owner, and make some private arrangements." And Rowan experienced a quick sinking sensation in the pit of her stomach.

"Ha!" The groom's expression was wry. "You're welcome to try it. This is the wizard Jannik's own horse."

"Oh, well, I won't bother him, then," Bel said, agreeably. "Now, then—" And she and the groom began to discuss prices, Bel haggling hard, in no apparent hurry; while Rowan stood, listening to them, trying to remain calm, and wishing very much that she could get out of there, quickly.

The arrangements were completed, subject to the head groom's approval in the morning. Bel bid the man a good night, and led the steerswoman at a leisurely pace down the row of stalls and out the door.

The instant they emerged, Will, who had tucked himself beside the door, grabbed Bel's arm, pulled her aside, did the same to Rowan, half-pushed them both around the corner and into the shadows. He swung Bel around, clutched her shoulder, hissed to her, urgently, "Is it? Was I right?" His eyes were wide.

The Outskirter nodded. "It's his horse."

He leaned back, flung out one arm as if to pound the wall behind him, stopped himself just in time. "Jannik's back."

CHAPTER TWELVE

"*H*e found your spells," Bel said. "He's neutralized them all."

"No," Willam said. "Not all of them. Not this soon. Something else brought him back." In the darkness, Willam reached out, found Rowan's arm, gripped it tightly, urgent. "It's you," he said, quietly.

"Will—"

"Someone went to Jannik, and told him—Rowan, you have to leave, now."

"If Jannik wanted Rowan, she'd be dead already," Bel put in.

"Will, that's true," Rowan said. She put her hand over his. "Jannik was right here, at the stables, not two hours ago. He could have simply strolled into the common room and killed me, or taken me away. But that didn't happen."

She felt his hand relax. "That's right…" He released her arm, leaned back against the wall.

"Then," Bel said, "Jannik is back because he's finished. He got rid of Willam's spells."

Willam remained stubborn. "No. Not so soon. Bel, there were *thirty* of them!"

The Outskirter scanned left, right; there was still no one else about. Then she took a step back and entered a stance that Rowan knew well: feet planted firmly, chin tilted up. "You're putting a lot of trust in those spells of yours. So, tell me this, Will—exactly how good a practitioner of magic are you?"

Will was silent.

Rowan had entirely neglected this possibility. She and Bel had no means by which to evaluate Willam's abilities. They had been placing all confidence in the skills of a runaway apprentice.

Presently, Willam drew a breath, released it; and when he spoke, it was calmly, with no sign of offense at Bel's challenging tone. "The jammers are simple," he said. "They either wouldn't work at all, or they'd work perfectly. And they did work. I watched Jannik ride out of town, not an hour after the first one was set to activate."

"Then he found them, all of them."

"No."

"It's the simplest explanation—"

"No it isn't," Rowan said; and it was the image of a man riding out of town on a horse that made her think of it, "that's not the simplest explanation at all."

Will and Bel subsided, and Rowan sensed their curious regard. "Willam," she said, "can the wizards create objects at will? Bring them into existence by magic?" Of course they could not; they would never need food, or new clothing, if that were the case. They would have no use for the common folk at all.

The question puzzled Willam. "No... Not really. They can make things appear... but the things won't be real."

"And while you watched Jannik ride out, did you happen to notice what he brought with him in the way of supplies?"

Silence, and then a soft, delighted "Ha!" from Bel.

Will laughed. "He's run out of food!"

"We," Rowan said to them both, "are panicking. We are panicking unnecessarily."

"Jannik will replenish his supplies, and ride out again in the morning," Bel said.

"Or in the afternoon; he's ridden all night. He'll want some rest, I should think."

"Or the next day," Will said; and his tone gave Rowan pause. "And if he's not gone by twenty-three hundred..." He allowed the sentence to trail off.

"Then you would have to abandon your plan entirely."

"No." He grew very still, and spoke quietly. "I'll try later. Without the maintenance routines to cover me."

Rowan did not like the sound of this at all. "How much riskier would that be?"

A long silence. Then Will's voice came from the shadows: "I don't want either of you anywhere near me if I have to do it that way."

Bel said, in a perfectly conversational tone of voice: "Let's kill him." Will startled. "And don't be squeamish," Bel went on. "He's an evil man. In fact, I believe that they're all evil. Even Corvus—despite you thinking that he'll let you get away with running off."

"Bel," Rowan put in, "we can't simply murder Jannik."

Bel ignored her. "You served a wizard for six years, Will, so you would know better than anyone—is even Corvus evil?"

Willam was a long time replying. "Probably," he finally said.

Bel was incredulous. " 'Probably'?"

"Yes." Will turned away. "Yes, he is evil." He turned back. "But Bel... they don't think like we do. Corvus doesn't think he's evil, probably none of them does. I don't think they even believe there *is* such a thing as evil. That, that the whole idea is imaginary, or... meaningless."

"It's not," Bel said. "You know that."

"Yes... but I think... I think that, as wizards go, Corvus is probably the best that we can expect of them."

"Wonderful. The best maggot in a pot full of maggots. And that's why you've run away from him." Will said nothing. "Since Jannik is evil, *and* he's in our way, I have no problem with killing him. By surprise, you said: would a knife in the dark do?"

"Bel," Rowan said, "no."

Bel's voice was harsh. "And tell me, lady, *why not?*"

It was Willam who answered. "Because the Krue won't let that pass. If they can't find Jannik's murderer, they'll take it out on the whole city. Or the next wizard of Donner will. Slado will send someone. And there's no one ready. But he'll send someone anyway."

"Someone inexperienced?" Rowan asked.

"Like Shammer and Dhree?" Bel said.

"Yes." The sibling wizards had been younger than Willam's present age. Abruptly, Rowan remembered Liane, a girl of some fifteen years, whose sole occupation at the fortress of Shammer and Dhree was to serve both wizards' pleasure.

Dead now, along with her masters.

Rowan forced the memory back. "Imagine Shammer or Dhree," she said to Bel, "with the city of Donner as their toy."

The idea disturbed the Outskirter, deeply. "All right," she said reluctantly. "Jannik can live. But we need to make certain he leaves in time."

Quiet, as all three considered this.

Eventually, Rowan said to Willam, "Can you affect the dragons yourself? Can *you* command them?"

"No," Will said. "I don't have the means, and I don't have the skill."

"That's too bad," Rowan said. She leaned back against the wall beside him, crossed her arms. "Jannik would probably consider this far more urgent if he thought that the spells did more than merely block his commands. If they actually allowed someone else to control the dragons, I suspect he'd dash straight back there, and wouldn't rest until he'd found them all—" He startled. "Will? What is it?" She could not see his face.

"Will—" Bel said.

He said, in a voice of immense astonishment: "That's it."

Rowan and Bel traded a glance.

"That's it." He threw his head back, laughed quietly. "That's it, that's *perfect!*"

Bel said, "You mean, you *can* take command of Jannik's dragons?"

"No." And he took Bel's arm, and Rowan's, and hurried them back toward the Dolphin. "But I know how to make him *think* someone has."

CHAPTER THIRTEEN

*T*he plan required twenty-four hours, and two horses. Fortunately, Bel had already reserved a pair. It merely remained necessary to alter the arrangement to include the extra time, and to substitute Willam for Bel when no one was looking.

Unfortunately, their funds were running low. The three friends pooled their resources, Will's and Rowan's contributions being very meager. They had money sufficient to hire the mounts and purchase supplies for the extended time, but only if Willam and Bel ceased to eat for the rest of their stay in Donner.

They considered the small pile of coins. "I could go back to begging," Will ventured.

"And I can pick a few pockets," Bel volunteered cheerfully.

"I'd really rather you didn't," Rowan said, affronted. "Aside from the morality of it, you might get caught and thrown in a cell. It would be inconvenient, at the least."

The Outskirter tilted her head. "I'll haggle some more. And you're a steerswoman. Perhaps we can get your horse without charge."

Rowan protested. "Food and lodging are one matter; there's no custom that requires people to give me free use of a horse for twenty-four hours."

"Yes, but maybe the head groom doesn't know that—"

"Bel—"

"So *I'll* do the talking, and you stay quiet and try not to look appalled and disapproving. And I can play on sympathy, too. You were sick yesterday—"

"I was not!"

"But everyone *thinks* you were. I don't know if you've noticed, Rowan, but for some reason people around here seem to like you, and right now they feel sorry for you. I say we should play on that."

The steerswoman continued to protest; but in the end, it seemed the only plan available, and Rowan surrendered.

They waited until dawn was near—not so very long a wait—and took themselves out to the stable yard. There, they watched while the head groom, a strong, weathered woman in her forties, gave the day's instructions to the stable hands.

"I like her face," Bel said. "She seems almost motherly. This might work." She turned back to Rowan, considered the steerswoman's expression disparagingly. "Maybe it would be better if you stayed over here, at a distance. Try to look peaked, if you can manage it—no, Rowan, at least *try*. And Will, be a bit concerned, and sympathetic—" She stopped short. "Ha."

Rowan was immediately suspicious. "What?" she said.

The Outskirter grinned. "I have an idea." She took Will's arm, and Rowan's, and pulled them closer to each other, spoke quietly. "Act cozy."

Rowan put up her brows. "Excuse me?"

"Act *cozy*. Here, Will—" She drew him closer. "Put your arm around her shoulder, like this—"

"Um—" He attempted to back off.

"And Rowan, lean in—" Bel pushed them together.

Rowan resisted. "Bel—"

Bel glowered up at her. "Rowan, no one will wonder if the steerswoman wants to ride out with a handsome young man instead of with me. And no one will wonder if they stay out all night."

"Um, Bel—" Will was definitely uncomfortable with this.

"Will, don't be a prude—" Bel maneuvered them both back into position. "—And since I'm such a wonderful person, and I've taken a liking to the steerswoman, I'm generously footing the bill for her little outing. But I've been spending my money like water, as everyone has seen, so I don't have enough for both horses. If we do it this way, I won't have to hide out all day, pretending I'm not here—" The conversation at the stable door ceased, and the group began dispersing to their duties. "All right," Bel said glancing back at them. "Now just stay back here—" She turned, caught Will's and Rowan's expressions, faltered. "Well..." She studied them dubiously. "Here." She pulled them both around. "Keep your backs to the conversation. Rowan, move in, put your arm around his waist; Willam, like *so*..." Bel stepped away, surveyed the result. "Just stand together like that. It should be enough, if they don't actually see your faces."

Bel left them and went to greet the head groom. Rowan and Willam remained in place. Rowan held on to Willam's waist tentatively, as if steadying some extremely tall object; Will held his arm about Rowan's shoulder in the manner of a person restraining a wet dog. They stared at the back of the inn as, behind them, Bel haggled cheerfully.

Presently, Will emitted an odd noise.

Rowan looked up and found that he was struggling to keep a straight face. He noticed her looking at him. He tried harder. He could not keep it up.

Laughter half-escaped him, suppressed into a series of truly ridiculous snorts. The steerswoman could not help it: she did the same—

At that, neither of them could maintain restraint. They laughed, breathlessly, silently, weakly hilarious, leaning against each other for support. "I think," Will managed to say between gasps, "that we'd better stop this, or we'll ruin everything."

"No, no," Rowan said. "No, this is better!" And she allowed herself to laugh out loud. There was a pause in the conversation behind them; then it continued, in a slightly different tone.

"Here," Rowan said, pulling Will halfway around, to allow their audience a better view. She stepped free, took both of his hands in hers, carefully composed her face, looked up at him. "Now, do you think you can manage to gaze longingly into my eyes?"

He said, as she had expected, "No—" and lost control completely, half falling back against the building, laughing helplessly. But she kept hold of his hands, watching him with genuine pleasure, and it seemed to her that the image they presented was perfect.

Presently Bel returned. "Well, that worked," she said. "I didn't think either of you had it in you." Bel waited, puzzled, through another spate of hilarity. "We have Rowan's horse free, and her supplies," she continued. "And they're only charging me one day for Willam's horse. I think the head groom just did it so that everyone can gossip about you two later."

Rowan said, wiping her eyes, "Oh, far be it from me to deprive"—she paused to catch her breath—"the staff of its entertainment."

While Willam went to retrieve the traveling gear from Rowan's room, a stable hand led out the horses: a pair of fine mares, one chestnut, one dapple gray. Rowan chose the chestnut, and introduced herself to her mount, rubbing its head, allowing it to snuffle at her hands. Then she checked its tack, testing the bit and the cinch. The head groom seemed reassured by the attention Rowan paid to these details.

At the open kitchen door, a small crowd of staff members watched, some standing, two seated on the doorstep. They observed Willam's return with a cheerful interest, maintained an amused silence as he passed them by, then entered into subdued conversation. Apparently, the gossip was not going to wait for Rowan's departure.

For this short trip, the steerswoman took only her cloak and bedroll, within which she had rolled a spare shirt and stockings, flint and tinderbox, and her sword. Her satchel held logbook and writing implements. Will's own bedroll was somewhat fatter, and definitely lumpy. His burlap sack was concealed within.

"This is good," Bel said quietly as she watched Rowan secure her sword to the saddle. "I can try to keep an eye on Jannik, from a distance… Do you think you'll need your cane?"

"No."

The undercook pushed through the group at the kitchen door, carrying two sets of saddlebags, which bulged temptingly. These she passed to the travelers. "That's two breakfasts, and two lunches, and a dinner. Each."

Rowan was genuinely grateful. "I'm already looking forward to them."

"Hm." The cook eyed her, up and down, so obviously assessing the state of her health that Rowan grew embarrassed.

She was glad to be distracted by a tug at her trouser leg: the handkerchief boy, holding up yet another folded bit of paper. Rowan adopted a serious expression, and with great formality accepted it. "Thank you very much." He grinned, then suddenly dashed behind the undercook, from which position of supposed invisibility he gave himself to a fit of giggles.

Rowan unfolded the paper, considered the depiction, and passed it down to Bel.

"Ha. Last night's boar."

"At least the poor creature seems resigned to its fate."

"More than resigned; look at that grin! No mean feat, with all those knives sticking out of it…"

Willam completed his own arrangements, and came over to the women. "Are we set?" he asked Rowan.

Set, for a pleasant ride about the countryside… "We're set," Rowan said, and turned to mount up.

At which point, faced with a horse whose back was as tall as her shoulder, she realized that although her left leg was adequate for walking and stair-climbing, it would definitely be unable by itself to hoist her entire weight up such a height. And no horse would allow her to mount from the right. She was about to ask for a mounting block when Will solved the problem by casually gripping her by the waist and heaving her upward— and Rowan found herself ludicrously sprawled across the saddle. She slipped her right leg around and sat erect—quickly, lest Willam decide that it would aid the deception for him to slap her on the backside. She gave him a warning look, which he accepted with a grin.

Then he mounted, and the two turned their horses, waved goodbye to Bel and the spectators, and rode out of the yard and into the street.

The sun was risen, but had not yet cleared the buildings. The air was cool, with that perceptible difference in temperature from the ground up that one only truly experienced when seated high on the back of a horse.

They moved along, down the cobbled streets with shops and homes on either side still shuttered or just stirring; and Rowan loved her mare, who responded so easily to her, moving with such strength and lovely economy of motion; and it was a beautiful day for a ride, with a clean blue sky above, clear and growing brighter.

And they were off to steal a dragon.

Rowan shook her head, feeling half unreal.

She urged her mare closer to Willam's, spoke across the distance. "I saw the undercook take you aside just before you mounted. What did she say?"

He put on a dignified expression and spoke in an admonishing tone. "I'm not to treat you roughly."

She chuckled. "Good advice all around, I should think."

There was no useful straight road toward the dragon fields; Greyriver was wide, shallow, and marshy at the banks. Past the city limits, Rowan and Willam turned east to drier ground, passing among shabby dwellings, hardly more than shacks. In the distance, mud-fishers poled their flatboats, their heads seeming to float above the grass as they threaded through the estuaries. Two blue herons stalked the grasses, imperiously indifferent to the presence of humans, protected by custom as signs of good luck.

Close to midday the travelers stopped at a small hill facing the river and settled down on its crest, allowing the tethered horses to graze below. Willam found a bottle of red wine in his saddlebags, considered it regretfully. "Not until dinner, I guess. We're going to need our wits about us." He replaced it, and brought out a string-tied package. "Now, is this lunch, or dinner, do you think?"

"It's lunch if you eat it now."

He settled down across from her, with a blue cotton table-cloth spread on the grass between them, one of its corners showing an embroidered red dolphin. He set the packet down on the cloth, and shook his head, seeming half amazed. "This is all just too civilized."

"I was thinking exactly the same thing."

"The last time I was here, it was the dead of night, blasting thunder, raining buckets, and I was cowering under—" He scanned the ground below, pointed. "—*that* bush."

Rowan considered the sky above them, which remained utterly perfect. "With any luck, this weather might hold through tomorrow night."

"Actually, rain might be better. I think this is dinner." This when the package proved to contain cold roast boar. "Oh, well... Less chance of people noticing us skulking around in the night, I mean," he continued, pulling a shred from the meat with his fingers.

"Perhaps," Rowan said; she had fish pastries and a baked potato. "But if we must begin our invasion of Jannik's home at twenty-three hundred, we'll need to see the sky. I'd hate to have to send Bel jogging to find the watchman every few minutes, to check the time."

He glanced at her, gave an odd, shy smile, then set the meat down on its wrapper, carefully wiping his fingers on the edge of the tablecloth. Then he reached into the collar of his shirt, pulled out and over his head a loop of string, with something dangling from it. He leaned across and passed it to her.

A simple bit of rough twine, its ends knotted together. Inside that knot, secured with crossing loops, was a small black rectangle, perhaps an inch and a half long, half an inch wide, a quarter inch deep. It had an odd texture, seeming both dry and slightly oily. Rowan turned it over in her palm.

Written on one side, in white: 81:11.

The steerswoman puzzled. She suspected from its texture that it was magic. She had on occasion handled a few shards and pieces of magical objects that had possessed a similar feel. A charm of some sort, then, or a talisman?

She glanced up at Willam, but he seemed merely amused. Rowan considered the rectangle again, turning it over and over, testing its seamless surface.

Magic animates the inanimate. This was the one clear fact that she knew about magic: not a true principle, but an observed apparent universality, and the only means she had to recognize and categorize it.

61:11, the numbers now read.

One small, distant part of her mind remarked to her, perfectly calm: There, you see? Magic. But the rest of her, body and mind, remained still, and stopped, and uncomprehending, as if some barrier had appeared before her, blocking her movement.

Presently, like an insect faced with a brick wall, and just as instinctively, she began to grope for the edges of the barrier. They had been discussing time...

Rowan rotated the rectangle in place.

11:19.

Really, she thought, she ought not be so very surprised. Nevertheless, she heard herself mutter, more breath than voice: "Gods below..."

Willam said, now solicitous: "Rowan, I'm... I'm sorry. I guess I'm used to that sort of thing . .

She looked up at him, perfectly amazed and silent. After a moment, he gave a small, helpless shrug. "It's a clock."

"I suppose it must be," she managed to say. She had seen a few clocks. They were huge, cumbersome affairs, involving levers, and pulleys, and tubs of sand or tins of water. They needed constant attention, and daily correction, usually achieved by simply watching the sky to note the moment that one or another Guidestar passed into the darkness of the world's own shadow. This a Guidestar would do at exactly the same instant, nightly, forever.

Rowan looked again.

11:20.

Eventually Will said: "Rowan—say something—"

"How can it *know?*"

"When it was made, it was told the exact time, at that moment," Willam said. "Since then, well—it's just counting. Really, Rowan, it's a very simple thing."

"Counting is a very simple action," Rowan admitted, in a distant voice. Simple, for a human mind. And for that of a wood-gnome, or a Demon, likely. And crows can count to three. And insects cannot count at all. And objects—

No: the clocks she had seen did count, after a fashion. Perhaps it was merely that magic had reduced the workings to such a tiny size. And sealed them completely within this little box. And perfected them, so that they would never need adjusting. And caused the white numbers to show themselves on the seamless surface, and to change, when appropriate...

She looked up at Willam: a man of only twenty years, kneeling on the edge of the cotton tablecloth, on the grass, on a hill, under the blue, clear sky; white-haired, copper-eyed, one eyebrow ragged, his right hand missing two fingers from a spell gone wrong in his childhood.

Rowan felt her balance slowly return. She said: "You made this?"

Willam made a sound of amusement. "No. I brought it with me."

"And Corvus won't miss it?"

He hesitated; and she realized then that he often hesitated, when Corvus's name appeared in a conversation. It seemed to her that he needed to make some internal adjustment before speaking. "No," he said, then shrugged. "There are a dozen or so of those, all over the estate. I kept that one on my nightstand." She passed it back to him. He regarded it in the palm of his hand a moment, twisted his mouth wryly, put it back about his neck. "Rowan, I'm sorry, I didn't mean to startle you. Really, it's nothing particularly fantastic."

"I suppose," she said, halfheartedly picking up a fish pastry, "that I must seem a little foolish to you."

"Oh, no!" He was sincere. "Not at all, the same sort of thing happened to me, too. Only worse!" He settled back, returned to prying apart the boar meat. "Corvus," he began; and again, that hesitation. "Corvus has a device," he went on, "like a bird. About the size of a hawk. It flies"—he made one hand go up, to demonstrate—"and it can move about," the hand tilted, as if catching and riding the wind, "and watch the countryside below it. One day—and it wasn't long after I first got there—Corvus let me see through the bird's eyes. Rowan," and he dropped his hand and shook his head, "it took me *days* to recover!"

"Actually," Rowan admitted, "it sounds rather wonderful." To see the whole of the land below, directly, without so abstract an intermediary as lines drawn on paper...

"It sounds it, yes, but it's another thing to have it happen to you! And with not much warning, either." He began on his lunch again. "One moment," he said around a mouthful, "you're standing in a room, thinking, Well, what's the wizard up to now?; and the next, you're hanging in the middle of the air—I wasn't really, I was still in the room, but it *looked* like I was up there. Nothing all around me, *nothing* underneath me, except, way, way down, the tops of trees, and the whole of the River Wulf with tiny boats on it, and the buildings of Corvus's estate. And then, the bird turned in the air"—his free hand demonstrated a banking maneuver—"which looks, through the bird's eyes, exactly as if the whole *world* was tilting over—" He dropped his hand again. "That was the last straw. I just collapsed on the floor, raving like a lunatic, and finally had to be carried out by the servants." He pulled another shred from the boar, but did not eat. He set it aside, pried a second, contemplatively. "And all I could think," he said, "when I got my wits back, that is—all I could think was that I'd somehow failed, and that I wasn't good enough to learn magic after all, and that Corvus would throw me out."

"But he didn't," Rowan said.

Will was quiet a moment. "No." He reached for the canteen of water. "Later," and he paused to drink, "later, Corvus told me that letting me see through the bird's eyes wasn't the right thing to do so soon. And that he hadn't taken into account my—he called it my 'context,' but he really meant my ignorance."

"I think 'context' is probably accurate."

"Well, call it what you like," Will said. "The thing was, Corvus knew how to teach the usual sort of apprentice, but he wasn't sure where to start in teaching me. So we went back to the things I'd already learned by myself."

"Your blasting-charms."

"That's right. We started there, and went on." He resumed eating.

Rowan remembered well the destructive power of Willam's spells, so blithely referred to as "charms"; but the little clock, somehow, seemed weirder to her.

A lightning strike might have an effect similar to the blasting-charms; an avalanche would be as destructive. So it seemed that the Krue could confiscate and command the very powers of nature, and this she was forced to accept as fact. But these were powers that already existed, independently.

The steerswoman could think of nothing at all in the natural world that would do so peculiar a thing as hang from the end of a bit of string and cheerfully, innocently, count.

They rested briefly after lunch. They had had no sleep the night before. When they moved on, the party atmosphere had completely vanished. *Dragons ahead*, Rowan did not need to remind herself.

And a very simple plan:

Ride to the dragon fields. Select a small dragon. Move it away from Willam's jammer-spells. Release it.

Once the dragon was clear of the spells, Jannik would again become aware of the creature, and able to command it—but he would not know why or how it had traveled so far, without his instructions. And his only conclusion would be that someone had been able, if only briefly, to take control.

Jannik could not allow that. He would return immediately to deal with the spells.

It had all seemed so very simple when they had discussed it that morning. Now, in the full light of day, with very real fire-breathing dragons ahead, the steerswoman began to suspect that the entire mission bordered on insanity.

She looked back. Will's horse was trailing hers, with Willam lost in thought, tilting his head from side to side a bit in a rhythm independent of the mare's gait, as if following some internal music. He stopped, sighed, shook his head.

Rowan dropped her mare back beside his. "Patterns," she said. Uncontrolled dragons, he had told her that first night, did nothing, or moved in patterns.

"Yes. And that's why we should be able to capture one."

"And the dragon we take won't"—she still found this hard to believe—"won't fight us?"

"It should ignore us, and go on trying to follow its pattern. But if we want it to stop, covering its eyes should do it."

He had explained this when explaining the plan: if unable to see, the dragon would assume it was injured, and would wait for assistance. However, Rowan herself had half-blinded one dragon during the attack on Saranna's Inn, and the creature had continued to fight.

But that dragon had been under command. This time matters would be different: "Because of the jammer-spells…"

"That's right."

Rowan was not reassured. "Can we kidnap one of the ones that are doing nothing?"

"If it's doing nothing, it might be dead," Will said. "Jannik won't even notice that it's gone." He glanced about, reined in. "I think we should leave the horses here. The dragon we set loose might catch sight of them, and attack."

"And they won't have the sense to stay still." They dismounted, led the horses into the cranberry bushes.

He grinned at her. "I'd forgotten that you've already met some dragons."

She could not be amused. The nameless woman in Saranna's Inn was standing in the back of the steerswoman's mind, behind her thoughts, burning.

"At least," Rowan said, as they tied the reins to a bush, "out here in the countryside our victim won't find victims of its own."

Past a collection of grassy hillocks, the mud flats appeared again. Between the mud and the hillocks: a wide marshy field, with a stand of scrub pine on its far edge, and another similar field visible beyond.

Willam and Rowan stood atop one hillock, Rowan tense, Willam with such brazen casualness that the steerswoman glanced at him, occasionally, sidelong. He seemed not to notice.

Below, in the near field: rather a lot of dragons.

The largest was bigger than a horse. The smallest visible, the size of a cat. Little pockets of motion on the ground suggested the presence of others, perhaps as small as mice.

They gleamed, green with glints of silver about the eyes, and on the taloned tips of their feet. The smaller dragons fairly glowed with vibrant color; the larger showed a darker green, with hints of dull pewter; and the very largest, the somber color of moss, with brown shading at the head, feet, and tail.

Their heads were flat, their snouts long, with wide nostrils that shut to slits when their breath became flame. Eyes were side-set, a deep garnet red, faceted like jewels, glittering.

Long necks wove, tails flailed. The smallest dragons half walked, half slithered, with a weasel-like sinuosity, sidling around each other and dodging the largest creatures, which moved with heavy dignity.

Most were in motion: either slowly or quickly, they roamed the field, often passing close by each other. There were occasional confrontations between like-sized dragons, involving threatening displays, screams and hisses, and gouts of flame directed toward the sky.

All of the creatures ignored the humans.

"I think this is not going to be as easy as we hoped," the steerswoman said.

Will said nothing.

Pick one; approach from behind, to avoid any flame. Cover its eyes. Carry it away.

Simple.

Madness.

Rowan mentally rehearsed the actions, selecting a cat-sized creature that seemed to be wandering outward toward the edge of the herd, imagining herself and Willam stalking it. But halfway to the edge, the small dragon paused, industriously scratched at the back of its head with one hind leg, turned about, and moved back toward the center of the group.

Rowan wondered what sort of flea or tick might call a dragon hide home.

Beside her, Willam let out a huff of frustration. "They're staying very close together."

"Yes…" There did seem to be some definite limit to their wanderings, an invisible circle beyond which they would not pass. "But they're not moving in patterns."

"No, they are," Will said, definitely. "But the movements are designed to look like the sort of thing they'd be doing naturally."

Rowan watched for a while. "It's very convincing." Too convincing; the animals gave every semblance of a collection of reluctantly social creatures, disliking each other but for some reason unwilling to separate from the herd.

Will hazarded, "I suppose I could just make a dash for the edge, grab the nearest small dragon, and get back before some other one happens to spit fire my way…"

The burning woman transformed into a burning man… "Willam."

He continued to study the scene below. She repeated his name, and he turned to her.

"Are you absolutely certain that these animals are... are completely caught up in these... patterns?" She had almost said *hypothetical patterns.*

He could not miss her distress, and said, with such kindly patience that she felt embarrassed, "Yes. Absolutely. They have no outside direction now, not from the controller spell, and not from Jannik. They can't decide for themselves what to do, they're too simple. All they can do is follow the pattern."

She would have to take his word for it. "Very well."

But he continued to regard her, seeming faintly disappointed. Then an idea occurred to him; and before Rowan could stop him, he stooped to the ground, rose again, and flung a small rock directly into the center of the dragons.

Rowan cried out, in a sudden flare of terror.

The stone struck the wide side of the largest dragon, bounced, and dropped.

Completely oblivious, the dragon continued its slow, imperious stroll through a collection of smaller creatures, which were squealing annoyance at its intrusion, scrambling to get out from under its feet.

Stunned, Rowan turned back to find Willam regarding her with a small, self-satisfied smile. He had another stone; he tossed it straight up, caught it, then shied it out among the creatures. It fell toward the littler dragons, skidded across several backs, then dropped out of sight.

When Rowan turned back, Will was holding out to her a third stone.

Before fear got the better of her, she snatched it from his hand, turned, and, with a sudden weird, fierce glee, flung it.

It struck a horse-sized dragon directly below its left eye.

The animal showed no reaction at all. It proceeded on its way, paused to scratch at the ground, then circled like an immense dog, and lay down, nose to tail.

The steerswoman gave a weak laugh. "You've convinced me." Willam grinned at her. She felt her heart slowing; she had not realized it had been racing. "Let's choose our target," she said, "and get this over with."

His amusement faded. "Well"—he turned back to the scene below— "that's the problem."

The dragons continued to keep close together; and there was the fire. "You'll have to choose a point in the pattern when none of them is breathing flame..."

Willam sat down in the grass on the hillock, pulled his knees close, wrapped his arms around them, and studied the movements in the dragon field, his expression intent, analytical.

Something dawned on Rowan. "You don't know what the pattern is, do you?"

"No... I'll just have to keep watching until I can figure it out. Or enough of it to know when it's safe to make a try."

Rowan was silent for a moment. Below, the dragons continued, wandering, writhing, facing each other off. "But didn't you see it when you were here before, placing your jammer-spells?"

"The spells have a range of about half a kilometer. I didn't have to get close to the dragons. Just near enough to set the jammers."

A silence somewhat longer than the first. "Will... is this the closest you've ever been to any dragon?"

He replied with a nod, still watching the creatures.

At least they would not be attacked while they sorted this out. Rowan sat down beside Willam, leaned back on her elbows in the grass. They both watched in silence for a while.

The wind picked up, bringing to them the cloying stink of the mud flats, and the scent of smoke; and then a small pocket of heat from a pony-sized dragon that, in an apparent fit of exuberance, had reared back to send a plume of fire toward the sky.

Eventually, Rowan said: "You don't know what the patterns are, but you do know something about their nature."

"Yes." He pulled his attention in. "They're lists," he told her. "Each dragon has a list that it's following, of movements and behaviors. When it reaches the end of the list, it will go back to the start."

Rowan could not fathom this at all. "These creatures are intelligent enough to remember a list?" She had expected something much simpler, as a dog might be trained to do a number of actions in a row, when prompted by a single cue.

"It doesn't take intelligence. Remembering things just takes memory. Even a book has that kind of memory. Just a place to hold something."

"But... they must then read the list."

"They don't read it. They just do it. Whatever is on the list, they do."

This remained incomprehensible. She decided that he must be using an analogy, one that unfortunately did not correctly communicate the principle.

The steerswoman struggled. "We have to watch for the point when they start repeating. Then, watch the whole pattern, all the way through."

"That's right." He went back to studying the actions in the dragon field.

"How long are the lists of actions?"

The pause told her that she would not like the answer. "I don't know. They can't be too short, or any fool walking by would notice that the dragons repeat."

"Then, this might take some time…"

They both watched. After some minutes had passed: "Nothing yet?" the steerswoman asked.

"No."

"I don't see anything, either." Nothing other than the natural movements of a group of animals. For a moment she studied Willam instead. He sat with his arms wrapped around his knees, his chin on his forearms, the copper gaze scanning the field below. He seemed to her to be very good at focus, and concentration; his attention never lapsed.

His lips were moving, silently. Rowan guessed his thoughts, and said: "I count thirty-two dragons. Not counting the ones too small to see clearly. But I notice that those haven't spit fire yet."

"The littlest ones can't. We can ignore them. And I think there are only thirty active dragons. Two of them haven't moved at all; I think they're dead."

There was no vegetation within the dragon field, no living thing other than the dragons themselves. Scorched ground, a number of boulders, charred skeletons of bushes. Nothing else.

"What do they eat?" Rowan wondered.

"Nothing at all," Will said.

"How can they grow?"

"They don't. They're each already the size they'll always be. Some of them are hundreds of years old."

In the field, two dragons faced off, screaming fury. It was an impressive display: the two backed and twisted their bodies, weaving their heads, now low, now high, studying each other, first from one side-set eye, then the other. Smaller dragons nearby scrambled away, giving out whistling calls of annoyance. Halfway across the field, the largest dragon lifted its head to watch, emitting a low rumbling.

The steerswoman found herself analyzing, hypothesizing patterns of dominance, drawing comparisons to other sorts of creatures—wolves, perhaps—

Lists?

"All of that"—Rowan indicated the confrontation below—"is on a *list?*"

Willam nodded. "This is good. When this part repeats, we'll notice it."

Rowan said, bemused, "We could hardly fail to."

She returned to watching. She continued to discern no repetition, no pattern.

Beyond the dragon fields, beyond the mud flats, the wide expanse of

Greyriver was visible, murky with the black mud transported by the current from farther north, which gave it its color and its name.

At the water's edge, Rowan sighted a blue-gray shape that by its posture and actions she recognized as a heron. She allowed herself a few moments to watch the bird.

In her arid homeland, so far to the north, birds were rare. When first she had traveled south, crossing the entire breadth of the Inner Lands to reach the Steerswomen's Academy, Rowan had been surprised on her journey, and then astounded, by the birds.

They were everywhere, tucked into every corner of the country: squabbling, hunting, fleeing and fighting, singing to the morning sun, and above all else flying. They seemed to her perfect little pockets of life, bright-eyed, intent, utterly certain in all their small tasks, and by virtue of this, utterly free. She loved them.

At the river's edge, the lone heron stretched its wide wings, canting them as if testing the air; then with one, two down-strokes, it lifted. Rowan hoped it would approach, and then saw that it would.

To closely observe the flight of so great, so nearly royal a bird, was a privilege. The steerswoman watched, feeling a poignant joy as the heron moved with its characteristic slow grace.

It acquired no great height, wisely conserving its effort, moving smoothly inland and nearer, until Rowan could count and name each of its long flight-feathers as it soared low over the dragon field.

Below, a number of dragons paused, lifted their heads—

The heron burst into flame.

Rowan was down from the hill, away, and halfway to the horses before she realized that Willam was not with her.

She stopped, looked back. She called his name, desperate. She stood a moment, shuddering; then she clenched her teeth and ran back.

He was approaching at an easy jog, which slowed when he saw her. She reached him, breathless. He wore a mildly worried expression. "That was interesting," he commented.

"Interesting?" She clutched his arm. "Will, the dragons are not moving in patterns!"

Willam said thoughtfully, "I still think they are, really—"

"That bird was not on any list!"

"Well, no, it couldn't be, could it—"

His complacency suddenly infuriated her. She shouted. "Your spells are not working! The dragons are acting freely! There are thirty of them down there, each one capable of burning us to death!"

He was astonished by her anger, but he did not reply in kind. He spoke with patient reasonableness. "Rowan, we threw rocks at them, and they never reacted. You leapt up and ran, and they didn't chase you. And right after they got the bird, they went back to what they were doing, like nothing had happened. There's something else going on here, some other factor that I didn't know about. It's just a matter of figuring out what it is."

In the face of Willam's calm, Rowan found herself caught between shame at losing her temper, and even greater fury at what now seemed to her a blind and thickheaded stubbornness. "Very well." She sheathed her sword—she did not recall having drawn it—and stepped closer, looked up at him, spoke harshly. "You've told me what you know about dragons. Now let me tell you what *I* know:

"A dragon reacts to motion. It can't properly see a thing unless that thing is moving—or unless the dragon's head is moving, which has the same effect. Its eyes are immobile, and side-set like a horse's, so it has a blind spot directly in front, as horses do. When the dragon is spitting fire at you, it cannot see you; when it sees you, it cannot flame you until it first turns its head—and from the look on your face, you didn't know *any* of this, did you?"

Her vehemence took him aback. "No..." Did Willam know *nothing* of dragons? Then he recovered, said musingly, "That part about seeing only motion is interesting..."

She threw out her arms. "That's why they burned the heron! And that, Willam, is why they will burn *us.*"

This reached him. He stood silent. Rowan said: "This plan is not going to work."

He thought for some moments; and then he took her by the arm, leading her off. "Let's go and check the jammers."

CHAPTER FOURTEEN

*T*he first jammer-spell Willam sought was not present: a small hole in the ground between two tree roots marked its previous position. Will hissed displeasure, looked about to orient himself, and led Rowan off again.

It took some minutes to find the next. Willam paused under a pine tree, peered up at its branches, received no satisfaction, and tried an adjacent tree of very similar configuration. "There."

Rowan stood below while Willam shimmied up the trunk. Once at the lowest branches, he reached up and tugged; pine needles hissed against each other, and bits of debris and dead needles briefly showered on the steerswoman. As she brushed them off her hair something else fell, something that fluttered, then thumped when it landed.

A length of cloth, very close in color to the tree bark; and a small cube, about three inches in each dimension, painted in garish colors. Rowan stooped to examine it, but could not bring herself to touch it, due to the truly hideous little face that grimaced up at her from the top surface.

"Go ahead," Willam said, and he dropped to the ground. "It can't hurt you."

Rowan forced herself to pick up the cube, despite her fear that the imp-face would come alive and speak to her. To her relief, it did not, although its expression of disgust and derision was very realistic indeed.

"The decoration doesn't do anything," Willam said. "It's just there because that's how Olin would do it. Er—" This as Rowan turned the cube over. On the underside the same imp was enthusiastically flaunting its hairy buttocks.

Will held up both hands. "That's not—that's not my choice, really! It's just, that's the sort of thing Olin would put there."

"I see." She examined the other surfaces, which displayed other offensive postures and gestures. "I know that Olin is a trickster, but I frankly thought he'd be more subtle than this."

"Well, generally." Willam took the cube from her; his flush of embarrassment was impossible to hide. "But doing this would be like Olin saying that undermining Jannik's spells takes no subtlety at all."

"Thumbing his nose at Jannik," Rowan said; and thinking of one image in particular, could not help adding: "So to speak."

"Please." He was turning the cube over in his hands, prizing at the edges. "I'm just glad it was this one that we found first. Some of the others are even worse—Here we go." The side with the face on it flipped up with a quiet click. Willam prodded at the contents of the box with his index finger. "It looks good. Here." He stepped closer to Rowan, tilted the box to show her.

Inside: a tangle of colored strings; a flat rectangle etched with copper lines; a pair of black insect-like objects, with their many legs rooted to the copper; various other objects similarly attached, some as small as apple seeds, brightly colored; and, filling the bottom half of the box, a squat black square with two metal studs.

Willam indicated. "Push that yellow button."

It did look like a shank button, pulled from some festive shirt. The steerswoman touched it hesitantly, attempted to gently push it aside. It did not shift; but when her fingertip slid across it, the button moved downward, into some slight recess. One of the apple seeds emitted a brief green glow.

Rowan, startled, drew her hand back; then, more cautiously repeated the action, to the same effect.

"If the spell didn't have any power left, or if it was set up wrong, that light wouldn't light. This one is working."

Rowan pressed the shank button down again, and once more, finding the obedient little light weirdly charming. She did it again. "And this box somehow stops Jannik's power over the dragons?"

"Yes. It sends out... something like a noise, that we can't hear, but the dragons can. It's really very loud. It's as if you were trying to talk to someone when you were standing next to a crashing surf, or a grinding millstone."

"I wouldn't be able to hear the voice."

"And the dragons can't hear Jannik's commands, or the commands sent by the controlling spell in his house."

They replaced the jammer-spell, and searched out others. They did not check each and every one, but selected a sample, spread out around the two dragon fields. All were, according to the test, functioning.

Through all this, Rowan was engaged in an internal struggle. The jammer-spells definitely existed, were definitely magical, and Willam seemed very at ease with them. Perhaps he was mistaken about their effectiveness against dragons—but if nothing else, he was capable of constructing a spell that emitted green light when prompted to do so.

That in itself was a wonder. Rowan felt the tug to believe in Willam's skill, utterly.

But the heron was no less dead.

They ended where they had begun, sitting in the grass at the top of the little hill. Rowan had insisted that they approach with stealth and caution. Willam had acquiesced. Their caution was unnecessary. The dragons ignored them.

They had brought along one of the jammer-spells; Willam set it down on his right side, away from Rowan, presumably to shield her from its offensive decorations. Rowan found his protectiveness amusing.

Then the two of them watched, again, to no result whatsoever.

At last Willam heaved a weary sigh. "Tell me, lady, what's the difference between a bird and a stone?"

"A bird is alive; a stone is not. A heron is large, a stone is small. A large bird moves slowly; a tossed stone, quickly. The bird flew directly above; the stone came from only slightly above, and to one side."

"Above," he said thoughtfully. "And slow." He searched his pockets, coming up with a handkerchief. Inexplicably, he began to tear at it, pulling its four turned edges free.

Rowan watched in confusion. "What are you doing?"

"Making a shoot," he said, continuing to tear; each edge was now attached only at a corner. "It's nothing magical; I've seen little children playing with them in The Crags… Or maybe they *are* magical… it's hard to tell, sometimes."

Rowan knew the term *shoot* only as applying to the hunting method of an Outskirts insect called a trawler. A trawler would construct a parabolic web, which it would fly like a kite above the redgrass tops. Small insects, unable to see the gossamer, would become stuck to the threads. When enough were trapped, the trawler would reel in its dinner.

Willam's shoot was a square of cotton with strings trailing from each corner. He searched in the grass for a small stone, rejecting several candidates before finding one that suited him. Then he tied the free ends of the strings to the stone, wadded up cloth and stone together, stood, and tested the weight of the combination in his hand.

He threw high. The cloth-wrapped stone arced up, and at the top of its trajectory, as it slowed, the handkerchief, predictably, unwrapped.

The stone drifted, downward, slowly.

It hung from the handkerchief, which had spread into a parabolic shape that cupped the air beneath it as it fell, pulled down by the stone—

Like a kite, with the weight of the stone in place of the tether, the stone's fall in place of the wind—

In a single, amazed, delightful rush, the steerswoman generated a flurry of equations: mass, gravity, shoot size, speed, all elements interdependent, all interacting, each element requiring the existence of the others, all of them making each one necessary.

It was lovely; it was clever; it was more than clever: it was elegant.

Although, Rowan realized with a touch of smugness, for best effect, Willam might have chosen a slightly heavier stone—

The steerswoman startled when the handkerchief burst into flame.

The stone dropped. Burned cloth fluttered. Ash floated, and dispersed. "Did you see that?" Willam asked.

"I... I'm afraid I wasn't paying attention to the dragons for a moment."

"They ignored it completely until it was about four meters above." He sat on the grass once more, arms around knees, thoughtful again.

Rowan felt a moment's pang, longing to pursue her equations; then she recovered. "We," she said, "are much more than four meters away. Possibly they can't see that far at all."

"Or they're just not interested. But they don't care about stones flung at them." He rested his chin on his knees, expression unchanged: intent, focused, calm.

And as she regarded Willam, it came to the steerswoman suddenly that there was a great deal going on beneath that immense calm, behind those wide copper eyes. As much, perhaps, and as quickly moving, as that interplay of calculations that had so fascinated Rowan a moment ago.

At this, he became comprehensible to her. He was neither blind nor arrogantly stubborn; he was merely certain, with a confidence born of long and careful thought.

"That big bird," he said. "It flew low over the dragons like it hadn't a care in the world."

So it had. "The dragons don't generally attack birds passing by." Else, birds would soon learn to avoid dragons entirely.

"But they attack birds now. So, that's different. And the only new element is the jammers."

The dragons, if nothing else, seemed to be stupider under the influence of the jammer-spells. "If they don't usually attack birds, then they must be able to recognize a bird as a bird. But no longer." She sat beside him.

"What *can* they recognize?" he asked, apparently of himself.

The steerswoman could not help but answer, if only with the obvious. "They recognize each other."

"Not really. They don't have to. They all know the pattern they're following."

He still believed in the pattern.

He knew magic.

And his mind, Rowan now understood, moved much as her own did.

The steerswoman accepted the pattern as fact, and the dragons as supremely simple, and recast the situation in terms of that knowledge. "The heron was not in the pattern they expected."

Willam turned to her. "That's it." He seemed proud of her finding the solution. "That's simple, it would need to be something simple. It's not a decision, it's just a reaction. The dragons will attack any motion that's not in the pattern." He stopped short. His face dropped. "You were right. This won't work."

"Unless we can move as quickly as a thrown rock... I don't suppose you have a spell that would do that? Cause us to move very quickly?" Some folktales of wizardly magic included such spells.

"No." He sounded as disappointed as she felt. "It can't be done. The best we can do is make something else move fast, and sit on it—or in it. But I can't do that myself."

His "we" confused her for a moment, until she realized that he was referring to the wizards. He was including himself among them again, by habit. She decided not to correct him.

Down below, a cat-sized dragon wandered toward the edge of the group, hesitated, scratched the back of its head with a hind foot, and turned back again. "Willam, I think they're repeating."

He made a disgruntled sound. "For all the good it does us."

Something was missing.

Rowan had been considering the situation very logically; she almost felt that one ought to be able to state it in terms of pure symbolic logic. She could not, quite; but the impression persisted, and along with it, the impression that something was definitely missing.

It happened sometimes, when one worked through a series of equations, following their progression and alterations to some conclusion, that one would sense, undeniably, that something was wrong. A feeling, perhaps, that completion was not present, that there must be something more. Half a shape, where there ought to be symmetry, awkwardness instead of elegance; the absence of, for lack of a better word, beauty.

But the matter at hand was not numbers and symbols; it was animals, and motion. Still—something was missing.

Lists; lists of actions, if not read from writing, then by some means memorized, and enacted by these animals. Like perfect actors, following perfectly a predetermined script. The same evening's entertainment, repeated endlessly... "How often is the program changed?"

She sensed Will's sudden attention, although he was a moment speaking. Then: "What did you say?"

She continued to study the dragons' movements. "Because it must be changed sometimes. Conditions will alter, and the script must be altered, too, to take that into account."

She turned to find the wide copper gaze regarding her, with an expression she was absolutely unable to analyze. From the airy realms of logic she suddenly came to earth, suddenly felt that she was speaking out of utter ignorance, and became embarrassed. "I'm sorry—"

"No..." he said, slowly, "no, you're right. The program would need to be changed."

She was relieved to find that they were at least using the same analogy. "How long ago was it altered, do you know?"

He gave this some thought, still watching her closely. "No, I don't... The dragons only enter this routine when they're completely out of contact with the controller. That's pretty rare. This may be the only time it's happened for decades..."

His tone, and his expression, were still odd. Rowan could not help asking: "What's wrong?"

"Nothing." His brows went up. "You're just surprising me, that's all."

She did not know how to feel about the statement. "Am I actually making sense?"

"Yes," he said, definitely. "A lot. Go on."

She turned back to the scene below. "Then"—*program* had communicated her meaning before; she continued to use the word—"the program was decided, and the script written, within the last few years, at the least. Because, as I notice, that small dragon is clambering on top of that rock to avoid being harassed by those two larger ones... but previously, the dragons were not in this field at all, were they?"

Willam considered. "The pattern takes the rock into account. The program has to date at least from when the dragons were moved to this location. What are you getting at?"

"I'm not sure yet." Actors, following a script of explicit stage direction; or dancers, with the dance predetermined, step by step.

Something was missing.

"Oh," Rowan said, in a small voice. She found she had risen, was staring down at the dragons, fascinated; watching not each individual movement, but the whole of it, the sum of the motions, the completeness that should, but would not be present.

Will was beside her. She did not turn. "What do you see?" he asked.

"... Nothing, yet..."

"What are you looking for?"

"… A hole…" He did not ask further, and she was glad of it; this took a great deal of concentration. But then, he understood what that was like.

"Ah?" An involuntary noise from the steerswoman, very quiet. She said, half to herself, "I think… that dog-sized dragon—it was acting oddly for a moment…" It had hissed, twisted, emitted a whistling whine of displeasure, backed off—from nothing.

Nearby, a smaller dragon suddenly startled, and scampered away—from nothing. "Willam—" Suddenly excited, she clutched his arm, pointed—"Those two pony-dragons, with the very brown heads, ten meters in from the edge."

"I see them…"

She released his arm. "Watch."

The pair were side by side, one desultorily scraping at the earth with a forefoot, the other watching the first with interest.

Simultaneously, both looked over their shoulders, hesitated, then separated, one to each side, leaving a wide empty gap between.

Willam said, in a voice of perplexity, "… What?"

Just beyond, a clutch of six little creatures the size of rats were writhing and weaving among each other.

They froze. They scattered. They did so in two stages: half a meter away, a pause, then another full meter. Rowan could not help but cry out: "Oh, lovely!" She could almost see the heavy footsteps from which they fled.

She turned to Willam. He was regarding her, drop-jawed. Rowan said: "Two of Jannik's dragons are dead."

Realization dawned, and he closed his mouth, slowly. "There's a *hole!*"

She was grinning. "Two holes. Two places in the pattern where a dragon is expected, but does not exist. Willam—do they really only know each other by their places in the pattern?"

They tested the limits of the problem. They sacrificed Rowan's spare shirt to make more shoots. One they tossed toward the edge of the dragon herd, incrementally closer and closer, to determine the exact range at which the dragons would continue to ignore it. Retrieving it repeatedly became increasingly more harrowing, until, at a distance of four meters from the edge of the herd, three dragons noticed and flamed the shoot to ashes.

Rowan found it rather more difficult to maintain a properly objective state of mind when the dragons actually spit fire; Willam seemed not to have this problem. But the steerswoman no longer doubted his calm, and she found his steadiness steadying.

They scratched a line in the earth, a large curve below their hill, marking the limit of the dragons' interest. They attempted to drop another shoot directly into the hole in the pattern, but this proved impossible, due to the unpredictable movements of heated air above the dragons.

And through all their tests, and observations, and preparations, the hole continued to move: an emptiness that wandered, paused, advanced and retreated. They knew it by the creatures around it, with every other dragon it neared behaving exactly as if the absence were a presence. A ghost-dragon, invisible.

The hole corresponding to the second missing dragon was much harder to track. It moved less steadily, it turned unexpectedly, it seemed sometimes to vanish entirely. Willam soon identified the difficulty: the second dragon was smaller than the first. Other dragons were less likely to clear a path for it. Furthermore, it seemed more aggressive than its size warranted, and confrontations were more common, with the outcome less predictable. The watchers decided to concentrate on the larger hole.

Stand just outside the perimeter. Wait for the hole to approach the edge. Run to the hole, and enter it. As quickly as possible, snatch the nearest small dragon, pull it into the hole, cover its eyes, pick it up—and run, before the hole moved back into the herd.

Speed was needed, and precision. But it was all so very logical.

"It looks like it might reach the edge over there, on the right."

"If you say so," Willam said.

She turned to him. "You can't see it?"

"Sometimes. I lose it every now and again."

"It takes looking at all the dragons around the hole." She turned back, and was a moment finding it again. But there: two large dragons, heads cocked, as if tracking the passage of an invisible third. Admittedly, the signs were sometimes subtle. "Very well. I'll do it."

Willam stepped directly in front of her. "You will *not.*"

"But—" He stood before her, appalled and unmovable. "But," Rowan said, "if I'm the one who can see the gap more clearly—"

"*No.* I'll do it."

"Give me one good reason why."

He needed to think, but did so quickly. "Dragons are heavier than they look, and I'm stronger."

"I'm not weak, and I'm fast, and I have a very good idea of exactly what I'll be doing."

He crossed his arms, regarded her with narrowed gaze. "Then I won't go in until you pass on to me that very good idea of what exactly *I'll* be doing."

"Willam, I'm the better choice, and you know it."

He hesitated. "Yes, you are the better choice. But"—he became stubborn again—"it's my idea, and my decision, and my responsibility. We're here because of me. If something goes wrong, and someone gets burned, it's going to be me, and not you. Because all this is *my* doing."

It was true; and were their positions reversed, Rowan would be exactly as insistent, and exactly as right in her claim.

A steerswoman could not deny fact. "Very well." He relaxed, relieved.

They cut a section of cloth from Willam's bedroll, to cover their victim's eyes. They discussed the moves, planned, rehearsed. Throughout this, Willam was very intent, with an edge of nervousness that worried the steerswoman. But finally, and rather abruptly, Will became perfectly calm, utterly composed. The steerswoman recognized this as the exact moment when Willam understood, completely, what he would do. No more discussion was needed.

They watched the hole, and waited.

Twice it moved toward the edge of the herd; twice it turned back, with Willam already in position, left behind at the perimeter. Once it seemed to march confidently to the very edge, and paused there for a long moment; but also at the edge a waist-high dragon and another as tall as Rowan's shoulder stood on either side of the hole, one eye of each pointed toward the perimeter. They would not fail to catch the moment of out-of-pattern motion when Willam dashed to the hole.

Rowan and Willam sidled along, just outside the limit of the dragons' interest, alert for another opportunity. They both saw it coming, and wordlessly moved into position.

Rowan intended to signal Willam with a slap on the shoulder when the moment arrived; she slapped air. He was already moving.

Three long steps and he was in the hole.

Willam stepped to the far end of the gap. Three smaller dragons were near, walking away, not quickly; Willam was quick. He grabbed one by the tail, pulled back mightily. The dragon slid back, claws scoring the earth. A flicker of attention from dragons farther in, but now all motion was only within the limits of the hole.

Willam's dragon writhed, twisted its head, but Will had it by the neck with both hands, pointing its snout away from him. He straddled the creature and forced it to the ground.

He leaned on the neck, hard. The dragon flamed, and Will turned his face from the heat, freed one hand, pulled the scrap of blanket from his belt. When the fire stopped, Willam pushed the cloth over the creature's face, held it in place—and the dragon went limp.

All of this took place in mere instants.

But in those same instants, other events occurred.

To the right, deep in the herd, sudden movement: two dragons, backing away from something. They neared the edge; they reached it; they could go no farther. They hissed, flailed their tails, and parted, one to each side, continuing along the edge, still retreating.

From nothing.

It was the second hole, the vicious smaller ghost, chasing these others. The one on the left was scrambling, backing, toward Willam.

He did not see it. He would not see it in time. It would cut off his escape. Rowan thought to shout warning, but they had not tested shouting, she did not know what shouting would cause.

Five steps, at a run, and Rowan was in the hole with Willam.

He looked up, startled, then terrified. She clutched his shoulder. In a whisper: "Don't move," and again, without voice: *Don't move, don't move...*

Then the dragon was directly behind them.

It was taller than Rowan. She stood frozen as it eyed her, head cocked.

No. It does not really see me, Rowan told herself, it does not, it does not... Its action was part of its script. It would not attack—as long as they stayed inside the hole.

Willam was down on one knee, motionless, the captive dragon limp beneath him. The blocking dragon wove its head, took a step, and another, toward them.

Rowan glanced over her shoulder. Ahead, a dragon as tall as her shoulder looked her way. It hesitated, rumbled in its throat, and shifted slightly aside.

Making way. The hole was about to move, inward.

Rowan shook Willam's shoulder, urgently. He glanced about, eyes wide, then pushed his captive forward on the ground, following the two hesitant steps Rowan took.

The dragon behind still approached, sparing a hissing whistle of annoyance at another that had crowded too near.

Two dragons behind, now.

In the other direction, a small dragon prodding at the ground with its nose lifted its head, startled, made to flee, hesitated.

There was nothing to frighten it, no threat here. But with sudden urgency it scrambled away, paused, and looked back.

Its head was cocked, one eye centered directly on Rowan. Then the head tilted farther, and the eye was watching, tracking—nothing.

The hole was still moving. It was large, Rowan and Will were still within it, but not for long.

Rowan reached down and back, blindly, trying to find Willam, to pull him forward. But then his hand was on her shoulder; he was already standing. She did not look behind. She stepped, and he stepped with her: forward, into the focus of the dragon's garnet eye.

The small dragon watched, warily; Rowan watched it watch, kept herself where it saw her, step by step. She walked, and Willam walked, walked, as slow as the great dragon whose empty space they inhabited.

Then the small head tilted sharply in the other direction, at something on the dragon's far side. The creature twisted, scrambled away, and was gone.

And the steerswoman was surrounded by dragons.

Small bright ones, half-slithering, half-walking. Larger ones, rambling about, eying each other. The largest, lying down, or standing with heads weaving, moving, slowly, with the smallest dragons scrambling away from the swing of heavy tails.

Rowan smelled them, a scent like hot iron, and oil, and the air before a thunderclap. It was hot in among them, then cool, then hot as their bodies shifted, blocking and admitting the breeze. For one moment the tang of the mud flats by the river appeared, like a voice calling freedom; then it was gone.

The hole was still moving, it must still be moving—but where?

There: were those two dragons studying each other? Or something invisible between them? Or that one, there, moving—away from her, or toward something else?

She tried to look everywhere, tried to catch the dragon-glances, tried to see paths being cleared for her to follow.

There was an empty area ahead, but no dragon seemed to be watching it.

Will's hand on her shoulder urged her forward. Rowan managed one quick glance back.

Willam had hoisted the captive dragon across his shoulders, and was standing half-turned, one hand on her shoulder. The copper gaze was wide, and frightened, but moving, scanning the dragons behind.

She had forgotten about him. She could not see everywhere, all the time; but she had eyes behind, Willam's.

Beyond Willam, a moss-green dragon was approaching, whipping its head sideways, and Rowan felt she could see the ghost-tail of her ghost-dragon flailing, the creature behind dodging it. She realized then what she had not noticed before: the dragons never actually touched each other.

But this was all she had time to note. The dragon drew nearer, and Willam's hand told her again to move.

She moved, forward, into the gap ahead of her.

Where next? How could she guess?

Motion: only motion mattered. Only motion was information.

The steerswoman forced herself to stop glancing about wildly. She gazed steadily ahead, watching with the whole of her vision, ignoring shape, ignoring detail. She noted only movement: flicks and flickers in the corner of her eye, shifts of large forms ahead and around, sinuous shapes close to the ground, and the glints of light on garnet eyes.

A flick on the right, which was the tilt of a dragon's head, its gaze tracking her; she followed the track. Quickness, down on the ground: small dragons hurrying out of her way.

She moved; Willam moved with her.

And it seemed to the steerswoman now that she entered some sort of perfect state, where, like a dragon, she saw only motion; where, like a bird's, her task was simple, and clear, and without options.

She seemed to herself to be hardly present. There was only motion, the sum of all visible motion, a mathematical operation that could not complete, unless she moved.

She moved when she must; paused when she must; waited; and moved again.

She did not know why she felt so very cold, in this heat; but she was cold.

She moved.

At intervals, the pressure of the hand on her shoulder told of the motion that she could not see, told her how to complete the sum, saying: *Move left. Pause now. Move back. Move back again. Move back.*

They reversed positions. The ghost-dragon had altered its route. Rowan led again.

They passed among dragons. They paused at the approach of large dragons. Small ones retreated from them.

It went on, and on. The steerswoman did not know for how long; time vanished. She moved as she must, feeding her actions into the pattern, reading the sum.

And then, the movements ahead: they did not give way. The sum of all motions told Rowan to move back.

She did so, with slow steps that lifted with a wet sound.

The hand on her shoulder said, *No.* She stopped.

But before her, little motions, low to the ground: small dragons. Not retreating. Approaching. Rowan stepped back from them again.

No. Rowan looked behind.

A shape, approaching, without hesitation.

Left: another shape, huge, not moving, not watching, giving no clue.

Right: no pathway being cleared.

Front and back, all motion slowly closed in. The hole was shrinking around them, vanishing.

Willam's hand pulled, hard. Off-balance, Rowan fell to her left—and then she was half-sprawled, half leaning, directly against some great, dark object.

Her focus broke.

Dragons, everywhere.

The blue of the sky above, and the green and silver of light on dragon scales, flashing, large and small dragons moving, slowly and quickly, claws and faceted eyes gleaming, all around. Their hides creaked as they moved; they hissed, whistled, and shrieked at each other. The air consisted only of the scent of them: Rowan saw, heard, breathed dragon.

Her shirt was wet with sweat, and she was trembling: not with cold but with a battle taking place in her nerves and muscles, the need to flee fighting the knowledge that flight would be suicide. Her very bones wished to run. Her heart banged like a fist against the walls of her chest. There was a sour taste at the back of her throat.

Willam was beside her, leaning back, panting and shuddering. He had shifted the weight of his captive dragon slightly off his shoulders, and onto the curved surface behind him.

The dark green, scaled surface.

They were leaning against a dragon.

The steerswoman made a helpless sound through her teeth, quelled it instantly.

The dragon's cold, hard form was motionless against her back. Its scales, under her left hand, were streaked with dust. Half-crumbled leaves lay in the fold of its foreleg. A small drift of ash had accumulated against its nose.

No breath stirred the ash.

It was the corpse of their own ghost-dragon.

It reclined, head on forelegs. It must have died in its sleep; the pattern must have included it walking to this spot, lying down, and sleeping.

The hole had not vanished. It was here. Will and Rowan were safe inside it.

For how long?

How long before the dragon was scheduled to wake, and the empty hole would move?

How long was the full cycle of the pattern, how long before the hole again reached the edge of the herd, how long before Willam and Rowan could escape?

How long had they been among the dragons?

She might guess the hour by the angle of the sun—but she could not spare the attention. She had lapsed, she had lost that perfect state of pure observation of the sum of all motion. She must get it back.

Do not look at individual dragons. Do not identify them as dragons. See motion. See only motion.

Motion beside her, as Willam wiped sweat from his face, leaned his head back against his burden—

Heavier than they look, he had said. How long could he carry it?

Don't think about that; see motion.

Details faded. Living dragons became, slowly, only shapes, then blocks of mass.

The masses moved. Movement was everything.

She saw waves, ripples of response. Eddies that swirled, then dispersed. Little jumps. The parting of great shapes.

And, some unguessable time later: movement away from the dead dragon's head, making way—

Blindly, she found Willam's hand. Together, they sidled around the corpse. When the hole left the dragon behind, they were in the moving gap once more.

They went on.

The shapes grew more numerous, and closer together—many more shapes, crowding close now.

Good. More motion: more cues.

In the grip of pure logic, Rowan walked, paused, backed, turned, moved.

Motion ahead, shifting the shapes. Motion approaching. Rowan stopped, waited; it grew nearer. She tried to back up.

No, Willam's hand said.

No opening to either side; and the movement ahead, a scrambling, still coming near. She tried again to back. *No.*

She glanced behind. One large shape that was standing still, not giving way.

The movement ahead became commotion; there were dragon-whistles, and hisses. Then it froze, and small glinting eyes turned on her, turned away, turned back.

Then the shapes ahead split, moved to each side, quickly, fleeing.

From nothing.

There was a gap directly ahead, and Willam's hands, both of his hands, on her shoulder, urging her forward. But Rowan refused; she stood solid; she tried, by stance and resistance, to tell him that the gap he saw ahead was not theirs to enter.

It was the second hole, the second ghost-dragon. Rowan was no longer the only missing parameter in the equation.

She could not guess the sum. She could not tell which cues belonged to her. She did not know what was happening, what should happen next.

The sum of all motions was failing her.

But the list: these actions were on a list, designed to look natural. If the dragons could act freely, what would they do? What would they do *now*?

Her dragon was large. The other dragon was smaller. It should defer to her, and back off.

But no: no such sign was visible. Instead, it seemed to her that the other ghost moved even closer, slowly.

Yes, it was smaller; but it was more aggressive. She had seen that, watching its path before. It would confront her.

And now, flickers of movement, the glances of garnet eyes, as the animals all around looked first to one ghost, then the other. Wondering about the outcome.

The second hole was a negative presence; she could not see its limits—until mid-sized dragons at the edge of the crowd whipped their heads back to avoid a flail of the second ghost's tail.

Tails moved for balance. The invisible dragon was moving left. Rowan shifted to the right, felt Willam shift with her; and from the corner of her eye she caught the motion of the dragons behind as they shied back from the swing of her own heavy tail.

She had seen confrontations; she knew how they went. Her adversary would now search, head weaving side to side, seeking an opening.

She turned slightly, adjusting Will behind her, remaining face-on, not allowing her flank to be exposed.

The crowd startled; the ghost was making its move. Not to one side, by the watching eyes: straight on.

Which way should she move?

No!

She was huge, she was the second largest dragon in the field. The audacity of this small, vicious animal—how *dare* it?

In her mind, she reared. She rose tall on hind legs, screaming hatred; she flailed with her front claws, threw back her head, and with one great breath sent a gout of white fire into the blue sky.

And all around, like a wave moving outward, green and silver flashed as dragon heads dropped, as dragons shied back, as dragons cowered from her, from her fury, from her power—

From nothing.

Through it all, Rowan had remained motionless, tense and silent, with Willam's hands damp on her shoulders. Merely two human beings, standing in emptiness, at the heart of a horde of dragons.

And the second emptiness before them, where the other ghost should now drop its head, retreat—

The creatures beyond separated like wheat stalks, turning their heads to watch the flight of the vanquished dragon.

Gazes flicked back to the victor. By hint and inference, Rowan saw her path.

She walked, and Willam walked, through dragons that hurried to make clear the way.

But ahead, jittering motion, a dragon with no room to retreat. It hissed, twisted, whistled fear, then found an opening and backed off. Another shape, close to the ground, startled at Rowan's approach, and scampered urgently away.

This was familiar...

Two shapes, side by side; abruptly, both looked back at Rowan, hesitated, and separated. Rowan led Willam between them, where a small writhing on the ground stopped, then spread out ahead: half a meter away, a pause, then another meter.

She knew this. The pattern was repeating.

Behind Rowan, Willam's steps now shuffled. His hand on her shoulder was heavy. She reached up and laid her hand over his, pressed down firmly, trying to communicate that he should put more weight on her.

He did so. He used both hands. She felt herself heavier; but she had been walking unburdened all this time. She would manage.

And she could remember now, from this point on, many of the movements the hole would make. She had been watching. She no longer needed Willam's eyes behind.

She led him on.

Later, at last, ahead, in the path that would be theirs: scuffed earth, footprints and claw marks left when Willam had first captured his dragon. And beyond that, when just one more dragon shifted aside, there was only open land from Rowan's feet all the way to the safe perimeter.

The hole in the pattern, the absent presence in the list of all actions, moved, as it must, to the edge of the dragon herd.

But although she could not see it, Rowan knew: the second hole was again not far away; other dragons were retreating from it, along the edge; one of them would soon move, as it had before, to close off the path to the perimeter. When the time came, Rowan and Will must move very quickly.

The time came. Rowan turned, pulled Will by the arms, hard, saying without sound: *Run!*

They tried. They were slow. Willam was too heavily burdened, his strength too spent.

They made it to the end of their ghost-dragon's space, but they staggered, and stumbled, and Willam was down on one knee. And the hole moved back into the herd, leaving them behind.

And there it was—the one dragon that before had cut off their escape, now standing between them and the herd, not ten feet away, facing left.

They were in full view of its glittering eye.

Dragons saw motion. For the space of three heartbeats, Rowan and Willam remained, frozen.

But the steerswoman saw from the movements within the herd, and knew from memory, that when this dragon was gone, others would be there, more of them: many bright, jeweled eyes to catch the humans' last break for freedom.

Rowan said, between her teeth: "Run." And she ran, herself—left, away from Willam.

The dragon saw her, head twisting to follow the motion, then turned its snout toward her.

She dodged, right. A wash of heat and light beat to her left. When the flame stopped, Rowan placed herself in the hot air of its passage, and ran up that corridor, straight ahead, straight toward the creature's blind spot.

Her sword was in her hand. She reached the dragon as it turned its head, and she swung with all her force directly at the glittering eye.

The eye shattered, cascading red shards, spitting sparks from within. The dragon writhed, backed, flamed again with no aim, twisted its neck.

She ducked under the head, struck at the second eye, missed. The creature saw her, tried to turn, to flame, but the blade caught on the edge of the eye.

Rowan held tight, and the dragon's own strength pried the entire garnet dome free of its face. Blinded, it froze, then collapsed, senseless.

But the pattern still moved, and now other eyes were watching. Rowan straddled the fallen dragon, holding its place in the pattern for the single moment she needed, raised her sword, dropped its point behind her head, used both hands, and flung it: up, high, arcing out over the herd.

Bright metal flashed twice in the low sunlight, spinning, then descending. Heads lifted and turned; from a dozen sources, flame fountained up—

Willam had her by the arms, stopping her flight. "You're clear, you're clear!" She did not recall having run. She looked at him, stunned and speechless.

They were outside the perimeter.

Willam was pale, and shuddering, his shirt drenched, his eyes wide; Rowan thought that she must look the same herself. He smelled of sweat, and oil, and mud; she thought she smelled of dragon-fire.

They stood, shaking and gasping. Then Willam said suddenly, in a wild voice, "What were you *doing?*"

And because it was a question, the steerswoman discovered that she could answer immediately. "Distracting them."

Willam made several attempts to speak, and failed. Eventually he found his voice. "It worked."

Rowan made a noise that perhaps ought to have been a laugh of relief, but it could not escape from the back of her throat. It sounded to her like something a very small dog would say. She dropped to a seat on the ground. Willam knelt down beside her.

The sun was low, and the air was cold. Very slowly, Rowan's heart calmed, and her breathing eased. "Where's our victim?"

Willam had his eyes closed. Without opening them, he tilted his head. "Over there."

About twenty feet around the perimeter, just past the line in the earth marking the safe distance: a sprawled shape, bright green and silver. Lying senseless and blindfolded, it looked, at the moment, rather pitiful.

Rowan nodded, dumbly. Her left leg was lying in a puddle, water seeping in over the high edge of her boot. She felt dull, weak, empty. She struggled to recover thought. "We should move it, before the sun goes down."

Willam's head dropped, and his shoulders slumped. His hands lay limp on the ground beside his knees, palms up. "Yes," he said, eyes still closed, "but I don't think I can carry it anymore."

CHAPTER FIFTEEN

*T*hey both carried the dragon, slung between them, leg-tied and suspended from a dead branch, looking to Rowan like the prize from a hunt in some heroic ballad. And it was, as Willam had predicted, heavier than it looked.

They went north away from the city, and inland away from the river, so that it would encounter no humans once it was set free.

The jammer-spell that Willam had kept was now tucked into Rowan's shoulder satchel; while being transported, the dragon would remain deaf to the commands of the controller spell in Jannik's house.

They found a place by a little stream with steep banks, where wooded hills rose above, now deepening with evening shadow, and smelling sweetly of pine; rather a pleasant spot, Rowan thought.

As they set their burden down, and Willam began to untie its legs from the pole, something occurred to Rowan. "When you take off the blindfold, it will expect the pattern. Nothing will fit. It will attack." Willam paused; this had not been anticipated.

They solved the problem by digging a small hole in the rising ground, and arranging the dragon with its head in the hole, its face pressed up against the earth. Rowan could not help but feel sorry for it.

When Willam carefully slipped the cloth free, the dragon remained inert. He and the steerswoman backed away, then climbed.

Up into the woods, high, and deep, until the stream and the sprawled green shape on the bank were just visible below through the pine trunks. Willam and Rowan crouched down behind one particularly large tree, and peered out from either side.

Rowan passed the jammer-spell to Willam. He opened it, glanced once at Rowan, drew a breath, then prodded inside the box with his index finger.

Far below, the green jerked, then writhed, struggled. The dragon found its feet, and lifted its head, shaking dirt from its eyes.

It cocked its head; glanced here, there, and about; scratched its nose with a forefoot. Then it began scrambling along the edge of the steep bank. "The controlling spell has it," Willam said, quietly. "It's sending it back to the dragon fields—" Then he stopped short, with a quick intake of breath.

The dragon had halted suddenly, and now stood completely still. Then it wove its head, slowly, side to side. Willam breathed: "And there's Jannik."

A tall broken stump was nearby; the dragon noticed it, and climbed up its ragged top, then arranged itself carefully among the splinters and sat up, front legs tucked against its chest. It paused, made a precise quarter turn to its right, paused again, and repeated, and repeated, until it had turned in a slow, complete circle.

No animal would do that. The wizard was now personally commanding its movements; and, the steerswoman realized, surveying the dragon's surroundings himself, gazing through the creature's own jeweled eyes.

Rowan and Willam remained very still.

The dragon's forelegs dropped. Then, with sudden animal nimbleness, it leapt from the stump, clambered down the steep bank toward the water. A moment later it could be seen splashing through the brook. When it reached a large, flat rock, it climbed and sat, tail curled, eying the surface with one raised forefoot poised, exactly as if patiently hunting fish.

Willam and Rowan exchanged a long look. Then, crouching low, they backed off and made their way up the hill, through the woods, and away.

They made camp by the roadside, at a site that had been used for that purpose before. A ring of stones already outlined the best location for the fire, and some kindly person had left a number of branches drying nearby.

Willam made the fire quickly with the help of a small bit of metallic powder that hissed into white flame when he spit on it. Then he collapsed full length on the ground, with a groan containing just enough theatrics to tell Rowan that he was not in serious trouble. "I can't believe we did that."

"I can't believe we even attempted it."

"That was the most horrible experience I've ever had in my life," Willam declared, with feeling. When Rowan did not immediately voice the same opinion, he raised his head and eyed her. "Not in yours?"

The steerswoman had several candidates to choose from. "Well…" She pulled the saddlebags from among the tack they had removed from the horses. "It was different from anything else. I've never before had an experience that was so, so logical and so mindless, at the same time."

"Logical and mindless." Willam lay his head down again. "That's magic."

They dined, he on fish pastry and a baked potato, she on roast boar and squash, which they heated on stones by the fire.

She wrote in her logbook. When Willam passed by after arranging his bedroll, he caught a glance of one page. He leaned forward and indicated.

"That word is misspelled." Under his correction, *shoot* became *chute*.

Willam sat by the fire, quiet, watching the flames. Despite his weariness, perhaps, like her, he felt that sleep would be long coming.

Logical and mindless, the steerswoman wrote. But so many things in the world were both logical and mindless. The swing of the stars above, for all their beauty, had no intent behind them.

High up, in the crystal dark, the Western Guidestar hung, glowing bright, seeming eternal. In the opposite side of the sky: the Eastern Guidestar. Watching, recording, waiting for commands from their masters—"Are they alive?"

Willam glanced at her, then followed the direction of her gaze. "The Guidestars? I don't know." He remained, face tilted to the sky. "I used to ask that—not about the Guidestars, but about other things." His voice was quiet, puzzled. "The things that move, and act. The things that watch, and choose, and decide. The things that speak to us…" A pocket of moisture in one burning log hissed, squealed, then snapped. "And whenever I asked that question, Corvus would always say: 'The short answer is no.' And then he'd give me the long answer. And Rowan," and he looked at her, shook his head, "it always seemed to me that the long answer really meant yes. So… I don't know." He picked up a stick of kindling, used it to prod at the heart of the flames. "I do know that they're not *considered* to be alive, and they're not treated as if they were. We create them and destroy them without a second thought…" A breeze from the river rose, making the fire flutter as if struggling against it, instinctively. "If they are alive, I suppose that's wrong. But what I really think—" He set down the stick, held out both his hands, first together, then slowly widening the gap. "—I think that the division is not as clear as we think it is. Between what's alive, and what's not. I think," and he watched as his own right hand marked off steps toward his left, "that there are… degrees, between. More, alive, less alive… I don't think that there's any one point where we can say, 'Here's where it begins…' " He considered his hands silently, then dropped them to his knees. "I suppose that's true of a lot of things. We mark off some point in the middle, and say, 'There's the division,' when, really, there are a dozen steps between, or a hundred, or a thousand…"

He grew silent. The fire sputtered, sent up sparks that died before they reached the sky, fell as ash, and rose again, riding the heated air. Rowan watched the light move on Willam's face as he gazed into the flames.

She said: "Willam… will you teach me magic?"

He looked up at her. "Yes," he said, and he seemed gently surprised, not by the question, but by the idea that she might think there could be any answer other than yes. Then he hesitated, and said, "But…"

175

"I know. You couldn't learn it all in six years; I suppose it'll take even longer for me to learn just what you know."

He gave her a wry look. "Actually, I doubt that. But—" He paused. "Rowan, if things go wrong tomorrow night, but we do still manage to escape with our lives, I'll probably have to run. And probably you and Bel should, too. In the opposite direction. It would be safer, for all of us. So I just don't know how much time we'll have together."

She had, for the moment, nearly forgotten their mission for the following night. And for all the hope that it offered her, she found that she now resented it. "Then... for as long as we are together."

He nodded, pleased. "All right." And then he laughed. "But I don't know where to begin!"

"Since we have so little time," Rowan said, "give me the heart of it." The phrase took him by surprise. "Is there one idea," she went on, "one principle, that stands at the center? Can you think of one sentence that is true of every aspect of magic? Is there even such a thing: one truth that underlies it all?"

She thought that he had never considered this before; it seemed that he was thinking, not to recover one key phrase that had been told to him, but to discern, among all the things he knew, the connections; and then to follow them inward, to the heart, the center.

It took some time. The copper gaze shifted, uncertain, as he sifted, perhaps, through everything that he had learned. At one point, he idly picked up the stick again, apparently merely for something to do with his hands, then sat gazing at it, brows knit, as if it contained the answer. Apparently it did not. Frustrated, he tossed it into the fire.

Then he stopped short; he looked at the fire, looked at his hand—and he had it. He turned to the steerswoman. "Everything is power."

She was frankly disappointed. "And, I suppose, power is everything." It seemed a typical wizardly idea, but she had frankly hoped for something less political.

"No." He leaned forward, intent. "Not the way you think. I mean *really*. Everything... *is* power."

This made no sense. "I think," she said cautiously, "that you're using that word in a way I don't know. Some things *have* power—"

"*Everything* has power; and everything also *is* power."

She rubbed her forehead. "I think that even six years won't do it. We're only at the first sentence, and already I'm lost."

He sat back, struggled with his thoughts. He tried again. "Power," he said, "is what everything is made of. You, me; the fire; rocks and trees; the world, the sun, the stars."

"But, I am made of matter... so... Matter is made of power?"

He shrugged, helplessly, almost apologetic. "Yes."

Take it as a working hypothesis, the steerswoman instructed herself. "Very well. Go on."

"All magic," he said, "is movements of power, or transformations of power. In fact," he admitted, seeming a bit surprised at the thought, "everything that happens at all is movement or transformation of power. And magic is what happens when you have a very close control over the movement or transformation of power, and can use it to do something complicated and difficult, something that wouldn't happen naturally, all by itself."

She was reduced to repeating his most incomprehensible statements. *"Everything* that happens is movement or, or transformation of... power?"

He was more certain now. "That's right." He considered. "The sun," he said, "sends power down to the world. And a flower on the ground will, will gather up part of that power and use it to—well, to do whatever it is that flowers do to keep themselves going. I don't know a thing about flowers, except that. And you, and I, we take in food, because we need the power that's in the food to keep ourselves going—"

I *thought it was the food that I needed;* but she did not say this aloud. "Go on."

"And that's a movement of power, from the food to you."

"But," she said, "a rock doesn't take in anything, it doesn't need power..."

"Except to exist. It's made of power. And"—something came to him—"you can give it more." He searched the ground around him, found a stone. "If you take a stone, and lift it," he did so, "and, say, put it on top of a boulder and leave it there," he indicated it with his other hand, "you've given it some of your power, and the power is stored there. And if, say, it then fell off—"

Rowan immediately recognized an example from her earliest training: a demonstration, with attendant calculations, of potential and kinetic—

"Energy," she said.

He blinked. "Yes. But, not in the usual sense, like liveliness, or get-up-and-go—"

"You mean," she said, and stressed the word, *"energy."*

He sat up straight, suddenly glad. *"Yes!"*

And they looked at each other, each immensely relieved. They shared, apparently, at least one technical term.

"The energy of the wind," Rowan said, "is transferred to the sails—"

"And the ship goes forward."

"And you tie a donkey to the turning bar of a mill—"

"And the donkey moves, and its energy is moved into the millstone—"

"—so it goes around—"

"—and you place your grain between the stones, and the energy, the power, crushes your grain."

"The energy from the stone, from the donkey, from… the food the donkey ate."

"Hay. A plant. Which took its energy from the sun. Most power comes from the sun, in the end."

"But," she said, and paused to consider all that had been said, "Will, none of these things is magic."

He took a breath to speak; but she spoke for him. "The division is not as clear as we think it is. There are steps between."

"A dozen," he affirmed, "a thousand. But it's just a question of degree."

A continuum. A line that one could walk, step by step, from the familiar to the more and more arcane. And at the end: magic.

Not impossible, not mystical, but natural and logical, as mindlessly logical as the swing of the stars, as the fall of a stone.

She had asked for principle; he had given it. She said: "Now something specific, to demonstrate. Something magical, in detail."

"I don't know how to begin, really…"

Her own context would be much the same as Willam's had been; and he would know best how to teach in the way that he had himself been taught. "Let's start with your blasting-charms."

The stone was still in his hand; he laughed, tossed it into the campfire, and a spray of sparks flew upward from the pulsing orange heart of the wood. Willam watched with pleasure. "Lady," he said, his copper eyes reflecting rising glints, "they're fire. They're just fire."

They began, then, with fire—according to Willam, one of the purest examples that existed of the transformation and movement of energy.

They spoke of substances, and the way in which fire acted upon them; and the differences between the substances, and their inner nature. They touched briefly upon where to locate certain of these substances, and under what conditions they might be found; Rowan was familiar with some of these facts.

Optimal substances were identified. Specific quantities were named, and proportions, and the actions needed to combine them. And here, the matter seemed to the steerswoman as straightforward as a recipe.

Then speed appeared. Speed was the key. Heat caused expansion—and some things burned very fast indeed.

When the amounts of substances used were no longer specified, proportions naturally transformed themselves into ratios...

Speed spawned derivatives: acceleration, and force. Force was large.

Substances became symbols.

Actions became abstract operations.

Symbol, operation, symbol, result...

And the result, in the end, was wild, raw power.

At a pause, when Willam built up the fire again, Rowan attempted to quickly copy into her logbook the scrawled writing in the dirt that she and Willam had generated. And it was only in the act of writing them down that she noticed: she was copying a series of mathematical equations. She realized then that for some time, she and Willam had been speaking almost entirely in formulas.

She looked about. Willam was breaking small branches across one knee, tenting the kindling and logs. The fire would burn quickly, but brightly. They needed the illumination.

Down at the riverbank, reeds rustled in a light wind; stars shone on the river, not mirrored, but transformed into quick flickers by the motion of the water. The loom of trees behind Rowan, the sound of the horses breathing and shifting in the dark: all were sharp, clear, fresh.

Rowan felt she had been on a journey: a distance long, but quick, and quicker as the countryside grew ever more familiar. She and Willam had been hurrying at the last, not from urgency, but from the sheer joy of the speed.

The new kindling caught, new flames leapt. Willam watched the campfire for a moment, almost fondly.

Then he settled beside the steerswoman again, and they went on.

CHAPTER SIXTEEN

*T*hey slept as late as they dared, breakfasted as quickly as they could, and made the best speed possible back to Donner.

They did not converse on the way. Willam seemed thoughtful and absorbed. Rowan remained alert. Jannik had been given reason to hurry to the dragon fields, and may have left at first light. Rowan and Willam might actually encounter the wizard on the road.

But there was no sight of him during the open stretches of the journey. When they came into closer landscape, among trees and turning roads, Rowan took the precaution of tucking her chain inside her vest. Should the wizard pass by, there was no need to advertise herself as a steerswoman.

The day grew cooler yet, under a clearing sky. Other than this, all seemed as on the previous day, as they approached the city's limits. Rowan's concern relaxed.

They took a different route into the city proper, swinging to the east, then down along the harbor. Rowan caught sight of *Graceful Days,* out past the shallows. The ship rode heavy, now; two transfer barges, light on the water, were crossing the shallows back to the wharves.

"Ahoy!"

Rowan shaded her eyes against the late-afternoon sun.

"Gregori!" she called back, and slowed as he approached the riders.

He was in the company of Enid, who served as supercargo on *Graceful Days:* a small, weathered, sun-bleached woman, who peered about with a sharp blue gaze, as if constantly calculating the mass and volume of every object her eye fell upon. She and Rowan had shared many a conversation on the voyage—somewhat limited in scope, but enjoyable nevertheless.

"Now, I didn't know steerswomen rode," Gregori commented as he and his companion fell in beside Rowan's mare.

"We do," Rowan said. "We can. We're taught to. But we rarely use horses in the general course of our work." It was one matter to request free food and lodging for a solitary wanderer, occasionally for weeks on end; quite another to include a large, hungry animal. Also, a horse was a tempting target for bandits.

Enid and Gregori turned curious glances at Rowan's companion, and before they could ask, he provided: "Willam. Rowan and I have been out riding in the countryside."

The steerswoman completed the introductions. Gregori regarded Will with obvious speculation; Rowan's poorly suppressed grin seemed to please him. Enid studied Willam openly, as if trying to determine how much heavy labor he was capable of. "Your eyes aren't pink," she said to him.

"Um… no…"

She had obviously thought that he might be an albino. "Good. Otherwise, you'd fry on the deck on fair days." All Enid's interactions with the world at large were filtered through her evaluation of their potential use to her ship, regardless of whether or not any such consideration actually applied.

"I hadn't expected to see you again," Rowan said to Gregori, as the four of them, on foot and on horseback, continued up the street past a chandler's, a rope-walk, a shipping office.

"Some cross-shipments were delayed. But we're loaded now. Wood from upriver, wine and preserved fruits from Donner. Some of the Alemeth silk stayed aboard. Rice from up north."

"Don't like carrying rice," Enid grumbled.

"It's not like we're filling the hold with it," Gregori told her. Rice, if it became wet, would expand and burst its sacks. In a hold otherwise closely packed, this could cause serious difficulty. Rowan took a moment to explain the matter to Willam.

"When do you leave?" Rowan asked the captain.

"Noon-tide tomorrow, or the day after. Take that much time to gather up the rest of the crew; what with the delay, who knows where they've wandered to?"

The literal-minded Enid chose to answer the rhetorical question. "The mate knows."

"Yes," Gregori said patiently. "And she's waiting for us at the Dolphin." The first mate was Gregori's eldest daughter, sister to Zenna. An idea occurred to the captain. "Rowan, you and your friend come along; I'll stand you both drinks."

"That happens to be exactly where we're headed, as a matter of fact. I've been lodging there. I don't suppose you've seen Bel about?"

This took him by surprise; he obviously did not know that Rowan and Bel no longer needed to behave as strangers to each other. "Can't say I have… Enid?" The supercargo made a disgruntled noise in the negative. During the voyage from Alemeth, Bel and Enid had acquired a mutual dislike. Bel had found Enid stolid, limited, and unimaginative; Enid, for her own part, had never forgiven the Outskirter for a particularly clever satirical poem the supercargo had inspired.

At the stables, there were no grooms about, but it was nearing dinnertime. Willam and Rowan removed the tack, found cloths for a quick rubdown, and left the mares tied in the yard. They entered the Dolphin by the back door, and the captain and Enid paused outside Rowan's room while she and Will dropped off their traveling gear.

Inside, on the table beside a new bouquet of dried roses, was a letter.

"Who knows you're here?" Willam asked.

"Zenna, and Steffie," Rowan said, bemused, "and everyone else in Alemeth..." She picked up the letter, whose paper was of high quality, and read the address:

Rowan, Steerswoman,
or
Zenna, Steerswoman
The Annex, Alemeth.

"That explains it. It must have come through the harbormaster's office. They've remembered my name, and found out I was staying here." Rowan did not recognize the handwriting, but it was very clear, and formal, likely the work of a professional scribe. There was no point of origin indicated on the envelope. She turned it over. "Ah." Only a seal, with a signet showing a crest: a ship, and a wolf's head.

Rowan held it up to show Willam. He recognized it. "Artos." The duke, in Wulfshaven. "And I guess I know what it's about."

"I suppose I do, as well." News of Willam's escape was bound to catch up with him sometime. And Rowan had specifically requested that Artos befriend Willam, so that the apprentice would not lose touch with the common folk. She set the letter back on the table. "Did you spend much time with Artos?" she asked Willam as they left the room.

Will looked regretful. "At first, some," he said. "Later... things got busy..." He could be no more specific in the company of Gregori and Enid.

Rowan led the others down the angled hall, up the narrow back staircase. Gregori found the tangled and inconvenient route amusing. Enid peered at the walls suspiciously, as if being indoors, on land, was an experience entirely new to her. Rowan knew this was not the case.

In the broad main hallway upstairs, they had room to walk more comfortably. "Quiet tonight," Gregori noted. Sound from the common room ought to have reached them by now.

"Perhaps everyone in town is still recovering from the feast. I should think that would take a couple of days."

"Not for my people. They'll eat a whole boar with all the trimmings, and want the same again for breakfast…"

They reached the main staircase, and began descending. Halfway down, a man stood, gazing down into the common room. He looked up, greatly startled, when he saw them, glanced back down, turned back again, seemed about to speak as they passed him.

A muffled voice from below caught his attention. He hesitated, then said, with what seemed like resignation: "Well, that's it, you'd better get in there, too."

Rowan was almost at the bottom of the stair. Enid had lagged. The man reached up, took Enid by the arm, pulled her down beside him. "Hey!" she said, pulling back.

"What's going on?" Gregori asked.

"Nobody knows," the man said, and he shook Enid by the arm, not unkindly, but to get her attention. He spoke quietly, urgently. "You—all of you, just stay quiet, and don't look for trouble."

And a thought came to Rowan, clearly: she should leave, should get out of here, now, quickly—but too late. There was someone else already behind her, a hand on her back, turning her, urging her forward; she was already entering the room—

"And where did they come from?" a voice asked.

The common room was quiet; but it was not empty.

Every seat was taken, with a few people standing, as well, between the tables or back near the walls. The chairs in front of the hearth had been pulled away, creating an open space that seemed almost a stage.

Two men were there. One stood slightly aside: a dark, heavyset man, whose wiry black hair was worn woven into a complicated braid down his back. By Lorren and Eamer's description, and by the air of concern, responsibility, and authority with which he regarded the entire room, Rowan identified Joly, mayor of Donner.

The other man paced; not nervously, but patiently, as if prepared for a long wait. He seemed mildly concerned, faintly disappointed. He was small, round, white-haired, dressed in green and silver.

Jannik.

The wizard paused and looked up as the guard urged Rowan and her companions into the room. "I said, where did they come from?"

The guard shuffled his feet, and was a moment finding his voice. "Must've come in the back door. Sir."

"Well, post someone there; we have enough spectators as it is." Jannik gestured vaguely at the newcomers. "Find someplace to stand, out of the way." He returned to pacing.

Get out, Rowan's instincts told her again. But the wizard was uninterested in her; he had dismissed her; she was merely a member of a crowd. She could not flee without drawing attention to herself.

Wait. Find out what's going on. Stay calm.

She composed herself. Rowan had no talent for feigned emotion. She resorted instead, as she often had in the past, to attempting to erase from her outward demeanor every trace of emotion. This she had learned to do; and at the moment it was the best she could manage.

It took such concentration that for a period she did not see at all clearly, only knew that Gregori was urging her to a standing place far back on the left wall, well away from the hearthside where Jannik continued his patient pacing, and Joly, composed but wary, watched him.

Rowan found herself among unfamiliar faces that glanced at her incuriously. Some people were standing, some sitting with half-empty mugs and tea cups on the tables around, and the remains of a few late or early meals. No one drank; no one ate.

Willam was beside Rowan. She tried not to look at him, for fear that her face would betray the significance of his presence. He remained half-seen, a tall shape beside her, a glimpse of white hair high in the corner of her right eye.

Rowan took slow and deep breaths, and began to calm, began to assemble the scene before her, began to search, unobtrusively, for Bel.

There. The far side of the room. Against the wall. The Outskirter managed to appear as disturbed and confused as everyone else in the room, but Rowan recognized Bel's stance: relaxed, easy, but balanced and alert. If action became necessary, Bel would be ready.

Rowan picked out other persons known to her: Ruffo, seated not far from Rowan; the mate from *Graceful Days*, and her husband, the ship's navigator, whose hand she held; two day maids; most of the serving staff; the head groom.

Ona was seated at a table to the front, among three other women near her age, who all resembled her strongly. Naio stood beside her.

Rowan heard Gregori ask, quietly, "What's on?"

Someone nearby replied, in a whisper: "No one knows. He came in, told everyone to stay put, and wait while—" Jannik paused, and without turning raised one finger; the person who spoke silenced. The wizard smiled thinly, then resumed pacing.

No one else spoke; but there were many glances, between friends, between strangers, and small shrugs of confusion. Naio rested his hand briefly on Ona's shoulder, and she looked up at him, then caught sight of Rowan across the room. She gave the steerswoman a small nod of acknowledgment; then something occurred to her. She blinked in thought, then quickly looked away.

When the wizard's pacing brought him back in Rowan's direction, Ona's gaze again shied off, as she tried very hard, and continued to try, never to look in the steerswoman's direction again.

Rowan desperately hoped that this was obvious only to her.

She must try to be more natural herself. Puzzlement would be the most natural emotion, and most people here were both puzzled and wary.

But if at this moment Rowan showed any emotion at all, it would be fear. She could not let that be seen. She closed her eyes a moment, attempted to become more clear, more truly calm. She managed to achieve a peculiar detachment. When she opened her eyes, she did what everyone else was doing: she watched the wizard.

He was a small man, about Rowan's own height, and not quite portly. His short hair was white, as was his beard, which was close, trim, and pointed. He wore dark green trousers, with silver piping; a white blouse, silk; a green-and-silver embroidered vest tight across the stomach, loose elsewhere. On the armchair nearby, a cloak, light enough to be purely decorative, spilled a bright glory of green satin and white raw silk.

Jannik paused his pacing, turned to address Joly. "Who else of the council are still missing?"

Joly said, "Irina and Marel." His voice was deep. There was no subservience in his stance. He seemed not afraid, but grimly alert.

"Would the messengers have reached them by now?" Jannik asked him.

"Yes," Joly said. "Assuming they are at home." Rowan found herself admiring his calm, his immense dignity. She wondered, suddenly and irrelevantly, at his history.

The wizard considered, mildly annoyed. He glanced at the crowd. "Well. You may as well make yourselves comfortable. This may take a while." Jannik began pacing again, with such perfect nonchalance that Rowan understood that it was all for show. The wizard was, in fact, enjoying himself.

A few people shifted uneasily: what, under these circumstances, might constitute making oneself comfortable?

Halfway around the room, near the street door, Beck blinked a few times, thought, gave the tiniest of shrugs, took a tray from the limp hands of a nearby serving girl, and began to collect empty mugs and dishes. His smooth efficiency astonished Rowan.

He had worked his way to the table in front of her before Jannik took notice. "What are you doing?" He seemed both aggrieved and amused.

Beck stopped, looked at the wizard, looked at the tray in his hands, and by way of reply, lifted it slightly to show exactly what he was doing.

"Well, stop it," Jannik said, and went back to pacing.

Beck shrugged—and, in a move conducted with perfect naturalness, casually handed Rowan the loaded tray, jerked his head in the direction of the kitchen door, and turned away, exactly as if instructing and dismissing some minor member of the serving staff.

Rowan stood a moment stunned. Then, as smoothly as possible, she turned and began sidling through the tables, carrying her load to the kitchen.

The door was before her, and open. At the far end of the kitchen, invisible from Jannik's perspective, the undercook, crouched under a preparing table, was beckoning urgently. If Rowan could reach the kitchen, she could lay low until this was over. Whatever might be afoot, it would be best for all present if the steerswoman were absent.

"You." Rowan did not need to wonder whom the wizard was addressing. She was merely ten feet from the kitchen. She stopped, looked back.

Jannik looked mildly annoyed. "What did I just tell that boy? Put that down."

The people around Rowan seemed not to recognize her. She must seem merely a new hireling, behaving stupidly.

Across the room, Bel was wearing a similar expression. But all eyes watched Rowan.

The steerswoman set the tray down on the nearest table. While doing so, using the tray as a shield, she slipped her ring from her hand, and put it into her pocket.

Her chain was already well concealed, under her vest. If no one spoke up, she would remain anonymous.

No one spoke up. No one spoke at all. The people waited, silent, watching as a bird watches a snake. And Jannik paced.

After a space of time, Joly, with careful precision, crossed to the armchair where Jannik's cloak lay, picked it up, rearranged it to lie across and down the chair back, and sat. Jannik paused to watch him, almost fondly, seeming charmed by the man's audacity. On his part, Joly displayed not the slightest trace of fear, only a dignified determination.

This show of calm seemed to reassure the crowd. Some relaxed slightly. One woman spoke quietly to a table companion, inspiring a sudden sharp glance from Jannik.

The woman silenced instantly, but Jannik continued to regard her for a moment, with an odd fascination. Then the wizard smiled a small smile, and paced away again.

Rowan noticed that Jannik had acquired, from somewhere, a pair of black gloves. She had not seen him don them; he was wearing them now.

The street door opened, held by a very nervous girl. Stepping past her, Marel entered. The wizard glanced up. "Ah, good, Marel. Welcome to my little gathering. Someone give him a chair, please: he's elderly." There was a commotion outside. Jannik said to the messenger: "What's going on?"

The girl stuttered, sputtered, was unable to reply, overcome at being addressed by a wizard. Jannik tilted his head at her. Some braver soul seated near the door spoke up: "It's Reeder. He wants to come in."

"Reeder?"

"Marel's son," Joly said.

"Oh, yes, that's right. By all means, let the fellow in." Reeder entered, uncharacteristically disheveled, breathless. The guard from outside, holding his arm, directed him to a standing place near the door and set him free. Reeder threw the man a wild glance, then scanned the room, finding Naio, and Ona, and eventually Rowan.

Jannik had already dismissed Reeder. He said to the guard, "Is there any sign of Irina yet?"

The guard was nervous. "She—the boy we sent—"

"Yes?"

"—Her family say she's up at her orchards. Sir."

"And *is* she?"

"Uh..."

"Never mind. Go out, close the door, don't let anyone else in. I think we have enough here. Let's see ..." He turned back, strolled to the hearth, paused as if waiting for the crowd's attention. This was entirely unnecessary; no one was looking at anything else.

The wizard made a dramatic and expansive gesture in Joly's direction. "Our honorable mayor." Joly's only reaction was the slightest narrowing of his eyes.

Another gesture took in several members of the crowd, seated in various locations. "The city council—well, most of them." The persons indicated spared each other sidelong glances. Then Jannik spread his arms to include everyone present, and smiled. "Disinterested witnesses—more than enough, I should think. And..."

He dropped his hands, spoke precisely: "Thorns in my side..." He sighed, as if sadly. "Well... at least one is present." And moving with such casualness that no one reacted, he took two easy steps to his left, reached out, and laid his hand on the center of Naio's chest.

For an instant Naio's brown eyes looked down into the blue of the wizard's—

Then: a sound, like the slamming of a door the size of the world.

Naio's limbs flung out, rigid; as if struck by some huge blow, he was thrown backward, crashing into a table behind him. The table overturned, and he fell to the floor.

The air smelled of smoke, and of mountain-tops.

Jannik turned, strolled away, one finger raised as if thoughtfully making a point. "Now, we have a problem," he began—

—exactly as if the people were not now on their feet, shouting, crying out, some pulling back, their chairs falling; as if others were not clutching at Naio, trying to bring him to his feet; as if Ona had not screamed his name, and thrown herself on him; as if Reeder had not emitted a strangled cry, and begun fighting his way through the tables toward him; as if Rowan herself had not made a noise, something between a shout and a choked wail of "No!"; as if others were not doing the same; as if panic and chaos did not fill the room.

The wizard stopped and looked back, suddenly expressionless. Joly, already on his feet, saw Jannik's face. The shock on his own transformed into something more urgent. He stepped quickly forward, put himself with his back toward the wizard, facing the crowd, his arms wide, hands out, in a plea for quiet, stillness.

The people subsided, almost as one, suddenly silent, suddenly still, but for a knot around Naio, who was sprawled on the floor with Ona holding his face, calling his name, begging him to answer; and a quieter knot around Reeder, as those nearby resisted shifting to let him pass; and another small pocket of movement, which it took Rowan a moment to understand was centered on Willam.

He was struggling to move forward; he seemed to want to get to Naio. Gregori had him by the arm, pulling him back. Will tried to shake off the captain's hand. Gregori roughly yanked him back, shoved him against the wall, spoke to him quietly, uncomprehending but urgent. Will stared, wild-eyed, and suddenly subsided, head down, eyes closed, fists clenched at his sides.

Rowan could not let this continue.

Jannik had paused in the center of the open area, watching Joly. Should he move a few steps forward, Rowan would be directly behind him, a bit more than ten feet away.

One kills a wizard by surprise, Willam had told Bel. It's the only way.

Her sword was with the dragons. Her field knife was in her pack, in her room.

The diners at the table in front of Rowan had dined on cold boar: three very sharp dinner knives were close at hand.

Wait, she told herself; and mentally addressed the wizard, in something almost like a prayer: *Keep looking where you're looking, but take three steps forward.*

Across the room, Bel took note of the steerswoman's sudden intensity, adjusted herself slightly.

With the crowd now stilled again, the mayor turned his attention to the people on their knees beside Naio. He caught the gaze of one man, moved his head infinitesimally: a question. The reply, as small, was a shake of the head.

Despite the smallness of the movements, Ona saw and understood. The wailing cry she gave out, with all her breath, seemed to come from somewhere deeper even than her heart; the core of her bones, perhaps.

Several things happened at once.

The wizard moved two steps forward.

Rowan moved closer to the table with the knives.

Reeder looked up from where Ona was clinging to her husband; looked up and then stood frozen, staring, pale, wide-eyed, past the wizard—directly at Rowan.

She saw his lips move: *You.*

Then he made a sound, but no word: a cracked noise, as if something had broken in the back of his throat. He pushed through the people, flung himself into the open space, toward Rowan.

But the wizard was between them. Jannik stepped back, and aside, startled, threw one hand up—

Then Bel, somehow, was beside Reeder. She clutched his arm, and spun him around. "Are you insane?"

Reeder struggled in Bel's grip. *"Let go!"* He managed to turn them both around again, and now Bel was in front of Reeder, between him and the wizard.

Bel said, "You can't attack a wizard!" But Jannik was not Reeder's target; did Bel not know that?

"No—" Reeder choked out, and tried to push past her.

"Listen to me!" The Outskirter had him by the elbows, did something, some move, some yank-and-twist that made the tall man stagger to one side, and fall to his knees, and Bel clutched his collar, shouted down into his face. "You can't harm him! Don't you know that?"

"I don't—"

"Think! *Think!*" Bel shook him. "The wizards have too much power, you've just seen that. Do you think anyone can stand against them? They can do what they want, do you think that anyone can stop any of them? One of *us?* Some member of the common folk?

"What do you think it would take, to stop them, to stand against them? Can you even imagine? All the things they can do, all the things they know—do you think we could ever match that? Do you think *you* could?"

Jannik had relaxed somewhat. He said, with a condescending amusement, "Oh, you should listen to her; she's making a great deal of sense."

"You know you can't. Who could?" Bel demanded of the man on his knees, the man gripped in her two fists. "Who in the whole world could ever know enough to strike against a wizard?"

Rowan watched as Reeder's face, open and unguarded, showed him beginning to understand... then understanding completely.

Bel relaxed, spoke more quietly. "Don't be a fool. Don't make this worse."

And Reeder looked past Bel's face, across the entire room; and for a long moment, he and Rowan held each other's gaze.

The steerswoman waited.

Jannik stirred, slightly, uncertainly: he seemed to sense something amiss. He looked over his shoulder.

But Rowan was no longer looking at Reeder; there was nothing to distinguish her from the others present; she was a face among faces.

Jannik's suspicion wavered, waned. He turned back to the crowd at large, considered them a moment, then spoke. "Well. As I was saying, we have a problem. You are all in a great deal of danger, and you don't know it." He paused, made a self-deprecating gesture. "And not from me, although you may not believe that at the moment."

He began to pace again, thoughtfully, gloved hands behind his back. Someone gave Reeder a chair; Bel helped him to sit.

"No," the wizard went on, "our problem, our *mutual* problem, is that this city has an enemy. You all know his name, although none of you has ever seen him." He faced them again. "It's Olin. That's right"—he strolled again—"the Red wizard, against whose forces some of our citizens fought so bravely during the last conflict." Rowan thought for a moment that he was referring to the battle Eamer had seen as a child, then remembered: the more recent war, when Shammer and Dhree had established their own holding.

"Perhaps some of you present took part in that conflict yourselves?" Jannik asked. He paused as if for response; predictably, none came. "No? Well, each of you knows someone who did, perhaps even a family member.

Perhaps a family member who did not return.

"But what you do not realize is that this Olin is causing trouble again. No, you've been mercifully ignorant of the fact. But I'll tell you now—" And here he became suddenly furious, suddenly terrible, as he flung out his arms, and shouted: *"He's trying to free the dragons!"*

Startlement from the crowd, then fear, passing by glances among the people. "Oh, you don't know," Jannik said, moving again, his steps now quick, agitated, "how I've been struggling against him, you don't know what strange battles, magic against magic, have been taking place, invisible to you, while you went about, so complacently, in your easy daily lives. You don't know—because I don't tell you of these things. You don't need to know of them. Those responsibilities are given to me... and only a wizard can stand against a wizard."

He turned to them again, a look of pained innocence painted on his face. "Haven't I always tried to protect you?" he asked. "Haven't I served this city, faithfully, for more than forty years? But now, Olin," he became spiteful again, "with his tricks and subterfuges, his little games—have you never wondered why he lives so isolated, in no city, nor even a town or village? He doesn't care about people.

"For him, it's all for amusement. The inconceivable powers of magic are his toys, and people—I think, sometimes, that he must laugh when they get in the way..." He paused, and seemed very sad. "Yes, I do think that sometimes."

Reeder sat watching Jannik with a fascination of naked hatred. Bel still stood beside him. And Willam—

Will had remained where he was, against the back wall. His pose seemed to have changed not at all. His head was down, his eyes closed, hands clenched at his sides—

His lips were moving, silently.

Rowan felt a sudden flare of hope, and a stab of fear: an incantation? Could Will possibly act against Jannik directly?

Trying to keep her face neutral, Rowan watched Will unobtrusively, watched his lips...

Willam was counting. He was merely counting. He had reached 612. When the wizard shouted again, Will startled, but did not open his eyes, nor stop his counting—

"A dragon escaped!" There were sounds of fear from the people. "Yes, Olin succeeded—briefly. And only with a great struggle was I able to cast the spells to confine it again, and send it back to the dragon fields. It had been heading toward the city!"

It had not been. Rowan and Will had been very careful about that.

"But this danger is not over. Even now, Olin is still trying to break my spells, trying to set the dragons free to wreak havoc on this city. The battle of magic continues... and yet"—he seemed to speak simply now—"here I am. And here you are. Why are we here? And what has this to do with—" He gestured. "—poor Naio?

"Naio had been cooperating with an agent of Olin." Muted sounds of disbelief from the crowd. "No, it's true. One of your number, one single wise citizen, had the sense to inform me. Through either malice or simple credulity, Naio allowed himself to be taken in by a minion of Olin's, and to assist in the undermining of my power. This minion, this wicked person, has been working under the guise of a steerswoman.

"What an excellent disguise that is! Steerswomen are harmless. Steerswomen are pointlessly curious, like children. Steerswomen are indulged by the common folk—sometimes, I feel, merely for the distraction and amusement they provide. And I have nothing at all against them...

"But I tell you now: this woman is a false steerswoman! She has been abusing your kindness, she has been working for Olin, and anyone assisting her"—his pale blue eyes grew hard—"is assisting Olin himself. Our enemy."

Rowan's vision shrank to a small space centered on the wizard. There seemed to her to be nothing else in the world.

Jannik still did not know that she was here.

"I see some of you are beginning to show... a touch of nervousness, shall we say? Some of you have also helped this person? Well... be easy. Naio was by way of example. Sometimes... I'm afraid that sometimes people do need an example." Sadly. "Yes. They have to be reminded. I'm going to assume that the rest of you were merely taken in by this clever person, and aided her in complete ignorance."

And every eye in the room was on Rowan.

There could be no escape. It would only take one touch of the wizard's deadly hands. In a struggle, more people might get hurt, in error or through negligence. Rowan must step forward.

And now the wizard, too, had turned and was looking in her direction—

But not at her face...

A tug on Rowan's trouser leg. She looked down.

A small form, a small face with a huge grin, a small hand holding up to her a folded bit of paper. The handkerchief boy.

Get away from him—or get him away from her. He must not be near when the wizard touched her.

But do not startle him. Cause no panic.

Rowan took the paper from his hand, unfolded it, gazed at the scrawled drawing with half-blind eyes, and said to the boy: "Thank you very much."

She raised her eyes to find the wizard Jannik standing directly before her.

He was looking, not at her, but down at the child, as if some interesting thought was occurring to him, and he showed a strange, hard-eyed amusement.

Rowan said, immediately: "Let him go." The wizard transferred his glance to Rowan, seeming amazed that she would dare to speak to him.

And, forcing herself to remain composed, she gathered her strength, drew a breath to speak further, to say, as calmly as possible: *I'm the one you want—*

"Sir. Wizard. Jannik." He looked back.

The head groom had crossed the entire room, was now standing in the open area, with no one around her, no comfort or support from anyone. Only Joly was nearby, behind her, watching her with open astonishment and admiration.

The head groom said: "Sir, he's only a child. He doesn't understand what's happening here. He won't learn from it. He won't even remember it. He'll just get scared, for no good end. Let us take him out of here."

Jannik studied her a moment, then scanned the crowd, slowly, evaluatively; and Rowan understood that he was deciding what act would best serve him at this moment. The boy, perhaps sensing Rowan's own tension, had shrunk back against her legs. Jannik looked down at him, raised one hand, and Rowan hissed an intake of breath; Jannik glanced at her, amused, regarded his own hand as if realizing that he could not, at the moment, safely tousle the lad's hair. He smiled at his own foolishness, and turned and walked away.

The groom passed him quite close, almost brushing against him as she hurried to the boy. Jannik himself politely stepped aside as she went by.

Arrived, the woman and Rowan regarded each other for a moment, the head groom with relief, Rowan with resignation. *Get him away from me,* Rowan told her silently, hoping the woman understood.

She did not. With a careful show of calm for the child's benefit, the head groom took one of his hands in hers, and very deliberately placed his other hand in Rowan's.

No. No, she would not use a child for cover, for protection.

But the groom was already trying to lead them off, and the boy was tugging impatiently at Rowan's hand.

The steerswoman looked around the room.

Jannik was playing at indifference and nonchalance, his back now toward her as he idly paced the edge of the crowd. Of the people, all eyes were on her, and at that moment Rowan realized Jannik's error.

He had hoped to inspire obedience by fear, and justify it with a show of reason. This was exactly the reverse of what he ought to have done.

There are some things they don't understand at all, Willam had said of the wizards. And among these, apparently: the heart of the common folk.

Because every face in the room was speaking to Rowan silently, saying: *Go.*

Even the faces known to her. Even those who knew her to be the steerswoman Jannik sought. Especially those.

Bel's dark gaze, saying: *Go;* Willam's copper eyes, half blind with concentration, as part of him continued, under his breath, to count, and the rest of him pleaded with her to leave.

And more:

Marel, seated near the door, urging her to take this chance; the two serving girls, wanting Rowan to do it; the head cook, frightened on her behalf.

And at the front of the crowd, at its very edge: Reeder, stripped of his arrogance and posturing, his pale green eyes unmasked, showing her what she needed to understand this:

Hope. Desperate hope.

What do you think it would take, to stand against a wizard? Bel had asked him; *Who, among the common folk, could ever do such a thing?*

The steerswoman had to live.

The boy tugged at her hand again. Rowan allowed the woman and the child to lead her.

They could not use the street door without bringing the boy close to Naio's corpse. They went toward the main staircase.

They were at its foot when Jannik spoke. "Wait." Rowan and the woman stopped, the boy looking up at them in annoyance. "I think only one of you needs to go," the wizard said.

The head groom stood with her eyes squeezed shut; and then, with careful deliberation, she let go of the boy's hand.

Rowan felt an emotion that she was utterly incapable of putting into words. She prepared to climb the stairs.

But the boy had finally caught the full force of the tension, and the fear, that filled the room behind them. Uncomprehending, and suddenly desperate, he flung himself against the head groom's knees, clutched them with one hand, buried his face against her trouser legs, whining: "Gramm*eee!*"

The two women exchanged a long glance. Then the steerswoman released the boy's hand, stepped away; and the people watched as his grandmother led him up the long staircase, and out of sight.

Rowan carefully composed her emotions, and her expression, and turned back to watch the wizard.

She would live to see him fall. She swore this to herself, and promised it to the people of Donner.

"Now," Jannik said, "our next step is quite obvious. In order to focus my attentions on Olin's direct attack against my protection against the dragons, I need this spying, this subterfuge, to cease. I want Olin's agent. I want the false steerswoman. I will deal with her"—here he glanced once at Naio's corpse, where Ona still knelt, her face buried against her husband's chest—"in my own way. Whoever among you knows where she is, speak."

Someone spoke, immediately. "I've seen her," Ruffo said.

Jannik smiled a broad smile. "There, you see? How simple. Ruffo, where is she?"

"She rode out," the innkeeper said. "Yesterday morning."

"Rode out?" Jannik's brows knit. "To where?"

"Well, I don't know that. Just riding around, for pleasure was what I heard..."

"Now, that's almost certainly not true," Jannik said, speaking as if to a child. "It was a ruse. Did you see what direction she went?"

"No, just out of the yard. On one of my best hire-horses, too, and for free, and if she's as false as you say, she won't be bringing it back, I'll bet, and who's going to pay for that?"

The wizard lost his smile. "I do hope that you're not actually looking to me for remuneration?"

Ruffo's bravado faltered, and he sputtered: "No, no, sir, I meant nothing by it—"

"He's just rattling on," Joly said to Jannik calmly. "He does that; it's just his way."

"Of course. Everyone knows how Ruffo rambles." Jannik scanned the crowd. "Who else saw her go?"

No one replied, but one of the serving girls began to jitter. The other punched her in the arm to settle her.

Jannik did not fail to notice, and fixed the pair with a sharp eye. "Yes?"

The jittering girl was beyond speech. Her companion screwed up her own courage. "We seen them go. We was helping out Sherrie, cleaning one of the back suites upstairs. Watched from a window. Out of the yard and north on Branner's Road, they went."

This interested the wizard. " 'They'? Someone was with her?"

The girl blinked, but could not deny it now. "That's so. Some fellow with her. No one I know."

"What did he look like?"

And the girl looked the wizard straight in the eye and said: "Small. Dark. Pretty little thing he was, too. I think she picked him up in one of the fun-houses."

The wizard spread his hands and addressed the crowd at large. "Now, there, do you see? Is that proper behavior for a real steerswoman? Consorting with a prostitute?"

"I guess a steerswoman needs her fun, the same as anyone else," Gregori said.

This inspired a glare from the wizard. "And have *you* seen her?"

"No."

Jannik was suspicious, but let it pass. "Who else?"

Someone stirred uncertainly at a back table toward the right of the room. The wizard said nothing, but tilted his head, eyes narrowed.

A middle-aged gentleman, well dressed, and a complete stranger to Rowan, rose formally and cleared his throat. "I saw them pass by my establishment, early yesterday morning. West, on Iron-and-Tin Street."

"Hm. And this, small, dark man... I don't suppose he is an employee at your own, ah, 'establishment'?"

"No," spoken definitely, "he was not." A moment's thought; Rowan was impressed by the man's composure. "But I wouldn't put it past him to claim to be. He came to me, two days ago, looking for work. I turned him down. The way he said it, that he'd do anything at all for money: it made me feel that he might be an altogether unsavory sort. I run a wholesome house, sir."

" 'Anything at all for money,' " the wizard mused. "I find that interesting. Very likely this minion of Olin lured him to work with her, promising some reward. I wonder if he survived the experience?"

Jannik waved the bawdy-house owner back to his seat, and turned away. "They were seen to leave; has anyone seen them return?"

There was no reply.

"The timing does fit..." Jannik said. "It was yesterday that the one dragon did escape, briefly. A very close call, it was, too. We were lucky. But I do wonder. I wonder about all those questions she was asking..." He paused; seemed to come back to himself; and, regarding the crowd, he sighed a sad and patient sigh. "Now, do you see? These people are working, not just against me, but against all of us." Abruptly and inexplicably, he looked up at the ceiling. A number of people in the crowd, Rowan included, could not help but do the same. "Hm," the wizard said, with apparent satisfaction. "Well." He addressed the people again. "I have no more time to waste here. I do need to go to the dragon fields, immediately, to try to rectify the damage, and restore the protective spells. And"—he glanced upward again, gave a small smile—"I need to get there rather more quickly than the usual means will provide."

Rowan felt a vibration in the pit of her stomach, like a note too deep to be heard, but loud enough to be sensed. She noticed a discomfort among the people; some of them looked about, perplexed.

Across the room, Willam, still counting, was looking at the ceiling.

"So," Jannik continued, and began to stroll across the hearthside again, "I'll be taking my leave, shortly, for a period."

Rowan's ears were ringing—no; the sound was outside her head. Like the highest notes of a demon-voice...

The people stirred, uneasy, as the noise increased. In the center of the room, Bel froze in the perfect motionlessness required in the presence of a demon; but it was no demon-voice.

Jannik spoke, now needing to raise his voice. "If the so-called steerswoman returns to Donner, whoever sees her will inform the city guard." Outside, a sudden rush of wild wind spun dust into the open street windows. "And the city guard"—Jannik turned to the mayor, spoke above the noise—"will hold her until my return."

Willam had transferred his gaze to the street door. Rowan did the same; and an instant later, it blew open, slamming against the wall, admitting furious wind. Door and windows spilled hard, white light into the room.

People cried out, shielded their eyes against dust and brightness. Some rose, tried to flee back from it. The wizard commanded: *"Stay where you are!"* The people froze; only Ona moved. Her face blank with her pain, she raised her head and stared blindly into the whiteness and the wind.

The light from the door dimmed. The noise subsided. The wind died. The dust began to settle.

Jannik smiled. "My transportation has arrived." And the stunned crowd, in scattered movements, slowly turned back toward the small, round, white-haired man. "I'll be leaving now—but I want you to remember something..."

He took a more formal pose, and his gaze moved across every person in the room. "I am your protector. I am the only thing that stands between this city and the dragons, and between this city and Olin's evil tricks. If you involve yourself in matters of magic, you set yourself against me.

"If you cannot behave correctly out of loyalty to the city, and gratitude toward me"—he paused; his blue eyes were hard, bright, sharp—"then do it out of fear."

He walked again, slowly, along the edge of the crowd, looking into each individual face as he passed. "Naio was working against me." The woman before him leaned back in fear. "It does not matter if he intended to or not." Another step, another face, an elderly man who trembled visibly. "Anyone meddling in the matters of wizards is my enemy." He had reached the end of the room; he doubled back. "I've shown you the results of meddling." A young woman covered her face as he walked by, then buried it against the shoulder of the older woman beside her. "I hope you never have to see such a thing again."

At the center, he paused before Reeder, who stared with open, unblinking hatred, and Bel, standing calmly beside him. "You should remember," Jannik told the people, "what this extremely intelligent woman told you." He passed on. "And you should remember what you've seen here tonight.

"Naio," he said, and now his eyes were on Rowan, and she fought to keep her hatred from showing, "was an example." He moved to the next person. "I don't like having to make examples—" He moved on. "But I will if I must." He had reached the left edge of the crowd, chose a single face, a burly man ashen with fear. The wizard stepped close, looked up, addressed the man quietly but clearly. "As often as is necessary." Jannik turned back. "And do not expect me to be so selective, so fair and just, the next time. I frankly cannot be bothered. I will make an example of anyone I choose, any time I choose, merely to *make you understand!*"

He moved his gaze across the entire crowd, slowly. "Anyone," he said again. Then he looked left.

"You, for instance," he said to Rowan. "You've been entirely too calm through all of this." He laid his hand on her chest. "You're dead."

CHAPTER SEVENTEEN

Gray...

Gray again, and shadows...

Gray, and shadows, and a roar like water, like the Dolphin Stair...

Gray again, and shadows, moving—
Rowan breathed in.

Light and dark spattered across her vision. The breath she had taken escaped...

Rowan breathed in.

Bel: weirdly shallow looking, two-dimensional, too bright. Her lips were moving.

Rowan exhaled, all at once, too quickly, leaving her so empty that at once she breathed in, just as quickly, and colors faded, and grayed...

Hands on her, a dizzying movement; then she was sitting up. The roar of water, and behind it, the humming voices of a hundred demons.

Bel's face, close, and Rowan was being shaken by the shoulders. She lost Bel's face, found it again.

Beside Bel, someone. A stranger.

No: copper eyes. Willam. He seemed surprised. How odd...

There was something she ought to do. She could not recall what it was.

Gray rose again...

Bel shook her, violently, shouted in her face, her voice tiny, distant: *"Breathe!"*

Rowan breathed in.

She kept breathing in, one continuous inhale; she wished that her body, the whole of it, was entirely hollow; that she might continue to breathe in, endlessly, to fill every corner of herself with air.

When she could fit no more, it all went out again, by itself. She missed it; she was empty.

It took her a moment to know what to do.

She breathed.

Willam was gone…

Bel said something. Rowan heard, but could not match words to sounds. Rowan looked at her, utterly uncomprehending; but from somewhere, she heard, quite clearly, Willam's voice, calling out urgently and inexplicably: *"Where are the sailors?"*

Abruptly, colors paled, and Rowan struggled weakly, for no reason she could identify.

Bel shook her again. "Breathe," the Outskirter told her; Rowan breathed.

She concentrated on breathing, in, out. It took all her will and intelligence to continue to breathe.

Bel turned, spoke to someone behind her. The person departed.

There were many faces, all around and above. Rowan was sitting on the floor.

"How do you feel?" Bel asked her. The steerswoman was dimly surprised that the words now made sense. But it took her time, several long breaths, to gather enough reason in herself to find the answer, and more to find the words to state the answer.

"My feet hurt." As if some cruel person were twisting both her ankles, and jabbing a knife into her heel.

"Wait." Bel turned away; the pain in Rowan's ankles vanished, and she suddenly found herself in control of her own legs. She drew up her knees. Her heel still hurt.

"See?" someone said, one of the people standing. "See, that was all a lie, what the wizard said."

Someone was behind Rowan, had been all along, supporting her where she sat. She looked up and back, and found a pale, dark-haired person whose name she could not retrieve.

Bel took Rowan's face in her hands, turned the steerswoman's head back, looked closely at her eyes. "Do you know where you are?"

Rowan was breathing more smoothly, now; but the act was sweet, and precious, and she would not burden it with words. She shook her head.

"Do you know *who* you are?"

Rowan nodded in Bel's hands. She felt cold, and damp, and suddenly wanted fresh air on her body, directly on her skin. The idea was irresistible. She tried to stand.

They helped her, as far up as the chair, and she sat, unable to rise further. She groped awkwardly at the buttons on her vest. Bel pushed her hands aside, and undid them, and removed the vest.

The steerswoman shivered, chilled by her sweat-drenched blouse. She wished she could remove it. Bel untied the lacings at Rowan's throat, opened the collar wide; it helped.

Bel stopped short and muttered something. Rowan looked down.

On the skin of her chest, red marks of broken surface blood vessels: five lines, in a fan shape.

"Bel," Rowan said, only because she was able to, only because the Outskirter was the one known familiar thing here, and it seemed to her important that she put names to things.

Bel looked up, grinned weakly. "That's right. How do you feel?"

The answer took some time. "Slow. Empty." She looked at her hands, then tried to push her sleeves up to her elbows. She could not do it.

Bel did it for her; the cold air was sharp on her forearms, but welcome. "Will thinks you'll be all right," Bel said.

Rowan nodded, distantly. "He was here..."

Bel looked right; Rowan followed her gaze, finding that her head moved in a wide, dizzying arc, and she struggled to orient correctly to vertical.

She could make no sense of what she saw. She identified, slowly, elements: tables, chairs, people, some standing, some kneeling or crouched on the floor. Some action was taking place—

The action had sense, order. Abruptly, as if with a snap, she recognized it.

Willam was kneeling on the floor beside a still figure, his hands, one atop the other, pushing down on the center of the man's chest, rhythmically. The man's head had been pulled back, and someone was breathing into his mouth—

It was the drill known well to every sailor, the actions to take to foil death itself, to pull back into the arms of life a person dead from drowning.

"He needs air," Rowan said, stupidly.

"Yes..." Bel said. And his heart, too, Rowan thought: his heart must remember what to do.

She realized that Bel's fingers were tight on her wrist, counting Rowan's pulse. At that thought, Rowan's heartbeat became discernible to herself, and she realized that it had been all along. But it seemed to be everywhere, in every part of her body. It was too forceful, and it was far too slow.

As Rowan watched, the man at the victim's head stopped, looked up, put his hand gently on Willam's shoulder.

Will twisted, shaking it off. "No. It's like drowning, but it's not *exactly* like. He could still come back."

If too much time had not passed, Rowan thought; but Will—and she remembered this, oddly, since she remembered nothing else—Will had been counting.

The man helping Willam gave up his place to a woman, a woman bleached and browned by sun. The man leaned back, watching Willam and the woman at work, then looked across at Rowan.

Salt-and-pepper hair, weather-darkened face. "Gregori," Rowan said. Identify, identify: match words to reality. The woman was—"Enid." The man on the floor: "Naio."

Gregori lifted Naio's hand, felt for the pulse, then studied the fingertips. He touched Enid's arm, once, and the woman stopped and sat back.

Will said again, immediately: "No."

"Lad…"

"No."

Gregori held up Naio's hand for Willam to see, then displayed the other. Rowan did not know why; from where she sat she could only see that the fingernails were black.

Willam stopped. His head dropped. Then he sat back as if falling back, and covered his face in his hands.

Enid moved away. Someone replaced her, but not to breathe for Naio; this woman laid one hand on Naio's cheek, and with the other gently stroked his long hair.

"Ona," Rowan said.

Movement behind her, then beside her, then passing her; but the man did not get far. Someone stood in his way, reached out gently to stop him.

An old man, and a younger one.

Marel, and Reeder.

"No," Marel said.

"Let me—"

"No…" Marel held Reeder by the arms, looked into his eyes, bright green to pale green. The two men were exactly the same height; Rowan was faintly surprised by this.

Marel said, quietly but distinctly: "Son… that's his *wife*."

The pale green eyes were blank with pain. Then Reeder closed them. Marel pulled a chair near, and Reeder folded down into it, and sat still and slack. Marel put one hand on his shoulder; and after a moment Reeder half turned, leaned, lay his face against his father. The old man held his son.

"You survived," someone said: a deep voice.

Rowan turned to see, but there were many eyes on her, and she could not tell who had spoken.

But a different voice spoke. "Because she's a steerswoman, she *truly* is. Steerswomen and sailors, so they say." A small man, in a shirt so yellow it burned Rowan's eyes.

What was it about steerswomen and sailors? "But," Rowan said, "the boots." She looked down. She was in her stocking feet.

Bel, kneeling before her, glanced back over her shoulder, and Rowan saw the boots standing behind the Outskirter. Their high shanks were flopped over.

Bel half turned, reached out, and tugged at one. It did not move. Rowan looked more carefully, concentrating.

The gum soles had melted to the floor.

Incredibly, someone laughed; laughed and kept laughing, utterly unrestrained.

The deep voice said: "She's mad!"

"No." Willam, now standing beside her, wiping his eyes with the heels of his hands. "That's normal. She'll be giddy, she can't help it." He stooped to her level. "Rowan," he said, "can you hear me?"

"Demons!" she declared, and that, too, was inexpressibly funny. "I hear Demons!"

Willam considered. "No, your ears are just ringing," he told her, as if speaking to a child. "That might take a while to go away. You were very lucky. You could have ended up deaf."

"Lucky," she confirmed, laughing happily, freely: lucky for the sweet air, that moved in her so easily now; for her body, which felt loose and weak, but present in every particular; lucky for the light she could see, the sounds she could hear—Abruptly, she remembered: fire in every nerve, each muscle clenched and knotted as if tearing from her bones, a blow, like a sledgehammer to her chest, and *pain*—

Bel was seated on the floor before her, holding her hand, counting her pulse. Willam was stooped beside her, serious, but showing a growing relief.

Above her, looking down: Joly, with Ruffo dithering beside him. "Gum-soled boots," Rowan said.

"You're the steerswoman," Joly said. "You're the one he wanted."

"But she *is* a steerswoman," Ruffo put in, "because, she survived, and that *proves* it. Jannik was lying to us all."

"No," Rowan said. She shut her eyes. Her wits were still scattered, like startled birds. She tried to retrieve them, coax them back, pluck them from the rafters and corners of the room—

Room. She was in a room. "I'm in the Dolphin," Rowan said.

"That's right," Willam told her. "Do you remember what happened?"

She remembered *pain* clearly, but was unable to recover what immediately preceded it. She puzzled.

"What did you mean by 'no'?" Joly asked her.

Will said, without looking up, "Give her some time. She's not all here yet." Beck appeared, with a small glass; Bel reached to take it, but Willam stopped her. "No. No alcohol. She could still stop breathing. Water."

"How do you know that?" Joly asked. He came nearer. "And how did you know what to do, what to try to do, for Naio?"

Then Willam did look up, his copper eyes unreadable. "Something like it happened to me, once," he said simply. "By accident."

Joly's gaze narrowed, and he glanced down, at Will's feet. Rowan wondered why, and she leaned forward to look down over Will's shoulder. Her movements were wide, clumsy, weirdly loose.

Gum-soled boots. Oh, clever. Good boy. "Everyone," she said cheerfully, "everyone should wear them."

"Happened to you? How?" Joly asked. Willam said nothing. "Meddling with magic?" Joly speculated. His eyes grew hard. "Then you're the one, the minion of Olin—"

"No one here," Bel said, "is a minion of anyone." She rose. "And when Rowan said no, she meant, *No, Jannik wasn't lying*—because he probably believes what he said. But it isn't so."

"But if she's the one he wanted..." His voice trailed off.

"You think you should just give her to him? Whether it's justified or not?" Bel moved, planting herself between Joly and Rowan. Seeing this, Willam rose, too, and placed himself solidly behind the steerswoman, resting his hands on her shoulders.

And despite the fact that the world consisted only of *now*, with memory before but shadows and mist—despite this, the steerswoman knew with perfect certainty that never before in her life had she felt so completely protected.

Violence before her, and magic behind her. With these, nothing could harm her.

"Right now," Bel said to Joly, "Jannik thinks Rowan has left town. There's no reason for him to know different."

"The only way he'd find out," Willam said, "would be from someone in this room. And you all know exactly what he'd do to her."

"But," someone said, "she'd live. The wizard can't hurt her, we just saw that."

"He can hurt her!" Willam said to the speaker. "If he had noticed she was wearing gum-soled boots, he would have just used more power. She would be just as dead as Naio." He turned back to Joly. "Although," Willam said, "if you handed Rowan over, I don't think Jannik would kill her quickly. No. I'm fairly certain he wouldn't."

Joly was a long time replying. "I have no intention of handing her over to the wizard." And he looked down at Rowan. "But she's very lucky that I didn't know, before all this, that Jannik was looking for her."

Rowan could not see Bel's face, but she saw when the Outskirter tilted her head slightly, heard the change in Bel's voice. "I like you," she said to Joly; this took him by surprise. "You remind me of myself. You'd protect your people. That's proper. But Jannik didn't give you the chance, did he, to protect your people? He killed first, talked later. That's what you're living with in Donner."

Joly considered these statements. Then he sighed, and pulled out a nearby chair, and began to sit.

Something he saw interrupted him. "Marlee," he called, across the room, "please stay here for the moment. Until this is resolved." He looked around; Rowan realized that the room was nearly empty. "Who has left?" A few names were mentioned, then more. "Are any of those people who know you by sight?" Joly asked Rowan.

In her mind, Rowan clutched at birds that were not there. She gave up. "Mayor," she said, honestly, "I'm not quite myself."

"Is she going to stay addle-pated?" Joly asked Willam.

"I didn't. Rowan." She looked up at him: directly up, which made his face upside down in her view. "What's the square root of four thousand and ninety-six?"

It had to be an integer; he was not likely to ask for a fraction. And 4,096 was not so very large a number. It was not worth working out the square root: she merely scanned squares of numbers below one hundred. "Sixty-four," she said.

"And the square root of that?"

Ridiculous: this took no thought at all. "Eight."

"She already has her wits," Willam said. "She's just still a bit stunned."

"How soon can she travel?" Will glared at Joly: a sudden, sharp anger. The mayor did not waver. "I want her away from the city. As soon as possible."

"Tomorrow morning," Bel said.

"No sooner than that?"

"We have business in town tonight."

Rowan felt Will's hands tighten on her shoulders.

Bel turned to Willam: "Will she be herself by twenty-three hundred?"

"Bel—" he protested.

"Their seyoh is working in the dark. That's wrong. He needs to know what's going on, in order to do what's right." Seyoh, Rowan thought: the leader of an Outskirter tribe. Joly, suddenly, did remind her very much of Kammeryn.

At this, the steerswoman realized that all her memory was in place. "I feel better," she told everyone. Although, apparently, she had not yet recovered her social graces; she had announced the fact as cheerfully and artlessly as a child.

"Good," Bel said. "Now, everyone listen." She glanced about, securing the people's full attention. Then she turned back to Rowan, and spoke in the formal mode. "Tell me, lady: why are you here in Donner?"

And at this cue, Rowan's mind, seemingly of itself, composed the information to answer. For a moment Rowan observed the process as if from afar; and then she entered it fully:

Kieran. Latitia. Unexpectedly, Slado.

One man turning good; another becoming evil.

An occurrence, one event happening on one specific night; and everything afterward falling from that, all the world shifting on that point.

One event. One fact.

The steerswoman said: "I'm here because power rests on knowledge. And no knowledge should be secret."

"Good." Bel took a chair, pulled it near, climbed up to stand on its seat. "Now," she said to the people, "listen to me."

And the Outskirter said, to Rowan's astonishment:

"Once upon a time…"

Bel told it all.

From its innocuous beginning, with Rowan discovering, in the course of her travels, the odd, flat, blue jewel; and becoming curious, as a steerswoman does; and asking questions; and finding at first as her only answer, the sudden interest of every wizard in the world—

Somewhere later in the tale, Rowan thought: I would have told it differently. She would have begun with the fallen Guidestar, spoken next of the destruction of the Outskirts, and what would result from it. She would have given them information.

But Bel, Rowan knew, was an artist. For her own people Bel had composed an epic poem, now circulating among the Outskirter tribes, moving across the land with a life of its own. The steerswoman was surprised that Bel had come to know Rowan's people so well that she could have constructed this: the Inner Lands version of the same tale, cast in familiar form, calling forth all the ways and manners of proper tales, drawing one in, moving the heart.

Rowan saw now that truly, this was the only way the story could be told. The information was intact, but participation in its unfolding made the knowledge each listener's personal possession.

The people listened.

At the point when Bel reached her and Rowan's first meeting with the fourteen-year-old boy with the talent for magic, the steerswoman realized that Willam was still in place, standing behind her, his hands on her shoulders. And it seemed to her now that it was more than protection; it was a declaration of affiliation. *He is with us. This is his story, too.*

Rowan closed her eyes, leaned her head back against him. When she opened them again, he had stooped down to study her face. "Do you want to sleep?"

She did not. She wanted to hear the tale, all of it. Perhaps Bel would continue, she thought, perhaps not stop at the present, but tell on: through all the struggles ahead, beyond the pain and terror that lay waiting in every dark adventure. Rowan wondered how it would end.

Willam was still regarding her, with solicitous patience.

The steerswoman said: "I'm so very tired."

He helped her to her feet, and the tale-teller paused, and all the listeners watched as Willam gently led the steerswoman away.

Rowan woke.

The room was quiet, and the light: a soft candle glow that did not flicker, but pulsed, once, twice, then steadied.

She was not alone. She said, uncomprehending: "Reeder?"

"Don't be alarmed." He looked up from his hands, which he had been studying idly. "I'm only here to ensure that you don't stop breathing in your sleep."

Rowan rubbed grit from her eyes. "But Willam, and Bel—"

"Your friends are occupied in discussions with Joly and the council, and the other remaining witnesses. My presence was not needed, as I've already made my position clear."

Rowan remembered, and sought words to adequately express her emotion. "Thank you for not betraying me."

He permitted himself a small twitch of a smile. "Thank the Outskirter."

She studied him. He seemed himself again: controlled, held at distance. Although, she noted, the disapproval he usually exuded was absent.

He accepted her scrutiny, perfectly composed. "You ought to go back to sleep. You have"—he picked up something from the table, something that trailed a string; he tilted the object to the candlelight—"four hours left."

Willam's tiny clock. Reeder set it down, and turned back. "Ah, yes, and I'm to ask you how you feel."

She took inventory. She felt, for the most part, a heavy weariness, as if she had been swimming for some long distance. Her ears still rang, but only faintly, a high, distant whine. The skin of her chest, below the collarbone and above her breasts, stung as if from some abrasion. She shifted a bit, pulled her collar forward, and looked down.

Still there: five lines on her skin, like the hand of a skeleton. She wondered if the marks were permanent.

Reeder watched with eyebrows lifted, as if mildly surprised that so dignified a person as herself would make so intimate an inspection in the presence of a stranger.

Her left leg ached dully; however one could hardly expect it to do otherwise, after two days' riding. Rowan was surprised that it was no worse.

But her right heel hurt. She sat up to examine it.

It had been bandaged while she slept. She did not remove the light wrapping, but considered the sensation of what lay beneath. It felt like a burn.

"He didn't even touch me there," she said.

"If you're inclined to make a more complete inspection, of all your body parts, please inform me. I prefer to be absent."

"My other body parts seem all to be in the right places," Rowan said, settling back thoughtfully.

"Fortunate. I'm to speak sternly to you if you show no inclination to rest; please assume that I've done so."

Rowan rubbed her face. "I don't think I could sleep..." Although, really, she ought to.

"I suggest that you lie still and close your eyes. Eventually, sheer boredom will work its effect." He leaned back in the chair, crossed his legs, adjusted the lay of his trouser leg. "If you feel someone shaking you, it will only be me, reminding you that air is necessary for life."

"I don't believe I'll ever forget that again."

She slept; it felt like forever.

She was aware, in her sleep, of a hand about to touch her. She woke a moment before it did.

Bel, with a satisfied smile, leaning back. "I see your instincts are all in place."

Rowan sat up, pushed her hair back. "How soon?"

"We have an hour to go. You should change your clothes, and wash up. You smell like a horse that's been struck by lightning." She paused. "Will doesn't want you going into Jannik's house."

"My wits are back," Rowan said, leaning forward to reach for her pack; Bel rose, and put it on the bed. "I'll probably limp, but I'm certain I can run, if we should need to."

The Outskirter nodded. "That's what I told him. But that's not it. He still doesn't want anyone else taking the risk. Especially now, especially you, after what Jannik did."

Rowan found a clean blouse, pulled her own over her head, and tossed it aside. "I am definitely coming."

She noticed Bel regarding her chest, narrow-eyed. "It looks far worse than it is," Rowan informed her. The steerswoman's gold chain lay draped across the skeletal hand, as if a ghost were trying to snatch it away.

"If you say so…"

The image reminded Rowan: "My ring." She rose, finding her heel painful but endurable, and reached into her pocket.

Nothing. She searched further; a hole…

Bel held the ring up, between thumb and forefinger. "Someone found it on the floor in the common room."

Rowan took the ring, slipped it on her scarred left hand. "Good," Bel said. "Now you're yourself again."

Rowan addressed herself to the ewer and pitcher, the soap and towel, that lay waiting on the table. Bel sat on the end of the bed, and pulled up her knees. She watched the steerswoman. "I've given Joly my names." Rowan stopped short.

Bel, Margasdotter, Chanly. An Outskirter possessed three names, the first used casually, the matronym and line name very sparingly. Knowledge of an Outskirter's names was proof of connection, and could protect one from attack by that person's tribe.

But Bel's own names meant far more. They were known now to all tribes, a password among all the Outskirters. "You don't think it's too soon for that?" Rowan asked.

"He's the leader of this city. His people will meet my people one day. When they do, they will know each other." Bel unfolded herself, and climbed off the bed. "Someone's bringing food, and strong tea. The boots are Enid's." She reached past Rowan to take Willam's magic clock from the table. "I'll go tell the others that you're up, and they should get into position."

Rowan was at sea. "Others?"

"We've enlisted some help," Bel said. "We need it."

Rowan washed, dressed. Tea was brought in, and toast, and eggs. The serving girl, with an almost proprietary air, insisted that Rowan eat immediately. "I won't take no, and that's a fact."

"Thank you," Rowan said, bemused. She recognized the young woman from the dining room, three mornings ago, and from the incidents in the common room. "You were very brave," Rowan told her.

The servant chuffed, and shifted her shoulders, pleased at herself. "And Jinny nearly giving it away, the goose. Had to think fast, or she'd have spilled. Think your hair will go white, like what happened to your friend? And is he planning to stay in town, do you know?"

"No. On both counts."

"That's a shame. I'll break the news to Jinny."

She left when Rowan settled down to the meal; and it occurred to the steerswoman that she would not have many more of the Dolphin's exceptional meals. Breakfast tomorrow, if all went well, and then all three of them must leave.

As she poured more tea, her glance fell on the letter, still sitting where she had left it. And because speculation on the coming events would do her no good, and she could use a distraction, she opened it, and arranged the pages to read while she finished eating.

The envelope had been addressed by a scribe; but the contents were in Artos's own hand, cramped but neat.

As Rowan expected: the news of Willam's escape—but also, many sad apologies on Artos's part.

Rowan had asked him to befriend Willam, and try to watch over him as best he could; the duke confessed that he had failed in this, that his good intentions had faltered in the face of his own duties, and the many requirements of Willam's. They had drifted apart.

Had Artos suspected that all was not well, had he realized that, for whatever reasons, life under the wizard's hand had become unbearable to Willam, every resource at the duke's command would have been called upon, nothing would have been too much to ask. Artos would have moved heaven and earth to help the apprentice escape.

Now, Artos said, Willam was alone, out in the wide world, fleeing. No one knew where he was, nor how to help him. Artos blamed himself.

Rowan wished that her words could fly through the air, to Wulfshaven, to whisper in Artos's ear, to tell him that their friend was not alone after all.

A knock on the door. "Rowan?"

The steerswoman folded the letter, set it aside, and rose to open the door.

Bel, her dark eyes intent, standing with the combination of ease and alertness that Rowan knew so well from the moments just before the Outskirter entered battle; and Willam beside her, his wide copper gaze serious, determined—and deeply, immensely calm.

Will held up one hand; the little clock dangled from it. He said: "It's time."

CHAPTER EIGHTEEN

*T*hey walked through the quiet streets of the city of Donner.

It was cold, as if near to winter, and the autumn constellations were winter-sharp, a spangling of stars high above the rooftops. Street doors were closed, window shutters pulled tight against the chill; and most of the city was asleep.

Rowan carried a lantern, partly shuttered, in one hand. Bel carried a sack of wheat flour from the kitchen stores at the Dolphin, slung across her shoulders. Willam carried his knotted burlap sack.

Bel's sword was slung at her back, in the fashion of the Outskirters. The sword at Rowan's waist was borrowed from the city guards' armory. Whatever weapons Willam possessed, if any, were not visible.

Only Bel's footsteps sounded against the cobbles, a small sound, seeming to vanish into the cold sky. Rowan and Willam, in gum-soled boots, moved silent as ghosts.

Up ahead, at a distance: one of the city guard, behaving exactly as if on duty as night watchman. When he reached East Well he shuttered his own lantern, leaned against the well, and withdrew from inside his cuirass a small bottle. He unstopped it, sipped. Its presence served as an excuse for his lingering.

He was a lookout, one of many.

When Jannik had departed from the Dolphin, he had done so by soaring away into the sky in a magic cart that Willam called a "flier."

The cart could bring Jannik back from the dragon fields in less than ten minutes. During the updates, Willam could not magically spy on the wizard's movements. He would not know if Jannik returned unexpectedly.

Bel had designed a warning relay.

One person was posted in the tower of the harbormaster's office, watching the sky to the northwest, in the direction of the dragon fields. Should she spy the bright lights of the flier, she was to shine a signal lantern at the street below. The man posted there would shine his own light to another person at an intersection farther along, and he to another, and another. The guard at the well was the last link, and would signal Bel, waiting outside the wizard's house.

The flier was fast, but it could not outrun a flash of light.

Someone had lent Bel a wooden whistle of the sort used by the barge tenders. It would be loud enough to hear from inside the house.

As they passed the well, the three friends nodded to the guard, as one did when passing a stranger. The man quickly hid his bottle and nodded back with a trace of guilt.

All for show. No uninvolved citizen need know what would happen this night.

At the intersection they turned right, and passed by the wizard's house. At the abandoned ruins next door they paused, glanced about, then stepped into the yard and positioned themselves against the remains of one wall.

Rowan set the lantern down, first flattening a place in the dry grass with her foot. Willam knelt beside it with his stolen clock in hand. "Four minutes," he said.

Bel set down the wheat flour and sat on her heels. Rowan leaned back against the brick wall. Willam remained as he was, watching time flick by.

"Two minutes," Willam said quietly.

No crickets sang; the insects had departed with the early snow, four days ago. Some small animal, a mouse perhaps, rustled in the grass, skittered past Rowan's feet, pattered briefly in the old floorboards, and was silent.

Then: "That's it. The updates are running."

Rowan had half expected some sort of perceptible effect: some sound, or sight, some sense of difference. There was none. The night was cold, starry, quiet.

Bel and Willam rose, collecting their burdens; Rowan took up the lantern. Trying to move casually, they returned to the street and turned back toward Jannik's home.

They walked up the front path; but at the portico, Willam stepped aside. "Rowan, you and I stay close to the wall," Will said. "Bel, you stand here." He positioned her beside and just under the overhang of the portico's roof, facing the street, her back against a supporting pillar. "That's an eye," and he pointed up, at an ornamental glass boss under the small peak of the portico's roof; Bel leaned forward to look. "The house saw us. It's trying to tell Jannik right now, but it can't reach him through the jammers. I can change its memory of us coming and going, but if you stay right here you'll be out of its sight, and I won't have to fix the part in between."

Will turned to the wall beside the portico, set his sack on the ground, unknotted it, felt around inside, and extracted an object.

A penknife. Rowan felt an odd impulse to laugh. She had expected nothing so prosaic.

With Rowan lighting his work, Willam counted bricks from the ground up, and at twelve he prodded at one with his fingers, then began to prize it with the knife. The brick slid out, then another, and a third, with soft scrapes that seemed loud in the night-quiet, and siftings of dust. Will inserted his hand into the opening revealed and seemed to grope. There came a *snick* from within, and a small creak. He waved Rowan closer, to direct the light into the niche.

A small metal door stood open on a little cupboard. Within, tiny specks of light, like distant red and blue stars, and the sort of small objects that Rowan had come to associate with magic: rectangular black insects, thin lines of copper, lengths of stiff, brightly colored string, which Rowan knew from past experience possessed copper cores.

Willam peered into the niche, gingerly probing with one finger. He pulled out two of the strings, left them with part of their lengths hanging outside. "Rowan, step back."

She did as she was told. Willam cut the strings, and waited, tensely. Nothing at all occurred.

Willam relaxed. "Good. Now…" He pulled from his sack a small canvas packet, untied and unrolled it. Inside lay a carefully ordered collection of tools, as tiny as a jeweler's. He selected one; but with his hands and face and the lantern so close to the little cupboard, Rowan could no longer see what he was doing.

Rowan and Bel both startled when the front door emitted a quiet *click*.

The women traded a quick glance; but Willam was already sidling up to the door. Staying to one side, he reached out, turned the knob, and pushed.

Warm yellow light spilled out onto the portico. This, despite the fact that the windows of the house were dark.

Willam blinked. "I'll fix that later; we can't have everyone seeing it. Bel—"

The Outskirter eyed the door, and the light, suspiciously. Then she picked up the sack of flour, hefted it, and heaved it into the opening.

A soft *thump* as it struck the floor. They waited.

Nothing.

Willam grinned. "Good." He replaced his tools in the packet, rolled and tied it. "I'd hate to have done all this and then get crushed by a simple deadfall." The packet went back into his sack. "Rowan, remember: when we're inside, don't say a word until I tell you that it's safe to speak." And with no further comment he picked up his sack, stepped under the portico, and entered.

Rowan gave Bel one more glance; the Outskirter was wide-eyed. Rowan followed Willam inside.

A foyer, paneled in old oak, the flour sack resting in the center of a mat of woven rush, itself showing the effects of many dirty shoe soles. Hooks along the wall held a hooded oil-skin cloak, a heavy one of dark green wool, and a rough-knit sweater. A brass stand in a corner beside the door contained two ornamental canes and a bright green umbrella.

Rowan found herself gazing at it in puzzlement, as if some part of her had believed that no wizard would ever need so simple a thing as an umbrella.

Willam was doing something to a wall-mounted lamp, reaching behind the frosted-glass shade. Three creaks, and the foyer went dark.

They waited for their eyes to adjust. Then Willam took the lantern and silently led Rowan inside.

The hallway lit itself on their arrival. Rowan could not decide whether this was ominous, or weirdly welcoming.

To one side: a parlor, still dark. Light from the hall lamp showed it comfortably appointed in dark blue velvet curtains, blue-green couch and armchairs, low tables, all arranged about a magnificent carved-wood hearth. To the other side, in deeper shadow, what seemed to be a formal dining room.

Willam ignored the rooms, glancing about the hall, seeking something. Rowan found it first.

She had seen one such in the fortress of Shammer and Dhree: mounted on the wall beside the dining room door, a tiny brass wheel.

She did not presume to use it herself, but waved for Will's attention, and indicated it. It was he who turned it, and the light in the hallway dimmed to darkness.

By lantern light, Willam led on.

Down the hall, past dark rooms on both sides, their uses indiscernible in the gloom. They found the staircase, which also greeted them with light. It was too far from the foyer's open door to show from the street. Willam allowed it to remain, and handed the lamp back to Rowan.

They climbed.

The second-storey hallway lit itself for them. Willam glanced quickly into the open doors of each room, then returned to the stairs, and indicated *Up*. Rowan followed him.

The light in the third-storey hall was cooler, softer, and only one door was open.

When they entered the room, there was light again, but not bright.

One lantern, mounted on a stand, sent a yellow splash onto a deep, comfortable armchair. On the table beside it lay a book, an abandoned tea pot, a cup and saucer. A small but pleasant brick hearth graced the wall, its mantel displaying a huge cut-glass vase filled with a riot of dried roses and statice.

A second, smaller lamp stood on the most beautiful desk Rowan had ever seen.

It was huge, ancient, constructed of rich bird's-eye maple, with contrasting geometric inlays of walnut and cherry. Rowan resisted the impulse to stroke it.

Willam moved behind the desk, and stood by the chair. He gazed around the room, then gave Rowan a glance whose meaning could not be misinterpreted: this was the place.

He set his sack on the floor, and opened it; from where she stood, Rowan could not see it, but she saw what he brought out as he lay each item on the desk. She watched closely.

A stack of small, flat, white rectangles, like half-sized playing cards, tied together with a bit of twine. A box, four inches by two by one, on top of which were mounted two brown wheels, their edges touching each other; on one end were two copper studs. A shallow paper cone, three inches across, its back supported by a thin metal cage. An object like a thick coin was mounted at the center of the cage, and from this trailed two more of the stiff, bright-colored strands.

The last item Willam brought out seemed by contrast the most inexplicable: merely a very small, old book, tied closed with a leather thong.

Willam picked up the paper cone by its cage, attached the free ends of the strands to the copper studs on the box. He arranged the cone to stand on its coin, open end up.

He laid out the white cards, in a single row. They were each numbered, simply, on one corner, 1 through 8.

Willam glanced around the room again, spotted something, indicated it to Rowan. She looked. Against one wall, by a bookcase: a short stepladder. She fetched it; he gestured that she should place it before the desk, and then that she should sit on it. She did so, grateful that he had thought of it. She did not care to stand for the next three hours.

When she was settled, Willam took a seat in the wizard's own chair behind the desk. He paused, then nodded to himself, picked up the card labeled 1, and leaned close to the box.

He touched it on one side; of themselves, the wheels began to turn against each other. With careful precision he placed the card, edge-on, at the point where the wheels touched. The wheels caught the card, pulling it forward between them.

The steerswoman was glad that she had seen something like the paper cone before, when she had dismantled a magic box while in Alemeth. So, she was not surprised at what happened next.

The cone said, in the voice of the wizard Jannik: "Access."

Rowan was, however, startled when the room replied.

From somewhere above came a voice, genderless, inflected in civilized tones, but seeming to possess no personality, no soul, no life. It said: "Password, please."

Rowan found she was clutching the sides of the stepladder in a desperate grip, to prevent herself fleeing the room. There will be more than this, she told herself firmly, and stranger still. She forced herself to breathe smoothly, seeking calmness, detachment, and clarity of observation.

Willam had caught the card again as the wheels released it, and without hesitation took up 2, and fed it to the turning wheels. "Equinox," Jannik said; then card 3: "Crocus."

Card 4 caused the cone to utter: "Solstice." Card 5: "Wild rose."

Willam used card 2 again, repeating: "Equinox"; then, card 6: "Chrysanthemum."

Card 4 again: "Solstice," and Rowan found herself running through a list of plants associated with winter.

With card 7, the voice of Jannik said "Mistletoe"; but Willam glanced at the box sharply. On the second syllable, the wizard's voice had wavered, warbled slightly. Will's eyes narrowed.

"Not recognized," the room said.

Willam repeated the entire process. Rowan again found herself admiring his concentration and patience.

When card 7 was being pulled between the wheels again, Will left his hand hovering above. In the middle of the word, he touched the moving card, briefly, precisely. The warbled syllable was steadied, somewhat. Then he waited, for what seemed to Rowan a long moment, but perhaps was not.

"Accepted," the room said. "Scan, please." Willam nodded, then took up the little book, untying the thong.

As he did so, a small, square inlay on the top of the desk slid aside. From inside emerged, unfolding, a thin metal jointed construct, insect-like, that first rose up and then angled toward Willam, and Rowan could think of nothing but the tail of a scorpion—

She was on her feet, and Willam glanced up, startled, not at the arm but at her. He held up one hand, his expression urgent, cautioning; he was not at all concerned by the strange device now pointing at him.

Rowan blinked, regained control, nodded. Willam looked significantly toward the door, then at her, questioningly. *Do you want to leave?*

Rowan settled down on the footstool again, in a marked manner. Willam gave her a very long, evaluating look. Rowan attempted to communicate both contrition and reassurance, which she found not at all easy with that poisonous-looking object pointing directly at her friend. But Will was reluctantly satisfied, and turned back to his work.

He opened the little book; but apparently the book itself was unimportant, as he set it aside after removing something that had been tucked protectively between its pages.

The object was about an inch square, as thin and flimsy as a slip of paper, although its color was of metal: silvery, shimmering, with rainbows refracting weirdly within, at a depth that seemed a bit greater than its actual surface.

Willam studied it closely, looked at its back, oriented it carefully, and held it up, less than an inch from the pointed end of the metal arm.

He waited. Nothing whatsoever occurred. He became disturbed, and then thoughtful. He examined the slip of silver again, back and front, considered, blinked, then shrugged in something like resignation.

Holding the slip by one corner between the thumb and forefinger of his left hand, he placed it over his own left eye, in the fashion of an eye patch, and leaned his face close to the point of the arm—a sight that caused Rowan to grit her teeth.

Red light emerged from the pointed tip, played across the slip of silver.

The room said: "Recognized," and the arm backed, bent, folded, retreated, down into its enclosure. "Good evening, Jannik."

Willam leaned back in the chair, pleased, then put away the silver slip and took up card 8.

The paper cone uttered in words oddly inflected, as if each one had been magically snatched from a different conversation: "Manual, input, only."

"Confirmed," the room said.

Willam relaxed, grinned across at Rowan. "We can talk now," he said—

The desk unfolded.

Willam startled hugely, but held up a hand to Rowan, said, "Wait—"

Side panels shifted, rose, tilted, moved back, around, behind. Slabs of curly maple and walnut unfolded, spreading around Willam as if seeking to embrace him, sliding across each other, and out from beneath each other.

When the motions finally stopped, Willam sat in the center of an array of levels, like a bee in the heart of a wooden flower—or, Rowan thought, like a master musician with his collection of instruments laid out all around him, each within reach, ready for a virtuoso performance.

Willam raised his brows. "This is interesting...," he said in a dubious tone.

"I take it you weren't expecting that?"

"No... I just hope I can recognize what I need. It has to be the most convenient..." He looked down. A section of the top of the desk had tilted toward him and shifted down to nearly rest in his lap. "This looks like the place to start." He looked up. "Are you all right? Because this is going to get a lot stranger."

Rowan surprised herself by laughing, if somewhat weakly. "I believe I shall be disappointed if it doesn't."

"All right." He passed his hands lightly across the surface in his lap, as if feeling for something. He found it, whatever it was, nodded satisfaction, and then arranged his hands carefully, and Rowan was reminded even more sharply of a musician. Willam seemed poised, like someone about to execute a complex composition on some keyboard instrument: a pump organ, perhaps.

Then his hands moved, graceful, precise. Despite herself, Rowan expected sound.

She got light.

Symbols, painted in pure light, from no visible source, appeared in midair. Ranks of symbols, lines of them, an entire block of them, hovered between her face and Willam's.

Things hanging in the air, Bel had said, after spying on Fletcher as he worked his magic in secret in the Outskirts. *Cold light.* Symbols, imparting information.

Will paused to study the shapes, nodded, executed another flurry of movement, considered the result. "Good..." He leaned back, now more at ease. His eyes flicked across the symbols, as if reading them—

Rowan realized that he was, in fact, reading them; that they were letters, and numbers; and that she had not recognized them because, from her perspective, they were printed backward.

She attempted to read them herself. The letters, although oddly shaped, were recognizable; but they formed no words she knew.

Will's hands moved again, briefly, and he looked up, anticipating the result.

To Willam's left, a lattice appeared, in crisscrossing lines of red light painted on thin air, each square of the lattice containing some tiny bit of writing, too small to read, but to Rowan seeming all alike—

But for one. Something was alive, trapped in the square, shifting and flickering. Rowan could not discern what it might be.

Apparently, neither could Willam. He corrected this by, quite simply, reaching across and plucking the square directly off the lattice, out of the air, and bringing it closer.

Everything is power, Rowan found herself thinking, as if repeating a litany, reassuring herself. *Power can be directed, controlled.* Will squinted at the tiny square, released it to hang in the air before him; then, using thumb and forefingers, he grasped alternate corners and pulled.

The square expanded.

Magic is what happens when you have a very precise control over the movement of power. The square was translucent, like a frosted pane of glass, and Rowan could see Willam through it. Movement flickered within the square's four borders, at varying depths, some of which absolutely could not be reconciled against the distance of Willam's face. The effect was dizzying.

It had no such effect on Willam. He watched, thoughtful, then looked through it at Rowan. "This is the dragon we stole," he told her. "It's the only one in contact at the moment."

She forced down nausea. "Very well."

He puzzled at her a moment, then seemed to understand, and looked apologetic. He took hold of the insubstantial square, and turned it around in the air to face her.

Depth suddenly resolved. Rowan saw a shimmering surface extending into the distance, humped dark shapes nearby. It was like a small window, or a magic mirror out of an old folk-tale, showing, as such mirrors often did in their tales, a distant view.

She recognized it. "The brook."

Where they had left the dragon. She was seeing through the eyes of a dragon.

And, she now understood, with utter amazement, she had before been viewing this scene from behind, not merely mirror-reversed, but with *depth itself* reversed, near to far, far to near. She found this easy to comprehend mathematically; in fact, it worked out with a satisfying neatness. But it remained freakish as experienced, as if, somehow, she had been standing on the far side of existence itself, viewing the entire universe from a point of view opposite to everything.

She had once before in her life experienced so great a shift, so complete a turning about and change...

A deep, bitter winter at the edge of the Red Desert. The air had been too dry for snow, but the ground itself froze, as it often did, so that it crunched and crumbled beneath the feet, and two sun dogs, nearly as bright as the sun itself, stood in the sky, illusory companions of the true sun.

Out of this cold, from the far, crisp distance, had wandered a strange figure. At first the people of Umber thought it to be a bear out of legend, with its strange humped shape and trudging gait. The villagers had sufficient time to speculate, with the cold air so clear. They gathered at the edge of town, young Rowan among them, wrapped in blankets and stamping her feet warm.

But when the figure neared it resolved into a person, bundled hugely against the frigid air, carrying an outsized pack; and when the person arrived in the common square, and pulled back the fur-lined hood, Rowan saw, amazingly, a woman.

A woman who traveled, alone, in the dead of winter. A stranger, brown-skinned, blue-eyed, the first person Rowan had ever seen whom she had not known since birth; either her own birth, or the other's.

In later years Rowan came to know her well, as both a merciless taskmistress and a gentle, sympathetic soul, with kind words for her young Academy students so far from their homes, and harsh ones for those who slacked in their studies: the steerswoman Keridwen.

But on that day she had been a stranger, with stories of far lands, odd and delightful facts, and an open, cheerful air that made her seem a bright star flickering here and there, in this corner and that of the great winter lodge—asking questions.

Questions, and more questions; she seemed to have no end of them.

Some were questions Rowan had herself asked, of her family and fellow villagers: asked and asked more, until they grew tired of her, and declared that she must be mentally deficient, to not know all these things as matters of simple fact, to need explanations for the obvious.

But when Keridwen asked, she was answered. And sometimes, questions were asked of her, always beginning: *Tell me, lady...*

Rowan shadowed Keridwen about the lodge, listening to the answers and explanations that had been denied Rowan from the time she was a very little girl—all of them delivered in formal, respectful tones.

At last, in the quiet of the evening, by the center fire, Rowan had gathered her courage to ask her own question: *Tell me, lady, why do they always answer you?*

Because I am a steerswoman.

And there had begun Rowan's life. She asked, and was answered.

Question followed question, ranging farther and wider and, later, deeper. And in the heart of the night, with everyone wrapped in their sleeping alcoves, young Rowan had asked: *Does everyone answer you?*

Every person I choose to ask. And not only people.

Rowan could not understand this. *Who else is there to ask, but people?*

You can ask the hawk how it hunts by watching it do it. You can ask the river how it flows by putting your hand in the moving water. These are answers, too. And Rowan recognized a truth she had always known, for this was how she herself asked, and was answered, when the village grew tired of her.

And more, the blue-eyed stranger went on: *Where the river flows from, how it grows, at what speed, where in the Land its path must go; how stones fall; where in the sky the stars must rise and set; what makes the seasons happen; all of these answers are being spoken for us, constantly. The universe itself is speaking, all the time.*

Young Rowan was not at all certain how literally she was expected to take this statement. *Why can't we hear it?*

First: you have to listen. And second—and the steerswoman smiled—*you have to know the language.*

The language was mathematics.

Rowan watched Willam: stark white hair, and copper eyes; hands moving across the panel in his lap; glance flicking here and there, where now six blocks of letters of pure light stood painted in the air around him.

What if, Rowan thought, you knew the language, or portions of it, so well that you not only understood it, but could speak it; could not only ask the universe, but *tell* it?

Instruct it. Command.

Magic.

She knew that this could not be done by writing down formulas, or by uttering them with her voice. Numbers and formulas were representations of relationships possessed by objects and forces. But by knowing the relationships with utter precision, and manipulating the objects, directing the forces—one could, in fact, command.

Everything might be power; but all power must move by the numbers.

"Here's where you can help me," Willam said. He leaned through the light-words as if they were merely what they were, light, and retrieved the square containing the distant dragon's sight. He shrank it between his hands, replaced it in its previous position within the red-lined lattice. "I don't know how many jammers Jannik has found so far, but we still have full coverage of the field. I don't *think* he can disable enough of them to make gaps before we're done here—but he might. If he does…"

"The house will be able to call to him, and try to tell him that we're here?"

"Well, no, not anymore. I've stopped that. But he might try to talk to the house himself, just to check. I'm not sure what would happen then, but we ought to stop what we're doing, and get out."

Reaching out, he took the entire lattice, turned it to face Rowan, placed it between him and her, expanded it slightly. His fingers danced on his lap panel, and the lines of red light dimmed slightly; Rowan found she could still see it clearly, while remaining able to see through it easily. "Now—" Willam glanced up at her, then looked again, puzzled.

"What is it?"

"You're awfully easy about this, all of a sudden," he said.

Rowan realized that this was true: she found the structure hanging in thin air before her not freakish, nor frightening, but intriguing, and lovely, in its way. "I've given the matter some thought," she said simply.

He leaned back, regarding her with something like amazement. "You know," he said, "you never stop surprising me."

"The feeling is mutual. What do you want me to do?"

He leaned forward again, indicating from behind the shrunken square he had replaced. "That's our dragon, outside of the jammers' influence. All of these"—his finger swept among the other squares—"are the dragons still in the field, inside the jammers."

With the lattice larger and no longer reversed, Rowan could read the little words. " 'Out of Range.' "

"Meaning, too far away for the controlling spell to reach. Which they aren't really, but the spell can't tell the difference. It just knows it can't reach them."

"Some of the squares say," and she puzzled over the unfamiliar word, " 'Offline.' "

He nodded. "Those are the dragons that are dead. If Jannik disables enough jammers—"

"The other squares will show what the dragons see."

"That's right." He sat back again. "The spell's not set up to warn me by itself, that's not how it usually works, and I don't have the time to figure out how to change it. And pretty soon I'll be too busy to watch the monitors myself."

She decided that he was referring to the array of dragon eyes. "I can do it." Arranged as it was, she could hardly miss any change in the configuration.

"Good." He gazed about, at the ranks of letters in the air. Within each block, the letters moved, marching along, shifting position, appearing at the lower corner of some invisible boundary, proceeding to the left, then up to the next line. "You know," Willam said, shaking his head, half disbelieving, "Corvus doesn't have anything nearly this sophisticated."

"Really?" And why would Jannik, she wondered, then realized. "Jannik inherited this from Kieran?"

"No..." Willam adjusted the position of two blocks, in order to view them more comfortably. "This is a lot older than that. It probably goes back to Donner."

Rowan was confused for a moment, then recalled that the city had adopted the name of its first wizard, out of gratitude for his rescue of the people from marauding dragons. Dragons almost certainly planted by Donner himself.

She studied Willam again. "Not to tell you your business, but shouldn't you be doing something?"

"It will get hot enough, soon enough," he said distractedly, then came back to his surroundings. "Actually, I set up these spells to search for me. They're checking the supposedly empty storage spaces for leftover pieces of records." Something occurred to him. "But…" He plied his lap panel again.

Something appeared to his far right, an opaque area three feet wide by three feet tall. "No, of course"—he seemed annoyed at himself—"the updates are running. Let's see if Jannik was looking earlier."

The dark area flashed into light, and color: mostly white, with spots and streaks of blue, green, brown, yellow, and at the upper limit, a ragged section of brick red. "Well, that's no good—" Something to his left caught his attention: one of the blocks of letters and numbers had ceased marching, and changed color from blue to red. Willam turned away from the complex colors, toward the simple ones. "We've got something." He pulled the block closer, directly through another section, still marching, which it had been half tucked behind.

Willam caused a square to appear, close by, its existence indicated merely by four white lines. This he picked out of the air as casually as if it were a pane of glass, and held it over the red-lettered section, moving it here and there. White letters appeared inside the square. "A fragment," Will said, "with no date. That's why the searcher brought it to me… It looks like a diary." He read, tilting his head from side to side, impatient. "Well, someone fell in love… with a truly wonderful man, la, la, and this does run on and on, and… it looks like the writer is a woman, so it's someone before Kieran." A few taps at his lap panel, and the red became blue, and marched once more.

"Did Jannik keep a diary of any sort?"

"If he did, it will show up." He indicated several of the blocks. "Those searchers are looking at the unused storage areas, for old information left behind. These"—he pointed—"are going through the indexed areas, looking for anything with a date from a month before Kieran died, through a year afterward. That one," to his far left, "is looking for the names of Kieran or Slado, starting from one end of the storage, and the one behind it is doing the same thing, starting at the other end. Ho." The second panel became red. "Let's see…" Willam pulled it forward.

Rowan found it useful to think of the blocks of letters as being written on invisible sheets of paper, pinned up on equally invisible walls, from which Willam would pluck as needed. It was only at this point that she realized that the invisible walls seemed to rise from the ranked flat panels of the unfolded desk.

But these pages searched, of themselves, wrote their findings on themselves, and would call for one's attention with a change of color when they found something.

Willam was passing his white-outlined ghost-square over the red symbols. He made a noise of amusement. "There you are."

She was not certain what he meant. "Me?"

He nodded, reading through the white square. "From... more than six years ago. The last time you were here in Donner. Slado's general order to find and kill you. Jannik's reply, that you were here, and he'd take care of it." He looked wry. "Slado sounds very annoyed."

She wanted to know his words, exactly; but something caught her attention. "Dragon."

He looked up. "I don't see it."

"Just for a moment. *That* one." She indicated, bringing her fingertip a fraction of an inch from the relevant square. She could not bring herself to touch it. "I saw a scene, briefly. Shapes moving, in darkness." She found it useful to think of a little window that had rapidly opened on a distant view, then immediately closed.

Will was disturbed. "He found a jammer, with no others operating nearby at the moment. Then another must have activated, almost right away. This is going too slow." He checked his searchers. "There's a lot of storage to go through. But if I make any more searchers, they'll start tripping over each other..."

He sat back, now tense. He glanced about, found nothing he could do; then his eye fell on the large square on his right, where the blotches of random colors still shone. "Well, let's make sure it's not a complete waste of time." His fingers moved on his lap panel; the colors altered in flashes, over and over. "It must have been clear sometime..."

Almost simultaneously, three pages of words turned red. Will turned away from the square of random colors. "We've got something, from the fragments." He pulled one of the pages forward. "It looks like words," he said, as if this would disappoint him. "Numbered lines, and lots of spaces." Rowan could see nothing of the sort, but Willam pulled the small white outline over it, which Rowan decided to think of as a magical glass that would translate from one language to another.

Unfortunately, gazing through the dragon lattice, through the back of the page of red words, and through the back of the translator, at words written backward, Rowan could not make sense of the odd-shaped letters.

"No good," Willam said. "A list. Something to do with flower bulbs." The letters went blue again, and walked up the page. Two more pages had gone red, waiting for Willam's attention. He reached for the nearest, but then noticed one of the farther ones. "There!" He stood. "I recognize that command." He plucked the page out of the air, remained standing. He did not use the translator, as if this were too urgent to bother with it. He read directly, blue light on his face. "Override—that's a command that means, 'Stop everything else you're doing, and only pay attention to this...'"

Rowan waited. Willam nodded slightly, then more definitely, talking as if to himself. "Override, there, yes... And shut down, and shut down... Delayed command, I don't know that one, but it's asking for a lot of power..." He sat, on the edge of the wizard's chair, reading eagerly. "Time to execution... and close all communication..." He looked up at her. "Would you like to know the exact second the Guidestar was called down?"

She said, with feeling, "Very much."

"At fourteen hundred thirty-eight, and twenty-three seconds. On the two hundred and forty-first day of the year. This is Slado, bringing down the Guidestar."

"A record of that event?"

"A record of the orders he used..." He began to set the block of letters aside; but then stopped short, raised his brows. "Do you know... ," he said, suddenly amazed, "if I had the right clearance... If I had the right clearance, I could bring one down myself, now." He recovered, studied the page again, closely. "What's just before this...?" He read, became disappointed. "Broken off. Just a fragment." He gave the page a shove and released it; it drifted up and back, then came to a stop high above the others, as if looking down on them, waiting. Willam turned his attention to another searcher.

For no reason Rowan could identify, this action caused her mood of acceptance to waver. For a moment, the crossing red lines through which she watched seemed solid, like the bars of a cage; the floating blocks of letters beyond, and now above, inexplicable and threatening; the man in the center, with his skin and white hair painted blue and red in the strange light, not only a stranger, but stranger than that, a chimera called forth by some magic spell—something, perhaps, other than completely human.

Something now possessing the knowledge to call down a Guidestar.

Power may move by the numbers; but the human spirit did not.

Nonsense. This was Willam.

She tried to recapture her mood of but a moment before. These lights—truly, they *were* beautiful, purer and richer than any colors she had seen before, their arrangement clean, a visible embodiment of the mathematics that must lie beneath them—

But it remained too strange to see such clarity and purity anywhere other than within her own mind.

She found her gaze drifting toward the large, multicolored square on Willam's right. Its randomness seemed more natural, its colors soothing. The blue, especially, seemed lovely, restful, almost calling to her in a voice she thought she knew. A swirl of brown specks within one blue area pleased her, as well—

She stopped short. She stared.

Eventually, she said, in a voice sounding distant to herself: "Do you have time for a question?"

"A short one," Will replied, half under his breath as he worked.

"Am I looking at the world?"

He looked up. Then he looked at the square, then back at her. He said, gently, "Yes. Yes, you are."

Wulfshaven was obscured by clouds, but the sweep of the Islands, in a patch of clear, glittering sea, indicated it. Donner was a glimpse of shoreline, Southport invisible, as was the Dolphin Stair.

The Western Mountains were a riot of browns under thin mist, twisted, seeming a pause in some ancient violence. The upper branches of the River Wulf emerged from the cloud cover, reaching toward their sources. In the far north, the Red Desert was cloudless, and as flat and featureless as Rowan remembered it, small arms of green farms encroaching its edges, with a few sunlit flickers of irrigation.

All foreshortened, not like a map at all, but exactly as seen by an eye hanging high in the sky.

She matched the angles. "The Eastern Guidestar."

"Mm." Willam had several red blocks waiting for him; he dismissed them after a brief glance, one after the other. "I'm sorry I can't find better weather for you, but Jannik only stored today's view. Do you want an overlay?"

She heard herself say, distantly, "I don't know that word…"

He replied by playing his fingers across his lap board; thin lines appeared across the view, outlining details the steerswoman already knew by heart. She gazed, scarcely daring to breathe.

"I'm going to give you the Western Guidestar," he said, casually, as if the star itself could be presented as a gift. Then, apologetically: "The change might make you dizzy."

It did not. But it showed her parts of the world no steerswoman or member of the common folk had ever seen.

Familiar parts of the world were slanted, compressed by perspective. The black outline of lands below the cloud remained, speaking to her with the logic of geography: mountains, here, with rivers twisting between; a collection of round lakes, like jewels from a broken necklace, their spill arcing across the land. And beyond, far to the west, under the clouds, an outline ragged and brutal, with nothing beyond—an ocean?

The steerswoman tried to burn the view into her mind, to reconstruct later, but then: "Dragons."

Will stopped short. He seemed a bit out of breath. "How many?" But he saw for himself. "Oh…" Seven adjacent dragon eyes showed tiny night scenes. "Wait…" They winked out, as if little shutters had come down on little windows. *Out of range*, the shutters read.

"That's not good… ," Willam said.

"How many jammer-spells altogether?"

"Thirty." Willam was disturbed.

"And you have no way, even from here, of knowing how many remain?"

"No." Four of his searcher pages needed attention. He returned to them, but kept glancing up at the dragon eyes.

Rowan did not want to interrupt his work, and waited before speaking further. In the interim, Will puzzled over the searchers without using the translator, selected two, sent them to join the one hanging high above, and set the others back to their work. Rowan said, in the pause: "Did you use any sort of pattern in arranging the jammers?"

Will grew still, and quiet. "No… ," he said; but it was with deep uncertainty. "I tried to be random—"

"You can't have been random." A truly random arrangement could not—

She struggled a moment. She had not had a real grip on the phenomenon of the jammers. They each had a range, she had been told; but range of sight, range of sound—these she understood. An object could block sound, and sight; but Will had said "coverage…"

She thought of the wizard's green umbrella, made huge, a half a kilometer across, with its handle rooted to the ground.

Then multiplied: thirty of them, crowded together, some folded, some open, with edges overlapping, creating solid shade beneath. Then some disappearing, suddenly; and some of the folded ones opening…

How many to maintain full coverage?

"Will, the jammers are *not* arranged randomly." The constraints of the problem delimited the solution. "And there's more than one way to discern organization."

"Like you did in the dragon fields." He thought, displeased, then became more confident. "No. Rowan, Jannik is nowhere near as smart as you are. He's not even as smart as *I* am! He probably doesn't use a tenth of what he has here, and he couldn't do what I'm doing, working behind the interface. I think... I think he was just lucky for a moment."

"Then let's hope this doesn't turn out to be his lucky day."

He looked around at his searching pages. "All right; let them trip over each other."

He caused more to appear, dozens. They stood tucked behind each other, crowding the air around him: bright butterflies of light hovering, as if in a frozen moment of time, magic words moving on their wings.

Willam worked; Rowan watched. When she became overwhelmed by strangeness, she turned her gaze to the view of the world.

With more searchers, Willam was busier, correcting them when they became confused. Or so she assumed; she did not interrupt to ask. But at one point, he did something that caused numbers to appear at the top edge of the dragon eyes, and indicated them to her silently. She watched them and soon decided that they represented the remaining time to the end of what Willam had called the "updates."

It was how much time they had left. Rowan was disturbed to note that nearly two hours had passed.

Pages began to merge. Will would pull one out of the air, lay it over another, and the two would blend into each other like soap bubbles. These he set aside. He had run out of convenient space in front, and had begun sending them to stand over the wood panels behind him. He was lit from three sides, by pure blue and red light, moving, and on one side, by the sweet light of the world itself, shining from his immediate right.

Twice dragon eyes flickered to life, then closed. Rowan drew his attention to them by pointing silently; he merely spared a glance each time, and continued to work.

Rowan watched the dragon eyes, watched the time, watched the world, watched the man working magic.

He moved quickly; she did not think she had ever seen anyone move with such precision, speed, and concentration.

With less than an hour left, there came a moment when none of the searchers presently asked for attention; Willam cast about, almost petulantly, as if he had grown so accustomed to speed that he could not now do without it.

He found nothing to do. He sat back, blinking, and noticed Rowan again. He checked the searchers one more time, then reached for the pages waiting behind him, pulled them forward, spoke quickly. "This is what I've got so far. The Guidestar that fell—Kieran was using it a *lot*, I don't know what for, yet. I've found some pieces of commands, some of them with dates and times still attached. It looks like he accessed the Guidestar almost every day." A searcher signaled red; he stood to see it closer, not bothering with the translator square. "Right"—he nodded as he read—"and this is one from the night he changed. And it doesn't look any different from the others—" Another searcher turned red. "And... that's another." He paused. "Same night." His gaze narrowed. "I can see the commands, but what follows them makes no sense. And it's that way with each one, so far."

"Your translator square is no help?"

He was confused a moment; then he reasoned out what she was referring to. "No, that's for words. I don't need it for commands. It just confuses things..." As if to confirm this, he picked up the translator, moved it on the page. "No." He set it aside to hang in midair. "It looks... it looks like this ought to be a pointer, to where something is stored"—he glanced aside at another searcher—"but when I look in the place, it's either empty, or has something else in it... and there are prefixes before that, that I just don't recognize."

Another searcher called for him. He glanced at it, glanced again, then brought it close. "And here's another." He set it beside the first, read, comparing the two. "Same thing," he said, helplessly. "Call to the Guidestar... access... these prefixes, the pointers—"

He stopped short. He glanced back and forth. "No, that can't be right."

He sat back, puzzling. He asked, apparently of himself: "How much storage space did Kieran have?" He sat up, plied his lap board again.

The light behind Rowan altered. She looked back.

Where the bookcase had been there now stood an entire wall of oak-faced filing cabinets.

Will muttered, derisively, "Oh, that's stupid; just *tell* me..." The cabinets disappeared. Rowan remained staring at the bookcases. And the very peculiar thing about it was how very prosaic it was, amid all this embodiment of abstraction. Merely bookcases, and then filing cabinets, here and then gone.

A noise from Willam called her back, and she berated herself for neglecting her dragon watch. But nothing there had changed.

Will had three more red-lettered searchers standing beside the first two. He noticed her, said: "From the same night," and went back to studying them, with frustration and urgency. "They *can't* be pointers," he declared, "because they're pointing nowhere! There are no such places.

They must be some commands I don't know…" He scanned the waiting red searchers. "More." He brought three forward. "Same night." He gazed at them helplessly, shaking his head. "It makes no sense. But look"—as if Rowan could discern anything by just looking—"some of them have times, and some of the times are just, just *moments* apart! What was he *doing?*"

He had struck some kind of wall in his understanding; Rowan recalled the many times she had done so herself. And because she had been thinking of her earlier, she now thought again of Keridwen, during Rowan's training. *When you reach a dead end,* the teacher had said, *you've made a wrong turn.* Go *back.*

"Tell me what a pointer is," Rowan said.

"Rowan—"

"Humor me. Talk quickly, if you must."

He seemed to realize that he had been short with her. "Sorry. A pointer is a number that tells you where some piece of information is stored, like, like a number written on the front of a box."

The vanished file cabinets; the number of drawers was limited. "And these particular pointers are pointing to locations you can't find?"

"Which is why they can't really be pointers."

Marel had sent his clerk into his old files for the records of deliveries… "If the locations are not in this building, where else might they be?"

He looked at her, astonished; then looked to his right.

The world itself stood before him, or a portion of it, as if this room were high in the sky, and the square an open window, looking down—

A mistake; Rowan ought not think of the view as down; her stomach twisted; she shut her eyes; she gripped the sides of the stepladder.

"How are the dragons?"

She forced her eyes open, suddenly terrified that she might have missed something. "Just the same one."

"Good—" He was standing; he leaned across the desk, his body passing through ghostly pages; he gripped edges of the dragon lattice, shifted it, turned it to angle toward Rowan from her right. "Here—" He turned back, took hold of the window open on the world, and moved it.

Toward Rowan. She felt she was falling—

"Here." He released it. It stood on her left, a hole in the air, terrifying. "Wait—" Will played the lap board, still standing. "Waitwaitwait… there." He leaned forward again, spoke quickly. "What you're looking for is structures—buildings, or roads—someplace where they shouldn't be. Take your hand—" He took it himself; it was limp in his grip. "Flat, like this." He arranged her fingers, moved her hand forward. "And touch it, so—" She was touching nothing, she felt nothing, only air—"And move, like this—"

The entire world shifted under her hand—or the window did. The view slid up; she was twisting in the sky, she was spinning, falling—

Instinctively, her hand pulled back sharply. Willam caught it again, brought it back. "Go slow... move smoothly."

Color slipped, left to right: blue, brown, green, white, weird, dizzying. In pure animal reflex, she flailed, jerked back, escaped Willam's hand.

He startled. "Rowan?" She turned to him, wild-eyed.

He had half climbed across the top of the desk and was leaning out toward her. "Rowan? Rowan, I'm sorry," he said. He made to reach to her again, then dropped his hand. "I'm pushing you too fast, I know. It's just...you were doing so well..."

He remained, waiting: a human form seeming to emerge from layer after ordered layer of cold, glowing symbols. The light of the world itself painted his copper gaze with blue, with white; Rowan could almost read the map of the world, reversed, in Willam's eyes.

And to his left, the numbers above the dragon eyes showed thirty-five minutes remaining.

Then thirty-four.

"I'm looking for Slado's place," Rowan said.

"Yes..."

"Let me try."

"Are you sure?"

"Yes."

He smiled, relieved. "Good. Someone has to." He moved back to his chair but remained standing, reaching down to the board. "I tried asking for it by name, but I don't think the name Corvus called it is its true name... It's important to have the true name..." His fingers moved faster, his voice grew distracted. "But..." One of the many pages erased itself, then spawned new writing. "Maybe I can find out if these pointers do fit..."

Rowan turned back to the magic window. Awkward, the steerswoman moved the world with her hand.

It was hard. Touch gave her no cue, no support. Her arm trembled, jumped. The view of the world leapt west, north, wildly. The sight was too strange; her vision seemed to fragment and reassemble randomly, dizzying. Her skin was damp; she tasted bile. She fought, focused, forced herself.

This was not the world. It was a map. She knew maps.

She tried again. The lovely colors jittered, jerked, a view all strangeness, no country that she knew, but then: "There's something here."

Willam glanced, dismissed it. "That's not it. That's the Grid. It collects power. Keep trying."

There was now no foreshortening, no compression of perspective. She was looking straight down. She knew where she must be: directly beneath the Western Guidestar. By clumsy leaps, she began to work back toward the Inland Sea.

She noticed that the soft pad of Will's fingertips against his lap board had ceased. She glanced at him.

He sat quiet, and very still, as if caught in a pause beyond which he could not pass. He noticed her regard with a flick of his eyes, said: "Wherever it is that Slado does live, the pointers aren't pointing there, either."

Then he leaned back slowly and gave himself to thought. Rowan turned back to the world.

She must work quickly. She could not work quickly. She worked, the only way she was able—

"Rowan, stop."

"No, I can do this—"

"No. Stop. Now."

She stopped. She turned back to him. He remained motionless.

An entire minute spun by.

Then: "Rowan, you have to leave."

"No."

He pushed his chair back, picked up his burlap sack, set it in his lap. "Please." But there was no pleading in his voice. He spoke quietly. He began drawing a number of small objects from his sack, setting them on the desk.

"Why—" Rowan began.

"There's no time to explain," he said. "Just go." He was assembling something, attaching the objects to each other, moving smoothly, swiftly, calmly.

Too calmly. It was that deep calm that he possessed when he knew for certain exactly what he must do. It did not comfort Rowan; he seemed to her at that moment like one who had made some ultimate decision, some final choice from which there could be no turning back.

It frightened her; and she would not leave him here alone. "Tell me I'll die if I stay," Rowan said. He looked up. "And don't lie to a steerswoman."

"Rowan, there's no time to—"

"Then *don't* explain. Will, whatever you need to do, just do it, and explain later." A small panel opened itself on the top of the desk, but Will had expected it, was already reaching for it. He pulled out a length of cord, attached it to his construction, tapped the lap board. There was a brief hum overhead, and a creak, and a rattle, then silence. He ignored the sounds.

"Rowan—"

"There's no time," she pointed out: twenty-six minutes remained. "just do it. Whatever it is. I'll be right here."

At this he flashed her one glance, a glance she could not read; then he turned back to his work. "You mustn't speak," he said, his hands continuing their quick work. "No matter what happens, not a word. Don't make any noise at all, none. Try not to move, breathe quietly—I have to trust you to do all that."

She did not reply. She composed herself for both silence and stillness.

And above all, calm.

The final component of Willam's device was a short rod. He attached it. Immediately, it glowed at the tip: a tiny red star.

At this, he stopped. He sat gazing at the little star, seeming to wait.

Presently, the star turned green.

Willam drew a breath, released it, sent Rowan one bleak glance. Then he closed his eyes, as if to clear his thoughts, as if to steady himself, as if to dismiss from his mind all thoughts of the steerswoman's presence.

He opened his eyes. He spoke to the small green star.

Willam said: "Corvus—I'm in."

CHAPTER NINETEEN

The paper cone spoke. "I trust this isn't trivial." The voice resembled that of the wizard Corvus. "You were only to contact me if—"

Willam interrupted: "Sir, the information we need is at Farside."

A pause. "That can't be right." The voice was thin, distant, with a continuous hiss behind it, like an ocean wave endlessly breaking.

"It is. I'm sure." Willam spoke quickly. "Kieran was accessing Gee-Three a lot—as near as I can tell, at least almost every night. But there was one night where he was using it for hours on end. Half the night. Until just before dawn—"

"The night Gee-Three came down?" the cone asked.

"No. No, that was later, that was Slado, Kieran was already dead." Willam became urgent. "Sir, the updates are almost done, there's no time to explain how I know this. The Guidestar falling—that was just *what* happened. This is *why*." The paper cone remained silent but for the quiet, unending hiss. "I found fragments here, with pointers, addresses for files, but the addresses are too high. There's just not that much storage here. They're even wrong for Central."

Still no reply. The young man waited, sitting alone in the near-dark, watching the small green star. All about him, and above, the ranks of letters of pure light stood, written on the air. Strange servants: simple, tireless, still innocently following Willam's last orders.

Willam said, helplessly, "Sir—tell me how to talk to Farside."

"You can't," the cone said. "Farside was locked on Gee-Three. Gee-Three is gone."

"Can't we use one of the other Guidestars?"

"No. The updates are running. The Guidestars are accepting only emergency calls."

"If—" Will seemed to cast about. "I don't know—if I could disguise my signal, somehow—"

"It wouldn't help. Farside was directly under Gee-Three. Gee-Two and Gee-Four don't overlap."

Silence again, but for the hiss from the cone: the sound of the sea, of darkness, the sound of the absence of pattern.

A minute passed. Then Willam said: "There has to be another way."

"No. You've done what you can. Erase your tracks, close up—"

"But sir, I'm talking to *you.*" The wizard did not respond. "And I'm not using any Guidestar. When Farside lost Gee-Three, wouldn't the automatics *try* to get help? If they couldn't reach a Guidestar, wouldn't they try something else? Everything else, every way they knew about?"

"After more than forty years..." The wizard's voice was thoughtful.

" 'They don't get tired,' " Willam said, as if quoting. " 'They don't get bored, and they don't get distracted.' And," he added, in apparently his own words, "they don't have hope—so they can't ever lose hope, can they?"

A pause, during which the unseen ocean briefly crested. The wizard's words emerged as the noise receded again. "—omething like a caretaker process—"

"That's what I mean," Will said immediately, eagerly.

"Perhaps... Stand by."

Hissing silence. Willam's neglected searchers were nearly all red now. Willam noticed, scanned their ranks, hesitated. He selected two and brought them close. Red flickered in his copper eyes as he studied them.

He glanced up, at the dragon-eye lattice.

Above the grid, the numbers showed seventeen minutes remaining.

Willam looked about, then down, reached under one of the wood slabs. There came a quiet sound, mundane, almost shocking in its familiarity: the sound of a drawer opening.

Willam pulled out a sheet of paper and a pencil. He wrote rapidly, glancing at the two searchers before him, and at the several that he had previously set apart, high above.

"Will."

"Here, sir." Willam stopped short, pushed pencil and paper aside.

"Look for something called 'broadcast' or 'receiver.' "

Willam glanced among the nearby searchers, settled on one, used his lap board. The searcher emptied of symbols, and new words appeared, arranged in short lines, like a list. Will shook his head. "Nothing."

"Try 'R-F' or 'short wave.' "

Result was immediate. "I've got it." Willam's hands moved, quick, graceful. "Do I need to shift the dish?"

"Stand by." A pause, then a thoughtful, dissatisfied sound from the wizard. "This is all new to me... No, it looks like you'll keep using the antenna... I haven't found yet how much power you'll need..."

"Maybe it will tell me itself."

Out of sheer nothingness, two objects appeared on Jannik's desk, lit by a spill of light from no source: a flat wooden box, with glass insets on its upper face; and something like a silver candlestick, with a squat mesh bulb in place of the candle. The glass insets seemed to contain simple graphs.

Will gave the objects a single glance of scorn and impatience, and caused them to vanish again. He muttered, "I can't even guess what that was supposed to be..."

"A problem?"

"No, sir. Just the interface construct. I'm behind it now." He pulled opposite corners of the transparent page, expanding it to four times its previous size. He studied it, occasionally tapping his lap board with one finger; the letters of light altered in rhythm, the entire block at once, flashing. "No..."

"Forget power for the moment; you'll start by listening... here's something. How high is the rod right now?"

"Fifteen meters..."

"Send it up as far as you can."

Willam nodded, worked; and from somewhere inside the house, a hum, which continued for a full minute, and ended with a faint rattle and creak. "Where should I listen?"

"I have no idea... Start at the bottom, work your way up..." Rapidly, Willam created a translucent square, and inside it a simple graph displaying a sine function. But the curving line lived, flailed, seemed to fight its confinement.

Calmly, Willam watched it.

Quiet, but for sound from the cone: the distant, endless ocean wave, as if time itself had frozen in the moment of its breaking.

Willam checked the time remaining: fourteen minutes. He closed his eyes, took several deep breaths, opened them; and then calmly, methodically, caused his searchers to vanish, one by one.

Red light diminished incrementally, flick and flick, until only those searchers Willam had set high above remained. The living light of the world's image on Willam's right began to dominate: cool, gentle, lovely.

"Anything?" Corvus asked.

Motion, to one side. Willam glanced left, froze.

Within the lattice of dragon eyes, more than a dozen little squares showed movement, shifting light.

"Will?"

"Stand by," spoken quietly, as if the distant creatures could hear him.

The shutters came down. *Offline.*

Will did not relax. "Jannik is starting to get good at finding the jammers."

"Then he's cleverer than we thought."

"Or we were not so clever as we thought…"

"And we're running out of time. No signal yet?"

"I'm still running through the frequencies…" Will hesitated, then picked up his pencil and wrote again, reading the high red letters intently.

Quiet, for a space; then the wizard spoke, a trace of amusement in his voice. "By the way, I had an interesting conversation with Abremio the other day."

Will glanced at the cone, continued to write. "Yes, sir?"

"He mentioned that he had located my lost pet in Donner, and did I want it back? I told him not to bother." Corvus became serious. "But you should be on the alert, Will. Someone, one of Abremio's people, is in Donner, and has spotted you."

Willam's eyes grew dark; but he spoke with careful nonchalance. "Two people, sir," he said. "And they're dead."

The wizard made a satisfied sound. "Good. Good work."

Willam did not reply. The graph writhed; the cone hissed.

Willam stopped writing, and set down the pencil. He gazed at the last red searchers above him, each in turn, his expression unreadable. Then he banished them.

All that remained were the world, on his right; the dragon eyes, angled off on his left; and the glowing graph before him. Its yellow line continued to move, weirdly alive, snake-like.

The snake froze.

"I've got something," Willam said. "The wavelength is ten meters." Moving quickly, he created a new square, outlined in blue. It remained empty. "But it's just a signal. It's not saying anything."

"A carrier wave. Ping it. Use all the power you have."

Will worked: a flurry of light taps.

The empty square grew blue letters, one by one.

Willam stopped short, reading; then he released a pent breath and collapsed back in Jannik's chair. "I've got it," he said weakly. "It's Farside."

"Good work!" The wizard sounded amazed, and very pleased indeed. "Now, getting past its security is going to be difficult. I'll try to walk you through it—"

But Will was already sitting up again, his hands were already moving, with uncanny speed. "Stand by."

"Will—"

"Stand by." He was scanning the penciled symbols on the simple sheet of paper as he worked.

"—Will, don't be rash, if you don't do this right—"

"I'm in."

A pause. *"What?"*

"I'm in. Stand by, it's asking me for everything, and trying to tell me all its problems, all at once... there." Will leaned back. "I sent a total override." He sighed, seemed to gather himself. "Right. Let's see about those addresses..." He began again; the blue letters and numbers vanished, and new ones appeared, flowing onto the magic page.

"Will," Corvus said, "how did you get past the security?"

Willam replied distractedly. "Worked around it."

"I'm impressed." And, by the sound of the wizard's voice, faintly disturbed.

Will seemed not to notice. "Thank you, sir. The addresses match. It's retrieving... Here we go."

Symbols, in pure, blue light, began accumulating in the air, within the abstract boundaries of an insubstantial, transparent page. "This is slow..."

"You don't have much bandwidth."

The dragon-eye lattice came alive.

Will was a moment noticing, another moment waiting, wide-eyed.

The movements in the lattice continued.

Willam slowly lifted his hands from the lap board. His copper eyes showed white all around.

"Willam?"

Willam did not move. He spoke quietly. "I think I'm dead, sir. The jammers are down, all of them. Jannik has contact."

Corvus said, quickly, "You're not dead yet. He may not have noticed you."

"The *house* knows I'm here!"

"Yes, and it thinks *you're* Jannik."

Sudden realization. "I can lock him out completely—" Willam made to address his lap board.

"No!" Will stopped. "If you do that," Corvus went on, "Jannik will *know* someone is there. Will, stay calm; we still might get through this without giving you away."

"But—"

"The house system is sophisticated, but not that sophisticated. It's a very stupid creature, like all of its kind. As far as the house is concerned, Jannik is perfectly able to give a command from his desk, instantly transport himself miles away, and give another command remotely. The house doesn't know any better."

Willam began to recover, cautiously. "What is Jannik doing right now?" Corvus asked.

Within the lattice, a sequence was occurring: a white outline appeared around one square, then moved to the next, and the next.

"Will?"

"It looks like some sort of status check for each dragon."

"That's all? He hasn't asked the house for its own current status?"

"No..."

"Good. Fix it so that if he does, the house will tell him that all is well." Willam did not reply. "Will, you just broke into Farside. This is simple by comparison. You're just panicking." The wizard's voice became steady, patient: the voice of a teacher. "I have every confidence in you. You can do this. Stay calm, stay focused. Ask for the house status yourself. See what it says."

Will lowered his hands cautiously, tapped hesitantly; a page appeared, with words scattered across its face. Willam blinked, then seemed to take in their meaning, and grew more certain. "It's saying that the desk is active, the antenna is deployed, and signals being broadcast and received." He worked, with a growing confidence. "And now... and now it's saying that they're not. And it will keep saying that, if Jannik asks..." He slumped back in the chair. "But only if he asks for an overall status. If he asks for some specific subsystem, and it's something I'm using, that will show up."

"I doubt he'll do that. Taking care of the dragons is about the limit of Jannik's abilities. Do you have any progress with that file?"

The page had filled; the lines of symbols were now shifting upward, as more were added at the bottom edge.

Only two symbols, repeating endlessly. Willam slowly grew disbelieving. "No..." A quiet, plaintive sound.

"A problem?"

Willam spoke to himself, under his breath. "No, no... it *can't* be empty..." He leaned closer.

"Willam?"

He seemed to remember the wizard's presence, glanced at the paper cone as if glancing at a person's face. "It looks *blank.*"

"Erased?"

"No... it's a file, it's marked as one, it's in Farside's own index as a file... but..." He spread his hands. "There's nothing in it."

"How many addresses did you recover?"

"Forty or so. But Farside has..." Willam tapped. "... more than ten thousand marked as Kieran's." The page emptied; blue light vanished from Willam's face, his eyes. "I'm trying another one."

The symbols began again: a handful of lines of apparently random numbers and letters, then: two symbols, repeating.

Will did not wait for the page to fill. "The same." He vanished the letters. "I'm trying another. They can't all be like that, not now, not after all this—"

"Willam, the updates complete in less than five minutes."

Will made a sound through his teeth; he fisted one hand. The blue letters, oblivious, continued placidly to collect themselves on the page. "This is too *slow!*"

"We can't make the files come across any faster."

"I can't *tell* if they're empty until I get them here!" He stopped short. "But Farside has them all—right now!" He worked quickly. "I'm setting up a searcher at Farside itself, to give me a list of any of Kieran's records that are not empty." A last tap, which had to it an air of finality. Will waited, unblinking, utterly still.

"It's one thing to pull out information already stored," the voice of Corvus said, "but to get Farside to—"

"All of them," Willam said.

A pause. "What?"

Will leaned forward, brows knit. *"All* the files have *something* in them." The wizard said nothing. "Maybe I just didn't wait long enough. Maybe only the beginnings are empty. Farside says *something's* in there!"

"Will, we're running out of time. Three minutes left. If you're going to give up, you should break off the contact now."

For the space of some thirty seconds, Willam stared, wide-eyed, completely still, through the pages of light and color, past the walls of Jannik's office.

Then: "Sir... how sure *is* it, that I would be spotted?"

The wizard spoke quickly. "By the Guidestars? Absolutely certain. Will they care, of themselves? I don't know. But they'll make records. I can erase the records. But not instantly. Do you want to go on?"

"How fast is 'not instantly'?"

"I can't stop the Guidestars from seeing you. But I can get into short-term storage, feed it a worm. The worm will eat the record. One minute left. Do you want to go on?"

"But if someone is watching, themselves, through the Guidestars, in real time—"

"They'll see you. If they look in R-F. Which they probably won't. But there's no way to tell. I can't risk being connected with this, Willam. If you do this, you can't come home. Do you want to go on?"

"But there's *something* there, in these files—"

"Do you want me to make this decision for you?"

The pause seemed far longer than the mere five seconds that passed. Will was motionless.

Then: "I don't need an entire file." And Willam again became a creature of speed.

"The updates are completing... now."

"I'm having Farside look at one file and pick out a section—"

"Guidestars are accepting normal traffic... Plenty to cover me..."

"—some part that isn't just null symbols—"

"I'm in. Western Guidestar. Will, you look like a bonfire!"

"—and it should send me that—"

"Feeding it the worm... It took it. Shifting to Gee-Two..."

"—Commands accepted. Searching. Here it comes—"

New symbols began to accumulate: numbers, letters, in pairs. Willam watched, flexing and bending his fingers as if they pained him, as if even this brief pause in movement were unbearable. "I don't recognize this..."

"Gee-Two took the worm." Audible even above the unending hiss: two harsh huffs, as if the wizard were breathing heavily after some great exertion. "That was not easy..." The hiss rose, as if the invisible wave were attempting to finally crest and break.

Will raised his voice against the noise. "I'm losing you, sir!"

The small green star at the end of the short rod by the paper cone flickered colors, settled on red. Only the hiss continued.

Willam remained disturbed, but turned back to the blue symbols, transporting themselves from the other side of the world. He watched, his copper gaze narrow, shaking his head slightly in disbelief at each new line.

Something occurred to him. He caused a new page to appear, half-tucked behind the blue symbols from Farside; and another, and another. On their faces, letters and numbers flickered wildly, continuously. Will made a sound between his teeth, of frustration, but continued to watch.

Abruptly, a leather-bound book appeared, materializing from nothing on the surface of the desk.

Will startled back hugely. Of itself, the book opened in the middle; the pages riffled themselves, rapidly, moving toward the end, but never reaching it.

Willam recovered, cautiously leaned forward, put out one hand, and stopped the pages. He read what was written; apprehension turned to relief.

The red star turned green; the voice of the paper cone became human again. "Willam!"

"Here, sir. I lost you for a moment."

"Yes. Atmospheric conditions."

"The house just linked to Gee-Two. But it's only receiving, not sending."

"Mm. Everyone's system is doing the same... Just re-establishing. All automatic." The wizard sounded distracted, as if some other action were taking most of his attention. "There's... I can't... I can't tell if anyone is trying to see you in real time. Too much traffic... I'm trying to watch your back, Will."

"Thank you, sir."

"Mm. I may not be able to..."

The book vanished, replaced by a live, miniature dragon.

Will showed only utter confusion. He worked his lap board, created a fresh page of insubstantial light, puzzled over what he read there. "It looks like Jannik is running a detailed diagnostic on the dragons..." The creature vanished, replaced immediately by another, then another. Will ignored them. "And he's relaying through the Eastern Guidestar to do it."

"He needs the bandwidth. Stand by."

Silence again, but for the hiss; the sound of night, the sound of emptiness.

"Will, access Gee-Two yourself. Something simple, low priority."

Willam moved his hands across the lap board; on his right, the world's image turned black, but for a few pale blue smears: starlight on water, on high clouds.

"Good. I can't tell what you did, but I've identified the routing code for Jannik's house—Wait." The sequence of tiny dragons ceased. "Will, did something else just come through?"

Willam looked, nodded. "He's reestablishing the dragon controller."

"All right. Has your link with Farside held?"

"Yes... but..." Will gazed, shook his head helplessly. "But I don't know what this is."

"What do you have?" Willam began reading off the symbols. Corvus interrupted him. "Will, I don't have your head for hex."

"Sorry, sir." Agitated now, Will cast about, could not find what he sought. Muttering annoyance, he recreated the white-outlined translator square. He plied it, shook his head, tossed the square aside. It floated, spinning slowly. "It's not words or commands."

"Can it have been encrypted?"

"I've been trying some decryptions. I'm not getting anything so far."

"Stand by." A pause, and some vague sounds from the wizard. "The traffic is easing. It's a little harder to... keep a low profile... Will, the files you checked before showed repeating pairs? But Farside pulled out some sections of difference?"

"Yes, sir."

"Are the differences scattered throughout the file?"

"Yes..."

"Will, you've gone too far behind the interface. It's an image."

Will's jaw dropped. He shut it with an audible snap. His hands moved, fast.

A heavy, ornate gilt picture frame appeared in the air before him. Will fairly spat in derision, but allowed it to stand.

Within the gilt frame, filling the upper quarter of the area: whiteness, and two small spots of black.

"What?" Willam seemed to address the frame. "That's it?" The frame continued to fill.

Will stared, utterly dumbfounded, then threw out both hands, brought them in as if to tear at his hair, stopped himself. "I don't understand!" he said. "I don't even know what I'm looking at!"

"Describe it." Willam did so, as the image in the frame grew:

Black spots, of various sizes, from small to tiny to mere flecks, seeming randomly distributed against the white. Some blots were sharp-edged, others fuzzy, as if seen with blurred vision. A few vague shapes in shades of gray: streamers, irregular blobs, hazy areas—

Corvus said: "Can it be a graph of some sort? A distribution?"

"I don't know... It would have to be a very complex function. And it doesn't have any axes marked." The gilt frame emptied, began again. "I've got enough of a second one to try it..." Willam watched; then his face twisted in distress. "The *same.*"

—As much the same as two depictions of randomness could be. But however they differed from each other, they were of a type, that much was clear. And there seemed, too, a sort of grace to the arrangement, something calming and satisfying. A visual harmony, perhaps, almost comprehensible, odd and innocent, like a simple song in some half-familiar language.

Apparently, this was not lost on Willam. "Can they... can they be some sort of art? Because, they're beautiful, but—no. No, because Kieran—" He tapped, checked the list presented to him in thin air— "Kieran made more than *fifty* of these, on this one night alone, and, and that's when it all changed! And later—" Willam grasped at the air as if grasping for some answer—"Later, he showed Slado, or told him about it, and Slado *killed* him, and brought down Gee-Three—"

"Will, I just saw something routed to the house."

Will glanced about, found the relevant page of light. "Um... Jannik asked for the house status."

"Let's hope your fix fooled him."

"I've got enough for another image..." The frame emptied, filled again. Willam watched, uncomprehending, fascinated.

A faint sound, distant but clear:

A two-toned whistle.

Will sat up straight. "Sir—"

"Something else… A moment…"

"Sir—" The whistle came again.

"—Will, stand by!" Willam froze. Corvus said, "I captured something, a command string sent to the house, starting with—" He began reading out numbers and letters.

Will was on his feet. "That's an override!" He reached right, pulled something from under the desk edge: papers, white, with blotches—

"I've diverted it, I'm holding it. But not for long, I'll be noticed—"

Willam had his sack open; shoved the paper in, swept objects from the desk: the cards, the box, the thong-tied book.

"How much time do you need to get out?"

Will thrust the handwritten sheet into his shirt. "Sixty seconds." He touched the board once; from above, a hum, a rattle.

"I can do that. Sixty seconds from your mark; say when. And good luck, Willam."

But Will stopped short, hesitated a fraction of an instant; reached back down to the lap board, tapped a furiously rapid sequence, glanced up at the dark image of the world.

Across its face, scattered widely in the night: red symbols.

In a voice of near-panic: "Will, did you just ping my link?"

"I pinged everyone's link, sir."

"That was massively stupid!"

"It couldn't make things any worse."

"Get out. Get out now. You have sixty seconds. Good-bye."

Will tore the speaking cone and rod from their attachments, threw them in the sack, slid himself straight across the face of the desk, through the light-letters, through the gilt-framed image, thumped to the floor, grabbed Rowan's arm, and yanked her to her feet.

She staggered; the sudden touch of solid flesh was startling. He pulled her upright; he gripped her shoulder; he said, close to her face: "Run."

CHAPTER TWENTY

*T*hey were out of the study, into the hall, to the stairs and then down them, with the house, ever helpful, lighting their path. At the bottom of the last flight, they stumbled through darkness, their eyesight still dazzled. In the foyer, they knocked over Jannik's umbrella stand, left it lying on the floor.

At the portico, Bel's hands found them. "No, not out in the street." She pulled them aside. "It's too open, he's high up, he'll see you." There were dim shadows of roof edges, black against the street cobbles, shifting slowly, weirdly, as if the entire world were one great ship changing its course.

Bel pushed Rowan and Willam against the wall. They stood gasping as the light above brightened, then lowered itself behind the house.

Bel peered around the corner of the building. Then she punched Rowan's arm. "Go."

They dashed in the shield of the house's huge shadow, across to the ruins in the next lot. They reached the half-wall they had hidden behind earlier, and crouched against the bricks in the dry weeds.

The place Rowan had flattened before was still there. She looked at it; it seemed unreal, inexplicable. "We forgot the lantern," she said stupidly.

Willam said in a small voice, "It doesn't matter. I can't believe we're alive." He slid down the wall to sit on the ground. Rowan did the same. She blinked about. The streets were too bright, the shadows too dark. The grass felt strange under her hands, sensation distant and disconnected from sight. Everything around her, persons and objects, seemed mere colored light, empty, insubstantial: interface constructs.

Rowan lay her cheek against the bricks, focused on their roughness, their scent. *Real. Solid.* The fact seemed abstract. She found she had turned her face to press her lips against the bricks; a moment later, obeying some instinct she could not name, she tasted them.

"I've seen Christers kissing the ground when they get off a ship."

She turned; Willam was regarding her, weakly amused. But when she did not reply immediately he became disturbed. "Rowan?" He reached out to her, but something, perhaps something in her eyes, made him stop. He remained, one hand half reaching, eyes wide. His white hair and pale skin seemed almost to glow in the heavy black shadows.

He had been working for Corvus. All this time, all along, he had been working for Corvus.

The steerswoman said, "I don't think I know what's real anymore." She turned away from him. "Bel?"

The Outskirter was prone, spying past the tumbled edge of the wall. "That thing, that flying cart"—she raised her voice over a rising wind that rattled the branches of the trees and bushes—"it's coming down in the garden." Dust hissed into the street, the houses now lit from a freakishly low angle, as if a small white sun were sinking to earth. Noise thrummed in Rowan's stomach, whined in her ears. The sound deepened, faded, but did not cease.

Rowan shifted forward awkwardly, trying to see what Bel saw. The Outskirter used one foot to shove her back. "Don't let him spot you," Bel hissed, "he killed you in the Dolphin."

"Can he see *you?*" Will asked.

"Probably not. But I don't think it matters. I'm not the only one looking." Across the street, shutters were open a crack, showing candlelight, quickly snuffed; at another house, the street door opened slightly, with a pale face half-glimpsed beyond.

"He's doing something with that cart, I can't tell what," Bel said. "He seems calm enough. It looks like you got away with it."

"No, he knows something was up. He sent a spell," Willam said. "He must think it worked. He thinks he's killed the intruder."

"Well, he's fussing away like he hasn't got a care in the world."

The noise rose again and the wind picked up, gusting wildly. Bel tucked her head down from the flying leaves and dust.

White light brightened. The long shadows sharpened, then shortened. Rowan looked up.

Low overhead, then arcing up and rising: an oval shape with four legs, like the underbelly of a huge insect with a lantern, impossibly brilliant, in place of its head. Smaller lights showed on either side.

The steerswoman was beyond astonishment. Like ship's lamps, she thought, distantly. Red for port; green for starboard.

The insect rose farther, became small, then tiny. The white light vanished abruptly, leaving only red and green, two colored stars that moved across the constellations, westward.

Willam reached past Rowan, tapped the Outskirter's foot. "Bel?"

"He's watching it go. I can see him, there's a red lantern lit in the garden." A pause. "Now he's walking up the path to the back door...

That's it." Bel climbed to her knees. "He's gone into the house."

Willam released a shaky breath. "We should get out of here—" He made to rise.

But Rowan put out one hand, caught his arm. He stopped. "Willam," she said, uncertain, then suddenly urgent, "that last spell, that"—she recovered the term he had used—"that 'override.' "

He was puzzled. "Yes…"

"Are you absolutely certain that it was *Jannik* who sent it?"

Will's jaw dropped. "No…"

A soft *whump;* a huge *crack;* and wind, as sudden as a blow, and as brief. A thousand tiny objects struck the wall beside Rowan in a weird, chiming hail.

A moment of utterly empty silence, as if the world itself were stunned. Then a hiss and a growing roar, and crackles. Shadows jumped and writhed from flickering light.

Rowan stood slowly and backed away from the wall.

The windows of Jannik's house had all burst outward. Smoke streamed from them, out and then straight up, vertical rivers of smoke, thick and black. Inside, light flailed wildly, red and yellow and white.

Willam was standing beside her, gaping at the sight. There were shouts in the distance, more shouts nearer, then many voices in the street.

Bel came to Rowan's side. "Ow." She was rubbing her face.

Will saw, grabbed and stopped her hands. "No, don't touch it, stay still, keep your eyes closed." He took her by the shoulders and turned her toward the angry light from the house. "Rowan—give me your handkerchief."

She passed it to him, now frightened. "Will—"

"Wait, wait." Seeming oblivious to all else, Willam brushed at Bel's face with infinite patience and delicacy. Each pass left threads of blood behind. "We need water," Will said.

They led Bel to East Well, pushing through the crowd now growing there, people gathering safely back from the heat of the wizard's house. Men and women in nightclothes, or wrapped in blankets; barefoot near-naked children; three of the city guard; and voices all around.

Their former lookout was shouting, pulling and pushing at people, forcing them into order. A bucket line, Rowan realized.

Once again, a starry night in Donner; once again, a burning building, and a bucket line… At least this time, only a wizard had been harmed.

And Bel—

Willam was patting Bel's face with the dampened handkerchief, rinsing, patting. Rowan said, "Will—"

"Stand by... ," he said distractedly.

Working for Corvus. "Willam!"

Bel said: "Rowan, let him be, I think he knows what he's doing." The Outskirter's aggrieved tone reassured Rowan immensely. "A lot of debris flew in my face, but I'm not in terrible agony. And I hope that handkerchief is clean," she added to Willam.

"It's better than glass getting in your eyes. Hold still."

"Meaning it isn't, I suppose."

The bucket line had evolved into order, but the volunteers hesitated when a voice spoke up in an authoritative tone: "Hold back. The wizard's house stands alone." A blanket-wrapped figure moved through the crowd and drew near. "Let it burn down, I say."

It was Irina. She caught Rowan's eye, nodded.

"I thought you were out of town," Rowan said, confused.

"Hmph. When a wizard sends for me, I am definitely not at home." Irina turned away, adjusted the blanket more decorously about her night shift, and stood watching the fire, reflected flame glittering in her eyes.

But the bucket line did go to work, relaying water to the house across from Jannik's and another nearby, where burning debris had settled on the roofs. The volunteers moved quickly, efficiently.

Willam intercepted one of the buckets. "Bel, keep your eyes closed, and dunk your face in the water." The Outskirter did so, came up sputtering. Will inspected her face carefully. "Your eyes don't hurt?"

"No. My face does." Bel's forehead and right cheek were covered with a multitude of small cuts. Thankfully, none was large, and none seemed deep.

"All right, then," Willam said. Bel dried her face on her sleeves, looked about, then at her friends, then at the wizard's house.

Orange light, flickering and pulsing in each shattered window. Smoke, streaming up into the night sky. Heat-shimmer, rising from the roof, making the stars beyond seem to twist and shift.

The roof tiles were blackening. As Rowan watched, yellow lines appeared among them, cracks, which widened. There was a pause, as if the building were itself drawing a breath, and then the roof collapsed, down through the third storey, and the second. A blast of wind and heat, from which everyone present turned away; and when they turned back, the house was a brick shell, holding only flame within.

Bel turned to Rowan and Willam. "I thought we decided not to kill the wizard."

CHAPTER TWENTY-ONE

"We didn't do it," the steerswoman said.

Rowan sat with Bel on her right, Willam on her left. Across the large table, crowding close and in some cases tucked behind each other, were the fourteen members of Donner's city council, and a few other trusted citizens.

The formal dining room of the Dolphin was dark but for two silver candelabra standing in the center of the table, and one window on the far side of the room. It stood open on a predawn sky of a dull dusky blue, where the last of the morning stars shone faintly.

Winter stars, Rowan noted distantly. The morning stars of autumn are the stars of winter.

Joly traced the pattern in the linen tablecloth with one finger. "I can't say that I'm sorry," he said, not looking up. "If ever a man deserved to die, it was Jannik." He raised his dark gaze to the apprentice and the steerswoman. "But if you did not cause the fire, even by accident..."

From the corner of her eye, Rowan saw Willam shift slightly. She ignored him; she could not bear to look at him. She said to Joly, "We believe that was Slado's doing."

Bel sat up. "He saw you?" Rowan turned to her. The Outskirter made a strange sight, cuts strewn across her face like red mud splashes, looking as if one could simply wipe them off. Bel had a clean cloth, and had been wiping. The marks remained, some of them still stubbornly bleeding.

"We stayed past the updates," Willam said, from behind Rowan's left shoulder. "I was so close... I thought, if I kept working for just a little longer..."

"The updates ended, and Slado saw," Rowan said to Bel. "However it is that wizards see these things, he saw." The steerswoman addressed the gathering at large. "But Slado also saw that Jannik, in the dragon fields, was calling magically to the house, and giving it commands from afar."

"Different commands," Willam put in. "Harmless ones. But Slado couldn't tell that."

"But he could recognize the spell taking place in the house itself. It was..."

"Big," Willam said. "Loud."

"Bright." *Will, you look like a bonfire!* "And its nature could not be mistaken. So Slado sent the house a command of his own. He told it to wait for Jannik to come home, and then destroy itself."

There was quiet for a space, and then Irina asked the obvious next question. "And did you find what you were seeking, you and your runaway apprentice? Did you learn this mighty secret?"

It was Bel who answered. "No. They would have said so immediately." She turned to her friends, disappointed. "You failed. You didn't find it."

"Actually...," Rowan said, and for a moment she regarded her own two hands lying on the tablecloth, locked together, fingers interlaced. "Actually, I don't know." And then she did look at Willam: she turned to him and looked directly into those familiar, beautiful, guileless copper eyes.

Working for Corvus.

The steerswoman held the wide gaze with her own, her face expressionless. "Willam?"

"Rowan, I think I did find it." He spoke as if speaking only to her, spoke with a desperate sincerity almost painful to watch. "What we saw, at the end—I really think that was it. But..." His hands moved vaguely, as if trying to grasp, as they had before, insubstantial light. "But I didn't know what it was. I didn't know what it meant. It was beyond me." He dropped his hands. "I was out of my depth." But then, faintly hopeful: "Rowan, did *you—*"

She turned away from him. "It was completely incomprehensible to me."

Quiet comments of disappointment among the council members; and Joly sighed. "Then all of this was for nothing." All the searching, questioning; the slayings done in darkness; the terror in the dragon fields; the revelations and hopes.

A friend's betrayal. Naio's death.

For nothing.

"That," Irina declared, "is your opinion." She took a moment to adjust her blanket closer about her shoulders, managing to convey, even in her night shift, a graceful dignity. "As I see it, 'all this,' as you call it, has had a wonderful result. Donner now has no wizard."

"They'll send another," Will said immediately.

Irina sniffed. "No doubt. But we know a thing or two about wizards now. This new wizard will be a stranger, and he won't know what we're capable of. We'll smile to his face and be oh-so-respectful, but all sorts of things can happen when his back is turned. We'll find ways to work against him." She looked about the room, and became outraged at some of the expressions she saw. "Well, *some* of us will, at the least! Persons with both courage and discretion. Are there none such in this room?"

Reeder, standing behind his father's chair, spoke without hesitation. "Here."

"And here," Marel said, glancing up at his son.

"Here," Joly said, leaning back, studying Irina with new interest.

Ruffo screwed his eyes shut tight, his face becoming a single immense wince. But: "Here," he managed to get out.

"If so, Ruffo, you will definitely have to learn to moderate your volubility," Irina said.

"Well, try not to tell me any important secrets."

"Secrets come with the territory!"

The bawdy-house proprietor laced his fingers, placed his hands on the table. "You would be amazed," he said, with some pride, "at the sorts of things my young men and ladies hear."

"Excellent! I believe we have the makings of a cabal in this very room. I'm sure that among us, we can find any number of small, secret, and subtle ways to weaken the wizard's power over us—"

Willam sat up straight. "Destroy the dragons."

All conversation ceased. Rowan turned to Willam in astonishment.

He seemed not to notice her. "All of them," he said to the people of Donner. "They're complicated devices. They're hard to make, and they'll be hard to replace. It will take time. And not only that"—he became eager—"it will take power, and material, and important resources away from other things that the wizards do. Destroying the dragons would cause all the wizards a lot of trouble, all around, for a long time."

No one seemed to know how to take this. Eventually Joly said, hesitantly, "But... how could we possibly accomplish such a thing?"

Will immediately stood and moved the candles to the far side of the table; and when he then reached down to the floor by his chair, Bel let out a single *"Ha!"* and clapped her hands.

Willam placed a small object in the center of the white tablecloth. "By magic," he said.

It was round, slightly smaller than a goose egg, and white. There was a dark band around its circumference with short vertical lines and corresponding numbers, like index marks.

Willam sat down again. All eyes remained on the object. "Right now," Willam said, "the dragons are on standby—" He caught himself, began again. "The control system is down—" He paused, thought. "The spell that tells the dragons what to do was inside Jannik's house. It was destroyed.

That means the dragons have no guidance, no instructions, and they can't leave the dragon fields, no matter what happens. Someone has to go there, and throw this charm right into the middle of the dragons."

The steerswoman sat stunned and speechless; but Bel had no such problem. She laughed out loud, the bright, hard laugh of a warrior. "It will shatter them! Like Shammer and Dhree's fortress, like that derelict boat in Wulfshaven! Dragons flying apart, in a thousand pieces—Will, that is brilliant!"

During this, Ruffo had slowly sunk down level with the edge of the table and was now eying the destructive charm across the entire breadth of the surface. He said, in a small voice, "Kill the dragons?"

Irina smiled sweetly. "Kill the dragons."

"Let me do it," Reeder said.

"Can you throw?" Irina asked him.

Marel said, "I've seen him fling a ledger across the entire length of the office and hit a dozing accountant."

"I'm sure you exaggerate."

"Well, perhaps it was only a tally board. Quite a distance, though."

Reeder casually leaned, and reached, and picked up the charm. Gasps and murmurs among the people, and those nearby shied back in sudden fear. Reeder ignored them all and coolly examined the object, turning it over in his hands.

Joly watched nervously. "That... small thing will actually destroy the dragons?" he asked.

"It might take more than one," Willam said. "I have a dozen with me." He looked Joly straight in the eye. "You can have them all."

Irina gazed at the ceiling with a dreamy expression. "Oh, I find my mind bursting with wonderful plans—"

"Don't use them on people!" Will's sudden vehemence startled them all, but for Reeder, who merely glanced up, brows raised. "Never," Willam said. His eyes were hard and bright. "That's wrong. That's *evil.*"

Joly recovered first. He said, solemnly: "We will never use this magic on people. I swear it."

Will required the same promise from each and every person present, ending with Reeder, who paused long, carefully studying Willam's face. Then Reeder reluctantly assented, with a single nod, and turned his attention back to the charm he held. "What are these markings?"

"That's a timer." Willam rose and went around the table to show Reeder. "If you use it, the charm will wait for a while before releasing its power. See? These markings are seconds, and next comes minutes—"

Rowan recovered her voice. "Willam."

"And you turn the ring—no, don't do it now—"

"Will."

He glanced at her once, then looked back again, caught her expression. And then he stopped: stopped speaking, stopped moving, stopped everything and merely waited for whatever the steerswoman would say next.

She had found her voice, but words were harder to come by. Perhaps it took only a moment; it seemed far longer to her.

"This is a wonderful idea," she said. The statement was inadequate to the depth of her emotion; but at this moment, she could do no better. "Thank you."

A small smile, almost shy in its quickness, but conveying in one instant pleasure at her praise, and relief, and gratitude. Willam turned back to continue Reeder's instruction.

A series of noises coming from Ruffo's direction evolved into "But—but—" and drew the council's attention. "But," Ruffo said, "what will the new wizard think, coming to Donner and finding all the dragons dead?"

Willam had the answer to hand. "Blame it on me," he said smoothly. "The escaped apprentice. But wait until I'm gone to use the charms—"

"Must you go?" Irina asked.

"Yes," Will said with regret. "I must. But if I can, if things ever quiet down, I'll try to come back in secret. And when I do"—he took the charm from Reeder's hand and held it up for all to see—"I will teach you how to make these for yourselves."

There was more discussion, and ideas arising, and plans made. But all of it was conducted among the people of Donner, and proceeded entirely without the steerswoman's participation, and without the Outskirter's, and, quite soon, without Willam's. The three friends watched for a while as these citizens of Donner devised strategies, formed subgroups, designed clandestine lines of communication, and regathered themselves into a new order.

Presently Bel leaned forward to catch Will's and Rowan's attention and tilted her head toward the door; and it seemed to Rowan that it was, after all, time to go. They waited for an appropriate moment, and made their good-byes.

Rowan found herself standing by the dining room door, clasping Joly's large hand, looking up into his dark, intelligent face. "I hardly know how to thank you, and all these people, for the help you've given us."

"I'm glad we did it. You showed us something, lady: something about ourselves that we didn't know before. You, and Naio as well…" He released her hand. "I believe Jannik was right, in a way. Naio was an example after all." He glanced back at the table, where people were continuing their work. "I think we've learned the lesson, now."

"We've started something," Bel said, as Rowan led the way down the staircase. "You may have failed in the wizard's house, but things have been set in motion here. But this is only one city... Rowan, your people need to organize, and they need a leader."

"I think you're right. The Outskirters have one now, and we need—" The steerswoman stopped dead in her tracks at the bottom of the stairs. She turned to Bel. "No. No, Bel, not me! I can't—"

"Of course you can't." The Outskirter's expression was disparaging in the extreme. "You don't have it in you. It would be a disaster."

"Well. Thank you for your candor."

"But you should keep it in mind, and keep your eyes open for prospects—"

"Bel," Willam said. The others looked back and up; he had lagged behind and now stood paused halfway down the stairs. "Slado is in the Upper Wulf Valley." Bel's jaw dropped. Will went on: "That's not where he lives, it's just where he is now. By the time you get there, or get word there, he'll be gone. It doesn't help any. But I have something else for you." He descended the last few steps to join them. "There are Krue among the Outskirters, and I can show you where they are."

Back in her tiny room, the steerswoman pulled the charts from her map case, located her single map of the Outskirts, and handed it to Willam. He glanced at it, then stopped short and regarded her, puzzled.

"I'm the only steerswoman ever to visit the Outskirts," she explained. The small chart showed only Rowan's own route to Tournier's Fault and back: a wandering line, a few clear landmarks, and vague indications of nearby geography as described to her by others.

Willam thought. "Then I need a blank sheet of paper, and something to draw with."

They used the back of the largest chart of the Inner Lands. It was too big for the table; they set in on the bed. Willam laid Rowan's little map of the Outskirts at its left edge, and knelt on the floor. "I used to look at the Outskirts a lot. But I'm not good at this." He moved the pencil, wide, sweeping movements. "The distances may be off, but I'm fairly certain about the landmarks..." A cluster of lakes appeared, high in the north, the source of a huge river whose course intersected with Rowan's own map and continued south. "This goes all the way to the ocean..." The coastline was merely a slash, and a scrawled label: **Oriental**. Will abandoned the ocean as if it were irrelevant and moved north again. His depictions were crude, the labels awkward and outsized, but the steerswoman watched as the unknown lands revealed themselves.

Then: "Right," Will said, as if finished; but he did not pause. "Here, and here." Two *x*s tucked among the numerous **Cat Lakes**. "Those are links."

"Wizards' minions," Bel breathed.

"No, not minions." He added another, south of a series of roughly sketched hills. "It's a different sort of link, more powerful than minions get. These are Krue."

The last thing Willam had done in Jannik's house, the action that caused Corvus such distress—"You…" Such an odd word; Rowan struggled to recover it. "You pinged the links."

He nodded, added another *x* northwest, quite close to the Inner Lands, one more far to the east. "It's like a question: 'Are you there?' The link will respond, by itself—it has to." He hesitated, pencil in the air, then added one more *x* near Tournier's Fault. "This one might really be two, close together." And he sat back on his heels, considering his work. Then he shook his head. "That's the best I can do. It went by so fast. There might be more, but I'm sure about these."

The leader of the Outskirters studied the scrawls and marks that located the positions of her enemies. "I'll send word. We'll find them." Bel's tone left no doubt as to their fate.

"Bel, think twice." The Outskirter turned to Rowan. The steerswoman said, "Fletcher was a wizard's man, but he grew to love your people. He turned. One of these might, also."

Bel's dark eyes moved in thought as she speculated. "More magic on our side?"

"As much as possible."

Willam rose from the floor, carefully rolled up the chart, and set it aside. He sat on the bed. Then he reached down the neck of his shirt and drew something out, and passed it to the steerswoman. Rowan accepted it hesitantly, but did not open it. She waited for Willam to speak, although she guessed what he would say.

Willam said: "Kieran's clearance."

The Outskirter let out a whoop and fairly threw herself at him, catching him in a huge hug, knocking them both against the wall. "Will, you're brilliant!" she declared, and laughed. "High clearance, you said before, all the way to the top—"

Will was attempting to extract himself, and to calm her. "No, no it's not that good, not anymore."

"But it's his authority!"

"But he's *dead.*" Bel backed off to sit on her heels beside him. Will went on: "When a person dies, his clearance is... canceled, negated. The spells won't accept it anymore." He looked up at Rowan. "But when that was done, Farside was already isolated. It never learned that Kieran is dead."

"What's Farside?" Bel asked.

"The third place of strong magic," Rowan said. "Will, this is why Farside obeyed you, once your commands reached it?"

"That's right."

Bel asked Willam: "What can this Farside do for us?"

"Nothing, anymore. I'd need the magic in Jannik's house to reach it again... But, I wonder. I wonder if there are other systems—other collections of spells that have been isolated for a long time. It seems to me that there must be. I know the wizards aren't as powerful as they used to be."

"How do we use it?" Bel asked.

"You can't. It isn't Kieran's passwords, or his voice. It's what comes after that, it's... it's what the spells translate Kieran's voice and passwords and scan into."

Rowan considered the acts done in Jannik's study, remembered a phrase. She said, "We'd have to get behind the interface."

He nodded.

"Willam, I can't possibly do that myself."

"I know. But I shouldn't be the only one who has it. Because somewhere, sometime, someone else might know how to use it. Because... because it's something powerful, that the wizards don't know we have."

Rowan opened the paper. Numbers and letters, in meaningless sequence. She found herself impelled to say, irrelevantly, "Willam, your handwriting is terrible."

At this, the man who mere hours before had nimbly manipulated bizarre and incomprehensible magics looked as sheepish as a child admonished by a teacher. "I'm sorry," he said. "I don't often write by hand."

"You generally write by magic?" Bel asked.

"Well, yes."

She grinned. "Clever boy. But what about the Krue in the Outskirts? Could they use it if they had it?"

"I don't know. It depends on what kind of link they have. But Rowan is right; if your friend Fletcher could turn against the wizards, another might, too."

Bel laughed. "Rowan," she urged, "make a copy!" She turned back to Willam. "One of them is bound to turn. You can't live as an Outskirter, be one of us, without learning to care about your tribe."

Tell her, Rowan thought; but she did not have the heart, at the moment, to quash Bel's enthusiasm.

Rowan sifted among the charts on the table, located her logbook. She flipped through it, looking for the first blank page.

"It's possible," Will was saying to Bel. "Those people are so isolated from the Krue. They'd have to form local attachments, it's only natural."

Loose sheets slid out of the book, lost themselves among the charts. Rowan retrieved them:

Slado, nursing his tea. Slado, standing by the wharves. Slado's portrait, left unfinished when young Ona fled. The handkerchief boy's primitive pastoral scene. Rowan slipped them back into the logbook, one by one.

"Some may have already turned, or be about to," Bel was telling Will. "The tale of what has been going on has been spreading among the tribes for four years now."

"And if Slado uses the heat again, they could die along with the Outskirters," Will replied. "One already has, that I know about."

Rowan stopped with the last drawing in her hands. She stared.

"Slado doesn't care," Bel was saying. "He never warned Fletcher—"

Rowan held up the drawing, face-out.

Conversation ceased. Bel and Willam regarded the picture, perplexed. They shifted their confusion to the steerswoman. Rowan said nothing.

Presently, Will spoke, tentatively. "... Horsies in a field?"

Rowan said: "The sky is white, the stars are black."

They remained confused; then Willam blinked, and comprehension dawned. "Stars?" He took the drawing. "Kieran... Kieran was looking at the *stars?*"

"Yes," Rowan said, definitely.

"Are you sure—"

"Yes!" That was why the images had seemed so familiar, had seemed beautiful. It was the beauty of the natural world, like the sweet sight of the world itself, from high in the air. And if a Guidestar can look down, why not up?

"Why black on white? Why not the way they would really look?"

"I don't know."

"But, why so many? Rowan, there were more than ten thousand!"

"Kieran was looking at the sky." She had no doubt.

"But—" Willam studied the child's drawing desperately, as if it were itself one of the magical images, as if it could provide the answer. "—but, *why?"*

"I don't know."

"Rowan, you know the sky," Bel said. "Where was he looking?"

Rowan thought, and thought harder, trying to recall; but no, she had recognized nothing...

But how could one, with the colors reversed, the view not known to be stars at all, and the entire scene viewed from behind, backward?

The steerswoman turned out the chair and sat. She closed her eyes. "Give me a moment." She concentrated: dots, blots, streamers, hazes... reverse it, match to known constellations...

She heard Willam moving about in the room; there came the sound of papers being shifted; and then something was in the steerswoman's hands. She opened her eyes, looked down. She said, in a small voice, "Oh..."

It was beautiful, rendered with that inhuman perfection typical of wizards' maps. A chart of the sky, black stars on white, but with nothing labeled, with every object mute and nameless.

She looked up at Willam. He said simply: "Hard copy."

But nothing was familiar. Rowan turned it about, and about again, to no result. "This might be in the sky of the far south. There are stars beyond our horizons that no one has ever seen."

"Try this one." Willam passed her another, handed hers to Bel, who studied it curiously. He held one more in his hands.

Rowan tried again, recognized nothing; and then she did, but not from her own knowledge. "Give me the first again." Bel passed it back to her. Rowan compared them. "They overlap."

They laid them on the bed, side by side. Rowan turned them about, testing orientations. "Here." She slid them together. Two charts overlapped diagonally, with the third centered on the section in common.

The steerswoman, the Outskirter, and the wizard's apprentice stood regarding the result.

Then Rowan lifted and dropped her shoulders. "Apparently Kieran was charting the sky." A wizard who loved flowers, and children, and the stars... But surely ten thousand overlapping charts would cover the entire sky many times over. Why such obsessiveness?

Accuracy, perhaps. By drawing each one fresh and comparing previous versions, errors would be obvious, and could be corrected on a master chart. Rowan separated the charts again, checked the overlapping area, and nodded. One chart did differ slightly from the other two.

Fifty, on this one night alone, Will had said to Corvus.

Rowan felt foolish. "Of course," she muttered, "he didn't actually draw these himself." It would take Rowan hours to make an accurate chart of even a portion of the sky.

Will looked at her in surprise. "No, they're not drawings at all. They're—it's hard to explain. They're images of what's really there. As if you could capture exactly what you see, and save it forever."

Rowan rubbed her eyes, which suddenly stung with exhaustion. *Magic*, a part of her mind whispered; *Impossible. Incomprehensible.*

No. She knew better now. Anything existing must be possible; anything existing could be comprehended. She understood Willam's blasting-charms. A similar logic must lie behind this.

Accept it; go on from there.

"If this is what Kieran actually saw," Rowan said, and pointed, "then, what is that?"

Willam and Bel looked. "Stars," Bel said.

"Four stars," Willam said.

"But they're not on this chart, nor"—she checked closely—"on this."

Four tiny stars, like the points of a tilted square, on one chart only. On the others, there stood in that position only a single star. "Will, what order were these"—*charts* would not do; she used his own word—"these images created?"

This presented a problem, as the images were not marked. Willam finally reasoned from the order in which he had passed them out.

In the relevant area, one star; then that star gone, and four in its place; then one star again. "These three images, all on the same night?"

"Rowan," Willam said, "these images were captured just *seconds* apart."

And the steerswoman knew that she could take this no farther.

There was information here; but she could not recognize it. This was—and she was certain of it now—the very answer they had been seeking. But she could not understand it.

Individually, each one of these captured views of the sky admitted of at least reasonable explanation. In fact, any two taken together did—because there were such things as new stars appearing where none had stood before, and she assumed that stars must sometimes die—

But all three images taken together in sequence immediately negated even the most extreme speculation.

New knowledge was built on earlier knowledge, built on knowledge learned earlier still, all of it growing wider, deeper, higher, and reaching endlessly farther. But these magical images represented information too distant from everything the steerswoman knew as true.

There were steps between: a dozen, a thousand.

Context: she had no context in which to understand this. Rowan considered long before speaking; so long that she moved the images from the bed to the table, sat down on the bed, pulled up her legs, and remained, gazing in the distance, and silent, for some time.

Bel watched her, disappointed, then leaned against the wall, crossing her arms. "Send them to the Archives," she said. "The Prime can put all the steerswomen there on it. Maybe together they can—"

"Willam," Rowan said, "if Corvus saw these images, would he understand them?"

Bel was immediately, sharply disapproving. "Rowan, we should think carefully before we do that. Corvus may have passed you by once, but I don't think it's a good idea to put yourself in his path again."

Willam seemed not to hear Bel. At Rowan's question, his face had become expressionless. He turned the chair out and sat, elbows on his knees, hands loose. He gazed at his hands, then looked up at the steerswoman. "I don't know. He's never been interested in the sky. I don't think he knows much about it at all."

"But, with his magic, would he be able to learn more about it, if he chose?" Willam only nodded.

Bel threw up her hands. "Wonderful! And whatever the wizards know, they keep secret. Let's give them even more secrets, shall we? Let's allow Corvus to figure all of this out, and just remain in the dark ourselves."

Rowan sighed. "Bel, this is beyond us. We need help."

"And why would Corvus help us?"

Rowan waited for Willam to speak; he did not.

Bel could not fail to miss this. She said slowly, in a dangerous tone: "Someone tell me what is going on."

"Willam," Rowan prompted.

Willam gathered himself to speak. He glanced at the Outskirter, but could not meet her eyes. He looked away. "Bel," he began; but apparently he could get no farther. He fell silent.

The steerswoman said: "Willam did not escape from Corvus. Corvus sent him here. Willam has been working for Corvus all along."

And the Outskirter seemed, at the moment, beyond words; but a word emerged nevertheless, weakly, on a breath not planned for speech: "What?"

Will closed his eyes. "This wasn't supposed to involve either of you, I didn't know you were here—"

Bel's breath found its force. *"What?"*

Rowan discovered that she had risen to interpose herself between Bel and Willam, and that the room was far too small for such sudden action. She found herself with her hands on Bel's shoulders, and Bel against the wall. Rowan wondered how long that would last.

Bel shifted her anger to Rowan, but at least used words first. "You *knew!"*

"I've only just found out. In Jannik's house, when Will asked Corvus for help."

"Corvus was *there?*"

"No. Only his voice was there. Bel, think of what Willam has done for us, working with us, helping us, giving magic to the people of Donner." Rowan moved to look the Outskirter directly in the face, and stressed her next words, "Willam is not our enemy."

Bel looked at Rowan, then glanced past her at Willam. Rowan did not know what the Outskirter saw, but Bel said, "No. No, of course he's not." And Rowan relaxed somewhat, and released her friend. "Will, what's the meaning of this?" Bel asked. "Why did your master send you here? Is Corvus working on our side now?"

"Corvus is playing his own game," Willam said.

"With you as his pawn!" Will did not deny this. "To do his dirty work, risk your life, and lie to your friends—and lie to a steerswoman!"

"I tried not to!" Will said. He looked lost, helpless. "I did, but it was so hard, I had to keep watching what I said, it was hard to keep track—"

Bel pushed Rowan aside; but there was no violence behind it. She stepped in front of Willam, and stooped down level with his face. He regarded her bleakly. "You're talking about words," she said. "I'm talking about actions. You did everything you could to make Rowan and me think you didn't serve Corvus. Will—what kind of power does the wizard have over you?"

"It's not like that—"

"Bel," Rowan said.

The Outskirter ignored her. "That blast Slado sent was meant for you! Is that how it is, then? Will you walk into danger for Corvus, lay down your life for him, betray your friends at his word—"

"It was my idea!" Willam threw out both arms. "The whole thing was *my idea!* Bel"—he turned to the steerswoman—"Rowan... Whatever Slado is doing, it's got to be as bad for the wizards as for the common folk, or why would he keep it secret from them? Bel, Corvus *is* trying to find out what's going on but, but he has to be careful. He can't let Slado know that he knows anything, and he can't let Slado know he's trying to learn even more!" He dropped his arms. "So, so after the last Bioform Clearance... I remembered that Slado had been an apprentice in Donner, *I* thought that there might be fragments of records left, and I said we should get into the house system and look for them—but Corvus wouldn't do it."

"He was afraid," Bel said, with scorn.

"What happened to Jannik could happen to Corvus. Just as easily. But then, I thought"—he laid his hand on his chest—"I thought that if *I* was the one to actually do it, then if it went wrong Corvus could deny that he knew anything. So we let on that I had run away." He leaned back, seeming suddenly weary. "And if everything went right, if no one noticed what I did, I could go back to Corvus with my tail between my legs. And Corvus would make a show of forgiving me, and take me back. The wizards would think that he was weak, and foolish, and a slave to his passions, and they'd gossip and laugh at him behind his back—but that's all they'd do. No one would be any the wiser." He looked up at Rowan. "I thought I could do it all myself. I thought you'd never have to know. But when it turned out to be *Farside*... I didn't know how to reach it. I needed his help."

During this, Bel had seated herself on the floor, and was now looking up at him. "What a clever plan," she said quietly. "And you couldn't trust us enough to share it?"

"It was safer that you didn't know," he said.

"How would ignorance protect us?"

"Not us, Bel," Rowan put in. "Safer for Corvus."

Rowan expected anger again; but from her place on the floor, Bel looked up at Willam, showing only deep sadness. "You think we'd betray you."

"I think you wouldn't have a choice. If the wizards thought you knew something—"

"You don't know me very well."

"I know them," he said simply.

From where she stood, Rowan could not see Willam's expression, but Bel could. Whatever the Outskirter saw there gave her pause.

Then abruptly Bel stood, reached past Willam, and picked up the sky images. She brushed into him as she did it; Willam did not startle, nor shy back. He seemed beyond action.

The Outskirter fanned the three images in front of the apprentice's face. "One man saw this, and turned good. Another man saw it and turned evil." She paused. "Which way will Corvus go?"

"I don't know. I can't know, without knowing what they mean." And he saw the disbelief on Bel's face; it seemed to break his heart. "Bel, I'm not lying!" he said desperately. "I *don't* know! I'd tell you, if I did."

The steerswoman said, "I believe him."

Bel turned to her. "He deceived you worse than me. You're the steerswoman."

"Corvus never knew that I was in the room." Bel was surprised, and her eyes narrowed in thought. Rowan went on. "Corvus could hear and speak, but not see. Willam never betrayed my presence. And, Will—Corvus never knew that you were using Kieran's clearance, did he?"

"No," Willam said. "I don't think he should know about that."

"Are you playing your own game, too?" Bel asked him.

He sighed. "I don't know what it is that I'm doing anymore. I think I'm just trying to help."

Bel held up the images again. "What about these? Will you show them to Corvus?"

Will regarded them, and was a long time replying. "Let the steerswoman keep them."

"Good," Bel said. "One Slado in the world is enough." She set them back on the table. "So, that's it. Now you run back to your master."

"I can't go back."

"Why not?" Bel spoke bitterly. "Slado doesn't know about you. He thought it was Jannik working all those spells—" She stopped. "Slado can't admit that he killed Jannik."

An escaped apprentice; a center of magic, destroyed; a wizard, dead.

Slado needed a scapegoat. Willam was convenient. Willam could not go back to Corvus.

"Well, you're a runaway apprentice, after all. You don't have a choice, do you?" Then Bel's voice lost its irony. "You're better off away from Corvus," she said. "I don't think it's been good for you."

Willam had in fact chosen, Rowan realized, but not here and now.

Corvus, when the updates were about to end, when continuing to work meant having no protection: *I can't risk being connected with this. If you do this, you can't come home.*

Do you want to go on?

Will had gone on.

Now he could not return. And—whatever else life under the wizard's command might entail—home, to Willam, was with Corvus.

Willam looked, at that moment, very alone.

Rowan stepped past the Outskirter, sat down on the bed near Willam. He glanced at her, said nothing.

"They're going to be looking for you."

He nodded.

Come with me, she wanted to say; but: "I have to go to the Archives." A letter would be insufficient. "That's... too close to Wulfshaven."

Another nod. "I understand."

Alone in the wide world, after all. "You'll have to run."

"Or hide somewhere." He made a small movement with his shoulders: not quite a helpless shrug. "Which is better?"

She twitched a small smile. "I prefer to keep moving, myself.

Although…" And she considered. "Establishing oneself in a small corner of some quiet place… making friends, accumulating a second history… It's good to have people around you, Willam. If trouble comes, you may find you have more allies than you knew."

Bel leaned against the wall, made a wry noise. "Well, pick one. He can't stay in one place and keep moving at the same time."

Rowan looked up. "Actually," she said, feeling a great relief at the idea, "actually, I believe he can."

CHAPTER TWENTY-TWO

Willam joined the crew of *Graceful Days*.

Of the ship's crew members, only Gregori, Enid, the first mate, and the navigator knew of Willam's presence during Jannik's gathering in the Dolphin, and his connection with the events surrounding the wizard's death.

"But the others will know that something happened," Bel pointed out as they walked down the street to the harbor. The day was bright, brilliant and clear, but the weather had become even colder. Rowan was warm under two sweaters and a scarf, with her steerswoman's cloak drawn about her. Bel had unearthed from her gear her piebald goatskin Outskirter cloak and boots. Gregori and the navigator had earlier spirited Willam away for an outfitting, and now he was dressed in secondhand sailor's clothing: a short, warm coat, heavy wool trousers, a rough gray scarf, and a knit stocking cap. He carried a battered duffel bag.

"The story has already flown around the city," Bel went on. "I'm sure the sailors have picked it up by now. They'll probably talk of nothing else for months." She spoke seemingly to the air; she rarely looked in Willam's direction.

"I'll try to act all agog when they tell it to me." Will spoke with a forced cheerfulness. It was a poor attempt, and Bel did not respond in kind.

They went on in silence, along the twisting streets, into the clamor of the harborside. When they reached the near end of the long loading wharf, Bel paused, and the others did as well.

Bel turned to Willam, and after a moment's awkwardness on both their parts, she put out her hand. Willam took it. "That actually was a clever plan that you and Corvus put together," Bel said, looking up at Will uncomfortably.

"I'm sorry it had to include deceiving you—"

"It didn't. It didn't have to." She released his hand, and stepped back. "You're away from them now, Willam. Try to remember what you are."

"I will," he said; but she had already turned away.

Rowan and Willam watched her as she walked off some distance, pausing before the open front of a rope-walk, as if idly, as if interested in the work going on inside. She waited.

"I don't have very many people in my life who are important to me," Will said. "I'd hate to lose one."

"It will be all right, Will. She just needs time."

"Yes. I wish we had some." He sighed, and turned to the steerswoman. "We always seem to be saying good-bye," he said. "Why is that?"

"I don't know," she replied, honestly puzzled. "It's only the second time we've ever done so."

He thought. "I guess it's because it's the last thing I remember, of you and Bel: us saying good-bye. For all those years with Corvus, whenever you came into my mind, we were saying good-bye."

"Whenever you came into my mind, I was wondering what fantastic spells you were learning." At this, his face fell, and he glanced aside for a moment. "You're going to miss it," Rowan said.

"Yes…" Spoken with regret, a trace of longing. "Some of the things I've seen, the things I've done… you can't imagine it."

"Stranger than the spells in Jannik's house?"

He nodded. "Stranger. More beautiful." Then he laughed a bit. "Not to mention light when I wanted it, music from the air, and a hot bath every single day. Yes. Yes, I'll miss it."

She almost did not ask, but then did: "Will you miss Corvus?" His expression became mixed, far too complex for her to decipher. "Was he…" she asked, awkward, "… was he a friend to you?"

"I don't know. Sometimes I thought that he was. And sometimes… sometimes I just couldn't tell at all."

"Hey! Ho! Attise!" They both turned.

It was Enid, leading two sailors jockeying a sack-laden wheelbarrow onto the wharf. "Move it," Enid said as the three passed by. "Last barge."

"I'm coming!" Willam called after her.

Rowan turned back, bemused. " Attise?' "

"I thought it would be a good idea to use a different name."

"And you chose Attise?' " It was the alias Rowan herself had used, when she had briefly resigned from the Steerswomen: the name she had been traveling under when Willam first met her. "I thought you *hated* Attise!"

"Oh, I did!" he said. "She was dull, rude, closemouthed, and condescending. But since then I've learned that she has a lot of good qualities, which it might be wise for me to emulate. Besides, someone once told me that if you use a false name you should pick one that, when you hear it unexpectedly, you just naturally turn around to look."

And this would be a good moment, a graceful moment, for them to part, and Rowan knew it. She discovered that she cared not at all for grace. She cast about for more to say, some way to delay events. "You're going to have to think of an explanation for your white hair," she pointed out. "And please don't blame it on a fright; you'd just be promulgating old wives' tales."

His mouth twitched. He pulled off his hat.

After a moment, he said, "No, go ahead and laugh. You'll just hurt yourself, holding it in like that."

She succumbed to a fit of hilarity. He was completely bald.

"It will grow back in its natural color," he said.

"And," she said, when she had enough breath to speak, "in the meantime, how will you explain—"

He put on a serious expression. "Lice."

She surrendered to laughter again. "But," she said, fighting for composure, "but, Willam, a person with one sort of lice might be suspected of having another sort—"

He held up his hands. "Let's just say I've done what's needed to keep up the deception, even in the close quarters of a ship, and leave it at that, shall we?"

"Oh, yes, let's."

He put the hat back on, much to her relief. "But speaking of close quarters…" He knelt by his duffel bag, untied it, reached in. "I'm going to keep the tools—I'll find some way to explain them—but I thought that if somebody got into my things, I'd have a hard time explaining the rest." He held out to her a small bundle: his burlap sack, now nearly empty, wrapped around the last objects tucked far in the bottom. "I thought you might want to study these. The card reader should work for a while, if you don't use it too often. You'll have to reattach the speaker."

She took the bundle. "The 'speaker' is the paper cone?"

"Yes."

They were quiet a moment; Rowan wondered if, like her, he was searching for some reason to stay for just a few more moments.

But she really must keep him no longer. "Well," she began—

"Are you going to put me under the Steerswomen's ban?" The beautiful copper gaze was both pleading and resigned.

"Oh, Will, I don't know," she said helplessly. "I've had no time to think this through. Everything has happened so quickly." In fact, their entire time together in Donner totaled less than four days. "But it seems to me, whenever I recall some of our conversations—I'm not certain that you ever did actually lie to me."

"I tried not to," he said earnestly.

"Yes. You spoke so carefully, sometimes." All the pauses, the obvious internal readjustments before speaking. "I really ought to have wondered..." And she ought to have mentioned it. Somehow—and she could not identify why she felt this—she knew that if only she herself had spoken of it first, and if she had used exactly the right words, Willam would have been able to tell her everything.

A call, inarticulate in the distance, but definitely the voice of Enid. "You have to go."

They embraced. Bundled against the cold as they were, the contact seemed muffled, distant. When they released each other, Rowan found and held his hand: a touch more formal, but by contrast far more intimate, far more real.

His fingers were cold. Three fingers: it was his right hand she held, the one he damaged as a child, by a moment's carelessness in the use of magic.

"Don't dwell on partings, this time," she said, and released the hand. "Think ahead, to the next time we say hello."

"That will happen," he replied, and shouldered his duffel bag. "The world is a much smaller place than you think it is." And he walked away; but once on the wharf, he turned back to call: "And when she's ready to hear it again, give Bel my love!"

When he turned away, he became unrecognizable: merely another of the many people on the wharf, a tall, broad-shouldered man in a blue coat and a stocking cap.

She would think him a sailor, if not for his stride. It was a land stride. But that would change.

She rejoined Bel, who was watching the activity inside the rope-walk. Bel eyed the sack. "What's that?"

"Some things he couldn't carry without arousing suspicion." They turned away and proceeded up the street, back toward the Dolphin.

"Magic?" Bel asked, when no one was near. She seemed both suspicious and interested.

"Yes. Although not of any real use to us. Still, I believe I can get at least one of these objects to work..." She mentally inventoried the contents. She stopped short in the street, unrolled the bundle, and reached deep into the sack.

"Rowan," Bel cautioned.

"I think there's a book in here... Yes." Her fingers located it. She pulled it out, stuffed the sack under one arm, and examined her find as they walked on.

It was the tiny book that protected the silvery slip. Its thong ties were loose. Rowan opened it at random, squinted at the minuscule writing. The letters were oddly shaped, and some recognizable only by context.

Bel watched her sidelong. "Any useful spells?"

"It seems to be poetry. Or songs… this one… it looks like the lyrics to 'The Sallie Gardens'…" Rowan chose another page…

"Ha. Now you're going to think that it's the common folk who were connected to the wizards."

But the steerswoman had stopped walking and stood dumbfounded in the center of the street. Bel turned back. "What's wrong?"

Rowan read out: "From where she stands—

—to where I stand
Is but a hand, a link, and a lock,
But there are doors, mine poor for
Being always wide—"

" '—I wait in stillness,' " Bel said, quiet, amazed. It was one of the ancient songs of Einar, the first seyoh of the Outskirters. " 'I wait in the speaking of grasses, in their voice.' " Rowan's eyes followed on the page, word for word. " 'I wait in the open of wander,' " Bel went on. " 'The world holds me, its smallest stone, but for the moment she comes.' " Now Bel could not help but sing it, if softly:

"The moment she comes to me,
The moment she comes,
Her eyes now light in light on dark,
Her voice a silent, known and humming
In my heart only: wider, call and empty.
Her fingers pulse the edges of the sky—"

"Not 'edges,' " Rowan said. She could not decipher the word; it was no word she knew. "I don't think it says 'edges.' Bel, how would 'The Ghost-Lover' end up in a wizard's book?"

Bel thought long. "One of the Krue living with the Outskirters heard it and brought it back, and wrote it down in that book."

"I suppose that's likely enough…"

And they continued on up the street. But the steerswoman was thinking: *Lock. Link.* And a voice that came *shadowing down the sky*. She began to wonder at Einar's ghost-lover, who seemed a woman with very strange powers, and whom only Einar could see, only Einar could hear.

270

They returned to Rowan's room, where they had stowed their traveling gear; but when they arrived, they found that the room was not empty. Two people waited there.

One was a young woman, dark-skinned, dark-haired. She stood with one hand resting solicitously on the shoulder of an older woman, who sat wearily in the room's ancient chair.

Ona.

"Oh—" Rowan said; and a moment later found herself kneeling on the floor at Ona's feet, holding both the small hands in her own, looking up into the pale face that seemed, so suddenly, very old. "I'm so sorry..." Inadequate; but all words are inadequate, at such a time.

"It's not your fault," Ona said quietly.

"If, if I had known..." It was painful to speak. "Ona, I would never have—"

"No. It's my fault."

"What?" Rowan could not understand this. "Ona, no."

"I knew," Ona said, and closed her eyes. Light from the window behind her haloed her hair with faint blue. "When you saw those drawings, that first night... I knew, from what you said, from what you didn't say... I knew there was more to it. I knew it wasn't just old gossip. I should have said something to Naio. But—" Her voice cracked; she bit her lips, waited, went on: "He was having so much fun..."

Tears came; the dark woman beside Ona had a handkerchief ready. Ona took it, and leaned against her.

Rowan looked up at the young woman and found dark eyes, a brown face very similar to Naio's. "Sherrie?" Rowan asked. The woman nodded: Naio's niece.

A period of quiet, during which Bel unobtrusively sidled over and sat on the bed.

Ona sighed and straightened again, still wiping at her eyes, and carefully composed herself. "He sent for her."

"What?" Rowan was lost.

"Kieran. He sent for that steerswoman."

She was a moment recovering the matter; it now seemed distant, irrelevant. Then abruptly, it did not. "Latitia? Kieran *sent* for her?"

Ona nodded. "When you left town, yesterday, Naio and I—" She paused again to master herself. "—we... we spent the day with old Nid. And it did take all day, Nid rambling and losing himself, and oh!" Here she laughed, the weak laughter of one exhausted from weeping. "You should have seen Naio, winkling old news out of Nid! Going over and over, circling around. It was so... so funny..." She pressed the handkerchief against her eyes again.

Rowan could only repeat, astounded: "Kieran sent for Latitia."

"Not by name." Ona removed the handkerchief, sat twisting it in her fingers. "Nid said Latitia said... There was a rider, who came across her on the road, looking for a steerswoman, any steerswoman. When she said she was one, he said there was a wizard who," and it seemed now that she quoted, " 'wanted a quiet word with a steerswoman.' "

"He was going to tell her," Bel said.

Rowan could hardly believe it. But: "Yes..." And if he had told Latitia, if Kieran had lived for just a little longer—

Whatever a steerswoman knows is freely given to all. There would be no secret. And all these terrible events might not have occurred.

Rowan closed her eyes, shook her head, sighed. She looked up into Ona's blue eyes. "Thank you."

"Naio wanted you to know. That's why we were here, yesterday..."

Quiet dwelt in the room for a space of time. Then Rowan rose, stood looking down on the silent woman, and on impulse kissed the top of Ona's head, gently. "We have to go."

"So we do," Bel said.

Rowan turned to her. "All right. Are you ready?"

"Yes," Bel said, and nodded, and did not move from the bed.

Rowan regarded her, puzzled. "What's wrong?"

"Where's our gear?"

The steerswoman looked around. Their packs were not present.

Sherrie tilted her head. "Out back."

The packs were in the yard, along with quite a lot of other gear, all of it being loaded onto the back of a horse.

Ruffo bustled up; he had apparently been waiting for them. "I was figuring," he said, "the two of you would want to make good speed, and that meant not stopping to look for food, or getting someone to give you some, so, so, there's all this. But it's too much to carry, isn't it, so, well... He faltered, then handed Rowan the leading-rein. "Anyway, she's got no master now."

Bel was delighted. "Jannik's horse!"

"But," Rowan said, "surely you can use her yourself, to hire out? Or sell her?"

"True, I could, but you could sell her later just as well, and don't tell me a steerswoman couldn't use a little ready coin every now and again, not to mention Bel, who nobody's going to feed for free."

"But—"

The steerswoman staggered at a shove from Bel. "Rowan, say 'Thank you.'"

"Thank you," Rowan said. She reached up to stroke the mare's soft nose, amazed and grateful. "I'll make certain she ends up in a good home."

"Good enough," Ruffo said. "The head groom tells me her name is Princess Alabaster of the Golden Cloud-Castle."

The mare nuzzled Rowan's palm, then bit her. "Ow!" The steerswoman drew back sharply. "I believe," she said, shaking the pain from her hand, "that I'll call her Sugar."

Beck, who had been securing Willam's bow to the side of a loaded pannier, stepped forward and held out to Rowan one of the Dolphin's linen napkins, its ends knotted. Rowan took it, and found it to contain a large number of sugar-lumps. She laughed. "Thank you," she said.

Beck grinned his huge grin and stepped back. "Be well," he said. "Stay safe." And he departed. Rowan gaped after him.

Bel, reaching for a sugar-lump, regarded her curiously. "What?"

"I've... never heard him speak before," Rowan said. "I was beginning to wonder if he could." The young man's voice was lovely: deep and resonant, seeming four sizes too large for him.

They bid Ruffo farewell, and led Sugar away, up Branner's Road, and left onto Iron-and-Tin. Somewhat later, they passed Joly, standing on a street corner in quiet conversation with the proprietor of the bawdy-house, and Marel. The three men glanced at the travelers, and Joly lifted one hand slightly, in unobtrusive acknowledgment; then they continued their discussion.

"The cabal is already at work," Bel noted.

When they reached the river dock, the ferry was already well loaded, with no passengers waiting, but for no apparent reason it had not yet departed. It did so the moment Rowan and Bel convinced Sugar to board, which caused Bel to smile happily, throw Rowan one significant look, and thereafter make a show of cheerful innocence. Rowan sighted the ferry captain, an immense, gray-haired woman who caught her glance, grinned, and surreptitiously winked. It was no one Rowan knew.

The ferry had pulled away from the shore and was halfway across the river-branch when Rowan suddenly recalled something. She made a sound of annoyance. "This sword isn't mine."

"Neither was the other one."

"But—"

Bel spoke aggrievedly. "Rowan, if you go back and try to return it, they'll just tell you to keep it. You know they will. And don't forget what Willam gave them. Even taking the sword, and the horse, and all the supplies into account, Donner still comes out ahead."

"Oh, very well."

And it was not until much later, in the shivering evening, after a meal by the campfire, with Rowan deep into a detailed description of all the events that had taken place in Jannik's house; and having reached the point in the telling when Willam used the magic voice-box; and having already reassembled it; and being about to demonstrate its use, as an aid to the telling, that they both heard it:

Two sounds, like distant rumbles of thunder.

They were faint, but crisp in the still, cold air. They echoed and re-echoed, across the river, against the distant hills, and farther on, passing from point to point, moving across the land, and fading at last beyond the limit of hearing.

This, despite the fact that the star-studded sky was perfectly cloudless.

Rowan and Bel exchanged a long look. The sounds had come, unmistakably, from the direction of Donner, and the dragon fields. Willam's charms were being put to use.

Then the steerswoman picked up from the rough, bare earth the white card marked *1*, and she carefully fed it between the little turning wheels of the box. The wheels caught the card, and drew it forward.

From out of the paper cone, the voice of the dead wizard said: "Access."

ABOUT THE AUTHOR

Rosemary Kirstein is the author of the Steerswoman series: *The Steerswoman, The Outskirter's Secret, The Lost Steersman,* and *The Language of Power.* Work is underway on Volume 5: *The Changes of the Dark,* and Volume 6: *The City in the Crags.* The series is projected to have seven volumes.

Paperback versions of the first four volumes were originally published by Del Rey Books.

Kirstein's short fiction has appeared in *Asimov's* and in *Aboriginal SF.* She blogs at www.rosemarykirstein.com, and can be found on Facebook as "Rosemary Kirstein -- writer." She occasionally tweets random non sequiturs on Twitter as @rkirstein.

Rowan's adventure continues, in this exclusive excerpt from
Volume 5 of the Steerswoman Series:

THE CHANGES OF THE DARK

CHAPTER ONE

At a crossing of ways, on the dark brink of morning, two women stood paused in moment of parting. The air spoke of ice coming soon, soon, and the sky was still full of stars.

Nearby, a pale mare shifted restlessly, huffing clouds of breath that drifted up into the chill, spangled dark. The women stood with their backs to a small campfire, allowing its light to fall on the map they held between them.

"I feel like a fool sending you out with this thing," the steerswoman said. "But it's the best copy I could manage so quickly."

The other woman said: "It'll do. In fact, it's neater than the original."

The map was a peculiar object, seeming very much concerned with landscape, but little with humankind. A river on the western edge possessed a name: *GREYRIVER.* A sprinkling of towns reluctantly acknowledged that people did in fact exist, and often lived gathered together: *Greyvale, Osterly, Redrunner.*

But further, to the east: hills with no name; mute, fragmentary rivers; an anonymous marsh. The labels that did exist no longer attached to towns. *THE DEEPMOST* might have been part of a river; *TOURNIER'S FAULT* seemed a crack in the earth; the *CAT LAKES* were a random scattering on the northern landscape, disconnected and mysterious…

But what drew the eye were markings which were not town, nor landscape, nor names. Merely a collection of X's —one centrally located, one to the east, one south at Tournier's Fault, and two tucked among the Cat Lakes.

"Bel, these indications can't possibly be accurate."

"I think we knew that already."

"And whole sections of the landscape are blank!"

"Good." Bel took the map from her friend and began folding it. "Those are the parts I'm not interested in. This way, I won't be distracted." She stooped to stow the map in her pack, currently resting on the cold ground. The pack was leather, well-worn, randomly patched and stuffed tightly full.

The steerswoman watched for a while. "And those wizards' minions are hardly likely to remain where they are while you're traveling," she added.

"Then it really doesn't matter that the locations aren't accurate." Bel looked up, caught her friend's expression, and laughed. "This is actually painful for you, isn't it?" She tied off her pack's flap, and stood.

"Rather," the other admitted, with some reluctance.

"Always the steerswoman. You're aching to have that map filled in. Rowan, I need to start somewhere. This is what we have."

"Well. Yes." She went to her own gear, loaded on the mare, and began opening a side-pocket of her own pack. "I think I can spare a smaller map that will get you to Five Corners —"

In an exasperated tone: "*Rowan —*"

The steerswoman turned at her name. Bel continued: "Rowan, this road will get me to Five Corners. Unless I fall into a ditch on the way. And from Five Corners, east will get me to the Outskirts. That's all I need to know. Once I'm in my own country, I can find my own people."

"Very well." Rowan gave up looking for a map. "But you might —" she began, then stopped herself, surprised. She was at a loss for words. Bel observed this, and waited.

Rowan recovered. "I was about to say," she said, "that you might not find it quite so simple to meet your own people, given that they tend to be scattered across the entire breadth of the Outskirts. But... that's not true anymore, is it?"

Bel was rather long in replying. "Probably not. Rowan, I won't know how far things have advanced until I get there."

"Of course not."

"I'll try to send word, when I know more."

"But word travels slowly. Facts can out-pace news."

"Yes. But you already know what you need to know: My people are *coming.*"

This had been known for some time. It was now a question of how soon; and what they might do when they arrived.

Sometime during the conversation, day arrived. It seemed to Rowan to have happened suddenly: the sky first night-black, now day-blue. There were no clouds.

Rowan went to the campfire, which was still snapping tiny flames, dim in the sudden morning. She kicked earth over it, and stepped on the coals, then spread the dead ashes, added more dirt.

Something occurred to her. "You could take Sugar," she said to Bel. Sugar was the mare. "You have the longer distance to travel."

Bel patted Sugar's flank, causing the mare to turn her head and deliver a suspicious glare. Bel drew back her hand. "She's better off with you. And she'd have nothing to eat in the Outskirts," Bel pointed out. "In fact, she'd be dinner herself, as soon as she got there."

"Yes, that's true. Well." It seemed the moment to part. But Rowan said: "'We always seem to be saying goodbye.'"

The Outskirter tilted her head and waited for explanation. "Something Willam said to me, when we parted," Rowan continued. "I didn't understand it then."

"And you do, now?"

"I believe so… When I think of you after this, if this is the moment that I happen to remember, then I suppose it really will feel like saying goodbye over and over."

"Ha. Pick a different moment to remember. One of the times I saved your life."

Rowan laughed. "Too many choices. Shall I pick the first occasion, or the most recent?"

"One in the middle. Or, better, that time you saved *my* life."

Rowan had to think. "Ah," she said at last. "Yes, that will do." She was delaying, she realized. "I've become accustomed to having you around," she told her dearest friend.

Bel became serious. "I have things to do."

"So you do. As have I. Then… goodbye."

"Try not to get killed while we're apart," Bel remarked, hefting her pack, swinging it about and slipping into the straps.

"Then we'll see each other again?" Rowan asked. It seemed to her, at that moment, not at all certain.

"Of course we will," the Outskirter replied, walking away; but she turned to deliver the last words: "One way or the other."

Rowan watched her go for a bit. "One way or the other." Then she took Sugar's lead, turned on to the Shore Road.

She traveled all day, camped again that night.

And in the morning, the snow began.